penny dreadful

will christopher baer

penny dreadful

will christopher baer

Lawson

Lawson Library
A division of MacAdam/Cage Publishing
155 Sansome Street, Suite 550
San Francisco, CA 94104
www.macadamcage.com

Library of Congress Cataloging-in-Publication Data

Baer, Will Christopher.
    Penny dreadful / by Will Christopher Baer.
        p. cm.
    ISBN 1-931561-81-8 (hardcover : alk. paper)
    1. Ex-mental patients—Fiction. 2. Ex-police officers—Fiction.
3. Missing persons—Fiction. 4. Denver (Colo.)—Fiction.
5. Punk culture—Fiction. I. Title

    PS3552.A3323P46 2004
    813'.54—dc22

                                                    2004015758

Paperback edition: November, 2006
ISBN 10: 1-59692-107-2
ISBN 13: 978-1-59692-107-8

                        Manufactured in the United States of America.
10 9 8 7 6 5 4 3 2 1

Book and jacket design by Dorothy Carico Smith.

for Elias

—*Why was the host (victim predestined) sad?*
—*He wished that a tale of a deed should be told of a deed not by him should by him not be told.*

—*Ulysses*, James Joyce

am near the end now and this notebook is falling apart in my hands. Damp, becoming pulp. The pages are swollen together and the ink bleeds. The ink disappears and I am not what I appear to be. I wanted to make that clear from the first, from the beginning. But failed, somehow. I tell myself that nothing has vanished, nothing is lost. The lies are chronological, evolutionary.

The dead are watching, listening. I wonder what they know.

The thing is that my consciousness drifts and I have forgotten exactly what I look like. I pass my reflection in a blackened window and I may not recognize myself. My reflection is now perceived as a threat, an ugly twin. My reflection is a dark nonperson, a stranger on the street and this is not an identity crisis as I understand the phrase.

Dear Jude. The mutation of self is normal.

But this is not a suicide note and I don't want you to feel sorry for me. There's no point in that. It has always been in my nature to stare at the sun, to step out into traffic. I am an unlikely suicide but I did want to get a good close look at death, to touch his matted hair and pass him by.

You should know that I am an alien, a stranger. I may ask you for a cigarette, for the time, for spare change. I may suddenly push you down an alley and steal your wallet, cut out your tongue. I may stop you from choking to death on a fishbone and I may have more than one name.

Did you know that your eyes tend to change colors. They slip from yellow to gray and blue and the change is irrelevant to mood, to disposition. The names are something like that. Phineas Poe. Ray Fine. Fred.

I wasn't thinking clearly when I came back to Denver. I followed myself back to Eve's place because I believed I would be safe there. I was equipped only with the small brain of a bird, the heart and bone structure of a chicken. I was a stupid chicken.

I was not quite self-aware.

The strangers in me are easily distracted. They are daydreamers, romantics. And therefore unreliable. They are often drunk and they don't always look out for each other. They pretend not to notice things. It always comes back to this business of drifting and I don't mean the way clouds drift. The way shadows drift behind the sun. It's a geological thing, a tectonic shift. The drift is not so easily noticed, but the impact tends to be profound.

Open your eyes, boy. Your eyes. Open your eyes and no more turn aside and brood.

— from a small blue notebook found on a Denver city bus, apparently the diary of Phineas Poe. This was the final entry.

Thursday

Goo:

The Trembler was young and fair, with red hair and stupid blue eyes and the pale furry limbs of a spider monkey. And shameless. The girl had no shame. She clung to Chrome as if grafted to his hip. Goo rolled her eyes and followed them down a road white with mist. Chrome was her boyfriend, technically. She liked to sleep with him. But she rarely hunted with him. It wasn't her bag. Goo was not a Mariner, and she didn't share his bottomless black hunger for tongue. Nor did she like to watch him go down on others, which Chrome very well knew.

They had found the Trembler under the 17th Street Bridge, crouched near a sewer opening. Alone and mute. She had obviously become separated from her little tribe, her pocket of the game. And when Chrome and Goo had come upon her she had pathetically tried to tremble them, which only made Goo more tired and grumpy.

Chrome, though. He had been unpleasantly cheerful all evening and apparently found the Trembler amusing so he had scooped her up like an injured sparrow. He had muttered something to Goo about having a delicious threesome, a sickening idea. Goo wished he would just take the girl's tongue quickly and cleanly and deposit her in an abandoned car, or behind a trash barrel.

But she could see that he was in no mood for the efficient kill.

The Trembler could be no more than sixteen, thought Goo. She was a newborn, barely an apprentice. Fashionably unclean, barbaric. The girl was dressed as some sort of prehistoric cave dweller, wearing a babydoll dress of raw suede and no shoes. Her legs were unshaven and she smelled.

Goo spat in disgust. She was an Exquisitor and was therefore expected to be a bit more elegant. She wore brown leather trousers, clean. She wore polished black motorcycle boots and a vest of fine silver chain mail. And Chrome, being a hunter, wore only black. Black jeans tirelessly reconstructed with black tape and rubber patches. Boots that laced up to the knee and a black T-shirt with the sleeves cut off. His head was shaved to black stubble.

Goo watched him drag the unprotesting Trembler along by the elbow, his fingers no doubt raising bruises in her flesh and from a distance he looked just like a boy who had found a lost kitten and was taking it back to his tree house to feed it milk and tuna or possibly cut off its feet and now Goo quickened her step and came up alongside him.

I'm going home, she said.

Nonsense.

I am, she said. I'm gone.

Chrome stopped, flicked his wrist and the Trembler stood upright, quivering.

Have you ever seen such a waif? he said. La jeune fille, exquis.

Yes, said Goo. The girl is exquisite. But I'm bored. I'm hungry and I'm tired and I'm going home.

The girl stared at them, unblinking. She was a wetbrain, thought Goo. She was a ninety-eight-pound victim of the Pale. Chrome growled, impatient.

Come, he said. There's a market ahead. I will buy you a loaf of bread.

They turned down the next street and Goo flinched at the web of bright lights. She didn't like the bright. It reminded her of day. But Chrome did not even look to see if she was following. He merely flowed down the sidewalk, as if he were made of water. The Trembler trailed behind, a balloon on a string, forgotten.

It was near dawn.

Maybe four or five in the morning. Traces of yellow and pink in the sky, like fine hairs. Which made it Thursday. There was a twenty-four-hour Safeway up ahead and Goo sighed. She could get a bite to eat and perhaps distract Chrome from the Trembler. Not that she was sorry for the girl, not in the least. Goo wasn't interested in the girl's fate, near or far. She was tired and she simply didn't want to watch Chrome eat a stranger's tongue.

Through hissing doors into terrible white light. Goo squinted, covered her face.

Chrome grinned, mocking. Le soleil cruel.

Goo hated him. His French was terrible.

But the store was empty, a morgue. She didn't want to flounder alone under the man-made light and so she followed them down a row of canned vegetables, her eyes focused dully on the Trembler's slender but dirty and needle-scarred legs.

The dairy section.

I thought we were buying bread, said Goo.

Chrome shrugged. He opened a glass door and withdrew a brick of Monterey Jack, which he thrust at the Trembler. Hold this between your knees, he said.

The Trembler blinked and Chrome shoved her up against the open door. He bit at her lips until blood ran to her chin and she opened her mouth.

The cheese hit the floor.

Chrome sucked at the girl's dirty face and Goo closed her eyes. She felt sick and reached for something to grab onto, pulling down a row of creamed corn. The dull clatter of heavy metal and she opened her eyes to see the Trembler fall to the black-and-white tile floor as if she were made of lead.

Blood gurgling from her mouth, too much blood.

What did you do? said Goo.

Chrome looked at her, puzzled. I took her tongue.

All of it?

He spat, and something flew from his mouth like a broken tooth.

Nah, he said. The tip is all.

Isn't that a little too much blood? said Goo.

Chrome winked at her, pulling a bit of stained plastic from his teeth.

Blood packet, he said. An ordinary theater prop.

Oh, said Goo.

The Trembler stood up, brushing herself off and smiling meekly. The red ran from her mouth, real and false. Goo wanted to gag but Chrome was watching. He was always watching her. She shrugged and turned to go, as if bored.

I stepped off the Greyhound from west Texas and looked around at a world shimmering with exhaust and dead air. Denver, unrecognizable. My mouth was full of fucking dust and I was home. Broken glass scattered on a parking lot of black tar.

Dull sunlight.

I stood for a few minutes with the other passengers, waiting stupidly for my luggage. I had no luggage. I had nothing much in my pockets. Two or three cigarettes and a book of matches. Stub of pencil and a useless hotel room key. One dollar and an assortment of coins, most of them pesos. One bright blue pebble that I had picked up on a sidewalk in the French Quarter because I thought it might be lucky. A mysterious coupon for cold medicine. I couldn't remember when I last had a cold.

I started walking and found myself counting my steps. Twenty-seven to the sidewalk, fifty-one to the corner. I needed to focus on something. I needed to find a phone booth and figure out where I was going.

Eve, I thought. I would go see Eve, maybe.

Little help, said a voice.

I looked down, surprised. A hunchbacked homeless man with a bloody nose and no hair squatted against a brick wall. I was nearly standing on his foot. There was a dog beside him, a pale arthritic mutt with a choke chain around its neck. The man worried the end of the chain between his fingers and stared up at me with hope in his eyes.

What do you need? I said.

The man began to cough and I patted my pockets, thinking I could either give him one of my three cigarettes or a handful of Mexican coins.

Lost, said the man. He spoke with a strange lisp.

I looked around. This is 19th Street.

You sure, he said.

Where are you going? I said.

Don't even know my fucking name, said the man.

I stared at him. I know that feeling.

Comfortably numb, he said.

Yeah.

I crouched down, careful not to get too close to the dog. Pulled out my sad pack of cigarettes and found there were only two. I gave him one, and he poked it between blood-stained lips. I lit a match and held it for him. He thanked me and I shook my head. There was only a fine line between us. The guy was younger than he looked, maybe twenty-nine. His fingernails were clean. His dog wasn't starving and I decided they were newly homeless.

Everything slips, he said. Everything slips away. I had a house and a car and they turned to fucking dust. Disappeared before my eyes.

I shrugged. Life is nasty and it seemed pointless to say so.

The stretch of silence and my knees began to ache. I couldn't help the guy. That cigarette was all I had. The sun slithered out from behind heavy clouds and the man whimpered at the sight. I stood up, dizzy.

Hey, said the man.

I turned. The dog lifted its head now and for a moment was not a dog at all. It looked like some kind of hideous bird.

What? I said.

The man opened his mouth and now I thought he would act like a proper homeless man and ask me for money, or at least offer me a crumb of wisdom. But then his nose started to bleed again and he said nothing at all.

Eve:

She wasn't sure what day it was, Thursday perhaps. Early morning. The sky was a web of gray and blue, as if it might rain even while the sun stared down. The day was otherwise unremarkable until Phineas appeared on her doorstep after thirteen months, his eyes narrow with apologies. He was asleep on his feet. He was dirty and stinking and still he didn't look so bad. The shadows and starvation were gone from his face. There was new muscle in his arms. His hair was long and tangled with fingers of red, as if he had been in the sun.

Words fail.

Her hands felt brittle at the sight of him, but she let him in. A voice in her head said very softly, with a touch of menace and despair: he can't stay here. He can't.

It wasn't her voice and she shook it off.

And he collapsed on the couch and slept while she undressed him, her hands never quite touching his flesh. She was tempted to touch the scar that coiled around his belly, to trace her finger around the dark red rope of alien tissue that had grown there. She stopped herself, she was afraid that she might wake him. The scar must be so cold, like the skin of a fish. There was a knife strapped to his left arm, a slender, pretty thing but very, very sharp. She hid it under a cushion. She pulled his boots off, his torn socks. She unbuttoned his pants and pulled them down, her fingernails trailing through his dark pubic hair. His penis was soft and meek and reminded her of mice sleeping in bits of grass and stolen feathers and she had a sudden peculiar urge to choke it in her fist. As if it were truly a mouse. Then his left hand twitched and slid between his thighs. He was protecting himself, even in sleep. And he should, she thought. He should protect himself from me. The urge was gone, anyway. She shrugged and covered him in a thin blanket and wondered if there was anything but rotten food in the house.

She dragged his clothes down to the basement in a pillowcase stained with pig's blood. The washing machine required quarters, which she did not have. But the coinbox had long been broken. She pried it open with a screwdriver, removed three quarters, then hammered the box shut again. One of her neighbors had left behind a small bottle of fabric softener and she didn't hesitate to steal it. His clothes would need a lot of softening. She stood over the machine for a few minutes, watching the water swirl and become gray.

It was time to go to work. To be fair, she was late and she wasn't so sure she wanted to go. She would love to put on her pajamas and drag the television out of the closet and watch a fuzzy movie, to fold herself in half and lie beside Phineas on the couch.

But she was weak, she was soft.

She could never resist, never. She would chew her leg off before she would stay home.

However. The house felt smaller now and she was changed. But not so much, yet. A wrinkle, a twist of color. Phineas had come back and she had no idea what she might do with him. She wondered what effect he would have on her. She wondered what he hoped to find, what he expected from her. Maybe nothing. Maybe he wanted nothing but a place to sleep for a few days. Then he would move on and would that be so terrible. She hadn't known him so well, really. They were connected though. By blood, by something.

She wanted to think about it and she walked around the small apartment, undressing slowly. There was no music and the ringing silence was a relief. Now she stood over him, naked. Her body was covered in bruises, new and old. She touched one, carefully. Yellow and blue and shaped like a star, a flower. She loved her body, cracked and torn as it had become.

She walked down the hall and dressed before a broken mirror.

Her pale splintered torso. Distended arms and legs, coming apart before her eyes. She watched herself fall and fall through the dark glass. She pulled on a black corset and thigh-high black boots. Hesitated, then chose a yellowed wedding dress that had been crudely altered and was now held together by safety pins and fell in a ragged hem a few inches above the tops of her boots.

Phineas still slept. She folded his clean clothes and left them at his feet. She tried but could not write him a note. Instead she left twenty dollars on the kitchen table with a menu for the Silver Frog, a Chinese place that delivered at all hours.

Down the creaking staircase and outside. Blue and black sky. She would take a cab down to Lodo but first she must walk a few blocks and relax. If she thought about it too much, she might cling to herself. She would be trapped, unable to play. But her breathing soon became easy, fluid. The street narrowed. And almost without apprehension, she transformed. Eve became Goo. And Goo was stronger.

I was awake, technically. But I didn't want to open my eyes. I was vaguely aware that someone was watching me. The skin had that familiar creepy tingle and I was naked, it seemed. On what felt like a couch. I was tucked like a dead man under a thin blanket. The material was very soft and smelled of tobacco and rain and skin. I reached between my thighs and gave my testicles a reassuring squeeze and briefly, I was twelve and just waking up in my narrow bunk bed at home with blue-and-white-striped sheets and pale blue walls around me and a whale mobile dangling overhead and my little dick cupped safely in my left hand.

I hoped I was in Eve's apartment.

The couch beneath me felt like velvet. Eve had a velvet couch, dark red velvet. I remembered that much. From before. But I didn't exactly remember arriving here. I must have walked twenty-two blocks from the Greyhound station in a drowsy sort of morphine stupor, even though I had been off that shit for six weeks or so, ever since I separated from Jude in San Francisco. It had been a long walk from the station, and stinking hot. I had decided it must be springtime. April, or possibly May. And who was watching me. It didn't feel like Eve. She must have undressed me, though. I tried to remember her hands. Her thin strong fingers.

I opened my eyes and stared into an unsmiling, androgynous blue-eyed face hovering a few inches from my own. The face sniffed at me.

Human, the face said. And apparently alive.

I sat up and waited calmly for the world to spin around. But the world appeared to be temporarily stable. Maybe this was an exaggeration, but I felt much better than I deserved to. The face grunted, pulled away from me and lit an unfiltered white cigarette.

Can I have one of these? I said.

Il est possible que.

I rubbed my mouth. The face was speaking French, apparently. Languages. I had studied German in high school and been pretty bad at it. I had spent some of the past year in South America and could spit out enough Spanish to ask for breakfast and not get shot. However. I hated the French and their slippery tongue. But I shrugged this away. I had no real reason to hate the French and could barely remember why I did. It had something to do with my grandfather and a prostitute during World War II and a mouthful of stolen gold teeth. Anyway. The unsmiling face before me was fierce and beautiful. It was probably male, I thought. If it were a woman's face I would likely be afraid of it.

Two slender fingers were extended, floating toward me. The fingernails were painted a bright yellow. Horrible, a horrible color. These were the fingers of a corpse, a vampire. A short white cigarette appeared before my eyes like a magician's rabbit. I took it between my lips and allowed the yellow fingers to light it for me. The smoke was bitter and harsh and I coughed painfully into my fist. As usual, I looked for black phlegm or chunks of lung in my hand and was relieved to find nothing.

What the hell is this? I said.

It is a Gitanes, the face said. The finest of French cigarettes.

I'm sure. But it tastes like shit.

The face was unamused. Then return it to me.

Thanks, I said. The tobacco is just a little stale, maybe.

Imagine, said another voice. The human is rude.

Right. I was fucking surrounded, then. I sighed and glanced around. My clothes were tucked beneath my feet. They were folded. I couldn't remember the last time my clothes were folded and somehow this made me feel incredibly lonely. I tried to compose my face but couldn't remember exactly what it was supposed to look like. I only wanted to take a shower. I wanted to be unmolested, unfucked with. But there was a shadow crouched in the window behind me. A boy, or a very small man, in raw brown leather clothes. His hair was long and white and he wore a string of bones around his throat. The room was otherwise empty. Okay, so there were only two of them.

Hello.

The man-boy smiled at me, a ring of sharp teeth in shadow.

I pushed the blanket aside and reached for my clothes. I felt hot, as if my blood was thickening. I pulled on pants and sat there, scratching my chest and not blinking. Trying to be cool, I suppose. As if I woke up on a strange couch with mutants staring at me every day. I wanted a cup of coffee. I wanted these two freaks to give me a little space.

I rubbed at a sore mosquito bite on my left wrist, aware now that my knife was missing. I told myself to wake the fuck up.

The unsmiling pretty face wavered before me, became solid again. A body formed behind it. A black, sleeveless shirt that appeared to be made of soft metal. Hairless, muscular arms with a few unreadable words tattooed on the pale, smooth underside of one bicep. Black pants held together by patches of rubber and electrician's tape and boots stained with mud. The man's hair was black and short and very soft, like the fur of a young black dog. The man was eerily calm and not exactly hostile. He was unpleasantly seductive, though. I guessed him to be about thirty years old. There was a fine web of wrinkles around his blue eyes. And those eyes were now staring obliquely at my chest, my exposed belly.

That is exquisite work, the face said.

What?

The scar, he said. Where did you have it done?

I blinked stupidly at him, smiled. It isn't meant to be ornamental, I said.

How did it happen?

On a lumber crew in Oregon. I stumbled into a tree pulper.

Ah, said the face. The wrath of Pan.

Excuse me. Who are you?

The face sighed. The wrong question, isn't it?

The man-boy began to whisper. A string of curses, or prayers. It sounded like Latin, maybe. One dead tongue or another. What the fuck. They wanted to spook me.

But how did it really happen? said the face.

You wouldn't believe me.

Try me, said the face.

I had an organ stolen, I said. And felt a slight flush. The story embarrassed me, somehow.

The face nodded sagely. Leggers, he said. Happens all the time.

I frowned. This was not the reaction I was used to. Most people looked at me with a peculiar mix of disbelief, horror and amusement. Nausea, basically. One woman actually hit me in the face when I told her about it.

Again, I said. Who are you guys?

I am rather more interested in who you might be, said the face.

Okay. I'm Phineas. A friend of Eve's.

Eve, said the face. I'm sure you mean Goo.

I opened my mouth, then closed it. Yes, I said.

I am Chrome, said the face.

The man-boy still whispered.

How do you know Eve? I said. Or Goo, that is.

I am her paramour.

Okay. I stood up and walked into the kitchen. I was suddenly very thirsty, and wondered how long I had been sleeping. I was shivering a little, claustrophobic. I didn't think I liked my new friends. Perhaps I wasn't meant to. Eve didn't want me here, maybe. And why would she? I barely knew her at all. The last time I saw her, she had just been raped with an assortment of household objects. By someone who was looking for me. She had probably hoped she would never lay eyes on my sorry ass again. Then I showed up on her porch, homeless and unannounced. And after I passed out on her couch she naturally sent these two along to give me a fright.

I opened the refrigerator and peered at its uncertain contents. A few unmarked items wrapped in brown paper. Meat, possibly. But Eve was a vegetarian, or so I thought. She was also a lesbian, the last time I saw her. Now she seemed to have a creepy Goth boyfriend with sharp yellow fingernails. His name was Chrome, for fuck's sake. The paramour. I licked my lips and reached for a jar in the fridge that appeared to contain water. And what the hell did I know. Maybe she was bisexual. Who wasn't a little bisexual at the end of the day, alone with the black fingers of memory and silence? The heart was a frail but curiously stubborn organ. I knew that much. This Chrome person, though. He was a nasty one. And not just dark and dreary. He was a skinny wolf lounging in the sun. The guy was for real. I sniffed at the water and my nostrils burned. It was not fucking water, okay. I leaned over the sink and took a long drink from the tap. Now my mouth felt a little better, but I was lonely.

On the table was a menu and twenty dollars, and I felt my spirits lift a little. Eve wanted to feed me, it seemed. Therefore, she was not trying to kill me. I smiled and licked my teeth, which felt mossy. How long had I been sleeping.

Be nice, I muttered. Be fucking nice.

I wandered back to the living room.

I'm going to order some food, I said. Are you guys hungry?

Chrome sighed. He sat on the couch now, his left boot resting on the blanket I had so recently slept with. And I have to say I was fairly aroused, my senses jangling. I felt sick, too. I concentrated on the fist of hunger in my belly. I stared at Chrome and I was confident that he was well aware of the effect he had on men and women. That he saw other humans as amusing toys. Everyone who ever came near him must want to fuck him or kill him or both. He had dark swollen lips that any supermodel would die for and blue eyes like seawater in the sun. And he smelled like metal, like salt and gasoline.

He was a tease, a torturer. Nothing more, nothing more.

Chrome stared back at me, smiling now.

The man-boy was busily examining the rest of my clothing. He sniffed a boot delicately, then licked the heel. He pressed the socks and shirt to his face.

What do they smell like? I said.

The man-boy grinned. Like a summer breeze, he said. Like chemical detergent.

Chrome spat. I assume Goo laundered them, he said. She is such a woman, sometimes.

I looked at Chrome's throat and wondered where the hell my knife was.

The man-boy grunted. The boots, however, taste of blood and feces. They taste of Louisiana. He glanced up at me. You have come from Louisiana, have you not?

Yes, I said. I was there last week. And I laughed, weirdly pleased by his cleverness. Meanwhile, my bowels felt like they were slowly stretching.

I lived there as a child, said the man-boy. My name is Mingus the Breather.

Well. I rubbed at my eyes and could think of nothing, absolutely nothing wrong with that. It's nice to meet you, I said.

Perhaps you would like us to call you Fred, said Chrome. Because you will be going to see Elvis, soon.

What? I said.

And then we can say: Poor Fred. He was a friend of mine.

That's not true, said Mingus. He won't see Elvis, necessarily.

I'm sorry, said Chrome with a sigh. But the man does not look well.

Nothing has been decided, said Mingus. No one's fate is sealed.

Spare me, said Chrome.

I smiled benevolently. As if I wanted to be nothing more than a gracious host. I picked up the phone and dialed the Silver Frog. My vision was swimming and I calmly ordered mu shu, dumplings, fried rice and eggdrop soup. Then hung up the phone and helped myself to another of Chrome's nasty French cigarettes. I blew a pretty sorry smoke ring and handed the cigarette to Chrome.

Our hands touched. Our eyes slipped over opposing flesh.

I laughed out loud. The tension between us was absurd, cartoonish. I might as well ask the man to choose a weapon.

Chrome merely yawned. Enchantez de faire votre connaissance.

I pulled on my boots and stood there, feeling awkward and clumsy, as if my limbs were suddenly too large for my body. I watched as Mingus patiently repaired a hole in my freshly washed shirt with a needle and a length of black thread. It was a maddeningly slow process, sewing. No wonder I never learned to do it. My mother had been no good at it either and as a boy my socks were always full of holes. Jesus fucking. My mind was about to crash into itself. I chewed at my thumb and wished they would leave. Otherwise I was going to jump out a window any minute now. The silence rose like water, swirling. Chrome stared and stared at me.

Do you like to hunt? said Chrome.

What do you mean. Like ducks? I said.

Yes, said Chrome. Exactly like ducks.

Goo:

She walked along a deserted street through shadows so soft she was tempted to grab at them, to pull them to her face. These were the dark sisters of clouds seen from the window of an airplane, she thought. She giggled like a foolish bird. Goo shook her head as if it were made of rags, disgusted with herself. She was thinking like Eve and she was still weak from the change, the glamour. The street she walked along did exist, she was sure of that. She had bent to touch it countless times. But the street was unnamed, and she could find it on no map of the city. In the end it didn't matter. There was cracked pavement beneath her feet, was there not? And now there were other voices, other bodies. They moved around her, a current. She was not entirely safe, though. Goo was vulnerable still, when out alone. She touched her fingers to her mouth and the soft tip of her own tongue reassured her.

Rain began to fall, a warm mist.

She turned down a tiny alleyway lit by gaslights and entered the Unbecoming Club.

You're late, pet.

Goo flinched. Hello, Theseus.

Theseus the Glove stood behind the bar in a murky green suit with flared lapels and narrow trousers. He looked like a woodland mortician. He did not smile at her. He did not offer her a drink.

The Lady Adore waits for you. And her patience grows thin.

But there is hardly a crowd.

Theseus nodded, staring moodily at the nearly empty club. There were several Mariners in the corner, playing knives and trumps by candlelight. Two lonely Tremblers lounged on a sofa, picking at their loose flesh. And a damp, foul-smelling Redeemer was perched on a stool at the bar, his nose nearly touching the cool yellow liquid in his glass. But there was a guttural swelling in the air outside and Goo could feel it in her fingers, her toes. The club would be full in minutes. The patrons would be hungry for her, for Goo.

And not for the first time she felt a little carsick at the idea.

Goo, she thought. They want Goo, not me.

Her pale splintered torso, coming apart before her eyes and falling through dark glass.

Eve, she thought. You stupid little bitch. She turned to the Redeemer at the bar and wondered what a few words of sympathy would cost her. My God. The man truly smelled. But he was not so pathetic and dirty as he looked at first glance. His hair stood up at freakish angles and was peppered with white. His face was long and sour, wrinkled. He looked like a pale gray prune. The man was old, maybe forty. And this was rare, she knew. The middle-aged were generally too gloomy and stubborn about reality for the game of tongues. The Redeemer looked at her now, his lips twitching into a smile. His eyes were red and scorched but still sharp and he was no wetbrain, she could see that. And he looked very familiar, he looked like someone.

Will you hear me, she said. Will you hear a confession.

The man sighed. As if amused. Why not, he said. I am a Redeemer.

Yes, she said. Do I know you?

No, no. I certainly don't think so.

But you look like someone, she said. What is your name?

Gulliver, he said. His hand was dry, with blunt fingernails.

Hello, she said. My name is Goo.

The Redeemer sipped delicately from his glass of Pale. He wiped at his lips, which were thin and rubbery and morbidly prehensile in appearance. His mouth was ugly but no doubt fantastic when it came to oral sex, she thought. A man could be very popular with lips like that. He nodded and rolled his eyes as if he could hear her thoughts and finally said, Well? What is your problem?

Goo sighed and glanced around, nervous and hating herself. Theseus didn't seem to be listening but she could never be sure. He seemed to be anywhere and everywhere at once. I'm not happy, she said.

Interesting, he said. I don't hear that one often.

Goo whispered, now. Sometimes I want to leave the game.

But why? he said.

I used to have a life, a dayworld life.

The Redeemer raised his furry eyebrows. Do you drink the Pale?

Rarely, she said.

He grunted. Good for you.

I love it here, she said. But I hate it, too.

The Redeemer was gazing at her with pity in his eyes and she wondered if he was thinking of her tongue. His eyes were gentle, perhaps. But the whites of them were laced with blood. Careful, she needed to be careful and now the Redeemer sighed. Who am I speaking to? he said.

Goo, she said. But she knew she sounded doubtful and he just stared at her.

This is getting silly, he said.

What do you mean?

Eve, he said. Don't you know me?

It was hard to swallow, to breathe. She wanted to get away from this man.

It's okay, he said. You can be two people at once.

No, she said. I don't want that.

Disappear, he said softly. Walk outside and disappear from the game.

Her left eyelid began to twitch, to blink uncontrollably. And she felt sick, she felt dizzy because that only happened when Eve was nervous, when she was paranoid and sleepless.

This world isn't real, he said.

My boyfriend would disagree, she said.

Theseus was glaring at them from maybe fifteen feet away and she wondered when he had slithered so close, and how much he had heard. She knew that he disapproved of the Redeemers and tolerated them only because they were necessary.

Her belly was exposed, her weak half.

She couldn't stand to look at him now. She backed away from the bar and dragged herself off to the dressing room, where Adore reclined on a mound of dirty pillows, rigid and bony. She often reminded Goo of a dead praying mantis. Adore had a headache, it seemed. She wore a woven silk ice pouch over her eyes and the room smelled of roses. The only light came from a green lamp that glowed like a fat firefly behind lace. Goo stood in the doorway, feeling like a wayward daughter. Her hair was a wreck and her skin itched as if she were covered in dry white soap. She was short of breath and confused. The Redeemer had not tried to kiss her, to take her tongue. And his advice had been very unorthodox.

No one ever suggested that you leave the game, no one.

Adore made a clucking sound. Gather yourself, girl.

I'm sorry, Lady.

Adore removed her ice pouch and regarded Goo with bloody eyes.

Don't be sorry, girl. You are an Exquisitor.

You flatter me, Lady.

I do not.

Goo cast her eyes away, embarrassed. She was only an apprentice. Adore laughed at her, a delicate and fluttering sound. She held out her hands and Goo moved to help her up.

Shall we take the stage? said Adore.

I found myself sitting on the floor of Eve's empty apartment, eating eggdrop soup in bright, unflinching silence. Eve apparently owned no television, no stereo. The only sound was my own manic slurping. At some point I must have thrown open the windows, praying for a little breeze or the distraction of traffic noise, but I couldn't really remember doing so. It was odd, but Eve didn't seem to have a telephone, either. Though I could have sworn she did have one. I had used it to order the food, hadn't I? And that was an hour ago, maybe two. But now I couldn't find a phone anywhere. It was a little maddening. I looked around and around, my head swiveling like a puppet's. I rubbed my eyes, disgusted. She didn't have a coffeemaker, a toaster. There were no electrical appliances at all. Maybe the food was delivered by fairies. Or else the phone was stolen by them.

I was alone in the apartment. Chrome and Mingus the Breather had apparently taken their leave. Faded from the scene without word or gesture. I could barely remember their faces, now. I wasn't so confident that they were real. They were too similar to the freaks that regularly populated my dreams. But if I closed my eyes, I could see Chrome in distorted flashes as he speared a dumpling with one yellow fingernail and fed it rather graphically to Mingus. There was fried rice scattered on the wood floor, as if I had been feeding imaginary squirrels. There were two untouched bowls of soup on the floor, and two spoons. I was Goldilocks, then. The soup is too hot, too cold. I wanted to write it all off as unexpected weirdness, nothing more. But I was dizzy, numb. As if I had suffered a mild electric shock. Or involuntary contact with two nonhumans. I forced myself to clean up the rice, to wash the bowls. I wiped my hands on my pants and stood staring at a long black wrinkle in my shirt, where Mingus the Breather had been kind enough to sew up a nasty hole in the fabric.

Well, then. They were real enough.

Here we go. I found this little blue notebook in the kitchen and not sure why, but I stole it. Eve had only written a few words on the first page, notes for a class and I couldn't be sure but it looked like Logic 101. And the rest of the book was blank.

I was going to rip that page out and start fresh but decided not to. The disconnected pieces of logic appealed to me, the odd little phrases. They comfort, somehow. And she has such fine crooked handwriting, like bugs crawling out of my head. Anyway. Not sure what I was thinking. It had been months since I wrote anything at all by hand. Not even a postcard to my poor mother. The rare signature maybe, on a bad credit card slip. Oh, yeah. I signed a lot of room service tabs when I was with Jude. She loved fucking room service. But the last thing I would have written by hand was probably an incident report for the department that was dull as a cloudless sky, I'm sure. That shit was deadly.

If I wanted to tell the truth, I would say that I stole Eve's notebook because I wanted to keep a record. And what use this might be is hard to say. I know this much. I can't really trust my memory anymore. Or my perception of what's real. And it's funny to think that I have never done this before. This will be my first diary. If you could even call it that.

Dear Jude. If I knew where you were I might send these notes to you.

But I should tell you that something bothers me and maybe it's nothing, nothing to worry about. I have my share of paranoid tendencies. As you know. Okay. I have been back in Denver for less than a day now and I'm looking over my shoulder like there's a contract out on my narrow ass. I can almost feel the crosshairs on my neck. It's not you, is it? I guess it wouldn't shock me. If you were out there. Following me, watching me from rooftops with the eye of a sniper.

Unless I inform you otherwise, I don't know what day it is. Which is why these notes are not dated. I don't even know the correct time. It seems I sold my watch a few days back. Anyway. It's only been a few hours.

I had to get out of Eve's place. The boyfriend was freaking me out. Did I mention she has a boyfriend, a sick fucker with bad clothes. His name is Chrome and he suggested I change my name to Fred. I'm not kidding. You would want to kill him on sight. He said something funny, though. He asked me if I wanted to go see Elvis and it sounded a lot like a threat. How about that. I'm going to Graceland.

You remember where you were when the news came on the radio that he was dead?

Late summer and stupidly hot and I was at Chloe's house. My first real girlfriend and she was trashy and not very smart and conditioned by her loutish stepfather to flinch when you looked hard at her or moved your arm too suddenly and was therefore happy to suck me off right on the couch whenever I dropped by with cigarettes or ice cream. Which I felt bad about but I was only thirteen and couldn't very well say no when she unzipped my pants and bent over me with the cool silence of a Catholic girl doing a few Hail Marys. We were watching the Stooges, I think. And the couch was covered in dirty laundry and I could smell the stepfather's socks and Chloe's head was busily twisting in my lap when they interrupted the broadcast to say that the King was dead. Chloe lifted her face then, her mouth puffy and red. She stared at the television, stricken and pale and she said, oh my mother loves him or she used to, before he got so fat and gross, you know. Then she resumed, she sucked me off like she was born to the task and actually swallowed my gunk. Which inspired me to tell her I loved her. I was thirteen.

Chrome:

He was hungry. Oh, he was violent. He slashed at the air with his long fingers and leaned to breathe obscenities into Mingus's left ear.

I want to hunt, he said.

Mingus glanced at the sky. It's raining.

Chrome muttered, not here.

They sat on a circle of grass overlooking the freeway. Chrome was on edge, he was bored. He began to play with Eve's telephone, picking up the receiver and saying: Yes, who's there? He had cut the cord and removed the phone from her apartment on a whim, thinking to confuse and alienate the sickly Phineas, whom he had found distasteful and oddly alluring.

He looked over at Mingus, who still stared like a simpleton down at the freeway. He was fascinated by cars, the poor thing. His favorite was the Saturn. He claimed it was the most graceful and godlike of machines. Chrome had to smile at this notion. He told Mingus that the Saturn was manufactured in Tennessee by unevolved humans.

Mingus was ignoring him, though. Which was not wise. Chrome stared at his own fingers. They were twitching and he realized he could easily kill his little friend. It could happen as suddenly as a violent sneeze, a brief involuntary convulsion. It was disturbing, really.

There's a green one, said Mingus. They are the prettiest, I think.

J'ai faim, Chrome said.

English, said Mingus. Speak English.

I'm hungry, he said.

It isn't safe to hunt by day.

Please, said Chrome. The Freds come and go.

Everyone comes and goes.

But the Freds stay in character.

As do we, said Mingus.

Ah, yes. But I am a bit more self-aware, said Chrome.

Chrome removed a garrote from his boot and twirled it on one finger. The black cord was soft and silky to the touch but strong as piano wire. There was a piece of wood the approximate size of his pinkie at either end, wrapped in leather. He could kill a bear with the thing, if he could only creep up on one.

You twit, he said. That was a Mustang.

My eyes are failing in this light.

How is your nose?

Fine, said Mingus. I can smell you.

Do you not smell meat?

Mingus frowned. A car had drifted to a stop nearby, an ordinary Toyota. It was perhaps a hundred feet away, parked under a little tree. The windows were down and two men sat in the front seat. The angles of their jaws suggested an uneasy discussion of money. Mingus would surely smell sex on them, like salt and fresh earth. Even Chrome could smell it. The sex was coming from them in waves.

We will not hunt a Citizen, said Mingus.

Of course not. You will sniff out an unfortunate Fred who has lost his way.

I walked out of Eve's place and felt better straightaway. The oxygen had been too thin up there, or too pure. And I had been talking to myself in no time, poking at my eyes with restless fingers. I did find my knife, thank God. It was hidden under a sofa cushion. I had tried and failed to write Eve a note. Thank you for the use of the sofa, the money for food. Thanks for washing my clothes. And I love your new friends...and fuck it. I had crumpled these aborted little notes and tossed them at the window. I would see her later, maybe. It looked like she was running around with a lot of freaks but why the hell should I care. She was hardly a proper little girl before, was she. And she was not a child to be looked after.

I had my own bellyful of problems, anyway. No money and nowhere to sleep, no job prospects. If I had three red apples, I might wander downtown and amaze the pedestrians with my juggling. I could gather enough spare change to buy a cup of coffee, maybe hang around a diner all day reading other people's newspapers. I could beg a ballpoint pen off a kindly waitress and use it to mark up the classifieds. A few months ago I had dreamed of a job at a gas station, a video store. I had wanted to change my name and shave my head and write bad poetry.

Yeah.

I rolled my eyes at the sky, at a blanket of gray. I didn't like poetry and I was not a good juggler. And I would first have to steal three red apples. I ducked into a phone booth and realized with some amusement that I bother to dwell on the irony. The call was free, at least. I told the emergency operator that I was a police informant and was in relatively grave danger. The operator was not amused.

This line is for emergency calls only, she said.

I'm going to be dead in five minutes, I said. Is that an emergency?

Your name, she said.

The angry flipper-boy, I said.

Hum of silence.

Phineas Poe, I said. Please tell Detective Moon to come get me.

Theseus the Glove:

The stage was black but for an egg-shaped spot of orange light. One of Goo's bare legs lay stretched there as if cut off at the knee. Her thigh-high boots were nowhere to be seen. Theseus reached under his jacket to pinch his left nipple. He had his doubts about this girl sometimes, doubts about her belief in the game. But she was lovely as a sleeping child when bound and gagged.

A gloved hand entered the egg of orange light.

Goo's leg looked as if it had been discarded, a piece of firewood. The hand began to stroke, or measure, her ankle with blunt, velvet fingers.

Theseus felt wet.

A small wire cage was shoved slowly into the orange light.

The wire cage had two doors. One of them was an ordinary door, with a hinge on one side and a latch on the other. The other opened like a set of flaps, with a semicircle cut out of each side. The gloved hands carefully pulled open these flaps and inserted Goo's bare foot into the cage. The flaps were then closed and the cutout circle fit snugly, if a little tightly, around her ankle.

There was a low, steady grunting from the crowd.

Money. This was silver in his pocket.

Goo's pale, arched foot was trapped in the wire cage. Now the gloved hand opened the rear door and a gray pigeon appeared, as if pulled from a hat. The pigeon was quickly pushed into the cage and the rear door latched. The pigeon crouched there, placid and dumbly staring.

The egg of orange light began to grow.

It widened to expose Goo's hips. Her other leg was crumpled, hidden. The tattered, yellow-white dress lay like dirty snow around her. Her arms were splayed and apparently powerless. She was not restrained, however. She was deliciously passive and Theseus wanted to laugh. The girl was dangerous. Her eyes were shut tight and her ears flattened, feline against her skull. There was a thin pillow beneath her head. The Lady Adore crouched at the edge of the light, near the wire cage. She wore leather pants and no shoes. The coiled black cloth around her torso resembled a bandage more than a shirt. In her gloved hands, she held a bundle of damp gray rags. Adore appeared motionless, barely breathing as the orange light swelled. Adore placed the rags at the rear door of the cage, perhaps six inches from the forlorn pigeon. She lit a match, and the little bundle began to burn. Theseus groaned, sweating.

The pigeon was frantic. It hopped up and down and sideways, like a grasshopper. Adore pulled a straight razor from the cuff of one velvet glove and began to cut and slash briskly at Goo's clothes. The pigeon threw itself against the wires as if it might kill itself, then abruptly stopped. Instead, it attacked Goo's trapped foot. The wedding dress fell away from the razor like paper.

The bird was a mad, thrashing blur. Goo's slim white foot was a web of trickling blood.

The corset was so thick that Adore was forced to hack at it. She peeled it away and Goo's belly was bleeding here and there, from superficial cuts. Her ribs were fine and shadowy. Her breasts were plump, her nipples red. Smoke from the small fire hung over her body. The pigeon was growing weak now, its gray feathers dark with blood. The Lady Adore cut away Goo's underpants and tossed them into the silent crowd. She reached into the cage and cut the pigeon's throat just as the orange light faded to black.

Theseus smiled, pouring drinks all around.

Multiple personalities. Don't freak out but I'm pretty sure I have them. Not a clinical thing, not a disease. But a distraction to be sure. There are maybe six or seven pretty concrete versions of myself knocking around in here and I mean it gets fucking crowded when everybody is drunk or talking at once.

And every so often the opportunity arises to assume another identity, to take another name and every time I want to run like hell, I want to run away from Phineas like his ass is on fire. Because I need a little personal space between him and me.

Distance. I need distance from the others.

But the other people I become are never strong enough. Or fast enough. Because Phineas wears them down in the end. He's relentless.

Early morning freak-out. I passed a construction site. Abandoned. Looked like someone was tearing a building down and then ran out of money. Their permit was revoked or something and the building was left half-standing and you could see this exposed brick wall that fifty years ago was an exterior wall but the building had been added onto and the wall was covered. There were old advertisements painted into the bricks, the kind that still said cigarettes were good for you. And rust marks in the wall shaped like the skeleton of a fire escape and windows. A few of the windows were boarded up and plastered over. But the boards were rotten by now. Rotten and the plaster broken through. And through a few of these windows I saw people moving around. Combing their hair and drinking tea and reading the newspaper and these weren't homeless people. They weren't crackheads or squatters. They were just people. They all had that sweet laziness about them, that oblivious air of someone who is watching television alone in a hotel room in his underwear and has no idea he's being watched.

Thought I must be dreaming. Thought I must be deceived by the light but they were in there, I'm sure of it. And you know what? When I see something like that, all the other versions of Phineas scratch their asses and pretend they didn't see a thing.

Fuck them, right. I sat with my feet in the gutter and peered through the iron gate into the black space below, looking for dead birds and lost skateboards, rotting pumpkins. I scribbled in my notebook and tried not to lament my lack of cleverness. The cars flew past me and I felt more and more like an alien. I was the only creature in sight without a bright, metallic shell. It had occurred to me that Moon might not be so thrilled to see me. But I had no one else to call. Crumb would offer me tea and an amusing story about a guy who came in complaining of stomach pains, who believed he had an ulcer when in fact he was carrying a bullet and was too drunk to recall being shot. I didn't need tea. I needed a job or a place to sleep. I needed a new pair of shoes, I needed a cigarette, and now Moon pulled up in a gray Taurus. The passenger window slid down and Moon stared out at me, his sour mouth twitching with amusement.

Jesus, he said. Get in the car.

Fortunately, Moon had cigarettes. And he seemed more than willing to drive around in forced silence for a while. His radio was broken, or so he claimed. We circled for a while, as if lost. It was a peculiar day. The sky was moody, inconstant. The light seemed to change violently from one block to the next and on one street it was actually raining. I shut my eyes and remembered driving across Nevada maybe ten years earlier. An empty stretch of desert, the highway glittering like a rope of black silver. The sun unblinking and the sky flat and silent as a stone. Peripheral vision fuzzy around the edges. A migraine, I thought. A hawk dropped suddenly from nowhere, swooping over the roof of the car and crashing into the luggage rack. In the rearview mirror I saw a brief windmill tumble of shredded wings, gray and white. As if the bird had exploded. And then nothing but my own face in the mirror and I had been baffled to see myself crying. How are you. How are you. I looked up and now we were sitting at a red light.

How are you, Moon said.

That's a good question. I'm a little confused.

Moon grunted and shifted the car into gear. I examined him. The same clothes, the same meaty face. The eyes vague and expressionless behind glasses but the mouth was vivid, quick. His mouth could be apologetic and menacing at once.

You look healthier, said Moon.

Yeah, well. It's been a year.

Is that all?

I'm broke. I need a place to sleep.

Oh, boy.

What did you expect?

I expected you to be dead by now.

We were driving directly into the sun. It lingered on the horizon, a sullen yellow eye. The sun refused to blink. Every tree and car and lonely pedestrian was skeletal and black, shadows come to life. A wheelchair rolled abruptly across the road, slow and wobbling, as if its passenger were unconscious. I blinked, waiting for Moon to touch the brakes. If anything, he sped up and we narrowly missed crushing the thing. I turned violently in my seat and saw that the wheelchair was in fact empty, drifting safely to the other side. There was no one on the sidewalk who might have pushed it.

What the fuck was what?

What was what, said Moon.

Moon pulled a cell phone from his jacket pocket and smiled sheepishly. He called the station and told someone to take his name off the board. He was taking a mental health day.

I was amused. Are you feeling unstable? I said.

Yeah. I was thinking of you, actually.

I appreciate it. Where are we going?

My place. You can sleep at the foot of my bed, with Shame.

Who the hell is Shame?

My cat.

Curious name, I said.

It was supposed to be Shane, okay. Like the gunslinger.

Oh, yeah. Steve McQueen.

Jesus. It was Lee Marvin.

Whatever.

Steve McQueen was a fine actor, said Moon. But he couldn't have handled Shane. The character was too rich, too complex. McQueen didn't have a true dark side. He was too good-looking, you know. He was a prettyboy. Lee Marvin, though. That motherfucker could act.

I sighed. How did the cat become Shame?

When he was a kitten, I had this girlfriend. And she had a speech defect.

Beautiful.

Chrome:

Mingus had a remarkable nose. Chrome was proud of him, truly. He adored the boy. In less than half an hour they had come upon a Fred wandering stupidly down an alley. A thin, starved-looking figure in dirty clothing who meandered along, chewing his thumb and peering into sewer grates and stopping now and again to ponder the contents of a garbage pail.

Chrome rubbed his palms together now, gloating. The alley was narrow and smelled of rot. The shadows were a dark, sinewy green. The shadows were lively. The Fred was perhaps fifty meters ahead of them but Chrome was unconcerned. He happened to know that the alley led to a dead end. And the Fred looked particularly weak, as if his brain had softened well beyond mush. A Mariner's nervous apprentice could bring him down with two fingers.

It was dreary, is what this was.

The best sport was of course a Fred who was self-aware, his nerves jangling with fear and his own new tonguelust. The self-aware would come at you with a piece of pipe, with teeth and boots. The self-aware were dangerous. And much more fun. In a pure hunt, thought Chrome, the hunter and the hunted must be properly entwined. They must be inseparable, of one heart and breath. They must be shadows joined, they must be lovers.

Chrome still twirled the garrote and bit at the air. He glanced at

Mingus, who was walking so slowly he might have been asleep. Mingus wasn't happy about this, he knew. It was a violation of the code of tongues to hunt by day. But it was a notion Chrome had been toying with for some time. Hunting in the light and among Citizens would surely increase the danger and thrill, the difficulty. He was bored silly with the stiff parameters of the game, the pious rules. And he was curious to see if anything would come of breaking the code. Besides. He was hungry.

Chrome was always hungry, always.

Mingus was a Breather, and therefore controlled his own tonguelust with the rigor of a celibate, which infuriated Chrome to no end. He spat with disgust as the Fred stumbled ahead and actually walked into a wall and bounced backward with all the grace of a rubber donkey. Fuck it anyway. The wetbrain would be a fast kill.

Mingus now leapt to grab at a fire escape, pulling himself up like a spider.

It will be a boring kill, he said.

Be quiet, said Chrome.

Mingus pulled a brightly colored yo-yo from his pocket, a Duncan. He flicked it down and back with hypnotic ease.

Walk the dog, said Chrome.

You know I can't do any tricks.

I will teach you, said Chrome. After I kill this poor Fred.

Moon's apartment was dark and relatively damp. He had very little furniture. I found I was not so uncomfortable at all. I had been a little worried that I might be. That we would be two unfamiliar men in a confined space, the smell of one overpowering the other and that any physical contact, skin touching actual skin, would be rare and awkward and tenuous. That we would suffer the crush of ordinary silence.

But I let myself fall easily onto a dusty sofa that was covered in equal parts with brown leather and fuzzy orange stripes. It was a hideous couch and I immediately liked it. I would sleep here, if I would sleep at all. I relaxed for a minute while Moon rattled around in the kitchen, cursing.

What are you doing in there?

I'm cooking, said Moon.

Oh, really.

Well. I'm heating a few cans of soup.

I nodded, gazing at a giant television that was so covered in dust I wondered if anything could ever be seen flickering on its screen. Other than the ghosts of dead baseball players and long unemployed actors. I wondered if Moon was in there mixing together several different and opposing flavors of soup: split pea and clam chowder and beef with barley, for instance. I hoped not. Moon came into the living room and tossed a narrow white box at me. It was a toothbrush, unopened.

Are my teeth green?

Moon shrugged. I went to the dentist the other day. It was free.

Thanks, then.

You shouldn't neglect your gums.

I won't.

Moon stared at me, apparently expecting me to run along and brush my teeth now, rather than later. As if I had a mouthful of dirt. I laughed and got up, thinking I might need to pee anyway. I repaired to Moon's little bathroom, brushed my teeth with Moon's generic toothpaste and poked aimlessly through Moon's medicine cabinet. Foot powder and witch hazel. Razor blades. A variety of pills and fluids that purported to deal with gastrointestinal distress. Generic aspirin. I spat gloomily into the sink, ever watchful for blood. I had a bizarre craving for a tall glass of cherry-red cough syrup with ice and soda water. The toothpaste left my mouth raw and I rinsed it repeatedly.

When I came out of the bathroom Moon was pacing, apparently agitated. I sat on the ugly couch and forced myself to swallow the unidentifiable soup Moon had given me. I wished Moon would sit down. He had taken off his jacket to reveal a blue denim shirt that was torn under one armpit. The sleeves flapped around his wrists, as if the cuffs had no buttons. He violently loosened his tie, his face red and puffing as he did so. He pulled a tiny Swiss army knife from his watch pocket and used the scissors to rapidly clip his nails. A skinny orange cat slinked into the room and came over to inspect me, the new human.

That would be Shame, said Moon.

Poor thing, I said. His name was ruined by a woman and now he looks like you never feed him.

He's just high-strung, said Moon.

I lowered my bowl of soup to the floor and the cat crouched over it, growling.

Moon, I said. You want to sit down, maybe? Relax.

I'm thinking about something. I think on my feet.

Okay. Do you have anything to drink?

Yeah. Next to the sink is a bottle of whiskey.

I went into the kitchen, glad for something to do. There was a mostly full jug of Canadian Mist on the counter. It was covered in dust and I wasn't surprised. The stuff was worse than poison. But I was a beggar, now. I was a jackal. I rinsed two glasses and poured several fat fingers of Mist into each. There were three empty ice trays in the freezer. I cursed and muttered and told myself the stuff would be equally putrid with or without ice. But I compulsively filled the ice trays at the sink.

I came back and gave one glass to Moon, who gulped the Mist in one swallow. Then choked.

Oh, he said. That shit is bad.

Christmas gift? I said.

Yeah. From a guy in Homicide named Tom Gunn.

What did you give him?

Tickets to a Nuggets game.

I guess you're even.

But these were good seats, man.

The fucking Nuggets, though.

Moon laughed. He sat down on a corduroy ottoman with a lurid floral pattern.

What's on your mind? I said.

Save it for later, said Moon. Let's get drunk.

Goo:

Adore smoked a clove cigarette, her eyes glowing red in the mirror like a cat's eyes in the flash of a camera. Goo felt weary, she felt ill and she hated it when Adore sat behind her like that because it was like she was surrounded by her. Adore was behind her and Adore was staring at her in the glass. There were two of them and one of these days she would smash this mirror.

Four walls were enough. In a mirror you had six walls, eight walls.

Goo was bleeding in a dozen places.

A young, nearly invisible girl knelt beside her, silently cleaning her wounds with a cloth diaper that she dipped into a pail of water and alcohol. The cuts were not deep, at least. She would not need stitches, and painful or not she was proud of the work. Goo watched herself smile in the mirror. She was in awe of Adore sometimes, and marked herself fortunate to be her apprentice.

It had been a beautiful piece, The Bird.

The crowd had been tortured into a state of distraction. They had paid good money to see her stripped naked and violated by Adore. But they were undone by their own fascination for blood and couldn't take their eyes off the bird eating from her foot. Then the lights had gone out and they could only sit and listen to the grunts and whispers of what may or may not have been two women sweatily fucking on a dark stage. In fact, Adore had noisily eaten a sandwich while Goo had lain in a blissful stupor. The victims were always shifting in the landscape of the game and now Adore was staring at her.

What? said Goo.

You spoke to a Redeemer, earlier.

She shrugged. Yes, so what?

What did you tell him?

Nothing. I told him that I was having boyfriend troubles.

Be careful, said Adore. You can't trust them.

Who can I trust?

Adore smiled. Are you still seeing that young man, that Mariner?

I suppose. Why?

Adore stubbed out her cigarette, deliberately.

You don't like him, said Goo.

No, said Adore.

The girl had finished with Goo's wounds and now moved silently to brush Adore's hair. Goo leaned back in her chair, still naked. Her clothes had been cut to ribbons, destroyed. It looked like she had been attacked by wolves and emerged remarkably unscathed. She would have to wear something of Adore's if she wanted to go home. That green dress with the gold thread, perhaps.

That's okay, said Goo. I don't always like him, either.

I think it's time for you to design your own piece, said Adore. I will be your victim, of course.

Goo was surprised. Are you sure I'm ready for that?

Adore didn't hear her because Goo's voice had fallen to a whisper. It didn't matter. Because she knew she was ready. She felt a thin, seeping wave of nausea but she was ready. It was Adore who might not be ready to exchange roles. Adore laughed and said don't worry, girl. I'm ready.

My first victim, said Goo.

That is, unless you have another victim in mind, said Adore. A young man, for instance.

Goo stretched her arms and winced at the ribbon of pain across her ribs.

I close my eyes and all I see is you, Jude.

Your hair is long and wet and you twist it in your hands like a piece of rope. You sleep topless on the balcony with those strange shadows falling across your belly. You have more money than you know what to do with and still you steal fruit from the market. You spend hours shooting green bottles in the desert with your back to the sun.

You ruined me for sex, by the way. I just can't be bothered anymore. I can't be fucked.

I remember something you said about serial killers and how the interesting ones are always very good kissers. I stared at you, stupidly I'm sure. I asked how many serial killers had you kissed and you laughed like the ghost of Lady Macbeth. You kissed me.

Moon was drunk, crashing around his apartment. He breathed wetly. His eyes rolled around, loose from their moorings. He was looking for something to punish, it seemed. He clumsily put his foot through a coffee table, panting. His foot became stuck and he fell heavily to the floor. I scrambled to move lamps and stereo equipment from harm's way. I remember, vaguely, that Moon was not really supposed to drink. There had been incidents in the past, nasty incidents involving borrowed motorcycles and flooded toilets and gouged eyeballs. There had been a rather notorious sword fight maybe ten years ago. But I was never my brother's keeper. The opposite, if anything. I could remember more than one night when Moon had prevented me from doing something stupid or fatal.

Moon now lay sideways on the floor, his foot wedged among the splintered remains of his table. He coughed for several minutes, then demanded angrily to know where Mary had gone.

I was patient. I promised him that I knew no one named Mary and Moon growled, then dropped the subject. I crouched next to him, patting his damp belly as if he were a wounded bear. Moon sighed sleepily and I quickly disarmed him. Moon carried only one weapon, and was known to disapprove of ankle holsters. But this Colt that he had carried at his hip for eleven years and had rarely fired was a regular monster. I hefted it, thinking I could easily kill a car with the fucker. I unloaded it, then slid the big gun under the couch. I currently had no gun, myself. I carried only the knife, and if it came to a knife fight I reckoned I was quicker on my feet than the poor coffee table, which had fared pretty well against Moon.

What happened, said Moon. What happened in Texas goddamn you.

Nothing much, I said. I watched a kid die.

And the woman, said Moon. The fuck happened to that crazy bitch.

I sat cross-legged on the floor. The carpet was dusty, hairy. It was pretty sticky in places. I stared at Moon's heaving chest and belly, at the stains on his white shirt and the limp, smeared tie. The white, hairy stomach flesh that gathered at his waistband. The green canvas military belt with unpolished buckle. The filthy white pants, the white socks. The black shoes with flattened rubber heels. Moon needed a woman in the worst way.

I leaned over and began to extricate Moon's foot from the shards of wood.

Jude, you mean. She's living in Mexico City, last I heard. Married to a nice banker and two months pregnant. She's happy as a clam.

Liar, said Moon. Fuck happened.

Ask me tomorrow.

You shit me.

Sleep, I said. Go to sleep.

Not tired. Let's go up on the roof.

I don't think so.

Fresh air. I can't breathe.

You can't even walk.

Okay. Lemme tell you a story. Moon abruptly began to frisk himself, grabbing at his pockets and crotch. Where the fuck is my gun? My gun, my gun.

I eyed the couch warily, hoping that Moon was too fat and soggy to wiggle over there. It's in the freezer, I said. With your life savings.

Okay. Shut up. Lemme tell you a story.

Yeah. Tell me.

Moon was a lump on the floor. His voice was thick, droning. I lit a cigarette and listened, my own eyes closed.

Thirteen, said Moon. Total of thirteen cops gone missing. But it's gradual. They fade. Not dead exactly. No bodies to speak of. They go undercover for a while and sometimes they come back but when they do they're not right. They're different.

Different how?

Like pod people. And then one day they don't come back at all. These are guys from Narcotics and Vice, mostly. Fuck them, right. But then two guys from Homicide. You remember Jimmy Sky?

Yeah. I never liked him.

Come on. The fucking Skywalker. You never met a cop so cool as him and he slides in dry as ice after a month undercover with a basket full of oatmeal raisin cookies he baked himself. Then he's gone for good. And nobody wants to talk about it.

Who's your chief?

Moon spat violently. Captain Honey, he said.

I laughed.

Moon muttered, the poor bastard is ninety days from retirement and doped up on painkillers. His teeth are no good. He tells me not to worry. Don't worry, he says. Meanwhile he's busy cutting shit out of the newspapers all day: comic strips and "Dear Abby" and coupons for cat food and his horoscope. You walk into his office and Captain Honey says hey, private. What's your sign? He reads you your horoscope and smiles at you like some kind of drunk priest. Then he slips you a coupon for forty-nine cents off Fancy Feast. He says you got a fucking cat, don't you? And the watch commander says there's nothing he can do about it. These guys aren't officially missing. Nobody knows shit. And nobody wants to go undercover, nobody.

A minute or two rattled past. I waited but Moon said nothing else. His voice had disappeared into the powdery air of sleep.

The motherfucker is asleep and maybe I'm jealous. Not sleeping so well lately. Not since I got off the junk. It's like the dark doesn't really find me.

I wait for it. I wait for the velvet, for the warm bottomless silence to come and wrap itself around me but the silence is indifferent and passes me by and I remember the velvet doesn't know me anymore, it doesn't want me.

And I think about other ways to get there. Bleeding to death might work. As long as I didn't cut through a major artery the long slide down to unconsciousness would likely be slow and sweet, something I could savor.

It's a funny thing to dream but sometimes I dream of going flatline. Not sure I would want to go all the way under but for a minute or two it would be pretty nice to take a look around and then swim back to the surface.

Thursday's child has far to go.

Mingus:
Red bricks on all sides. The smell of earth and clay and men sweating. The smoke of a thousand cigarettes. Sunshine and tar. The noise of a bulldozer, loud as fury.

Mingus chomped at his tongue. He was too easily hypnotized by his own sense of smell. The pain in his tongue cleared his head. His legs were asleep and dangling from the iron fire escape. He put away the yo-yo and leaned forward to watch Chrome lazily finish off the Fred. Mingus chewed at his thumbnail, his head still spinning from the scent of Chinese take-out and the strange Citizen they had encountered at Goo's.

That one would bear watching, he thought.

At the end of the alley, Chrome still whispered into the Fred's ear. Mingus stopped himself from summoning the smell of the Fred's damp, fishy hair. He was plagued enough by the real.

The Fred lay curled like a baby in ash and black gravel. He was almost asleep, his hands limp and white. Chrome stroked the back of the Fred's neck, his lips moving softly. He was singing a French nursery rhyme, Mingus was sure of it. Frère Jacques. Chrome was terribly disappointed that he had not been born French. He spoke often of jumping a ship to Paris, of starting their own subterrain there. But it would not be so easy. One did not just withdraw from the game and Chrome's French was hopeless.

He was the cruelest of the Mariners, without question. Chrome garroted the Freds, pulling them down like sick deer. But he didn't kill them straightaway. He calmed and comforted them. He promised not to hurt them and he lulled them to sleep. He made them feel safe in his arms. Then he went for the tongue.

The others were so greedy for tongue that they killed without pause.

The wind rose, flooding Mingus with a sickening spectrum of odors, each of them dense with borrowed memory. Mingus pinched his nostrils between thumb and finger and watched as Chrome knelt beside the Fred, brushing bits of filth from his clothing. He gently buttoned the Fred's jacket to the throat, then patted him on the cheek with the odd, faraway smile of a father who is about to strike.

Mingus closed his eyes because he didn't need to watch, to see.

He could imagine well enough. Chrome would take the man's face in his strong hands and bend forward, as if to kiss the mouth. He would force the jaw open, wide enough to count the Fred's teeth. He would suck the Fred's tongue from his mouth as if it were an oyster, then bite it softly at the pink root and stop himself just short of severing it but still he would draw blood. He would own the Fred's already blurry soul. He would swallow, his eyes flashing silver. Mingus could already hear the Fred screaming, or trying to. His hollow, shrunken voice like the bark of a baby seal.

Mingus opened his eyes and Chrome stood tall over the Fred, skinny and shining. His arms hanging loose. His face and chest were bloody, streaming red and black. Mingus felt cold and rushing dizzy as he saw but couldn't believe what he saw.

The Fred lay motionless, his throat ripped open.

Chrome has killed the man, truly killed him. Mingus coughed, staring. There was a shivering fist in his throat. He felt like he was falling down a brightly lit elevator shaft. This couldn't be. This was a game, a fantasy. The taking of tongues was painful, yes. A little bloody sometimes. But it wasn't real, it wasn't real. What had the motherfucker done. What had he done.

What have you done?

He looked away, then back. This couldn't be what it seemed and now Chrome walked toward him, his face a red mask. He held something shiny in one hand, like a badge.

Mingus, he said. Je me suis égare.

Long shadows. I reached for the jug of Canadian Mist and took a small, bitter swallow. Moon grunted and pulled himself up to an approximate sitting position now, with considerable effort. I ignored him, tried to digest his story. The thing was decomposing in my head and it sounded perfectly fucked up. It sounded like the paranoid tale of some accident-prone cross-dresser who had played with himself too much as a boy and his Baptist mother had burned his fingers on the iron when she caught him at it. In a few months or years, Moon would sound like any other twitchy bastard with a theory about how the phone company had started the Gulf War.

But maybe there was something to this. Maybe cops were disappearing and no one cared. Anything was possible.

Anyway.

I had a pretty good idea what Moon was asking for. He wanted me to be a canary, a fragile seeker of bad air. Moon wanted to send me underground, then watch to see if I would come back or disappear. And why not, right? I was a nonperson. I was untouchable. I had no money, no hope. I wasn't officially dead yet, but I was close enough. I knew the terrain, as well. I swallowed another mouthful of Canadian Mist. I had spent more than one day undercover busily deconstructing myself. What was another day, or two? But I couldn't quite see Moon's eyes. I couldn't trust him. I flicked on a reading lamp that I had moved out of Moon's path of destruction an hour ago. It provided a small circle of light that Moon now leaned into.

You can sleep here, he said. For a while. You'll need another address if you go under.

I shrugged, undecided. Yeah.

What do you say?

What is it that you want me to do, exactly?

Moon chewed at his lips, rabid. I want you to find Jimmy Sky.

What about the other twelve guys, I said.

I'll get you a gun, said Moon. A car, maybe. Any equipment you want.

The other guys? I said.

Fuck the other guys.

What's so special about Jimmy Sky?

Moon shrugged. I can scrape some funds out of petty cash. Mad money.

Mad money, I said. Oh, boy.

Yeah, baby. You're gonna have the time of your life.

I nodded, sinking onto the couch. There was one small thing that troubled me. Maybe it was nothing. But I was lying, earlier. I had never heard of a cop named Jimmy Sky. It sounded a lot like the name of a comic book hero, like someone's secret identity. It sounded like a lame superhero, some second-rate character like the Green Lantern. Now there was a pussy if ever there was one. The Green Lantern. A prettyboy with a magic ring.

Goo:

Limping, she was limping. What time was it. The sky had gone red and pink, like an exposed membrane. It couldn't be much past midnight, could it. But it felt like dawn, like the sun was rising. The air against her face had the warm kiss of fever. She crossed the street, barely aware of passing cars.

She told herself to slow down.

It couldn't be morning yet.

When she reached the other side, there was a faraway noise in her head like a hushed whisper, a ghost of fingers in her hair. Goo became Eve. Her apartment building loomed ahead, black. As ever, there was the knife of disappointment. The regret. She didn't want to share herself with Eve.

Eve bore new bruises, fresh cuts.

Her apartment was empty and the air brittle.

She took off her coat and hung it carefully on a hook, then stepped out of Adore's green dress and let it fall to the floor. Her body was numb, as usual. The transition wrecked her sometimes and she would easily sleep for fifteen hours without dreaming. The game was swallowing everything around her with the silent fury of a televised hurricane. Eve had no friends, no family. She had no job anymore and school was a pale, foreign memory. Three classes, she had paid tuition for three classes. Maybe four. One of them was Logic, she thought. Logic, yes. She had chosen it because it satisfied a Math credit, which seemed funny at the time. But she couldn't remember the last time she even went near campus. At least five, maybe six weeks ago. Dizzy. She was a little dizzy. It might not be such a bad idea to withdraw from the game for a while, to catch her breath. Eve glanced over her shoulder. There was no one to hear her disordered thoughts, no one but Goo.

She went into the kitchen and opened a can of tuna. Walked back to the living room and stood in the dark, eating tuna straight from the can. Her face in a black window, looking back at her. The sheen of oil on her lips. She might not want to leave the game, she might not be able to.

What had the Redeemer said? It's okay to be two people, two people.

Bone-white curtains swirled around her and she realized slowly that Phineas was gone. There were crumpled bits of paper on her floor. She picked them up and each one bore her given name.

I wondered dimly what time it might be. I had reluctantly sold my watch two weeks earlier in Memphis, to a nervous, razor-thin guy named Duke in a downtown pawnshop. Forty bucks for my father's antique diving watch. And Duke had insulted me. He said the watch was barely worth ten dollars, because there was no way it was still waterproof. I was fucking lucky to get forty, according to Duke. There had been a wide, unfriendly silence as I wondered how much the watch was worth to me and how badly I needed to get to Denver. A black fly buzzed past my face, then landed on my wrist. It strolled up my arm, looking for a bite to eat. Duke had stared long and hard at the fly, his head bobbing as I tried in vain to explain that water resistance was really not the point. The watch was a valuable relic, an ode to an earlier age. At which point Duke had wiped his bright red nose and glared at me and said that the forty was about to fucking disappear. Duke had the bright, acidic stink and glow of a meth addict and I had to admit that I could live with forty.

Now I was awake. I was damp and hungry on Moon's couch and I had no useful concept of time. The sky was black through the nearest window but that meant nothing. I had to pee, however. Maybe it was close to morning, maybe not. There was always the chance that God would cancel the day. That God would say fuck this noise and just shut down the whole operation.

I don't believe in God, exactly. I believe in gods. I tend to think there are any number of godlike creatures running around up there and that none of them is all-powerful. None of them is Santa Claus, okay. Most of them have dark intentions, cruel purpose. They want to be wrathful, but they don't quite have the juice. They have good days and bad days. On good days they can lay waste to a fishing village in Honduras or if they're feeling fat and prosperous maybe stop a bus full of kids from diving into a gorge but mostly they just fuck around and stir things up.

Anyway. Take a long look at your own hand. The slender claw, beautiful and cruel. A team of expensive scientists working around the clock couldn't design a more effective piece of machinery. This is what Hamlet was going on about there in Act Two. *Man delights not me, nor woman neither.* Because at the end of the day the hand does what you want it to. It saves the bird with the broken wing from drowning. It snatches the kid out of oncoming traffic and it pulls the trigger that ends the life of someone who deserves it or doesn't. The hand does crosswords and lights cigarettes and feeds the fish and pinches your nipples when it gets bored. The hand is God.

I'm a fool, of course. But in the bright or anyway less shadowy regions of my heart I think I was hoping to come home and find a little space. Which is funny, don't you think. *Home* is a word with such uneasy and fragile and ultimately menacing overtones that anyone else on the planet would have fucking known better.

Moon wants me to find a missing cop named Jimmy Sky and I have a pretty good idea that no such person exists but Moon has been such a faithful protector in the past that I can only nod and say yes.

The queer thing is Moon's tone, his voice. One minute he seems really very worried about the health and welfare of his pal Jimmy Sky and the next he is about to chew his own lip off just talking about him and I catch a vibe that maybe Jimmy was no friend at all and what Moon really wants is for me to find the Skywalker hiding out in some shitty motel room so that Moon can put a bullet between his ears or failing that, maybe find the fucker already dead somewhere so Moon might have the private pleasure of spitting on poor Jimmy's remains.

And I guess it makes no difference to me, as Jimmy Sky is no friend of mine but still I wonder because the whole thing feels slippery and wrong and maybe I'm walking down a road that goes nowhere good.

Imagine you were in my shoes. What would you do, Jude?

Chrome:

He was shivering and wet. The water was so cold. His skin had a far-away brilliance, like he had stuck his bare arm into the snow and left it there. He huddled in the dark mouth of a suburban driveway, using a sleeping Citizen's garden hose to wash the blood from his face and hands. He felt absurdly calm. He had done it, he had touched the ghost. He had killed and it wasn't make-believe. The Fred had been a policeman and if he wanted to, Chrome could certainly tell himself and anyone who cared to listen that it was self-defense. The policeman had pulled a gun on him. He had been a threat to all of them, to the game. But that wasn't it at all. The man had been a Fred. He had been passive, a slug. He had barely known what planet he was on. Chrome could have simply bitten the man's tongue and disappeared as he had done countless times. One tongue, taken by force. Two points. Two more points. But the accumulation of points no longer interested him. He had lost count long ago and he had known this would happen one day. And when he nipped the Fred's warm tongue and tasted blood, he had felt everything at once. His skin, bright and tingling as if he could peel it off and give it a shake. The small hairs on his neck. The enamel of his own teeth. He felt like time had folded around him and come to a complete stop. He and the Fred had been trapped together in a window, a bubble. They had fallen into one of those little plastic paperweights filled with water and artificial snow and the Fred's throat had been soft and white and sweetly exposed and Chrome had been unable to think of any reason not to sink his teeth into that skin and simply pull it open. The blood had washed over his face, it had filled him with a sickness and joy that were fleeting. It was like an orgasm, of course. But the comparison was such a cliché it pained him to consider it.

He was a werewolf, a ripper.

He grinned. Très diabolique, non?

Now he took off his shirt, rinsed it and put it back on. He glanced down at the street, where Mingus paced nervously along the sidewalk. The Breather was freaking out, truly. He had looked at Chrome with such horror and disbelief that Chrome had laughed out loud. Mingus had seen what he did. He had seen him kill and Chrome hoped this would not be a problem.

Dead face yawning. My own warped face in the mirror. I had acquired the habit of examining it whenever I found myself alone in a bathroom. Otherwise I tended to forget exactly what I looked like. I promised myself this was not such a bad thing, and hardly a clinical condition. I looked like no one and it was nothing to worry about. I pissed confidently into Moon's toilet, then climbed into his shower. The pipes groaned and the water was so immediately hot that I felt a little faint.

Moon had a surprisingly dainty assortment of hair products. Honey and clove shampoo. Conditioner made from dead silkworms, pasteurized goat's milk and raw egg whites. A silicone-gel hair thickener and eucalyptus hair mist. The poor bastard's hair was thinning, wasn't it. It was turning to ash. Moon's hair was vacating. The water crashed down and I dreamed on my feet. I saw Moon through the shower curtain, his hard white belly jutting against the sink and his face moist with sweat. I watched as Moon mournfully tugged another grassy fistful from his skull, then checked his gums for bleeding with a sigh. I watched him give the cat a bowl of dry food and leave the radio on to kill the terrifying emptiness in his apartment and I hoped that he felt a little better when he was out on the street. That he was suffering nothing more than the melancholy dreaminess of a distracted, middle-aged cop. And I wondered, as Moon must, how many years did he have left before he stumbled, before he stepped through the wrong doorway and shuddered from the tug of a bullet never seen, never heard.

Now I pulled on pants and wandered through Moon's apartment, my hair wet and smelling like a field of poppies from Moon's shampoo. The average person has a serious accumulation of shit. Personal shit and sentimental shit. Valuable shit and shit they don't need. But Moon had almost nothing that was his. Nothing to remind him of anything or anyone. He had a couch, a chair, a television. He had a screwed-up cat. He had a broken record player. He had a punching bag, a heavy one. It was covered in a year's worth of dust, though. Dead skin and cat fuzz and pollen. I gave it a passing jab and choked in the sudden, swarming cloud. Moon has a dartboard but no darts that I could find. There were no photographs, no trinkets. There were no books. I remembered that Moon bought one used book at a time and when he was done with it he traded it for another one.

The apartment was just silent. A wide pocket of nothing, a vacuum.

I could feel a mild panic attack coming on and I suddenly wanted to be sure that Moon was not dead or gone. I walked down the hall to the master bedroom and nudged the door open. Moon slept flat on his back, snoring softly. A small television was placed precariously atop a tower of milk crates. A lonely weatherman blinked on the screen, colorless and muted. The crates contained socks, underwear. The orange cat lay coiled around Moon's big bare feet and when I entered the room the beast gave me a look of profound indifference. I allowed myself to sit on the floor, my back to the cold wall. I smoked a single cigarette, dropping the ashes into my cupped hand. The weatherman gestured meaningfully at a swirl of cloud patterns. I stared long and hard at his frosted television hair and finally decided that it must be an expensive toupee. I watched Moon sleep and I had a feeling that he regularly slipped away in the broken light of the weather channel. This pale emptiness is what I had wanted so badly, when I wished my wife would die. It's what I couldn't bear when she did.

There was a clock beside Moon's bed, a pale red digital. Two minutes past five. I hoped the sun would come up quickly. I hoped something interesting would happen on the weather channel. Moon flopped over onto his left side, grunting. I moved closer and stared at his face, at the infinite twitching of his eyelids. His breath was terrible, oozing from his wide nostrils and thick, parted lips. Moon was two or three days past his last shave and I could see the beginnings of gray in his beard. It becomes him, I thought. There was a sudden change in temperature and I jerked back, afraid that Moon might wake to find me leaning over him like a killer. But one window was cracked, and a breath of cold air had merely entered the room. Shame stretched, then leapt from the bed. He glowered at me briefly, his eyes green and yellow. Then stalked out of the room with a lazy flip of the tail.

I wandered after him, stupidly eager for company.

Eve:

A shaft of yellow light in an otherwise dark apartment. Eve crouched in her closet, sifting through papers and discarded shoes. She wore thin black sweatpants and a T-shirt with the sleeves cut off. If she were normal, if she were someone with houseplants and a cat and a nice boyfriend, then she might have just come home from the gym. Her heart still thumping from aerobics. She would be drinking a vitamin-enriched smoothie and her rib cage would not be laced with cuts, she would not be stiff with bandages. Eve wore no underwear and no shoes and she didn't feel at all sexy. Eve was tired, worried. She was annoyed, as well. She was worried about Phineas and she didn't want to be.

As a small child, she had spent hours upon hours in her mother's closet. Trapped, she had imagined herself a spider. She had loved the four walls, the dangling clothes that hung like cheap, shrunken tapestries. Her mother's clothes had always seemed to be moving, touched by an impossible breeze. She would look behind them for a window, a portal. But there was only another wall.

When she was nine, she began to have dizzying nightmares about open space, fields of wheat surrounded by wide gray concrete. Nothing ever pursued her. But the emptiness had been unbearable and she always woke choking, as if she had swallowed half the sky. She would then crawl not to her mother's bed for comfort, but to her mother's cramped closet. Then had slept like a kitten on a heap of dirty laundry that smelled of smoke and fried food.

Now she found what she was looking for. A flat wooden box, taped shut like a cozy little coffin. Eve slit the tape with her thumbnail and removed the bald, naked Barbie doll from her childhood. She had an idea that she might use it for her piece. That Goo might use it. Eve glanced at her watch. She frowned and lifted it to her ear. It had stopped again. A dead piece of metal on her wrist. She tossed it aside and wondered if Phineas was okay, if he was coming back. She noticed there was a strange feeling in her stomach, a peculiar flutter, when she thought of him.

Shame swirled around the kitchen, murmuring. He twisted himself seductively around my leg. He was clearly hungry and there was no cat food to be found. I dug for a while through Moon's barren cupboards and eventually offered the cat some corn flakes. Shame stared up at me, disgusted.

I shrugged. Aren't you used to this, I said.

There was a crusty jar of peanut butter in the fridge. I scooped out a spoonful and wedged it into a coffee cup, which seemed to satisfy Shame. I knelt, then stretched out on my belly alongside the creature, who made a fairly nasty sucking sound as he worked on the peanut butter. His eyes flickered, warning me not to touch him.

The floor was yellow linoleum, torn and ravaged by Moon's feet, but it felt cool against my skin.

Moon had been drunk last night, raving. But he had offered me a job, sort of. The whole business was borderline craziness. It was nonsense and it wasn't. Moon wanted me to go undercover and look for a few lost cops. As if they were merely trapped on the wrong side of the wardrobe, with the lion and the witch. They could be anywhere and the disappearances could be unrelated. These were cops, though. And cops weren't known to disappear. They went mad, some of them. They got stabbed by their wives. They ruined their livers. But they generally showed up for work.

I watched the cat eat. I thought about it and I tended to think that thirteen missing cops was a case for somebody else, somebody who still had a badge, for instance. If there was any truth to Moon's story, then it was something heavy. It was FBI territory. The kind of case that I was more likely to make worse than better. The kind of case I would be sorry to fuck up. But if Moon really wanted to set me up in a motel room with a pocketful of walking money, then I might as well look into it. I could sniff around.

Why not? I said to Shame.

The cat had finished his breakfast and was now hurriedly cleaning himself. He looked pretty pissed off at me and I decided that the peanut butter was maybe a bad choice. Like glue in those old whiskers. I tried not to laugh, as I was pretty sure that animals didn't much like to be laughed at by ignorant humans. Shame gave his genitals a cursory lick, then glided from the room without a backward glance.

I could not live here, clearly. The cat didn't like me.

Mingus:

Pinched his nostrils between thumb and finger. Breathed through his mouth and stared bleakly at a patch of grass. He had alien memories, images that couldn't possibly be his. A tiny house in the suburbs, painted a dull peach color that had faded to an unpleasant flesh tone. The same color as every home around it. Each house had one sad midget tree in the front yard, a skeletal sapling that would never grow taller than five feet. Trees that provided no shade.

Mingus shuddered as a thin man entered his mind, whistling.

The man wore bright blue suspenders and a torn white shirt. The shirt was tucked carefully into khaki shorts. The man had long, strangely hairless legs. He wore destroyed black penny loafers with no socks. He pushed a lawn mower and sang softly to himself. There was a child in the background, a boy with hair so blond it looked white. The man was familiar, yes. The man was his father. His father. Mingus clutched at his face, his mouth and nose. He'd never had a father.

But he resembled the thin man.

I never had a father, he said.

Chrome punched him in the belly and suddenly he couldn't breathe. Chrome, whose hands were still wet. How does that feel, he said.

Mingus sputtered, unable to speak.

Image of the thin man faded. Boy with white hair was gone. He glanced fearfully at the patch of grass before him and nothing happened. His head was empty, thank god. The bliss of forgetting, of never knowing. He wondered if he would ever control his sense of smell and the terrible rush of images that he could not be sure were his own. The brutal memories that devoured him. He was aware that

Chrome was sitting very close to him. He didn't want to look at Chrome for fear of seeing blood. He was reluctant to breathe and he wanted to be careful when he spoke, very careful.

I'm better now, said Mingus finally. Thank you.

My pleasure, said Chrome.

Friday

I managed to brew a pot of coffee in Moon's wrecked kitchen. There was no milk to be found and the sugar had a few bloated ants crawling drunkenly through it, and more than a few of their cousins that looked to be dead, overdosed on sugar. But what can you do. In some countries, sugared ants are not cheap. The coffee was too thick and black, it was like oil. It tasted of ancient, frozen rubber. I added a fistful of sugar and dead ants and sucked it down.

I attempted to clean up the living room for a while, pushing garbage and dishes and clothes and general debris into various piles but soon lost interest in the project. I ended up just kicking the broken table into a corner. Then I started looking for something to read. The phone book, a dictionary. Even a little junk mail. Bored, restless. But I didn't much feel like venturing into the city. Not sure what I was afraid of. I was feeling shy or something. I didn't want to face the hum and buzz of technology. The drone and clatter of machinery. I was forever hearing false gunshots in the distance.

It crossed my mind that Eve might be worried about me, or rather I hoped she was. I would have called her, but she didn't have a phone. She didn't even have a toaster.

The sun was coming up in a hurry and I contemplated the social order of ghosts. If any of them were still out and about they had better take cover. Because it seemed to me that a stray phantom caught drifting the streets past daybreak looking washed out and pale with less than frightful hair would be tortured by his peers.

I sat with my feet up on a windowsill, my eyes peeled for any inter-esting neighbors to spy on. I am not a pervert, exactly. If I spotted another human in a compromised position with the shades up I would surely turn away. I was only bored out of my mind and lonely. But there was nothing much to see. An old woman came out with a small bag of garbage and walked to the curb in a painfully slow shuf-fle, so slow in fact that I was tempted to run downstairs and give her a hand but this would probably just frighten her and I had alternate visions of the poor woman either suffering a heart attack and collaps-ing at my feet, or beating me senseless with the black leather pocket-book she had curiously chosen to bring with her to the curb.

I smoked the last of Moon's cigarettes and finally gave up on any action from the windows. I made another search of the living room for something to read and came upon a drawer that contained a rel-ative mother lode of unpaid bills and one grimy, water-stained and thoroughly abused leather address book. There were a hundred names and addresses in there, including one heartbreaking entry for Phineas and Lucy Poe that was crossed out with a slash of blue ink. And while almost every other name in Moon's book was that of a cop, not one of them was Jimmy or James Sky.

Chrome:

They sat on a damp beach, waiting for a bus that would never come. Mingus was beside him, hunched over like he had a belly full of angry butterflies. Chrome smiled, or gnashed his teeth. He wanted to tell Mingus to slow down, to taste life and now he whispered it, softly. Taste it, he said. Taste life. But Mingus wouldn't look up. Chrome shrugged and licked his lips. There was a touch of dried blood just beneath his nose, caught in his whiskers like chocolate milk. Everyone loves chocolate milk, he thought. Oh my. How restless he was, how like a child. His arms and legs were bouncing, quivering. As if his molecules were coming loose. He was trembling like a wee little girl. It's just juice, he told himself. It's juice from the kill, from the real. The real.

Oh, yes. He was happy. He wanted to go back to the alley and look at the dead Fred again, to look into his flattened eyes and say thank you. And he realized that true killers always love their victims. They love them. They love them for sharing that last breath. Evolution would never dispense with murder, not if love was involved. Chrome was on fire. He wanted to walk for miles. He wanted to kiss the ground. But he had to think of Mingus. The poor little troll was trembling beside him. He must be exhausted, thought Chrome. And he was visibly upset. He was probably wrestling with his conscience or something. Chrome would have to come down to earth, for his sake. The Breather needed sleep, he needed to feel safe. But what did he need, what did Chrome need? Maybe a little sex would calm him down, a little love. He poked Mingus with a bony finger.

I have blood on my upper lip, he said. It smells like sea salt. It smells like the tiny golden hairs on the back of a woman's neck. It smells like a kid with a sunburn.

You bastard, said Mingus.

I'm sorry. The mind wanders, doesn't it.

Please. I'm a wreck. I need to get inside, to sleep perhaps. To dream.

Are you sure you want to dream? said Chrome.

In my dreams, I have no sense of smell.

Interesting. I am color-blind in mine.

Mingus grabbed at his leg with the small, powerful fingers of a monkey and Chrome jumped.

Let go of my leg, said Chrome. Damn you.

I want to go home.

We don't have a home.

A motel, then. A flop in the subterrain.

Chrome softened. He pried Mingus's fingers loose from his pants with a sigh and now he thought of Goo. She had strong fingers, too. Chrome did need a touch of love. And his friend badly needed sleep. Chrome sighed as it began to rain. He patted Mingus on the head and told him not to fret.

Then he smiled, feeling wicked. Look at the sky, he said. It's purple. Almost the color of a plum. A ripe, sweet-smelling plum. A bruise on the ass of a little child.

Mingus groaned.

Then again, said Chrome. If I were dreaming, I suppose the sky would look sad and gray.

Please, said Mingus.

Chrome still held the little man's hand. Thick callused fingers, with fairly chewed nails. He gave the hand a squeeze and said, come on. Let's get inside.

Not quite seven and Moon was miraculously awake. If not, there was an angry and very clumsy burglar crashing around in the bathroom and blowing his nose for about five minutes with what seemed to me truly morbid gusto. The toilet was flushed several times. Then more crashing. Moon came into the living room finally, panting. I looked up from the newspaper I had stolen from his neighbor.

The Nuggets won, I said.

Uh. What happened last night?

You killed some furniture.

Moon gazed without recognition at the shattered coffee table. He nodded and stared and I was struck with the uneasy sensation that

Moon had no idea who I was. In a minute, the wheels would grind in his head and he would know me for an interloper. Moon would find his strength and leap upon me, beating me about the head and face with extreme prejudice and evicting me from his cage.

You, said Moon. You disarmed me last night.

I nodded. You were something of a menace.

Where is my weapon, please?

The freezer.

Yeah, said Moon. Is there more coffee?

If you want to call it that.

Moon shrugged and ambled away and soon he came back with a cup of the sludge in one hand and his big .45 in the other. The gun looked strange and ghostly, black steel gone smoky with frost.

I blinked. How do your fingers feel?

And after a moment of silence, Moon laughed. Pretty fucking cold.

Don't put it in your mouth, I said.

Don't worry.

Moon settled onto the couch. He wore a fresh pair of white pants, a blue shirt. The familiar fish tie was crisply knotted. His socks appeared to match. His thin hair was slicked back and he looked much like an eccentric football coach. He looked like himself.

Did I tell you a story last night, he said. By any chance?

A wild story, I said.

Moon sat there, nodding at me. I tasted the remains of my own bittersweet coffee. Room temperature. The same temperature as my own skin. Tingling. I felt a headache coming on and touched my fingers to my eyes. Maybe it was just loneliness.

Moon is fucking crazy, I thought.

Jimmy Sky is missing, said Moon. I know that much. He raised his frozen gun to his own ear, grinning as he made a hollow popping sound with his tongue. Or dead maybe. He's gone to see Elvis. Poor fucking Jimmy. He was a friend of mine.

What? I said. What did you say?

The bastard, said Moon. I want you to help me find him.

What's this about Elvis?

Moon's eyes were flat and dark. I miss him, he said. I miss Jimmy.

Okay, I said. Okay.

Eve:

Alone in bed, sleepless. The sky beyond her window was the thin, nameless color of thick glass and she felt temporarily trapped between night and morning. She lay on her back, tracing two fingers over the length of her body down from the sensitive throat and hollow place above her collarbone, tugging at her nipples until they were hard and then moving on to examine the bruises along her rib cage, the tender places where Adore had nicked her flesh and now she pressed one finger into these sores until the pain was fine and bright. She stroked her belly, her hip bones. She trailed the tips of her fingers lightly, lightly along the inner thigh before moving to touch herself through the thin cotton of her sweatpants and with the other hand moved to stroke one breast in small circles close to but not quite touching the nipple and now she was wet and her hips were moving involuntarily and she slipped her hand under the edge of her pants and through the soft patch of pubic hair and the odd half-formed thought that she really needed to trim down there skated in and out of her head without quite being heard and now she had two fingers inside herself moving in slow collapsing circles but soon a shadowy person emerged in her mind, a ghoulish figure who somehow had Adore's thin dark body and long fingers and Chrome's sweet, wet mouth and the cloudy blue eyes of Phineas Poe and still the face belonged to none of them. Eve stopped and her breath came in blunt short gasps that pulled painfully at her bandages. She rolled over, frustrated and cold and her thoughts flying to what Adore had said last night. That it was time for Goo to do a piece of her own, to choose a victim. It wouldn't be easy, for the choice was not about lust or hatred or domination, but a kind of awful tenderness. And the victim must somehow recognize the difference.

I was glad when Moon finally said he might go to work. After a prolonged search that involved a lot of cursing and banging around, Moon produced a spare key and I told him I was going to need some money. Moon snapped his fingers and closed one eye. We were standing in the kitchen, a few feet apart. Hands empty, dangling. Shame brushed past mewling. His fur bright with static.

Money, said Moon. Of course. He grinned too widely.

He opened the cabinet beneath the sink and poked around. Roach killer and empty mason jars and Ivory liquid and one rotting blue sponge. Moon still hummed to himself and the tune was familiar. It was unlikely but I could have sworn this was from the soundtrack for *2001: Space Odyssey,* the opening scene. Two monkeys were fighting over a piece of fruit, or possibly a female. They circle each other, shrieking and spitting. Then it occurs to one of them that he might use a chunk of wood to his advantage. To escalate things. One monkey crushes the skull of another and he is so pleased with himself, with his discovery. He dances around in his enemy's blood and the camera pulls back for a wide view. Dark silhouettes that could be human. Kubrick. He wasn't always subtle but he knew what he was talking about. And now Moon had found what he was looking for: a slightly mildewed cigar box. There was a shadowy, conspiratorial glow in his eyes that I didn't care for. Moon removed a brown envelope from the box and handed it over.

What's this?

Moon didn't smile. We should talk later, he said.

With that, he turned and waddled down the hall to the elevator. His pants were too short and his wide buttocks swung like loose freight. He looked like the fucking white rabbit. He was neurotically cheerful and at least two hours late for work.

I sighed and opened the envelope to find a plastic evidence bag containing maybe an ounce of coke. Maybe less. I was hopeless at eyeballing weights. I shook my head in disgust as my nose began to itch. There was also an array of credit cards and ID under various names. My favorite was Ray Fine. I could be Ray Fine for a while. There was no cash in the envelope, however. Moon seemed to think that I could easily peddle the coke for a little spending money. It was not exactly what I had been hoping to do this morning but I would have to manage. I am so bad with drugs, though. I'm terrible at selling them. I always manage to get myself ripped off and whatever slim profit I come away with is most likely to find its way up my nose. Of course, there was no investment in this case. It was all profit and I should really taste the product before I tried to unload it. What if it was a lot of speed and aspirin and somebody wanted to gut me for burning them? That wouldn't do at all. I merrily chopped out a couple of skinny lines with Ray's platinum Visa card and of course had nothing at all to use as a tube, not a single dollar bill to hoover them with. This was perfect. The lines wiggled on Moon's chipped counter and I was sure that I would sneeze and blow them away before I could find a tube of some kind. I opened my wallet and got out my social security card. It was a little soft and ragged but it did roll up nicely. The coke was pure and fine and now I couldn't feel my own tongue. And what do you know but I decided I was suddenly pretty cheerful and thought a walk was just what I needed.

Besides, the apartment had settled into a mid-morning gloom that I really couldn't bear.

Mingus:

Four doorways and he had come this way before. These were the runnels beneath Los Angeles. Dark, with pockets of burning steam. Land mines. And blackened corpses lay everywhere. Four doors. One of them had the faint red glow of a laser trip wire. Immediate death. As for the other three, well. That was the question. Aliens waited behind two of them. And the fourth held a medkit, possibly a key. He couldn't remember. Okay, okay. He checked his health. A sliver of yellow. He could take one, maybe two shots and he was meat. No problem. He just couldn't afford to choose the wrong door. But if he did, he was by God taking a few aliens out with him. The ugly lizard boys. He checked his weapon. A chaingun, with twenty-nine rounds. Fucking worthless. He could easily waste that firing at shadows and he scrolled through his weapons for something better. Flamethrower: always a lot of fun but unreliable. Shotgun: two useless shells. Nine millimeter: full clip. Rocket launcher: suicidal in such close quarters. The nine it was, then.

Now.

Which door did he like. He closed his eyes for a moment, trying to think.

Pounding, pounding. Someone was pounding on the door.

Mingus opened his eyes and his perspective had changed somewhat. It was still a first-person shooter but he could see more of his body than he should have been able to. His feet, his legs. His abdomen. And his hands, which were empty. They weren't holding a weapon and this wasn't what he thought it was. This wasn't a video game.

This was life, or something like it.

The top of a flight of stairs, a white lightbulb. A single moth darting around it. Chrome was beside him, leaning against chipped gray plaster with a look of mild irritation on his face.

Where are we?

Chrome smiled at him. I'm at Goo's place, he said. Or rather, I'm waiting outside of Goo's place. I'm lurking in the shadows. I don't know where the devil you are.

Yes, I'm sorry. I was in LA, in the sewers. Hunting aliens.

It's nice to have you back, said Chrome.

It was an overload, a crash. A temporary aversion.

Well, then. If you are breathing freely again, why don't you tell me if Goo is in there or not.

Mingus sniffed. She's inside. She's listening to us.

Chrome leaned against the door, his cheek to the wood. Come on, love. Open the door or I will blow it down.

Silence.

Then Goo's voice, muffled. I'm not in the mood, Christian.

Chrome flinched at the sound of his given name, his dead name. Mingus tried and failed to catch his eye. And he realized he was afraid. He stood alongside Chrome with a permanent bellyful of fear and he was getting used to this. This fear wasn't going anywhere. Mingus could smell the girl inside, faintly. She smelled of shampoo and dried sweat and chamomile tea. She smelled vaguely of bitter flowers and Mingus decided she wasn't wearing underpants. The girl smelled like blood. She smelled angry.

Maybe we should go elsewhere, said Mingus.

Chrome shook his head. Open this fucking door, he said. I'm not joking.

Another silence. Long and bright.

Then the door cracked slowly and Goo stood there, barefoot. She held something queer in her right hand, a naked headless Barbie doll.

Mingus held his breath but it was too late. He was in the backseat of a car with a little girl, a sister or cousin. She was small, with dark skin. Nine or ten. She wore a red bathing suit and her legs were long and thin as a deer's. She had no breasts at all and her hair was still damp from swimming and she held a Barbie doll dressed in little tennis whites. The windows were open and the wind crashed through the car. His ears were ringing. His skin was tender, burned. Mingus was choking on something. He has a mouthful of something like sawdust. He glanced at his hands and saw that he held an oatmeal cookie with soft plump raisins staring back at him like dull black eyes.

Dear Jude.

I didn't want to leave you but I couldn't sleep anymore. And don't fucking laugh at me, okay.

I'm west of the Mississippi now. Two days, give or take. I remember train stations, rust. Lies. The memory is edited into a knowable body that defies logic. The land between us is dead skin. There are no peacocks, no maneuvers. There is no invulnerable green.

I was kicking a nice little morphine habit and what did I expect, a soft rosy glow and the soothing hum of furry woodland creatures and one long foot massage to lull me to sleep but that wasn't it.

It rains. It pours.

I could handle the withdrawals no problem. They were painful and horrifying and endless but that was pretty much what I expected. As advertised.

I would like to sleep in a tin shack with you. Under a tin roof that leaks.

What got me in the end was the notion that you were secretly the Dread Pirate Roberts. You know that flick, *The Princess Bride*?

The sky is endless, blind, ravenous. Enduring every shade of gray. Hunger. I pray for geometry, for logic.

I was the farmboy, Westley. He stupidly believes in true love and is captured by the Dread Pirate Roberts who decides at the last moment not to kill young Westley and instead takes him on as his valet and personal gofer and every night Roberts very cheerfully says to him: Good night, Westley and sleep well. I will most likely kill you in the morning…good night.

If I were an archeologist, I would never label my finds. My tender and dusty shards.

Good night, Phineas. And sleep well. I will most likely kill you in the morning.

Chrome:

Eve was annoying him. She was wary, and wouldn't ask them to sit down. Chrome considered this rude, but he decided to ignore it for now. He was reluctant to criticize her, to provoke her. He drifted through her place lazily, as if he might buy it. Mingus stood on one foot, then the other. Chrome saw Eve give him a quick, disappearing smile. She was fond of the poor Breather, Chrome knew. She felt sorry for him.

Chrome rubbed his tongue along the inside of his teeth.

Goo, he said softly. Why are you so unfriendly?

Don't call me that, okay.

She stared at him with cool disregard. That's the real trouble with her, he thought. She wasn't afraid of him. He touched one finger to his left temple, and hoped he would never have to hurt her. She didn't appreciate him. The stupid girl had no idea how exhausting it was, to play the part of a cool and charming psychopath all day. How difficult it could be to stay in character. She had no fucking idea.

He stared at her and saw that she still held the doll in her hand, a headless doll. It was an ugly little thing. The hands and feet appeared to have been mutilated. Then he noticed the tiny pink shaving of plastic on the floor. She had whittled away the hands and feet, sharpened them. He did love her, in a distracted way. He loved the notion that she would carve a doll into a weapon.

What shall I call you, he said.

My name is Eve, she said.

Surely not.

I'm at home, she said. And when I'm home, I'm still Eve.

Chrome took a step toward her. My love, he said.

Her lip curled. Oh, boy.

Chrome laughed. He heard the thin, glassy sound ring from his mouth and he knew he was not faking it. He really was amused, wasn't he. This was fun. This was a truckload of monkeys. Eve took a step back, against the door. He didn't really care if she thought it was any fun.

Are you not my devoted? he said.

Only in the game, she said. Not here.

Oh, no. You wouldn't call our world a game, would you.

Mingus made a chirping sound and ducked away, into the bathroom. Perhaps the closet.

Chrome shook his head sadly. You've frightened him.

What do you want, she said. I'm tired.

Perfect, he said. We, too, are weary. Mingus, especially. He was hoping to sleep on your sofa. And I was hoping to sleep with you.

Funny, she said.

Chrome shrugged. He glanced around the living room at the open windows, at the sunken velvet couch. The scraps of paper on the floor. The bits of Barbie. The menu for the Silver Frog.

Where is your friend? he said.

Eve shook her head. I knew it. You were here, weren't you. What did you do with him?

Nothing, love. We did nothing to the poor man.

Eve chewed her lip, apparently considering whether to believe him or not. It was remarkable, really. When she was Goo, she adored him. She glowed. She couldn't keep her hands off him. But this wretched Eve persona treated him like a diseased dog.

Acceptez-vous les chèques de voyage?

Fuck you, she said.

You love it when I speak French.

She sighed. I really don't. And I think you just asked me if I accept traveler's checks.

Give us a kiss, he said.

No, she said.

What's the trouble, love?

I might want to stop, she said.

What? he said.

The game. I might take a holiday from the game.

Preposterous.

Maybe you should sleep elsewhere, she said.

Chrome growled. He heard himself growl. He lunged at her without thinking. Though he supposed he intended to force her to kiss him. Not a pretty thought. Not for a man of his demeanor. But as he grabbed for her pale throat. Eve raked the headless doll across his face like a knife. He howled and stared dumbly at her. He touched his face and found blood there, a fine mist of red. Oh, he loved her.

Now where the fuck was I. The dubious end of Larimer Street, where the economy is based on bail bonds and waste storage and a steady traffic of lost and stolen goods. There are no trees on streets like this and the sun crushes the weal without fail. The sun is bigger out here on the perimeter, it's wider.

Shadows are rare.

I drifted, and allowed myself to consider a few possibilities. I could cut the coke jealously and sell it by the gram. The money would be endless and plentiful but I would of course have nightmares about it. I would have night sweats. I just didn't have the constitution anymore for that sort of thing. I could probably venture into a sex and disco scene tonight and sell it by the nickel to college kids. But that would be too hideous and depressing for words and I would probably fuck it up anyway. I would soon find myself distracted by some shiny little girl with manic blue eyes and plump, unrestrained tits and the cat would run away with the fiddle and I would start giving the coke away. The thing was, no one really did coke anymore. The beautiful people were all dead or pregnant or in grad school. Heroin and meth were cheaper, and more interesting. And crack. Now, that shit was reliable. It would never go out of style. Not as long as the lepers could afford it. The lepers tended to be less fickle. Nobody much wanted coke, nobody. But of course if you had a little coke to spare, then everybody wanted some. Because everyone is sentimental when it comes to drugs. And greedy. The blue-eyed girl I had yet to meet would cling to me like a weightless sloth and I would have a thousand new friends and my own nose would be crusted with blood the next morning, my penis sore and chewed apart. And then Phineas would have no coke, no money. End of discussion. I should really try to sell this bundle in one pop, to somebody who could move it rather painlessly. Or to someone who might spend his weekends throwing money around in Aspen, where coke is still casual. There aren't a lot of ski racks on the cars at this end of Larimer Street, however.

Moon:

Plump, stately Detective Moon hit the street with a mean hard-on for something sweet. Maybe a piece of pie, or sticky bun. His first mistake was turning on his police radio in the car. Bad fucking habit, that was. Another thing he would have to work on. It didn't matter. He could easily turn it off and go about his business. But the first call he picked up was an officer down. He sat in the front seat of his rancid Taurus, dimly registering the details and wondering if he knew the guy. Hungry or not he couldn't very well ignore this.

Let's go.

He put the car in gear and drove south. It looked like it might be a hell of a beautiful day but a cop was dead, or dying. Like a brother. Moon nibbled at his tongue and watched the sky. He spat. He had no brothers, not really. The sky was safe, wasn't it. White and endless with a smackerel of blue tucked into the corners. He made the scene in no time, five minutes or less. Two black and whites blocked the mouth of an alley. Moon eased his car to a stop and sat there. He hadn't lifted a fucking finger and he was already soaked with sweat.

Out of the car, get out.

Through the yellow tape and down the alley, his shoes grinding in dirt and gravel. Red brick walls with ancient fire escapes. Eyes to the front now and there was the body, a lump of black and brown. Moon counted three uniforms and a photographer, the medical examiner and his assistant. And lurking on the edge of the scene like a pale green stork was a Homicide dick he had reluctantly been partnered with lately, a stiff British guy named Lot McDaniel. He gave a long whistling sigh, his throat gurgling like a fucked pipe. Lot McDaniel. Of all the cops he might run into this A.M...son of a whore. How he hated that fucking limey.

And now McDaniel came skittering toward him, all ghoulish and pale.

Moon, old fellow. Don't believe we've seen you in a day or two.

The bastard, thought Moon. He always laid the accent on thick when he wanted to get up your ass.

Yeah, he said. I've been sick.

McDaniel sneered. Oh, my. You aren't sick of police work, we hope.

Shut up, said Moon. What's the story?

Yes, well. Tragic bloody thing. Narcotics officer name of Mulligan. Throat ripped out and he didn't suffer much, as they say. No badge, no gun on his person. Dead since last night at least.

Ripped out how?

Bare hands, old boy. And teeth. The coroner says it was a fair imitation of an animal's kill.

Fucking hell.

McDaniel shrugged. Come on, then. Have a look.

Yeah, said Moon. But his feet weren't so cooperative and it was a moment or two before he could drag himself along behind McDaniel. The uniforms ducked away as they approached, lighting cigarettes and murmuring about hockey. The medical examiner was lazily packing his gear. He nodded at Moon with an empty face. The photographer snapped one last shot, and Moon flinched like a little kid at the sudden flash, the exploding bulb. He crouched down, wheezing. His shirt was dripping. The dead man lay on his side like he was having a nap. Brown hair razored short. Black jeans and a brown leather jacket, buttoned up to the collar. His hands were in his fucking pockets and his throat was a bloody mess. It was pure hamburger. Moon took a long look at the guy's face and saw that he was young, maybe thirty. Thin, sunken cheeks. Black eyes and a crooked nose and this dead man was no one he knew.

Not too healthy, was he? said Moon.

McDaniel coughed. There's been no bloodwork done yet, of course. But he has the look of a user, no question there. An off-duty incident, possibly. Two junkies scrapping for the same bag or something along those lines.

The guy's got his hands in his pockets, said Moon.

McDaniel sniffed. It's only a theory, don't you know.

What's his first name?

Fred, said McDaniel. His name was Fred, I believe.

Fred Mulligan, said Moon. I'm sure he deserved better.

What do you think, McDaniel whispered. Does he look familiar?

No, said Moon. I've never seen him before.

Moon felt hot. His face was sweating now. His face. What kind of god would give him a sweating face. Oh, he was a fucking wreck and he only wanted something sweet for breakfast. There was nothing he could do for dead Fred Mulligan. Nothing he could do and McDaniel was crouched very close to him, too close. His long, white hands hanging from his bent knees like two sleeping doves. McDaniel smelled of rosewater and boiled sugar. Moon stood up, wiping at his damp face with one dirty sleeve.

What about Jimmy Sky, said McDaniel. Do you think Jimmy killed him?

You, said Moon. You motherfucker. Jimmy is no killer.

Jimmy Sky, said McDaniel. His voice dripping scorn. What kind of name is that?

McDaniel stood up now and Moon glared at him for a long twisting moment and maybe his eyes played some kind of trick on him or maybe the clouds were shifting fast up there but something happened to McDaniel's face. His nostrils were suddenly three sizes too big and there was a ridge across his forehead and his skin was like leather and those were fucking fangs jutting up over his lip. He looked like a dog, a dog-man. Then the shadows relaxed and his eyes went normal and McDaniel wore his own thin-lipped pale face.

What do you know about Jimmy Sky? said Moon.

Not much, said McDaniel. I know you won't find him, though.

Moon lunged at him with a vague idea of thumbing the bastard's eyes out and McDaniel snorted, stepping sideways. Moon fell against a rack of garbage pails with an embarrassing crash. He lay there in a heap for two seconds, three. He gazed up at the sky and thought of poor old Charlie Brown and how often the round-headed kid had this very same view of the world. Moon shoved himself back to his feet, panting. McDaniel hopped forward with the dainty footwork of a ballet dancer and punched him in the throat with an elegant, blinding left-handed jab. And Moon went down again, easily.

Take the day off, said McDaniel. You look like shit. You look a lot like our dead Fred, there.

I walked in the heart of downtown. Where the tall, mirrored buildings gleamed. One of my friends was a lawyer of sorts, with an office in the labyrinth. Griffin, the smiler.

I moodily kicked at a piece of broken glass, spinning it into the street. I wondered if the fucker was still my friend. Maybe not. The last time I saw him was two or three years ago. Griffin had dragged me to some very popular but hateful nightclub that was so packed with mad, happy people that the one unisex bathroom was like a furious game of Twister. People had been living in there, growing rapidly old as they exchanged drugs and money without pause. They had chatted on cell phones, smoking and drinking. And they had noisily fucked each other in the stalls. It was nothing out of the ordinary, right. But that shit gets pretty tedious, after a while. I had finally gone out to get some air, to urinate in peace behind an abandoned car. Griffin followed me, and I clearly remember asking Griffin in a sleepy voice what time it was and Griffin turning to face me, grinning. His eyes like wet black stones.

What time is it, said Griffin.

Menacing.

What the fuck. The fuck.

I had just stared at him, blank and probably smiling. And in a moment of universal weirdness, Griffin pissed all over my legs. He shook his dick at me, then breezily told me to fuck off and walked away. He hailed a cab and left me standing there in damp, stinking pants.

And I had ended up going home with a drunk little bank teller who apparently was equipped with no sense of smell. I apparently collapsed on her kitchen floor without fucking her, which annoyed her. She called the cops on me, then herself went to sleep before they arrived. Two moody beat cops did show up, an hour or so later. They banged on the door until I woke up and let them in. They smirked when I identified myself. The bank teller was by then mostly naked and snoring on the couch. The uniforms looted her fridge and made a big show of checking out her body, cheerfully deriding my lack of taste.

They gave me a ride home and I crawled like a rat into bed with my wife, Lucy. She wasn't dead yet, then. But she was dying pretty efficiently. Cancer and depression were ganging up on her without a bit of mercy.

And I had not seen Griffin again after that. I didn't expect him to have changed much. Nobody changes, really. Griffin would literally pounce on this coke.

Now traffic swelled around me. The noise and shock of over-population.

Vertigo, nausea.

It was boring to freak out all the time. If I could only remind myself to concentrate, nothing rattled me. I was a cool one at heart, really. Oh, yeah. If I was dead, maybe. Then I might relax. Downtown always troubled me. I was careful to avoid the pedestrian mall, the gauntlet of gift shops and juice huts along which senior citizens and random tourists gamely refused to buy ugly overpriced T-shirts while sullen kids reclined in the shade, begging for spare change.

Griffin worked in a handsome brown slab of a building. It looked like a coffin standing on end.

I walked into the lobby and was immediately surrounded by mirrors. A security guard leered at me while I patiently checked out my reflection. I wanted to tell him how fucking pitiful it was, how tiresome, this irrational urge to confirm my existence in one mirror after another.

The guard eyeballed me as I walked to the elevators but that was all. I was obviously no one to worry about.

The elevator was empty and way too big. There was room enough to spare, I reckoned cheerfully, for a dozen commuters plus a nice herd of actual sheep. I stood in the middle and looked at my feet as the box rose slowly, endlessly to the sixteenth floor.

A female receptionist coldly told me to wait.

I waited. I sat on a blue leather loveseat as the woman whispered to Griffin through her headset. There were no magazines in the waiting area. There was one gloomy painting on the wall that could be anything: a gray-and-black landscape of a Scottish moor, a chemically altered examination of a rain cloud. After a few brief moments of study, I concluded that it could only be a giant human brain, floating in a sea of alcohol. I asked the receptionist how much the piece might cost. She looked me carefully up and down, and I knew what she saw. A skinny drifter with ragged clothes and a desert tan, uncombed hair and gray lips still numb from the wind. A paranoid, lonely fucker who badly needed new shoes and who kept rubbing his nose as if it were numb and dripping. A person of dubious means. Not someone who could begin to pay Griffin what must be a very handsome retainer.

Eve:

She lay flat on her back, still wearing sweatpants and a T-shirt. No concept of time. She was like a child and a few minutes could mean anything. Hours were arbitrary. They weren't real. She sighed. It was maybe nine o'clock, or ten. The light had that flat, midmorning quality that she usually hated. She hadn't slept in more than twenty-four hours and she wasn't really tired. She felt a little bit jet lagged, really. Day was night and so on. Boring. Her body was just confused by the sudden shift between worlds. The night before was hazy in her mind.

Adore leaned over her.

The swing and flash of the razor. The frantic wings, the swelling orange light. A Redeemer with the lips of a monkey and now the touch of anxiety when she tried to remember everything that happened and it's only a game, she told herself. It's a game.

She turned her head to look at Christian. He was curled naked on his side, facing her. His limbs were too stiff, unyielding. He was pretending to sleep.

There was a spot of dried blood on his cheek, a splash of rust. She had cut him pretty good. He now had a nasty jagged scratch across the bridge of his nose and one eyelid, like he had tangled with a cat. That eyelid might permanently droop, she thought. Which would either make him look very stupid, insane or sleepy. He wouldn't like it at all. He had blubbered a few meaningless French phrases and accused her of trying to maim him, to blind him. Eve had merely shrugged and reminded him that she didn't like people to grab her. And that she enjoyed fucking with him, with his mind. She couldn't help it.

Christian was sexy, very sexy. Beyond sexy. He was one of those guys that sucked people into his wake, male and female. It was nice to be near him. He smelled good and he was talented in bed. But he was melodramatic when it came to the game of tongues and his face had turned fairly purple when she mentioned that she might just quit. A lovely shade of purple.

But she did feel a little sorry for him, and so she had calmly made up a bed for Mingus on the couch, her heart fluttering foolishly at the sight of an indentation in the crushed velvet that might have been left by Phineas. His head, his bent elbow. His foot. Jesus Christ. She was such a simple girl and all she wanted was a big brother. Mingus thanked her silently and laid himself down, pale as a monk.

Then she had allowed Christian into her bed.

He shed his clothes in a hurry, like she might change her mind.

But there wasn't going to be any sex, she told him.

Oh please, Goo. Give us a break.

She wondered if he was aware that he constantly referred to himself as a collective. If this was merely a peculiar side effect of the game. This apparent splitting, this fragmentation of selves. Because she often thought of herself and Goo as separate but equal.

Meanwhile, Christian had fiddled with his penis until it became hard and red. He showed it to her with creepy, boyish pride, as if he thought she couldn't possibly say no to such a handsome sight. Manifest destiny, or something.

I am not Goo today, she said.

This made him whine.

Eve finally told him to jerk off, if he must. But not to come on her. And not to poke her or prod her with it, or casually try to slip it in while she was asleep. She wasn't kidding. Christian had played with himself for a while, sulking. Then pretended to fall asleep.

That was a half hour ago. Maybe he really was asleep. Eve blew on his eyelids and he didn't flinch. She squeezed his soft penis like it was a peach and she couldn't decide if it was ripe. His penis was pretty long, when hard. About nine inches, he had told her once. He mentioned it casually, as if he were bored by the subject. But he had measured it, of course. Nine thrilling inches. It was too skinny and curved, however. It was what she imagined a dog's penis might be. The way it stabbed painfully into her uterus, sharp and bony.

Christian now began to snore.

She hesitated, then reached out and touched his hair. It was very confusing, this relationship. She didn't know if she liked him at all. But when she was Goo, she loved him. She wanted his children. It was a game, okay. She was playing a character. Eve stroked his fine black hair and her fingers caught in a funny tangle. His hair was matted with something. She worked her fingers through it and they came away sticky and brown. This was dried blood.

Eve closed her eyes.

Griffin appeared through wide sliding doors that literally purred open, cool and silent. It wasn't bad but a really sinister whooshing noise would have been much more effective. He wore a glossy Italian suit the color of bloodwine and it seemed he had begun shaving his head since I last saw him as his skull was now the same pale creamy pink as my own bare ass.

Are you going bald? I said.

I am bald.

Yes. I can see that.

Griffin extended his hand. There was a small tattoo on the inside of his wrist, like a black coin.

Was your hair falling out, though?

Yes, he said. It was like plucking feathers from a dead chicken. He shrugged. I decided to shave it instead. The girls seem to like it.

I'm sure.

Griffin stood there, unbending. His hand still hanging between us like a knife and a knife given as a gift will always bring bad luck. I stood up and shook his hand and the contact was cold but weirdly lacking pressure. Griffin's eyes drifted to focus on my eyebrows and I wondered if that was just a lawyer thing. Or did he truly want to avoid the eyes. I stared back at him, smiling with some reluctance.

Griffin bowed his head slightly and I hesitated, then touched the man's scalp. Oily and hot, almost feverish.

What do you want? said Griffin.

Oh, well. I'm back in town. Thought I would say hello.

Griffin smiled the smile of a gorilla, a chimp. He showed way too many teeth and a ridge of pale gray gums. That's funny, he said. That's a killer.

I shrugged, uneasy. Why is it funny?

Because you don't like me, said Griffin.

No. Not at all.

The receptionist was staring at us throughout this exchange, her lips parted. A bright glow of sweat in the thin blond fuzz along her cheekbones. Eyes glazed and blue, she chewed on her tongue and she looked mesmerized, as if she was home alone, watching a little soft porn on cable. Griffin flicked a finger at her and she abruptly began to type.

Nice, I said.

Let's go in my office, Griffin said. I have champagne, of a kind.

Moon:

Moon was parked on a swiveling stool at Lulu's Dough-nut Shoppe. His throat was killing him, literally. It felt like he had swallowed a mouthful of glass and what the hell happened back there.

He had provoked McDaniel, apparently. The motherfucker had a tight little ass, an irritating accent. Bad teeth. And very fast hands. Moon sighed and shifted his own ass around, trying to get comfortable. His hefty buttocks fairly melted over the sides of his stool. Moon knew what his father would say. Old man Moon would suck on his false teeth and swear that McDaniel would be speaking German right about now if it wasn't for us. And learning to like it. Maybe so, but that does me no good. He wondered if McDaniel was up to something nefarious or just fucking with him. Moon realized he was an easy target these days, what with his poor work habits and his body odor problems. Anyway. Jimmy Sky was nobody's favorite cop, but he didn't kill people. He especially didn't kill other cops.

Moon had a headache. He would worry about it later. And he would watch and wait for a chance to pay McDaniel back for this sore throat. He would wait years, if he had to. One day the motherfucker would fall asleep in the wrong place and wake up with his hat on fire and his hands cuffed to his feet.

Okay, then. He wanted to get drunk and concentrate on his breakfast. He had been coming to Lulu's every morning without fail for years. Lulu was long dead, or never existed. Wiley, a man who claimed to be her husband or stepbrother, ran the place now. He was a grumpy little man who was deadly serious about doughnuts. He wasn't interested in anything else. Wiley always wore strangely colorful clothes. He was a peacock. Today he wore a purple T-Shirt with black-and-white pants and yellow shoes. He was a freak, maybe. But he made the best doughnuts in the city. And he spoke very elegant English in a snotty voice, like a college professor.

Moon had once asked him about the inexplicable hyphen in the word "doughnut."

Wiley had merely shrugged. He said that Lulu had always been too liberal with punctuation, as if this had been an irreversible condition, something he had learned to live with.

Moon stared down at his place. Four fat doughnuts, arranged like the face of a clock. Blueberry at twelve o'clock. Maple swirl at three. Cinnamon at six and honey glazed at nine, to clean the palate. He drank coffee with a splash of bourbon and chased it with concentrated orange juice. He didn't smoke before noon, or he tried not to.

Dead cop with throat ripped out. Like a wolf had done it, a wild dog.

Moon finished his coffee and took a pull of bourbon straight from the pint. He lit a cigarette and noticed that his palms were sweating, they were dripping. It had been quite a while since he had been drunk like this, in public. He felt a stab of something like guilt. What the hell. He had no wife, no therapist to answer to. He was a cop, by God. And he was the only cop in the place. His fellow officers didn't care much for Wiley and his fruity clothes.

Black eyes and crooked nose and a face forgotten already. Hands in his fucking pockets.

Moon wiped his hands with a napkin and fought down a mouthful of bile and he knew he was out of shape, okay. It took a little strength, a little staying power to get drunk so early in the day. Intestinal fortitude. Moon swabbed out his mouth and tongue with the sweaty napkin and tossed it aside in disgust. He had the intestines of a little old lady. He was irregular. He had maybe one successful bowel movement a week, and it was pretty painful. It was rough. The bathroom was his personal torture chamber, lately. It was like he was passing a fucking stone in there.

This was a lot of bullshit, though.

Moon wasn't worried about his bowels, or his own guilt. He could shake off guilt like it was nothing, like a coat of morning dew. Moon would rather have a belly full of guilt than a touch of the flu, any day. But now he was distracting himself from the truth. And the truth was, he was a little worried about Poe. The guy was his friend, yeah. But he was a freak. He was purely section eight. Poe was a delusional fuckup, okay. He had been bounced off the cops for being too schizophrenic and was suspected but never implicated, never charged in connection with the shooting death of his wife.

And most recently he somehow got himself mixed up in the alleged transportation and sale of his own illegally harvested organ. That was a good one, wasn't it. That was a humdinger.

There were sixteen motherfuckers just like Phineas Poe, hanging around the methadone clinic and the homeless shelter right now.

Sixteen guys with no money, no cigarettes. Sixteen guys with their brains spilling out of their skulls one teaspoon at a time.

And what did he do first thing this A.M.

Moon rubbed his belly and thought about it.

Oh, well. Nothing much. He gave the bastard a handful of false identities and a lump of confiscated coke and turned him loose on a missing persons case that didn't officially exist. He could only wonder what sort of mayhem would come of that.

Wiley glanced up from his crossword. He cleared his throat politely and licked his lips, as if it was a great effort to speak. What ails you, Sheriff? he said.

Nothing, said Moon. I feel just like a king.

You have hardly touched your doughnuts.

Moon stubbed out his cigarette and plucked the blueberry doughnut from his plate. His stomach heaved momentarily, but he ate the thing in three quick bites.

Jimmy Sky, where was Jimmy Sky.

And five minutes later Moon crashed out of Lulu's, the glass door bending before his bulk and splashing onto the sidewalk. He broke the fucking door, shattered it. He was probably bleeding. There were tiny white fragments of glass on his arms and shoulders. It was in his patch of hair. Fucking hell. He inspected himself for cuts and scratches, cursing the door. The thing must have been defective. He turned to look at Wiley. And Wiley was nonplussed. In fact, he was turning orange about the ears and neck. He looked like one unhappy tangerine.

Hey, said Moon. Hey, Wiley.

Wiley stared at him, disbelieving. You are a menace, he said. A danger to yourself and others.

Moon pulled out his wallet, a bulging chunk of leather that smelled of feet.

He knew that it smelled of feet because he had sniffed it, just the other day. He had been trying to isolate a putrid, cheeselike odor that kept wafting from his body. He was sure it must be coming from his crotch, from the sweat and funk and decay of his package. But he had been sitting at a stoplight at the time and he could hardly bend over far enough to smell himself, what with the steering wheel in the way.

Moon smiled to himself. He couldn't bend over that far if Yoda himself was sitting on his neck, croaking a lot of Jedi nonsense at him. Luminous being we are…yeah. He might be luminous, on a good day. But he wasn't too fucking limber. Then it occurred to him. His wallet was pressed up against his ass all day, absorbing his unpleasant juices, his various gasses. The funk had to be coming from his wallet. And at the next red light, Moon yanked it out and had a good whiff and almost threw up right there.

Now he flipped the stinking thing open, taking care to keep it well away from his face. Sixteen dollars. Hardly enough to replace the door of a dollhouse. And his credit cards were in ashes, lately.

He pondered a moment.

Tell you what, said Moon. I'll write up an armed robbery report and your insurance will cover it, no problem. You could get a better door out of the deal.

Oh, sure. And they won't hesitate to cancel my policy.

Hmm. That's no fucking good.

You're drunk, aren't you. Since when do you indulge on duty?

Moon grunted at him. I'm thinking.

The forecast is for rain, said Wiley. Thunderstorms, you bastard. You have ruined me.

Okay, said Moon. How about this. I broke the door myself.

Wiley frowned, irritated. You did break it.

Yes. But I broke it in the line of duty, you see. In my zealous pursuit of a purse snatcher. You can bill the department. Okay? Tell them it was lead glass, stained glass. Whatever. Tell them it was a five-thousand-dollar door if you want.

Griffin's office was about what I would expect. Cool and sterile, with uncomfortable iron furniture. A thick, silent carpet that was such a powdery light blue that it disappeared like the far end of the sky. The sky merging with clouds. Griffin casually uncorked a magnum of something called the Pale. The label looked suspiciously postmodern, with bright ruthless colors.

California? I said.

Not exactly, said Griffin. Then he shrugged. It's two hundred dollars a bottle.

What the fuck. I hate champagne anyway.

Griffin's eyes were flat. You will like this.

I turned away, the glass fizzing in my hand. There were no law books in the office. The walls were gray, with a faint sparkle. The walls were like dirty silver, unadorned by art of any kind. Griffin had an excellent view, however. I stood before his massive window and looked out over downtown Denver. Half of the city seemed to be under construction, deconstruction. This was a sign of prosperity, this effortless ravaging of old, failing stone. A few years ago, Denver had not been looking well. It had been downright ugly, in fact. Emaciated and sickly.

Not anymore, by god. Denver had acquired a baseball team and the city was reborn. If they told you it was beautiful, then it was beautiful.

It's beautiful, I said.

Griffin sneered. Like a postcard.

I sipped at the Pale and it shivered down my throat like mercury, cold and thickly sweet.

What is this? I said.

Wormwood and licorice, said Griffin. With a drop of cyanide. Don't ask.

Absinthe? I said. You are full of shit.

Oh, I stink of it.

I took another drink and the glass felt heavy in my hand. I put it down on the coffee table and smiled. I was a little dreamy, like I had just exhaled a lungful of nitrous oxide. The silver walls rippled nicely. Griffin relaxed on the couch, heels drumming noiselessly on the carpet.

So, he said. What's going on.

Yeah. That's a good question.

Griffin smiled and smiled. His eyes were dilated and I saw him again, turning to spray my legs with urine. With urine.

You pissed on me, I said.

What?

The last time I saw you. You pissed all over my pants, like a dog.

Griffin shrugged. Maybe. Who remembers these things.

It's not something you forget. I fumbled with my zipper. If I emptied my bladder all over that ugly fucking suit right now, would you remember?

What's wrong with this suit?

You look like a big, paranoid grape.

Griffin finished his drink and the smile on his face was elastic.

Okay, I said. I have some coke I want to sell.

Coke, said Griffin. Please tell me you're joking.

I know. It's embarrassing.

Griffin sighed. Let's see the shit.

I pulled out the police evidence bag and Griffin laughed. He clapped his hands.

I have always wanted one of those bags, he said. It would be perfect for my toothbrush and hair gel and shaving gear. I could keep it in my briefcase.

You don't have any hair.

Skull gel then, he said. I like a shiny helmet.

I found myself nodding stupidly. I shrugged, pulled myself together and scooped out a fat bump of coke with one finger and sucked it up my nose. The eyeballs tightened promptly. I licked my finger and offered the bag to Griffin, who tasted it without blinking.

Not half bad, he said.

Do you want it?

Griffin yawned. Four hundred for the shit and two hundred for the evidence bag.

Four hundred? I could cut it up and sell it for five times that.

Good luck, he said.

Give me eight hundred, I said.

See you later, Phineas.

Okay. Okay, I said.

Yeah, he said. The thing is, I don't really want any coke. This is charity. This is like serving soup to the homeless.

Oh, well. I love a good bowl of soup, I said. Three hundred for the bag, then.

I hated myself and Griffin was practically asleep, he was so bored. He shrugged and produced a roll of new bills. He peeled off six or seven hundreds, losing count. He smiled and tossed two more bills on the table.

That's nine, I said.

What's the difference. Have you had lunch?

I watched as Griffin transferred the coke to a gunmetal snuffbox, carelessly. A fine white shadow of spilled cocaine caught the light and

Griffin noticed me watching.

Oh, he said. Would you like a last taste?

I hesitated, sniffing. Of course I wanted some. But I shook my head, mute.

Good, he said. That's good.

Griffin dropped the little box into a drawer. He folded the evidence bag into a small square and tucked it into his breast pocket, his eyes fond and bright.

Of course, he said. You're lying.

Yeah, I said. Let's have lunch.

Griffin sniffed, wiping at his nose. I want to show you something, he said.

Okay.

I was a bit clammy, shivering. I thought the air-conditioning was much too cold and I wasn't the least bit hungry and so I just nodded dumbly. Griffin walked over to the big window, his arms and legs hanging weirdly loose. The sun was crashing through the glass like a live thing and Griffin appeared to be held together by thread and I squinted at him through a maddening self-contained haze. I felt like I had wandered onto the set of one of those Roger Rabbit videos where some of the characters are real and some are animated. Griffin was definitely animated. I stared at the big window now, hoping to find myself in the open sky beyond but instead the light shifted and I saw a very peculiar scene in the reflection. I saw myself, standing in about the same position but wearing fairly ridiculous clothing, with a funny gray hat and a slash of white bandage across my face. Griffin looked exactly the same, but was standing on the wrong side of the room with his back to the window and there was a third person in the reflection, a long-legged man with limp yellow hair who wore a three-piece suit of soft brown leather and held a gun in one hand. The gun was aimed at me, at my head.

Do you see him, I said. Do you see him, Griffin.

Griffin turned and smiled, or maybe his reflection did because now the physical Griffin placed both hands on the window and pushed, muttering softly the word "poof." And I felt my mouth drop open as the entire sheet of glass fell from its frame and floated down toward earth with the lazy, carefree silence of a paper airplane. The glass was crystal-bright and somehow invisible and it swooped and glided back and forth, a pale deadly shadow. And it seemed to fall forever. I leaned out to watch the glass dive into a throng of pedestrians and cut three people in half and now I felt my head bump against the window. I touched it gingerly, with the tips of my fingers. It had never fallen at all. Griffin smiled and smiled.

Eve:

She woke from a drifting sleep and she couldn't breathe. Christian was sitting on her chest, staring at her like she was a bug. He was naked, slim and hairless. She was pretty sure he shaved his chest.

Eve never had a brother. But when she was a kid her best friend was a girl named Minna who had an older brother, a hulking bully named Guy. He had wanted to be a wrestler and his breath always stank of bananas. Guy had been truly manic but never depressed and his fingernails were always chewed to raw, moody shreds. Guy's favorite game had been to sit on his sister's chest, pinning her arms down with his knees. Then he would pinch her nipples and drool yellow spit into her face. Eve and Minna took care of him, eventually. Eve had gotten some codeine tablets after she had a root canal and they saved a few just for Guy. Minna made root beer floats one Friday night and dissolved five of the little white pills into Guy's float. He passed out before ten and they stripped him naked, then soaked his genitals and one eyebrow with Nair, the infamous hair dissolver. Guy woke up with no pubic hair and a painfully sore left eye. The Nair had dripped into his eye, apparently. It ruined his eyelashes and he could have been blinded, probably. But Guy always left them alone after that.

Eve wondered what Christian would use on his chest. Vitamin E and aloe, she decided. And as he was so scornful of technology, he probably used a straight razor. One day, he might lose a nipple.

What are you smiling at? he said.

You, she said. You have a nice chest.

Oh, he said. Now you want to be friendly.

Not really.

Well, said Christian. We don't have time, anyway.

He rolled sideways and off the bed. He stood there, distracted and chewing at his lower lip. Eve realized with some surprise that he actually looked worried. And there was one thing about Christian that he liked: he rarely looked worried.

What's the matter?

Your apartment, he said. It's slipping.

Eve sighed. Fuck you.

She had heard of this, of course. The whispered stories about badly spooked gamers, obsessed tonguelovers who never slept, who stayed in character too long. Their worlds were compromised and their reality began to slip. The idea was that if you lingered in the sub-terrain for too long, you might never leave. And some claimed to have lost their identities, their jobs. They showed up for work one day and no one remembered them. Their credit cards were suddenly invalid. The explanation for this seemed simple enough to Eve: a lot of gamers and tonguelovers were also computer geeks, hackers. And it would be child's play to tamper with the virtual reality of one of your enemies, thereby erasing his job and identity, his bank account.

Virtual reality was reality. The game of tongues was something else, a peripheral reality.

But it was not so easy to explain the physical slip. A few of these mad gamers claimed that losing one's identity was nothing, it was a joke. The physical slip was the real nightmare. They believed that their apartments and cars had literally become unstable, that they were fading. Disintegrating. Their material possessions actually ceased to exist. The walls around them got fuzzy. They suffered molecular decay.

Eve shrugged when she heard these stories. She scratched her nose. Drugs, she thought. It can only be drugs. Though she was well aware that the elite gamers like Mingus and Christian were pretty clean. They sucked down a lot of coffee and cigarettes and popped a little ephedrine. And the Pale, of course, nearly everyone consumed a mysterious liqueur called the Pale. Everyone but Christian. He never touched it, and he sneered at those gamers who seemed to depend on it.

Come on, said Christian. We'll show you.

Irritated, she slid out of bed. Her feet were bare and cold and she was pretty sure she had been wearing socks when she went to sleep. Christian had a mild foot fetish, or Chrome did. He often slipped her shoes and socks off when she was asleep or otherwise distracted. She didn't mind it so much. Odd as it may sound, she liked the way it felt when he nibbled on her feet. But she was annoyed this time.

Christian, she said.

He pounced on her, knocking her to the floor. His lips were pulled back to show fine white teeth and his eyes were like the blue edge of flame. Those teeth aren't real, she thought. Not real. They must be caps. The dig of pain in her chest and he was hurting her now. His teeth were impossibly white. Erik Estrada. He's got the teeth of Erik Estrada, she thought. What kind of grown man calls himself Ponch?

Thin red shiver of pain as she tried to breathe.

He may have cracked one of her ribs. Punctured a lung. The pain was like a claw, ripping at her from within. Eve took another experimental breath and as she opened her mouth Chrome lowered his mouth to hers. He sucked her tongue out of her mouth and held it between his teeth and his pull was very strong, he could swallow it, he could turn her inside out. He didn't bite her tongue but he owned it for a moment. He owned her. The tongue is the soul, she thought. The soul. The tongue is ugly, vulnerable and not well-hidden.

Chrome released her. Don't call us by that name, he said.

Okay, she said.

He helped her up, his face calm and friendly. As if she had slipped on the wet floor and he were merely bending to her aid. Eve jerked her hand away and looked around for her slippers. Her feet were cold and she felt raw, unclean. She wanted to pull a sheet over her head. Christian briskly pulled on his black jeans and said, come on.

She followed him into the living room, sighing when he told her to avoid a small circle of carpet in the hallway that he had marked with baking powder.

It's unstable, he said.

Eve rolled her eyes. But she stepped around it anyway, then stopped. The carpet did look strange, fuzzy and wavering. She bent to touch it and Christian pulled her away.

Don't, he said. It could be a vortex.

Are you serious?

He didn't answer, but she knew he was disgusted with her. He always treated her like a dim-witted child when it came to the game of tongues. He had no patience for what he called her failure to see what was real. Eve rubbed her eyes, wondered if she was dreaming. This didn't seem possible, logical. But at the same time, she didn't find it so alarming and she felt herself glowing, detaching. She felt like Goo.

Oh, no.

Yes, she said. Her skin was tight and cold.

She was on the verge of becoming Goo, without trying. Horrible and sweet at the same time. Because she loved herself as Goo, really. She forgot that sometimes. Mingus was in the kitchen, pacing back and forth like a nervous uncle. He was waiting for somebody to give birth. He looked at her, briefly. He sniffed her but said nothing. Eve realized from a vague distance that Mingus was reluctant to stand in one place for too long. And it looked like he was keeping his distance from Christian, too. She thought of the dried blood she had found in his hair.

In the living room, Christian pointed to the wall behind her velvet sofa. It looked like gray fog, a curtain of mist. Christian took a coin from his pocket and tossed it at the wall. The coin vanished.

Fleurs du mal, said Christian. We have to get out of here.

Eve stared at the wall, thinking that she would certainly have to move the sofa. That wall wasn't going to keep the rain out, was it?

What? she said.

We want you to get dressed, he said. Quickly. And bring whatever you can carry. We won't be coming back here.

But I have a six-month lease on this place. If I disappear, I lose my deposit.

A small brown bird flew through the wall from the other side and crashed to the floor. It flopped there, dazed. It appeared to be a starling. Christian looked at the bird, then at Eve. He laughed out loud, almost howling. He picked up the bird and snapped its neck.

Believe me, he said. You have already lost your deposit.

Griffin wanted to walk and I really didn't mind. My head was a mess. My head was dusty, full of fuzz and cat hair. I could use the fresh air, no question. I needed a few minutes before I had to sit at a table with my face three feet from Griffin's and his unbending smile.

And I suddenly felt like talking.

Maybe the coke had loosened my wheels, I don't know. Whatever the reason, I told Griffin most of what had happened to me in Texas. I told him all about Jude and how she made me feel like a slug on a razor blade. I told him about the morphine, the lost kidney. I told him about Horatio and how I killed him with a kiss. I told him too much, maybe Griffin didn't say anything, but he did laugh inappropriately a few times.

Griffin took me to a place called Rob Roy's. A dark, silent underground grotto where the waiters were stout, elderly black men who wore bow ties and never smiled. They didn't offer you a menu. And you were clearly a freak if you ordered anything but whiskey and a porterhouse steak. There were no women in the joint, none. A lot of crusty old men, though. They shoveled the bloody meat into their holes like they had never heard of heart disease: they were lawyers, judges, and newspaper writers, and a few drowsy cops.

What year is this? I said.

Griffin looked around, beaming. Nice, isn't it. It's 1955. Hitler is dead and the economy is a house on fire. My dad is sitting over there with Judge Waters, drunk as a fucking pig.

It's freaking me out.

Relax, said Griffin. Drink your martini. Or have another one. I'm buying.

Why are you being so friendly?

Griffin rubbed his naked head, his helmet. He shrugged. The walls of Rob Roy's were dark red and in that burgundy suit he nearly melted into the background. I could only see his eyes and teeth. The soft glow of his skull.

I sank back into the flexible haze of my own head. Griffin and I had gone to the same college, a shitty state school in Memphis. I didn't know him then, not really. But I had heard the stories. Griffin had this little girlfriend, a high school dropout. She was seventeen and after she moved out of her mother's house, Griffin sneaked her into his dorm like she was an illegal pet. He got her pregnant and then went homicidal because she didn't want to have a baby. Meanwhile, the girl did not have such a good reputation. She was a kleptomaniac, she was suicidal. She was white trash, she would give you a blow job if you bought her a milkshake. And she was illiterate. But this was a lot of bullshit. I met her only once and had liked her right away. The girl was sweet and tough, with the voice of a dead jazz singer. She wanted to be a photographer. Her name was Lisa and she was maybe a little too infatuated with Emily Dickinson, but I could forgive that. She was seventeen, right. Then she had a miscarriage and Griffin lost his mind. He knew she had gotten an abortion, he knew it. And so one night he tried to set her on fire, while she slept. Griffin did six months in jail and because he was only nineteen and his daddy was a powerful man in Memphis, his records were sealed. Lisa changed her name and got a job, an apartment. Then Griffin came out of the county farm on good behavior and started hanging around abortion clinics. He started following girls home. And on a rainy day in late April, he knocked on Lisa's door. He was smiling the same punishing smile. He wanted to give her something, he said. He offered her a bloody pillowcase that contained the head of a murdered prostitute. The prostitute, he claimed, was a killer of babies. But Lisa never blinked. She was expecting him, she said. Lisa surprised him, she did. She shocked the hell out of him. Lisa produced a gun and shot him and suddenly

Griffin wasn't smiling anymore. There was a hole in his arm the size of a half dollar. Later it was discovered that the pillowcase contained the head of a dressmaker's dummy. Griffin didn't press charges and the case was dropped.

And when I met him ten years later, Griffin was a slick young lawyer in Denver, working in the DA's office. He was arrogant, seductive, ruthless. He was a very good lawyer. I knew he might be a psychopath but what the fuck, right. I struck up a conversation with him anyway. A dark November morning. We were sitting on the courthouse steps, maybe ten feet apart. It was bitterly cold, unpleasantly cold. It was starting to snow. I had come outside to smoke, to get away from the press and the bureau chief and my own lawyer and everything else. Griffin was sitting cross-legged, with an expensive and famously ugly Italian leather coat wrapped around him. He was smoking a cigar. I glanced at his face and saw that he was a little hung over. Maybe a touch of the flu. Anyway, he looked like shit and I didn't feel much better. I had been testifying on a case that involved cops and the secret assassination of a local heroin king who had pretty much deserved to die, and the trial was dragging along like it would never end. Griffin was working an unrelated case, something to do with animal torture. It was boring him to death.

I said to him, didn't you go to school in Memphis?

Griffin had smiled. The smile that made me feel queasy. Like I just stepped on something dead, a bird or mouse bloated from the rain and now I couldn't get its guts off my shoe. But I went out drinking with him that night, and Griffin soon became something for me that every cop needs. Griffin became my ally, my confessor.

Wake the fuck up, said Griffin. Your food is getting cold.

The waiter had come and gone. I looked down. Before me was a wide, metal plate that held the biggest, ugliest lump of meat I had ever seen. Beside it was a deformed brown thing that appeared to be oozing sour cream. I slowly comprehended that this was a baked potato.

Do you have a girlfriend? said Griffin.

What?

Other than the organ thief, I mean.

I ignored him. I poked and prodded at the steak. It was not so bloody at all. In fact, it looked burned.

Your wife is dead, he said. Over a year now.

That's right.

What's your story? said Griffin.

No. I don't have a girlfriend.

Good. Very good.

Why? I said. Why is that good?

Griffin didn't answer. He ripped into his steak, barely looking up for the next five minutes. I stole another glance at my place and was positive that I couldn't eat this piece of meat. My teeth felt fragile, just looking at it. I wondered about Eve. She certainly was not my girl-friend but then I wasn't sure what she was. Whenever I was near her, I felt like I should protect her but such a notion would only make her laugh. She was much more likely to save me, to catch me when I next fall at her feet.

Eve had this dark energy around her, swirling but not quite visible. The ring and shadow of myth. Her voice was ageless. Eve was delicate, childlike. I easily imagined she could be sexy, brutal.

She had the bottomless eyes of someone at war.

Now where the fuck was my brain taking me. I was slipping down the ugly slope of bad poetry. I must be a little dreamy from that funny drink, the Pale.

Because, said Griffin. If you had a girlfriend, you would lose her before tomorrow comes.

How, exactly?

I wonder. Do you believe in ghosts? said Griffin.

What do you mean, like Casper the friendly?

Griffin delicately wiped a drop of reddish grease from his lip.

No, he said. I'm talking about the underworld, the walking dead.

Yeah, well. I see the walking dead every time I look out the window.

Griffin chewed briefly, staring at me. Listen, he said. You motherfucker. I'm not talking about urban despair. I'm serious.

Okay. Have you recently seen a ghost?

No, not exactly. But I have seen things that you won't believe.

I lit a cigarette and felt cold, thinking of the ghostly creatures I had seen in the torn-down building. Drinking tea and smoking cigarettes on a forgotten Sunday. *The Lone Ranger* crackling on the radio.

Ghosts. They didn't have a care in the world.

Try me, I said.

Griffin had finished his whiskey and now he growled at the waiter for another one. He looked weirdly angry, confused. I wondered what in the hell he was up to.

Tonight, he said. I want you to come out with me tonight.

Where are we going?

To the other side of darkness.

What is that. A disco?

That's a scream, said Griffin. You fucking kill me.

Moon:

Moon was aimless and hungry, driving around with a big emptiness in his stomach. His stomach was positively echoing. He wished he had brought along those doughnuts. But after taking out Wiley's glass door he had been too embarrassed to go back in and ask for a take-out bag. Almost noon, now. He had sixteen dollars, right. That was enough for a big lunch. Moon had a taste for cow. He wanted a hamburger, a big one. And a milkshake or two. He still hadn't checked in at the station and he was maybe three hours late for his tour. Hey, fuck it. That's cool. He had a thousand sick days lined up like little yellow ducks. And there was one of his favorite burger shacks, straight ahead: Millennium Burgers. He shifted around in his seat, wishing the seat belt didn't have to choke him. There was nowhere to park but that's why he became a cop, right. Unlimited parking. He rolled the Taurus into a loading zone and detached the offending seat belt. He rubbed his throat briefly, then tossed his sunglasses on the dashboard. The seat belt was still tangled around one thigh and he struggled with it a moment, then clambered violently out of the front seat. The seat belt tripped him though, and he nearly landed on his face. Fucking thing wanted to kill him. Moon drifted away from the car, muttering. Then turned back. He wondered if he still had that butterfly knife in his glove box. He leaned into the car, his butt hanging into the wind for the world to admire, and dug around until he came up with a knife. It was a big motherfucker, with maybe a seven-inch blade and a shiny brass handle. The blade was tucked within the handle and the handle was supposed to come apart like wings. Hence the name. If he was slick, he could whip the thing out and the handle would flicker apart like a butterfly in flight. But he wasn't very slick. He couldn't even remember where he'd got the thing. A shakedown, probably. But one of his buddies might have given it to him, as a gift. Cops generally had a pretty bloodless sense of humor and any one of his pals would have hooted at the thought of him trying to flash that knife without cutting off his own nose. Anyway. He opened the knife carefully now and cut the seat belt loose at both ends. Then stabbed the blade into the driver's seat cushion, cutting the beast from belly to throat. Yellow stuffing gaped from the wound and Moon felt better. Much better. He pocketed the butterfly and tossed the dead seat belt into a sewer grate, then proceeded to the Millennium, whistling as he walked.

Dear Jude.

Something is very wrong with Griffin, I think.

And this is a guy who's never been quite right. He came to the house once when Lucy was in the worst days of chemo and we were watching a baseball game, very casual on an otherwise dead Saturday afternoon and Griffin is eating pistachios. He brought over a sack of them and he's eating them one after the other and tossing the shells into an ashtray and he comes cruising out of the blue and asks Lucy if she's lost a few pounds. And she's sitting in the rocking chair with a blanket pulled over her in the middle of fucking summer and a scarf around her head like a turban and he knows perfectly well she's been sick and he goes on to say that he liked her better with a little meat on her but the way he says it you can't be sure if he's a complete psychopath or he's just living so deep in his own skin that he truly forgot.

I don't know what was in that drink he gave me but it feels familiar. It feels a little too good and I would have to say it's in the narcotic family. But a distant relation. Faint. The way ice tastes when it's been washed in vodka.

Anyway, Griffin paid the tab and instructed me to be at the Paramount around midnight, to catch a swing band called Martha's Dead.

And just as I began sleepily to contemplate whether Martha was involved in a state of being or ownership in relation to the dead, the grinning bastard kicked me under the table and said hey, maybe you can use that little kidney story to get close to some nice pussy.

You know. Milk the girls for a little sympathy, he said.

I stared at him and now it dawned on me that Griffin didn't believe me. He didn't believe a fucking word. It was really too bad that I don't have a few vacation snapshots of Jude sunbathing on a brick patio in an impossibly small bikini, the sky behind her yellow with Texas dust. Jude smoking a cigarette beside a fountain while tourists swarmed around her. Jude throwing money at a beggar. Jude standing in the ocean, hands white and skeletal at her sides. And one shot of Phineas and Jude together, fondling each other in a café. A sweet old lady from Minneapolis took that one. It was a ridiculous story, after all. It was pure tabloid. And why should I care if anyone believed me or not. I walked out with Griffin into gray sunlight and before he turned to go, Griffin touched my arm.

It was a simple thing, a touch.

Like we were friends, like we didn't need words between us. Maybe it was true. I tried to remember how things really were before the urine incident but everything was obscured by smoke and drugs and loud music and faces. Disconnected torsos. The memories disengaged and I was watching a movie on a grainy black-and-white television without sound.

Tomorrow, said Griffin. Tomorrow you will understand.

What? What will I understand?

Griffin shrugged. You will live in another world.

He walked away from me with unfailing arrogance, his legs furious and fluid in those slim purple pants. His smooth, round skull floating at his shoulders. I tried to reconcile this image with the smiling, slithering Griffin who had peed on me with impunity. There were but flashes of his previous selves, of the Griffin who decapitated a mannequin and offered the head to his estranged girlfriend. Of the Griffin who improvised wildly in the courtroom, the Griffin who was at once adored and hated by judges.

Moon:

Now that was fucking better. Moon felt a thousand times better. Nothing like a belly full of undigested meat to set him right. And he loved that bread they used for the buns, fresh sourdough rolls that were never exactly round like those creepy processed buns at McDonald's. Fuck those processed buns. The Millennium buns were properly deformed lumps of bread, often bearing strange tumors. And the Millennium gave a fellow a serious chunk of meat that weighed a quarter of a pound after it was fucking cooked and the fat had dripped away. Then topped with real cheese and fried onions, pickles and jalapeño wedges on the side. Moon had to pass on the waffle fries today. He had been feeling a little bloated of late, and was trying to lay off the starch. But he did soak the burger down with two vanilla shakes. Now he was walking back to the car, laughing at himself a little bit. He had been so hungry that he killed his own seat belt, for fuck's sake.

Droning down the sidewalk, he was on cruise control and feeling good. He was happy, of all fucking things. The hell was wrong with him. Maybe he would go down to the station and poke around, see if there was anything interesting on the board. Hey, now. What the fuck was this? His foot was stuck in something. A wad of green chewing gum that some sociopath spat on the sidewalk. The gum had melted in the sun and was now smeared nicely along the underside of his shoes. Fucking beautiful. Moon sat down on the curb, muttering. The next time he saw a guy, or a little kid even, spitting his gum on the sidewalk…dead. The offender was fucking dead. Moon finally took the shoe off and scraped at it with the handy butterfly knife. Then he heard voices, loud. Maybe two men and a woman, talking at once.

You stupid, stupid fuck.

Listen listen listen.

Whoa, now. I can't breathe with you in my ass.

Tommy, Tommy. Let's go, please.

Moon swiveled around to scope the cracked glass window of a coin-op laundromat. Four or five people were gathered around the change machine, shoving at each other. Okay. This was just what he needed. A random dose of pure foolishness. Moon replaced his sticky shoe and stood up, breathing hard. He walked into the laundromat and everybody froze. He sighed. Did he really look that much like a pig?

What's the trouble?

Everyone was silent and Moon quickly catalogued them. A skinny Latino girl and her white boyfriend, who had the pale, downcast eyes of bystanders. They were already backing away, as if to say: this really isn't our problem. In fact, we were just leaving. Moon shrugged and let them go. He turned to the other three. Black male in mid-thirties, shaved head and nose ring. Wearing blue hooded sweatshirt and sunglasses, black pants and sneakers. He looked angry, sullen. White male in early twenties. Long dirty blond hair and a beard. Filthy bluejeans, no shoes and a torn white T-shirt that read Zippy the Pinhead for President. A small, white female with black hair, braided. Middle twenties and wearing peculiar clothes: soft leather vest that buttoned to the throat, no shirt. Her arms bare and white. She wore a dark red or black skirt, knee-length and made of something like velvet. It was thick and heavy and the colors seemed to shift. A wide belt around her waist, with little beaded pouches dangling from it. Brown leather boots that laced up to her knees. She was staring hard at Moon, as if she knew him. Her eyes were gray as stones, with a touch of blue around the edges.

What's the trouble? he said again.

The woman smiled but said nothing.

This motherfucker, said the black male. He pointed at the white boy. This dumb cracker is trying to get change out of the machine with a piece of lettuce. I need to dry my clothes for work but I can't get some change because of this fool. He's got a pocketful of lettuce, he's got a damn salad in his pants and he wants to try every damn piece of lettuce, one after another. How am I supposed to put up with that?

The white kid grinned, scratched himself. He was a picture of bliss. There were indeed several wilted pieces of lettuce at his feet, and another in his left hand.

Well? said Moon.

Yeah, said the white kid. I'm cool. I'm minding my own shit when this person starts invading my space. Fucking up my head, you know.

Right, said Moon.

He stepped up to examine the machine. The dollar slot was slimy with green and black juices and bits of chewed lettuce. It looked pretty well ruined. Maybe not. He pulled out a dollar and tried to feed it into the machine. The machine promptly rejected it. The machine started blinking, like it was maybe going to explode. Moon sighed and wished his armpits would stop dripping for five seconds. He wanted to help somebody, he really did. He probably had a few quarters in his pockets, but he might need them later. He never knew when he might pass a video arcade. He regarded the fucked machine briefly, wondering how much trouble it would be to smash it open. He had a tire iron in the car, but the idea of going out to get it and coming back to pound on this machine for a while made him weary beyond belief. He did have a gun. But that would be a rather extreme solution, even by his standards. He glanced at the woman.

What's your story? he said.

She shrugged. I'm not involved. But I was curious.

About what?

I wanted to see if the lettuce would work. And I was curious to see which one of these two was going to get stabbed over four quarters.

Nobody's getting stabbed.

The woman sniffed. I smell blood on somebody.

Okay, said Moon.

What about my money, said the black guy.

The machine seems to be broken, said Moon. It won't be accepting any regular money today.

Motherfucker, said the black guy.

Easy, said the white kid. It's all good.

The black guy was rubberband fast. His left fist lashed out and Moon barely registered the shadow of movement, the recoil. But the white kid was already on the floor, bleeding from the nose. The black guy looked at Moon with mild brown eyes.

You gonna arrest me or something? he said. Because I'm gonna be late for work.

Moon shook his head, smiling. He wondered if the black guy could teach him to move like that. It would come in handy the next time he said hello to McDaniel. The white kid was choking, or giggling, at his feet. Moon glanced down at him and the kid was already bobbing his head to some internal hippie music. The kid stared at the blood on his hands and shirt for a moment, then tasted it wondrously, as if it might be raspberry syrup. He clearly didn't remember being punched in the face.

Arrest you for what? said Moon.

The woman tapped the black man on the elbow and he turned,

surprised. As if he hadn't noticed her there. She didn't smile, exactly. But her eyes were bright.

I have four quarters you can have, she said.

Thanks, he said. Thank you.

She pulled a handful of coins from one of her little pouches and sorted through them. Flashes of gold and sparkling bits of colored glass. She sells seashells, Moon thought. He couldn't help but stare at her and she was probably used to that. The back of his neck felt clammy just being near her. But that could well be the Millennium burger, or the bourbon. There was a lot of bad juice in his bloodstream. To put it mildly.

The woman separated four quarters and gave them to the man. He offered her a dollar but she shook her head, she turned and walked away.

Time to kill and money in my pocket and what would I do with myself now. It might be a good idea to go test the waters down at Moon's precinct but I was nervous. I needed a disguise, a wig or some false teeth. I wasn't walking in there as Phineas Poe, that was for goddamn sure. The roof might come down on my head. I wondered idly what Ray Fine might look like. Maybe old Ray could pass for a private eye.

I laughed at myself, now.

Because cops love to talk to private detectives. Oh, they do. They love it. And in five minutes Ray Fine might easily say the wrong thing and find himself in a holding cell with a handful of his own teeth and a dent in his head shaped exactly like the yellow pages.

No shit.

If Ray was going to be a private eye, he would have to dress like he still lived with his mamma, like he might be Norman Bates. He would need a mustache and maybe some ugly glasses that he paid fifty cents for at a yard sale. A carelessly constructed but psychotic geek. A guy that limped.

Okay, okay. This wasn't so bad. I might well enjoy it.

What else.

Ray would have a history of scoliosis and bad feet. His pants should be too short and possibly unzipped, but he would look like a guy who might get violent in a pinch. A guy that you wouldn't want to push into a corner because he might just stab you in the throat with a ballpoint pen, with his keys. Ray should be goofy enough to appear harmless, smart and relentless and creepy enough to get some answers.

That was my plan, such as it was.

I would become Ray Fine and Ray would go talk to Captain Honey and feel him out about my pal Moon and his tale of lost cops.

I started walking and things got slippery, fast. Passed a bus stop and saw four or five women dressed up like vaudeville whores. Leather granny boots covered in dust. Thick skirts that fell to the ground with fur and feathers stitched into the hems. White blouses with complicated hook and eyelet buttons cut low and square across heaving bosoms. Truly. These were tits that laughed at gravity, they fucking sneered at it. These women were each strapped into some kind of corset or bustier that not only aimed their nipples at the sky but gave them eighteen-inch waists as well, right. A wonder they could breathe at all. They carried little paper umbrellas and wore incredible sunbonnets that glittered with beads and colored glass and rose petals. Two of them wore snug little lace pinafores at the waist and the others had black feather boas coiled around their necks. Their faces were painted in terrifying monochrome red and blue and pink and their hair hung in exquisite ringlets and curls. I thought they must be on their way to a costume party and wasn't going to say a word as I was already gawking shamelessly at them but as I passed they commenced to whistle and hoot at me openly. One of them stepped in front of me and gave my arm an exploratory squeeze, you know. Checking the bicep for muscle. Whether she liked the specimen, I can't say. But she sighed and whimpered and asked if I was looking for a good time and her tone was pure Scarlett O'Hara.

Breathless and swooning.

And finally I said, has there been a ripple in time and they just giggled like mad chickens and she said my, isn't he eccentric? And by now they were all pawing at me and blowing into my eyes and touching me and one of them said it was just two dollars a throw. Which meant I could fuck all of them for eight dollars if only I had the strength.

And one of them was actually getting to me. She was small and dark with a mouth the color of fire and her waist was insane, maybe eighteen inches at the most. Pale yellow breasts, heavy and round. The bright smell of mint about her. She had me by the hand and I felt pretty weak, she had me in her grasp and my brain was still chanting two dollars only two dollars but the whole thing was freaking me out and finally I pushed through them like a spooked horse and when I turned to look back, they were gone. One of their bonnets lay on the sidewalk and just as I turned to go back and touch it the wind came up and lifted it up and away and I watched it disappear beyond a dark scaffold of trees.

Moon:

The dark-haired woman lingered on the sidewalk, thin arms crossed over her chest as if she couldn't decide where she was going. Maybe she was waiting for someone. Of course, she might be waiting for her clothes to hit the rinse cycle. Moon hesitated in the doorway of the laundromat, watching her. He liked the way that heavy velvet skirt hung from her small waist, a physical shadow. It caught rays of the sun and spun them away in fragments. She was not waiting for him, for fat sad balding Detective Moon. That much was pretty clear. He was Charlie Brown. Not quite as bald, maybe. But much fatter and clumsier and plagued by nastier and certainly more powerful bodily odors. The little red-haired girls of the world tended to flash past him like flying squirrels. They rarely touched the ground and generally remained unaware of the large, slow-moving and oafish members of his species.

But one never knew.

Maybe she was in some kind of trouble of her own and needed to talk to someone. A sympathetic cop, for instance. Moon shrugged and glanced at his reflection in the window. His fly was at least zipped and his shirt was clean. What more could he ask of himself? He swabbed at his face with the sleeve of his jacket, wiping away any remaining traces of hamburger grease.

Can I help you? he said.

The woman turned. What?

Help, he said. Do you need any help.

She frowned. No, thank you.

Moon fumbled with his car keys, then dropped them. The ring of metal against pavement. Moon poked at the keys with one foot, suddenly reluctant to bend over and not sure what he was afraid of. Take your pick. His pants could easily rip open at the crotch. His body might choose that exact moment to produce some unsavory noise or odor. And he was well aware that he grunted like a pig giving birth whenever he bent to tie his shoes, but he couldn't seem to do anything about it. The woman smiled at him, or allowed her lips to curve slightly in his direction. Moon blinked at her. He showed her his gold shield, casually.

I'm not a pervert, he said. I just thought you might need a ride somewhere. This isn't such a good neighborhood.

Her eyes burned brightly. I live just a block from here.

Oh, well. Moon scratched his head, briefly. Helplessly. His left foot spasmed suddenly and he kicked his own keys into the street.

Your keys, she said.

Yes.

The woman bent quickly, like a bird. Black hair like spilled ink. The long braid swinging lazily around her neck. The twitch of muscle in one bare shoulder. Now the keys jingled in her palm.

She's fluid, he thought. Fluid.

What's your name? he said.

Dizzy, she said. Dizzy Bloom.

Nice, he said.

My great-grandmother was Molly Bloom.

Who?

Now she laughed, softly. Did you not read *Ulysses* in college?

Moon was paralyzed, stupid. Her wide gray eyes tugged at him like gravity and he tried to remember exactly what he had studied in college and came up blank. Sociology, wasn't it? He spent two years reading a lot of depressing German philosophers, then dropped out to join the cops.

Never mind, said Dizzy.

She took a step forward and placed the keys in his left hand. His fingers closed reflexively. The woman sniffed him and the smile vanished from her face.

It's you, she said. The smell of blood comes from you.

What?

Be careful with knives, she said.

Moon felt his head wobbling around on his shoulders, as if it wasn't properly attached. He felt cold. And he had a sudden case of the creeps. He wanted to get away from this freaky bitch. It was too bad, because she had incredible eyes but there was something wrong with her.

I'm sorry, she said.

I hit a thrift store first, a cavernous place called Lost Threads.

The stink of mothballs and a rat-faced clerk wearing army fatigues. Pink Floyd seeping like loneliness from hidden or buried speakers. I counted sixteen mannequins, most of them naked and missing crucial limbs. They made the place feel unpleasantly crowded and somber at once. A mirrored disco ball glittered overhead. There were heaps of clothing everywhere, unsorted. Whole families could be burrowed in among these piles armed with sleeping bags and mosquito netting and collapsible stoves, waiting for the apocalypse. I could almost feel their eyes on me, infuriating little needles. The razor whine of imagined voices. I wandered around for a half hour and came up with an armload of clothes that might fit.

The clerk ignored me when I asked if there was a dressing room. But that was okay, really. I wasn't proud. I could blend in with the mannequins. I tried on a few things and finally settled on an outfit that Ray Fine and I could both live with. A pair of black and blue Depression-era pinstriped pants made from an unidentified material that flared slightly at the ankles. These were a good fit, actually. They made me feel taller. A hideous, mostly white rayon shirt with a big floppy collar, a possible blood stain on the left breast, and an incongruous surfer motif: a coiled, naked woman on one sleeve and a big orange sunset on the back. A muddy brown unabomber sweatshirt that zipped up the front. An ugly but weirdly stylish wool blazer, bright pea green in color and equipped with seven mysterious pockets. And topped off by a charcoal gray fedora with grease stains along the brim and a mangy feather stuck in the band. I briefly coveted a pair of silver and green Doc Marten clown shoes but they were much too small. My own cracked and dirty work boots would have to do.

Ninety dollars, said the ratty clerk.

I gave him the money and wondered if there might be something secretly wrong with these clothes. That they might be pox- or lice-ridden, for instance. But at that price, I could live with a little infestation. I had had lice before and I was bound to have them again. It wasn't my problem, anyway. These were Ray's clothes. I asked for a shopping bag or something to carry my old things in, but the clerk ignored me again. I was barely visible, it seemed. I glanced around and spotted a black plastic garbage sack on the floor, bulging with donated clothes. I dumped the contents on the floor and immediately a furious white moth flew into my face. I killed it by reflex, then tossed my old clothes into the bag, tipped my new hat at the ratty clerk and was gone.

Dizzy Bloom:

The smell of cat, of a solitary man. And dust, a lifetime of dust. Boiled tomatoes. Tobacco and whiskey and unwashed socks. Blood, above all. The burned copper stench of blood. She could see the cat now, sniffing at his toes. She could see a television, a twist of leather. And another man, thin and hungry and staring.

Oh, she had a headache. Blue and crushing. A rain of brittle flowers. Her vision shrinking and she was looking through a fish-eye lens and then everything faded and she breathed with relief. She hated this, she did. She never asked for this. She never knew what to do with what she saw.

Dizzy walked through a fine white mist and hoped it wouldn't rain before she made it home.

Yesterday she had touched a woman, a Trembler.

Dizzy took one breath of the woman's ash-white hair and suffered a prolonged vision of her five or ten years into the future, sobbing and ripped apart as she gave birth to a damaged child, a mongoloid with fused spine. But somehow beautiful. It was still a child, a little boy-child and he was amazing and fine when he took his first breath. Even though he wouldn't live more than a year. She couldn't bring herself to tell the Trembler what she saw. It would have accomplished nothing and besides, the Trembler had been heavily drugged. She had been a puppet, a ninety-six-pound ghost. Her flesh had not been her own and her mind was porous.

And besides, it had been Dizzy's choice to tell or not tell. She had owed the Trembler nothing, for the game of tongues described no parameters for the Breathers. They were unbound by the laws that guided the other players, that gave them purpose. For most of them, this was not a problem. They drifted through the game as bystanders, witnesses. They were free to help or ignore the other players as they wished. But Dizzy was the rare Breather who saw not the past, but the future. Fortunately for her, she was not tormented by every breath she took. Thank God for that. She was not plunged into an unknown and possibly terrifying future by every drifting scent. Her visions were rare, unexpected. And so she functioned well enough. The hardest to bear was the unwanted glance into someone's last day. Even with the game, death could be very real and the scent of it left her ill for days. But when she ventured outside the game and into the realm of Citizens, she was at times visited by terrible and confusing visions. She could never be sure if what she saw was real. The Citizens were said to be unaffected, untouched by the game and any visions that swelled from them must therefore be mistaken. But no one within the game could ever agree on this. Only the Gloves knew, and they only smiled when asked for the truth.

The poor policeman. Overweight and lonely and worried about his hair. His blood had seemed real, very real. As if he had been bleeding from an unseen wound along the thigh, the ankle. And perhaps he was not an ordinary Citizen at all. There had been a fading but distinct glow of the glamour about him, the almost visible smell of flowers. He had worn the fuzzy look of the unaware Fred.

Dizzy turned down her street, walking quickly now. She wanted a bath, she wanted bubbles and steam and a small glass of wine. She wanted to shed her clothes and be alone, to sleep. Tonight she would not enter the game, and she would not drink the Pale.

Her mouth was sore but her head was clear, the brittle blue flowers forgotten. The taint of blood was gone. Dizzy sighed and looked to the wide yellow sky and reminded herself that blood was not always the end. It may come of nothing, a cut finger or crushed nose. There were black clouds in the west, seeping into the yellow and she could only hope that the fat policeman suffered nothing more than a mishap with his razor.

Home, she was home.

Dizzy opened the iron gate, started up the flagstone path. Her house was a three-story Victorian with wild roses and creeping vines and a slightly leaky roof left her by her grandmother. She saw the first shadow on her porch, then another. There were three of them and she sighed, but she was not surprised. The game had come to her. She would at least have a bath. But she might not resist the Pale.

The first shadow came down the steps to greet her with empty hands. He bowed to her and she recognized him. Chrome, the Mariner. She didn't know him well, but she had heard rumors of him.

That he was a fearsome hunter, collector of a hundred tongues. And that he was a gentleman, a charmer of men and women. Dizzy shrugged. She was not so easily charmed. On the porch behind him was Mingus, a gentle Breather. The third shadow was a young girl, thin and dark and unknown. Chrome introduced her as Goo, apprentice to the Lady Adore.

Welcome, said Dizzy.

Dear Jude.

Don't worry about me. The pain is gone. I can tie my own shoes without whimpering. I have gained a few pounds and people don't stare at me in the street. I don't horrify myself in the shower.

My grandfather had this three-legged dog, a pit bull named Chaucer. And he was a fucked-up animal, he was beyond tragic. Chaucer was a hermaphrodite. I'm serious. Male and female genitalia and neither of them functional. Chaucer was sterile, thank God. A truck ran him down when he was a pup, which is how he lost the leg. And it seemed like that dog would never die. Poor fucker had arthritis, glaucoma. He had bald spots in his fur from a hundred old wounds and most of one ear was missing. He smelled of death, of sewage. He was a sweet old dog but terrible to behold. And if you shoved him into a corner and made him fight he would calmly chew your arm off without blinking because he still had all of his teeth and he just didn't give a fuck. That old dog had no worries. He had already been crushed by a red pick-up truck on a partly cloudy Sunday morning and lived. He had a worthless cock and a dried-up pussy and he could never gratify himself but he was still walking around.

That's me, sometimes. That's your Phineas.

And sometimes I think my heart will give out on me. Everything tastes strange and there's a faraway muffled thumping in my ears and I keep looking at the sky, thinking it's thunder. There's a storm coming. But it's not thunder. It's my own stupid blood hammering away and I'm just having a panic attack.

Oh, yeah. You might think you're cool and confident but you live on the narrow, on the hot edge of metal in the sun and you're walking down the street in these clothes that you bought for someone else and you catch a glimpse of yourself in the black windows of a parked car, your reflection is suddenly kicked back in your face and it's not you at all. You're lost, you're lost and here comes the panic.

Here it comes.

Ray Fine:

Don't fucking worry. Stay in character and don't piss anyone off and you will be right as rain. Phineas whispered these last unheard words of advice to his new parallel ego and retreated safely into the shadows to watch and listen. I'm not here, he said. You are on your own.

Ray Fine smiled wetly at everyone he passed. Ray is one of those sad guys who can't quite keep his mouth closed. His lips were forever parted, as if he had a problem with his sinus, as if he were simple. And he limped, as expected. Not terribly, but with enough hobbling and spastic shuffling that he might well crash into a mailbox at any moment. His clothes were very bad. The clothes of someone who might be seen howling prophesies at traffic. He wore a charcoal fedora with a diseased sparrow's feather tucked into the brim. He wore a pea-green jacket and a brown, hooded sweatshirt. A white polyester shirt under this, untucked. Outlandish blue-and-black bell-bottoms that people actually stopped to stare at. He had a ragged mustache that burrowed between his mouth and nose like a pet mouse, and he wore glasses with yellow lenses and black frames held together by a piece of wire. A brand new digital watch with a price tag still dangling that he had purchased for five dollars at a drug store. Ray Fine was another rambling, harmless freak. And he knew it. He limped up the steps to the Ninth Precinct, loudly saying hello and good morning to everyone he saw. A few people even said hello back to him.

Once inside, Ray Fine became mysteriously unobtrusive. He lost the limp for a moment and walked briskly past the desk sergeant, who was busy with someone else and who, if he noticed Ray at all, might have assumed he was an eccentric lawyer. Two rookie uniforms turned to stare at him and he winked at them. Ray Fine knew where he was going. Ray continued down the hallway largely uncontested. Now he muttered to himself and allowed his head to wobble on his shoulders. He was a delirious monkey. He placed one hand over his mouth as if he might vomit. This seemed to help a lot. Now everyone ducked out of his way. Ray turned a corner and resumed his limp.

He smacked his lips and worked his tongue around his mouth, perhaps fishing for debris left over from his lunch. He passed a pretty assistant DA and gave her a friendly thumbs-up, then came to an elevator and merrily pushed the already glowing Up button.

He pushed it five or six times, to be sure.

Two detectives, fat and thin, and a brightly colored secretary stood waiting for the same elevator, and now they turned to peer at him and politely look away. Ray Fine took this opportunity to fart silently and step to one side, his nose twitching. The secretary wrinkled her upper lip and glanced with disapproval at the fat detective.

The elevator arrived and Ray graciously climbed aboard last.

Three please, he said loudly. I'm going up to Homicide, you know.

Ray extended his hand. Ray Fine, Special Adjuster #616.

The what?

That's right. There's a problem with the conglomerate eleven two tone appropriation policy. Big problem, big as a fucking house.

The secretary cocked one eyebrow in disbelief. I don't think…

Ray hooted at her. Easy now, little Debbie. You don't want your face to get stuck that way, do you?

The fat detective grinned as the doors opened on the third floor. No one moved a muscle as Ray Fine darted through and turned to give them all a two-fisted thumbs-up just as the doors hissed shut.

Moon:

He was not crazy, not crazy. Sometimes he wanted to get away, sure. To take off his shirt and sprout wings from his humped and painful shoulder blades. His wings would at least be white, he thought. His wings would be deceptively pretty. He wanted to fly high and wide, out across the plains where the high yellow grass would bend and dip in the wind. Moon sucked in his breath, confused. Brief shudder and thump as his head smacked against the roof of his car. He had jumped a fucking curb. Nearly crushed a lightpost. Oh, boy. That's right. He was temporarily without a seat belt. Tufts of yellow stuffing floated up to his face and he tried to grab them with a clumsy paw. He had to get a hold of himself. Maybe he would drop in on the department shrink. The idea made him want to choke up his lunch but what else could he do? He was trashing doughnut shops and making sad eyes at hippie girls in the street and disemboweling his own car. He was killing himself, which he might not mind so much but it could take a while to actually finish himself off. Moon opened the car door, inspected himself for injuries. Nothing to speak of, really. An egg-sized lump on his forehead that would likely be colorful tomorrow, but he could always wear a hat. He stepped back to survey the car. Three wheels on the sidewalk, nose shoved into a wooden post. It was possibly an acceptable parking job, though it might impede pedestrian traffic. He considered moving it, straightening it out a bit, but his throat tightened up at the idea and he had to flail his arms for balance. Fucking wings, for god's sake. He looked up and down the street for moral support and while his might have been the only car on the sidewalk, it did have unexpired tags and a decent paint job and well, fuck it. Moon was a half-block from his building. He would go home, have a cold shower. He would pluck the clumps of dead hair from his bathtub drain. He would brush his teeth and wash his face with witch hazel. Then he would drink a single beer and have a grilled cheese sandwich, with bacon and onions. Maybe Phineas would be there. They could have a good laugh about the lettuce incident and then walk down the street to move his beached car. Right, then. He made sure his doors were locked and turned to go home.

But he hadn't gone ten feet when a shadow fell across his path.

Good day, said the shadow.

A tall man in an overcoat, the sun behind him. Not a breathing shadow. Moon wrenched himself sideways and got a look at the guy's face. Long, wet lips. Fucked-up looking hair, like it was cut by a drunk with a kitchen knife. But at least the guy had some hair to speak of. The guy was about his age, maybe older. Wearing a black raincoat. For about two seconds, Moon thought he was maybe going to flash him.

But the guy just looked at him, his head crooked.

Do I know you? said Moon.

I don't think so, the guy said. My name is Gulliver.

Well, then. What the fuck do you want.

Nothing at all. I was passing by and couldn't help noticing that your head is bleeding.

Moon blinked. There did seem to be a slow leak just north of his left eye, a warm trickle. He grabbed at his skull with one hand and it came away red.

Huh, he said. That little chicken wasn't crazy, I guess.

Excuse me?

Oh, said Moon. I met a very strange girl, earlier today. She said she smelled blood on me.

Interesting.

Anyway. I wrecked my car just now. Must have cracked my nut on the windshield.

The man leaned close, sniffing. I smell nothing, he said.

Moon jerked his face away. Who asked you?

The man shrugged. The girl was a Breather, perhaps.

What?

Don't be thick, man. I can see you're in the game.

Moon took a step back.

It's okay, said the man. I don't want your tongue. But I'm very good with a needle and thread, if you want to stitch that cut.

It's a scratch, said Moon. It needs a Band-Aid, maybe.

I might help you become self-aware.

You're some kind of pervert, right?

The man shook his head. He smiled and his teeth were like bones in the sun, cracked and yellow. Moon was disgusted. He was offended. He didn't feel sorry for people who couldn't take care of their teeth. Maybe it was just a desperate response to the loss of his hair or the foot odor problem but he seemed to brush his teeth about five times a day, lately.

The queers don't usually go for me, said Moon. I'm too butch, or something.

Or something, said the man.

Yeah, said Moon. Thanks, though.

The man sighed. You won't last, he said.

Ray Fine:

They ducked into a restroom, hissing at each other. Pushed and shoved to the sink and ran cold water over their hands, eyeballing the mirror all the while. You want to settle down, or what? You're a maniac, you're out of control. The idea was to be foolish but inoffensive so just settle the fuck down, okay. If you can't be half normal then you're toast. This is my body, right. What's left of it. And if you get the shit kicked out of it then you can go back to living in a cigar box under Moon's sink.

Fucking right.

Then to the urinal for a nervous pee. Ray Fine and Phineas shared a laugh, then Phineas backed off. He gave Ray a final dirty look and let him leave the bathroom in peace to try his own luck with the desk clerk.

She looked like an unforgiving hag. Face like a slab of ham, bright pink and bloated with fat. Thick burgundy hair piled on her head in the shape of a barrel. Ray Fine gritted his teeth and put on a happy face. Behind the hag was a steady hum and bustle of typewriters and telephones and cops going about their business. Phineas felt cold, watching from a distance. He was in the nerve center, such as it was. A trickle of sweat down his back and jangling nerves from skull to fingertips. He hadn't been this close to so many cops in over a year. He didn't like it. He didn't like it at all.

Ray tipped the fedora. Hello, Ma'am.

Flicker of suspicious eyes and a mouthful of gum. Yes?

Yes, well. I need to see Captain Honey right away, posthaste and tout de suite. Life or death and he's expecting me. Ray Fine, from the mayor's office.

The hag shrugged, pushed an intercom button. She bent over it with her pink face. Ray Fine to see you, sir. From the mayor's office.

Long pause, crackling silence.

Phineas squirmed in the dark. Ray Fine grinned confidently.

Nadine, what? The mayor, did you say? Christ on a pony. By all means, send him in. Wait, wait. Ask the poor fellow if he wants a cup of coffee, or a nice danish. Then send him along.

Nadine rolled her eyes. Would you care for a danish? Apple or cream cheese.

Is that real cream cheese?

Hardly.

Ray Fine smiled. Tempting, but no. And don't get up, please. I know the way.

He looked straight ahead as he made his way through an orgy of closely confined odors, of contorted faces. Past the squeals of swiveling chairs, the hiss and purr of fax machines and the groans of his own nervous belly to Honey's office. He looked directly at nothing and no one. Phineas couldn't handle the eye contact and Ray didn't much like it, either.

Captain Honey sat behind his desk in a handsome black wool overcoat. He looked pretty coherent. Freshly shaved, with a single dot of blood on his left cheek. What remained of his hair was combed smartly over his naked scalp. His eyes were blue and clear. He had one foot up on his desk, though, and he seemed to be wearing tennis shorts with no socks. And upon closer inspection, it looked like he was wearing a plaid bathrobe under the wool overcoat. Moon had not lied about the coupons, by the way. The man's desk was littered with coupons. The walls were wildly decorated with old comic strips. Marmaduke. Beetle Bailey. Ziggy. And scarily prominent was the insidious Family Circus. Phineas closed his eyes, wished he could go to sleep. Ray Fine smiled and sat down.

Good morning and what can we do for you, private? said Honey.

Ray glanced at his watch, it was nearly five in the evening. Honey was staring at him pretty intently for a confused old guy. Ray Fine stuttered. Oh, well. It's a question of human interest.

How's that? said Honey.

Ray took one rattling breath, smiled, then commenced to babble. The mayor wants to improve the police department image, you know. He wants the people of Denver to feel safe and happy. He wants them to say hello and good morning and God bless you when they pass a cop on the street.

Honey gnawed at a hangnail. I like it, I do. It sounds like a grand idea.

The first order of business is to profile one of your brightest and bravest, to make one special cop look like the guy next door. Our sources say that Detective Jimmy Sky is your finest officer.

Sky, did you say?

That's right.

Oh, dear. I don't think I know him. No, I don't.

He should be attached to this squad, said Ray.

No, no. Jimmy Cliff is a singer. A Jamaican fella, I believe.

Jimmy Sky, said Ray.

Honey thumbed his intercom button. Nadine? Is there a detective named Sky on my squad?

She sighed mightily. No, sir.

Honey smiled. There you go.

Interesting. Let me ask you this, then. Have you had any officers go missing of late?

Honey's eyes darkened, as if a stray cloud had passed before his brain. He leaned forward, one bony finger poling at the air before him. Listen boy, he said. I never leave this office. Except for weekends, that is. I sleep on a fold-out cot like a goddamn soldier. Nadine has all my food brought in by long-haired little shits on bicycles. And I pee right into a mason jar when I need to relieve myself.

Ray took off his hat, ran one hand through his hair. He was sweating.

Believe you me, said Honey. I would know if any of my men were missing.

Of course you would.

Captain Honey closed his eyes and leaned back in his chair. Before long, he was snoring.

Ray Fine sat there a while, nodding. It occurred to him that old Phineas was probably crawling out of his skin right now.

Dizzy Bloom:

Warm inside and dangerously cozy.

The girl called Goo was curled on a nest of pillows by the fireplace. Chrome had gone to take a shower, a cold shower. Dizzy had asked him very politely to save a little hot water for her bath and he gave her a nasty shivering look, saying softly that he took only cold showers. Mingus sat cross-legged in the bay window, his nose shoved defensively into a book of Dorothy Parker's short stories. Dizzy moved in shadows about the room, lighting a few scented candles and turning the radio to a gospel station. She kept looking at Goo. Wondering who she was in real life, how she came to be here and how deep she was in the game. Goo didn't fidget, she noticed. She didn't pick at her fingernails or play with her hair. Her hands were restful, solemn. Dizzy glanced at the ceiling and wondered what Chrome was doing up there. He could be spitting onto every clean towel, he could be masturbating on her bed. He could be using her toothbrush. He could be taking a shower. The pipes were droning but cold water was fairly endless. Dizzy moved to sit beside Goo. The girl smelled of musk and brown sugar, of dried blood and Band-Aids. A rich, intoxicating presence and thank God she threw off no visions.

Are you hungry? said Dizzy.

Goo stretched her thin legs and smiled without speaking. Dizzy looked at her closely now. A short, wild mop of black hair. Dark, soft mouth and gray eyes. Heavy boots. Brown suede jeans and a little black sweater of silk or fine cotton with short sleeves. The sweater didn't quite cover her tummy, and when she moved, it rose a little. Dizzy again smelled dried blood, and she saw the white edge of adhesive tape. The girl had a bruise on her left arm, another on the side of her neck. But this wasn't unusual. She was an Exquisitor's apprentice.

Do you eat meat? said Dizzy.

Goo sighed. Yes. I do now.

What's the matter?

Do you know why we're here?

Dizzy shrugged. One of you is running from something.

My apartment is slipping.

Really?

Yes. It was disappearing before my eyes.

The girl spoke in a clipped, halting monotone. She stared without blinking and Dizzy realized she was in a mild state of shock.

I saw a car disappear once, said Dizzy. It just melted away.

How is that possible?

Physically, it's not. As far as I know.

Physically.

Dizzy grinned. Useless distinction, isn't it.

I want to sleep, said Goo. I want to wake up and be normal.

How long have you been in the game?

The girl hesitated. As if she couldn't quite remember her real life, her past. Then she shivered. A slow flush of color in her cheeks. Not long, she said. A little more than six weeks.

You're just a baby, said Dizzy. You will be okay, eventually.

Dizzy lifted one hand, or allowed it to float sideways. She began to stroke the girl's hair, dragging the soft black curls through her white, crooked fingers. After a minute or two of thick silence, Goo touched her wrist and asked her to stop. Dizzy wasn't offended. Some people don't like to be touched. Dizzy excused herself, slipped away to the kitchen. She tied an old apron around her waist and began to chop onions, thinking she would start with a nice spinach salad. Then perhaps grilled shark steaks.

Excuse me?

Dizzy turned to find Mingus standing in the doorway. Hesitant, as if he was afraid to intrude. Mingus was so strange. Otherworldly, even within the game. It was hard not to like him. He was small, frail. Not more than five feet tall and barely a hundred pounds. He was maybe two pounds heavier than she was when naked and wet. Thin blond hair, almost white and hanging over his dark eyes. He had the sweet face of a boy, soft skin and red lips. He had possibly never been with a woman, although she knew he was about her age. Dizzy was twenty-nine.

Come in, she said.

He moved closer, he moved slowly. He was worried, frightened. Dizzy took a deep breath of him and he was a whirl of scents, most of them not his own. She saw nothing but dark skies.

What is it?

I'm a bit worried, he said.

Dizzy put down the knife, wiped her hands on a towel. Mingus glanced uneasily at the ceiling, then back at her. The shower was still running. The pipes groaned and whistled. Mingus went to the refrigerator and got out a piece of ice. He sucked on it as he spoke.

It's awkward, he said. It's about Chrome, you see. And I don't want to cause alarm without good reason, but he took down a Fred, yesterday. Under the sun. We were not within the game.

Dizzy shrugged. That's risky, of course. But not so unusual.

No, said Mingus. That's not it. He killed the man. Literally, I mean.

An iron skillet fell from Dizzy's hand, crashing to the floor. It barely missed her foot. Mingus stared at her, sucking nervously at the ice.

What? said Dizzy. What did you say?

There was blood, he said. A lot of blood. I don't always trust my eyes but I'm sure it was real. The man's throat was gone and I think Chrome wants to make the game real. Or more so.

Dizzy put one hand over her mouth. Have you ever seen the future?

No, he said. Never.

What about Goo? she said.

Mingus frowned. What about her?

Have you told her this? said Dizzy.

No, he said. Chrome is my friend, my ally.

The girl should know who she sleeps with.

The kitchen was shrinking around them. Pots and pans, a dead wandering Jew. A microwave oven she didn't know how to operate. Crystal champagne glasses that had never once been used. A black-and-white photograph of two strangers, apparently just married. A television that baffled her. She had no idea where it had come from.

Fuck me, said Mingus. I can't deal with this, you know.

And your Glove, she said. Who is your Glove?

Mingus shook his head. I have a Genetics midterm in one week.

Who? said Dizzy.

He sighed. Theseus. You know it's Theseus.

Okay, said Dizzy. Tonight we will talk to him, we will tell him about this.

On the street again, my belly ripe with acid and funk. I hated every bend of light. I pulled off the damned mustache that had been tickling my poor nose like a dead thing. Tossed it in the gutter. Fuck that thing. It had been a mortal struggle not to sneeze every five seconds. I removed the glasses, too, but tucked them into my jacket pocket. You never know, I might want them again.

I had intended to meet Griffin at the Paramount as Ray Fine, but there was really no point other than to amuse and confuse. And Ray was not such a reliable persona, was he. Too fucking daffy. I was much better off in my own skin. I would wear Ray's clothes, though. I felt kind of cool in them. I glanced at my new watch, then frowned and plucked off the price tag. It was early and I had plenty of time.

Ducked into a video store with the idea that I might rent a copy of *Shane* and put a smile on Moon's face. We could watch it in the raw sleeping hours past midnight and drink more of that Canadian poison. Funny thing, though. I found the video on the shelf and as my eyes flicked over the credits on the back of the box, I couldn't help noticing that Lee Marvin did not play the lead. It was Alan Ladd, presumably the father of Cheryl and what was in a name, right? Nothing. But it was weird and I decided not to rent the thing after all.

Outside, I hailed a passing cab.

I relaxed in the back and counted my money. I couldn't be wasting too much of it on luxuries like taxis, at least for a while. Was not sure what I was going to tell Moon. That Jimmy Sky doesn't exist and maybe the two of us should take a little vacation down to Florida? A little quiet time, that's all Moon needed. Moon wasn't going to like it at all. He believed in this shit. He believed that cops were disappearing and coming back like zombies. And one of them Jimmy Sky, his friend. Missing or dead. My stomach hurt. I would have to be careful with the old bear. Remember the coffee table, I thought. And then I saw myself smile in the rearview.

Very strange.

Maybe I should take Moon out with me tonight, to see this swing band with Griffin. Those two would get along like a heart attack and a bottle of ether. It would do Moon a world of good, though. Maybe he could hook up with a nice, middle-aged single lady. I would have to keep an eye on him, though, and not let him get so drunk.

Now I glanced out the cab's window. Larimer Street. A few blocks from Moon's place. The cab passed a vacant lot and a length of cyclone fence and then I see a gray Taurus parked crazily on the sidewalk and wedged against a lightpost. Had to be, I said out loud. Had to be Moon's car.

Let me out here.

I passed the cabbie a few bills and walked over to the abandoned Taurus. It wasn't so badly wrecked. The tires were still sound and the front end was maybe a little wrinkled. Nothing to worry about. I touched the hood and it was pretty cold. Peered through the windows and noticed that the driver's seat had been gutted like a goddamn big fish. Yellow stuffing everywhere. Now that was odd. I frowned. There was no blood, at least. Maybe it was nothing. I touched the door handle and what was this? The same unsettling wave of warm dizziness that I felt at Eve's place. Like a plastic bag had been slipped over my head and I couldn't breathe. I didn't like this at all and recoiled, flexing my hand. I looked up and down the street and started walking quickly for Moon's place.

Goo:

Something she needed to do, something important but she couldn't quite remember what because it wasn't her problem, it was Eve's. Never mind, never mind. Hum and holler. It would come to her, or it wouldn't. She sat up and took a good look around. Dizzy Bloom had a nice place. Asian rugs and a thousand books, dried flowers and dark wooden furniture, abstract sculptures and a glowing tank full of exotic fish. How did she maintain all this if she was forever stepping in and out of life? She was a Breather, though. And like Mingus she would be less affected by the Pale, by the lure of tongues. She would have that creepy ability to accept both worlds as real. To let two violent colors merge and become one.

Goo watched her now, as Dizzy laid out a white tablecloth on the floor and arranged dishes and silverware. Dizzy looked so solid, she looked permanent in her flesh. Graceful, silent. Long dark hair and white, white skin almost pink. Leather jerkin buttoned to the throat. Hard to tell if she had breasts or not. Her skirt was full, swirling. But the leather knee boots made her look tough. Dizzy glanced up, saw her looking and Goo could only smile, unashamed.

Mingus cleared his throat and Goo was startled. He was so quiet that she forgot about him sometimes.

What? she said.

Chrome is still in the shower, he said. It's been half an hour.

Goo shrugged. I'll go check on him, if you want.

Please.

Upstairs, she followed the sound of rushing water. Through what appeared to be a guest bedroom with pale green grass cloth on the walls. A queen-sized bed with a puffy white comforter like a small cloud. Roses on the bedside table.

Can't we just live here? she thought.

Eve. That was the sort of thing Eve might wish for. Goo crawled onto the bed, let herself sink into it. She rolled onto her back and felt her body slowly loosen. Her muscles were wound so tight all the time. The shower pounding in the bathroom. His skin would be cold as ice now. Bright with goose bumps. Goo was vaguely aware that Eve hadn't been so nice to Chrome earlier. She could make up for that, though. She kicked off her boots, slid out of her pants. She dropped the black sweater to the floor and lay back on the bed, naked except for the white bandage taped to her ribs. The sound of water crashing and she touched herself, waiting for him to come out of the bathroom. Two fingers inside her, moving in circles. Okay. She didn't want to wait. She rolled off the bed, tiptoed to the bathroom and pushed it open.

Chrome, she said. Come to bed.

She threw back the shower curtain and no one was there. An empty stall, shower pounding like tiny hammers on porcelain. Goo hesitated, then turned off the water. The bathroom was small, with exposed wooden rafters and a tiny little sink. She felt like she was on a boat. Cold and she wrapped her arms around herself. The window was open and she supposed it was just wide enough for Chrome to wiggle through.

He often disappears, she said. To no one, to herself. It's nothing.

But she remembered the blood in his hair, thick and matted. She looked down and the porcelain tub was white as snow. Goo backed out of the bathroom and dressed quickly.

Moon's front door was open just a crack, just enough for a sliver of light to escape down the hall. I saw it as I came around the corner and pretty much shrugged. I relaxed. Because I knew something had happened to my friend. Something bad. Moon was dead, maybe. Or else he had gone completely mental. Moon was fucked up. I could feel this in my teeth. If it had already happened, then there was nothing I could do about it. There was no reason to feel bad about it.

My second thought was: I hope Shame hasn't run off.

I edged close to the door, my knife in hand and wishing I had a gun. Eased the door open and the smell was dreadful. The smell of copper and salt. I stepped inside and my heart became a fist. There was no doubt, then. None at all. I moved through the kitchen and into the living room and nearly fell to my knees as if slapped in the head by a giant's meaty hand.

The room was red, now. Dark with blood.

I forget sometimes how much blood a single body can hold. It's astonishing, really. I pinched my nostrils and looked around for the body. Moon must have been bled like a pig. His throat cut, his body hung upside down. But there was no body. As if he had shriveled down to a handful of flesh and the killer just dropped him in his pocket and walked away. I turned in circles, reluctant to walk through Moon's blood. There was little sign of struggle, aside from the smashed coffee table which Moon himself had smashed. Which could mean everything or nothing. Moon knew the killer. Moon had been asleep at the time, or drunk. Moon had put up no fight. The thud of tiny feet and the cat swished past me.

Shame, I said.

The cat was a firecracker of nerves.

I whispered to him, my hand outstretched. I put the knife back in the sheath under my sleeve. Finally, the cat came to me and allowed himself to be held. I cradled him in one arm and stood up. I turned around once more. My eyes full of blood. I took two steps and a tall, thin man in a white hat came out of Moon's bedroom holding a gun in one hand, a half-eaten sandwich in the other. I stopped and stood there, still petting the cat.

Okay, I said. Are you going to shoot me?

Identify your fucking self, the man said.

He had an Irish accent and seemed pretty angry. He was about to chew his own tongue off. The man stepped closer now, the gun held chest-high. The gun was black, an automatic. It was not Moon's gun but that meant nothing. The sandwich looked to be peanut butter and jelly. The hands holding gun and sandwich were gloved in latex and the man's clothes were not bloody at all. Nobody carried latex gloves but cops and cat burglars and medical examiners, and nobody helped himself to peanut butter and jelly from a dead man's pantry but a fucking psychopath. I allowed my brain to skate around this unhappy equation for a moment and decided the man was probably a cop, mainly because he walked like a cop. He was even wearing a white hat. He was Irish, for that matter. And if he was a cop, he might have heard a thing or two about me, about Phineas Poe. And not liked what he heard.

I hesitated, sighed. Ray Fine, I said. My name is Ray Fine.

And what are you doing here, Mr. Fine?

I'm a friend of Moon's.

The man lowered his gun. Hmm, he said. I believe you.

Why?

That cat wouldn't let me touch him. And he fucking knows me, right. I've been here a hundred times. But he seems to love you.

Yeah, well. I fed him this morning. Who are you?

Lot McDaniel, Homicide. I was Moon's partner.

Really. He's never mentioned you.

McDaniel shrugged. I said I was his partner. Not his pal.

Your name is Lot? I said.

That's right, love, Lot. It's a fine, biblical name. Genesis nineteen.

The guy who staggered away from Sodom in disgrace, I said.

McDaniel sniffed. The very same.

Unlucky, don't you think?

How do you mean?

His wife became a pillar of salt.

Exactly. She was unlucky, not him.

Maybe, I said. But your mother must have had a nasty sense of humor.

My mother was a lovely woman.

The Bible is a telephone book of suitable names for a boy, I say. Peter and Paul, for instance. Thomas. John and Michael.

Those fuckers, said McDaniel. They were dreadfully overrated. The apostles in particular. Unemployed fishermen and layabouts, all of them. While poor old Lot never got a fair shake.

I shrugged. I'm pretty sure he had sex with his own daughters.

McDaniel was fuming. Those wee bitches, they got him drunk. They ganged up on him in the dark. And the poor fellow was feeble. Blind in one eye, too.

Whatever, I said. It might explain why the name never caught on.

Numb and sick. I would really rather be standing somewhere else. Anywhere else. Outside, for instance. My eyes were watering now, from the blood. McDaniel was staring at me, his nostrils flared. And he was toying with the gun.

The cat twisted away from me and jumped to the ground.

McDaniel still stared at me.

Something wrong? I said.

A word of warning. I hate that little Americanism, that expression: *whatever*. To my thinking, you may as well just say fuck you and be done with it.

Brief, awkward silence.

I couldn't decide whether I should apologize or run away.

Okay, I said. The smell is making me faint.

McDaniel smiled. Soft in the belly, are you?

I told myself to ignore this. Where's the body?

In the bedroom, said McDaniel. And not what you would call a handsome corpse.

Do you mind if I take a look?

Detective McDaniel smiled and looked at the sandwich in his left hand, the gun in his right. He took a bite from the sandwich, chewing thoughtfully. He put the gun away, then produced an engraved business card. He offered it like a gift and I had no choice but to hold out my hand.

As a matter of fact, said McDaniel. I would mind. I would mind very much. I need to preserve the integrity of this scene. Forensics are on their way, and all that. You've seen your share of police dramas on television, I suppose.

Oh, sure. I used to watch *Barney Miller* all the time.

Then you understand. I can't let you blunder about back there.

No, of course not.

McDaniel pressed the business card into my palm as if he hoped it would lacerate the flesh. I was feeling ill now, very ill and fucked up. I pocketed the card and backed away, hoping I wasn't going to throw up. I couldn't remember ever coming across a cop who carried engraved cards but I would rather not suspect this guy. It was on the tip of my tongue to ask if McDaniel knew anything about Jimmy Sky but now my brain was coughing slowly into action, like a motor with faulty connections. The motherfucker was eating a sandwich. He was a real freak, he was one giant bad vibe and you never saw his badge, never saw his badge. But then you never asked to see it, did you. And so what if the man carried fancy business cards. Maybe he was a little strange. Maybe he came from a snotty family or went to an Ivy League school on a rugby scholarship. Maybe he wasn't Irish at all. Maybe he was fucking British.

Why don't you call me tomorrow, McDaniel said. If you think of anything useful?

Yeah, I said. I'll call you tomorrow.

McDaniel took another bite from his sandwich and stood there chewing and smiling and obviously wishing I would get the hell out. And I didn't want to hang around. Because I was going to be sick any minute. I hurried back through the kitchen, arms wrapped around my stomach and now I could feel it coming. Eggdrop soup and mu shu pork and Canadian Mist and not much else. I threw up patiently in the kitchen sink and remembered something Moon once said: a gentleman never throws up on his shoes.

Yeah.

I bit down on my tongue to stop myself from sobbing and I didn't think I could stand it if McDaniel came in with his white hat and a mouthful of sandwich and dryly handed me a box of tissues. I stood over the sink, bitterly wiping bile and snot from my lips and wishing I hadn't given all of that coke to Griffin. I opened the refrigerator, looking for something to drink. There had been a single grape soda on the top shelf this morning and I was glad to see it was still there.

Next to it, though, was something very odd, something that was not there this morning. A used paperback copy of *Ulysses*.

Chrome:

He was hungry and his lips were parched but this was when he felt most alive. Hunting. His face and hands were painted black and as he passed through a black doorway he knew that only his eyes were visible. He slipped through a crowd of theater-goers and none of them noticed him. A woman with bright orange hair and a string of pearls passed two inches from him, her breath mingling with his and he was sure he could poke his tongue in her ear and duck away and she would turn slowly, she would turn like a cow trapped in mud. She would decide she had imagined it. He could cut her throat and disappear.

The dark was coming on now and this was his favorite time of day, when the sun was nearly gone, when the sun was failing. The sun was too weak to cast shadows and already he could make out faint gaps between the dayworld and the game. He stopped, melted into a doorway. Allowed his eyes to relax so that he might number these gaps: a blurred patch of red bricks, a shimmering pocket of air, a window so purple the glass looked like a pool of spilled ink. If he stepped through any of them, he would likely find a pocket of the game. He was tempted but his intended quarry was out there somewhere, another Fred with a badge. He was perhaps very close. It was a shame he couldn't have brought Mingus along, but the poor Breather was showing himself to be too stiff, too moral to be good company.

The obvious suspect is Jimmy Sky, of course. Moon is so hot to find the guy it's like he's got a crotch full of spiders and wham, not twelve hours later Moon's own apartment is washed in blood. A kid could figure it out. So it must not be right.

Anyway. I have yet to confirm that Jimmy Sky is a real person.

It happens all the time, this panic. The worst thing is the urge to dart out into the street like a rabbit. I have to push and prod myself along and find a little corner store where I can buy a carton of milk and maybe a pack of bubble gum. Then outside and find a bench, a patch of grass. I sit down and drink the milk slowly and breathe, breathe until the blood slows down and the milk is gone. Then chew my gum and blow a few bubbles and I'm fine.

On my way to Eve's place now because my head is full of bad voodoo and I want to be sure that everyone I come in contact with does not wind up dead. Because I am not Clint Eastwood, you know. As much as I might like to walk around town and calmly kill every asshole that has ever done me wrong or looked at me funny. A bullet between the eyes and a face full of black tobacco juice and I'm back on my horse.

I'm fucking gone.

But that's not me. I'm not Josey Wales. Maybe something's lacking in me, something is lost.

Oh, yeah. It looks like I'm going to be reading *Ulysses* this weekend. That's right. James fucking Joyce. I've read it before. Or to be correct, I have tried to read it in the past but always failed. I was too stupid, too lazy. I was too drunk. It's a difficult read, no question. But I love it. I love the elasticity of time, the doubtful state of reality. As if reality were a liquid. And you can only imagine my delight when Leopold Bloom trots off to a funeral with a fried kidney in his pocket.

Dear Jude.

Moon is dead. Perished.

I sit on a curb, staring. The blue notebook in one hand, a black felt-tip pen in the other. But every word is a struggle. I watch cars pass with the dull wonder of an animal that wants to cross the road but is so mesmerized by the noise and speed and lights that its ears lay flat and its eyes achieve a glossy sheen and soon the beast has no idea how it ever came to sit beside this road.

Now a bus rattled to a stop. Angry black exhaust and I climbed aboard. I regarded the other passengers with profound suspicion but no one else got on or off. I sat down and waited for the bus to move. But it just sat there, trembling. The driver must have disappeared for a pee or a smoke. I was not fond of buses. I always felt like I had been physically erased when the doors hissed shut and the driver was taking me to hell and I recently spent two horrifying days on a slow-moving Greyhound and fuck it anyway. I could have taken a cab to Eve's place but I was feeling thrifty and altogether too mournful about Moon to hurry anywhere. I pulled out *Ulysses* and opened it to a random page and read: beingless beings. Stop. Throb always without you and the throb always within. Your heart you sing of. I between them. Where? Between two roaring worlds where they swirl, I. Shatter them, one and both. But stun myself too in the blow. Shatter me who you can…oh, that was fine. That was lovely.

Eyes upon me and I lifted my head.

A young man, nineteen or so, was staring at me with the flat cold eyes of a fish. But the boy was not staring at all, I realized. The gaze was unfocused, fixed on a spot above and to the right of my head. The boy was blind. I felt a slight flush and opened my mouth to apologize, but this was unnecessary.

What does your tongue feel like? the boy said.

I hesitated, hoped the boy was speaking to someone else. But of course he wasn't. He was speaking to no one. He was possibly unaware that he had spoken out loud at all.

Silence.

A woman sitting near the boy got up and moved to another seat.

Your tongue, the boy pleaded. What does it feel like?

Excuse me? I said. It feels like an ordinary tongue.

Mine is soft and slimy, said the boy. And warm. Do you think that's right?

Again, silence. The other passengers stared at the boy with the satisfied horror and joy of the unafflicted. The boy stuck out his tongue and flapped it up and down and sideways, tasting the air. I found myself smiling and moved abruptly to sit beside the boy, surprising myself. I was sure that I had made no sound but the boy quivered slightly, as if the small hairs along his arms and neck were so sensitive that he could detect a molecular shift in the air around his body, the slightest change in temperature.

Why do you ask? I said.

Because it's all I think about sometimes. The boy stared straight at me and I was briefly alarmed by the way his face contorted as he spoke, the way he sucked and chomped at his lips. Then I realized that the boy must have never seen himself in a mirror and so his facial muscles were free to wiggle and twist with the unbound chaos of a monkey's.

It's all you think about, I said. How can that be?

The boy nodded violently. Yes, yes. It fills my head, you know. It sleeps there in the dark of my mouth like a beast. Warm and soft. And unpleasantly slimy. And I want to know if that's right.

I might not have chosen the word slimy, I said. But yes. That sounds about right.

The boy seemed relieved and said nothing more. But I was uneasy. I remembered a Charlie Brown comic from childhood in which Linus became aware of his tongue, to the point that he could think of nothing else. And the more he tried not to think about it, the more his tongue conspired to swell in his mouth, to become a limp of oppressive flesh. Lucy listened to this story, sneering as she was wont to do, then walked away. Moments later she was clutching at her throat and cursing her brother, for now she too was aware of her tongue.

I stared straight ahead, consciously licking at my teeth.

Theseus the Glove:

My, my but that was close.

He took one last bite of his sandwich and dropped the crust into Moon's overflowing dustbin. Theseus sighed, wondering if there was anything he needed to tidy up before his fellow officers arrived. It was his own error, of course. Damn his police instincts anyway. He had called this in too quickly, before he had tasted the blood and identified it as cow, not human. Before he had searched the apartment and found no body. On top of which, that idiotic Ray Fine person had blundered in at precisely the wrong moment.

Theseus scanned the living room again. A fine mess, but not extraordinary by Moon's standards. The blood was dreadful of course, but he barely noticed that anymore. He took a deep breath of the pungent air.

It was sweet as milk.

Of course. He rather liked it. But fucking hell. He could only assume that Moon had faked his own death but why he had done so was quite another matter. The man may have simply lost his nut and the real shock was that it hadn't happened sooner. Lord knew the fat bastard had been on the edge. Moon had been literally melting. But perhaps he was only trying to evade the game.

Theseus cursed, now.

He had been so confident that Moon was unaware of his rather unique status within the game of tongues. This was an irritating and unexpected twist, to be sure. Another one. That murdered Fred had been enough for one day, thank you. And unless he was blind as a newborn, the two were connected.

His eyes hurt, just considering it.

Theseus didn't have much time and truly he would rather just disappear, or at the very least give the impression that he was too horrified by the apparent death of his partner to be of any use. Theseus glanced at his watch and calculated that while the coroner would likely realize straight away that this was not human blood at all, he would not be able to confirm it until he got back to the lab.

But this was of little consequence. As a police matter, this scene barely interested him. It was the game that concerned him.

And Ray Fine, also. Ray Fine was a concern. That fellow was certainly not as stupid as he appeared.

Detective McDaniel? said a voice behind him.

Theseus willed his face to become pale and crushed. He should appear to be in shock, after all. His partner was dead, his body apparently stolen for some vile purpose. He rubbed at his eyes and forced a tear and turned to face the uniforms that had arrived.

Yes, he said.

It was easy enough to break into Eve's apartment, what with the door standing wide open. Her things were exposed to the elements. And having just come from Moon's place, my stomach fairly churned at the sight of it. My stomach became a wide black hole and escape velocity was doubtful.

But I wasn't so worried, really.

Somehow I knew she was just gone. Vacated. Most of her clothes and all of her furniture remained, but I could tell she wasn't coming back.

Now I poked through her bedroom with peculiar reluctance, with an older brother's nervous fear and vague arousal that I might stumble onto her diary, her vibrator.

There were clothes, mostly. And shoes.

And a thousand small fragments of Eve: strange little drawings and a collection of pocket knives, polished stones and bottle caps, a few Wonder Woman comic books, chewing gum and nail clippers and ribbons, matchbooks and foreign coins and panties and various girlish items that I couldn't quite name. She had left in a big hurry. I drifted into the living room, sat down on the floor in pretty much the same spot where I had eaten my eggdrop soup yesterday. I told myself not to worry about it. Eve was a tough little bird. She would turn up, undamaged.

Eve/Goo:

The candles had burned low and the gospel was nothing but static.

The food that Dizzy had prepared for them lay mostly untouched on the floor and she thought it was a wonder that gamers never starved. They ate like such nervous birds. But the three of them had already gone through half a bottle of the Pale. In an hour or so they would leave the house without comment and drift into the game. Mingus and Dizzy sat on the floor, facing each other but not speaking. They spoke, but not in complete sentences. One of them would produce a word from black depths, an image. The other would then examine the word, taste it and roll it around on the tongue. Then sigh, nodding.

Goo was not terribly worried about Chrome.

She didn't quite love him, not enough to worry. And he was known to disappear. Mingus was worried, though. Obviously. She had seen it in his face when she came downstairs and said Chrome was gone. The way his lips had curled and his hands clutched at nothing. But he wouldn't say why. Goo lit a cigarette and paced around. She felt cold, disconnected. She felt like Eve.

Are you performing tonight, said Dizzy.

Yes.

Have another drop of the Pale.

Goo shrugged. No, thanks. It makes me too clumsy.

What's the matter? said Mingus.

I don't know. I wonder where he's gone, that's all.

He could be anywhere, anywhere.

And you have no idea?

Mingus hesitated. He sniffed and looked at Dizzy, who now pulled uneasily at her hair.

Tell her, said Dizzy. You have to tell her.

Goo felt her throat tighten. A small cold fist inside. Tell me what, she said.

Mingus spoke in a halting monotone. Chrome killed someone yesterday, a Fred.

She smiled. But he does that every day. Twice a day.

No, said Mingus. Not like this.

What are you saying?

He took this one beyond Elvis, said Mingus. It was real.

He killed somebody, said Goo. Dead, you mean.

Dead, said Mingus.

His hair, she said. There was dried blood in his hair today. But I thought it was fake, or cow's blood. I thought it was part of the game oh shit.

Are you okay? said Dizzy.

No, she said. I'm not.

She was not okay. Faint, she felt faint. Her voice seemed to come not from her mouth but from her belly or spine. The words flickered between her lips like moths. This will be the end. The end of the game, thank God. Two candles drowning and the room got a little darker. Goo sat down, or fell. She fell into someone's strong arms. Dizzy, perhaps. Oh, no. Goo was slipping back into Eve's disorderly mind. A velvet couch, a Barbie doll. Shadows and starvation. Thin dark rope, alien tissue. The red skin of a fish and now she remembered. Eve wanted to warn Phineas about the apartment. And for that matter, she had better tell him to watch out for Chrome.

Oh shit, she said softly. This is insane.

Insane, said Mingus. He looked numb, he looked like he was made of wood.

How could he kill someone? she said.

Dizzy shrugged. Easily, she said. I'm sure it came easily for him.

Eve took a couple steps back. She felt like she was dreaming, like she had been dreaming of a birthday party two minutes ago and unwillingly stepped through a window into this other dream. She was lost.

But shouldn't we do something, she said. We should tell someone, report it.

Yes, said Mingus. I'm going to tell Theseus, tonight.

Dizzy nodded. He will take care of it, I'm sure.

But she didn't sound so sure at all. Eve wanted to go back to the birthday party. It was nice in there. Ice cream and cake and funny hats. They had helium balloons and she wanted nothing more than to shrink her voice down to munchkin level.

Do you have a telephone? she said with some effort.

Dizzy blinked. What an odd question. I think so. I have no idea if it works.

The telephone rang and my mouth dropped open. The phone. What fucking phone. There was no phone, I was sure of that.

The phone rang insistently and I followed the noise to the couch. Beneath one cushion was a little portable. I shook my head in disgust and pulled it out.

Hello.

You are there. It's me, she said. Eve.

Hey, I said. Where are you?

She hesitated. I'm at a friend's house.

I nodded, realized she couldn't see me nodding.

Everything okay? I said.

Yes, she said. And no. The apartment isn't…safe.

I glanced around. How's that?

Oh, well. This may sound strange.

This is me, I said. This is Phineas you're talking to.

She laughed. Okay. The apartment isn't stable.

What do you mean, Eve?

Don't ask me how, but it's sort of disintegrating.

I glanced down at my feet and the wood floor appeared normal enough.

Are you okay? I said.

It's hard to explain, she said. But look at the wall behind the couch. It's like…fading. The molecules are breaking down.

Uh-huh.

And there's a hole in the floor, near the bathroom.

Eve, I said. Are you high, or something?

Listen, she said. This is not a joke. Look at the wall.

I lowered the phone and stared at it. Fucking crazy. I felt crazy, like I was really holding an apple in my hand and Eve's voice wasn't real at all and she only existed in my head.

Nevertheless.

I walked back to the couch and hesitated, then reached out to touch the wall. It was pretty ordinary textured Sheetrock, and it felt very solid. It was real. I knocked on it with my fist.

Eve, I said. There's nothing wrong with the wall. Where are you?

I can't tell you, okay. I'm sorry. Please get out of there.

Where are you? I said.

Something else, she said. You met my friend Chrome, yes?

Yeah, I said. He seemed like a really nice guy.

He's dangerous, she said. If you see him, walk away.

Dial tone.

Eve, wait a minute.

Dial tone and I wondered, not for the first time, exactly what sort of research had gone into the selection of that particular sound. The military had been involved, no doubt. The psychological discomfort that the dial tone caused was no accident. The phone company did not want the sound of a dead connection to be pleasing and Eve had hung up on me. I chewed at my lip and nearly tossed the phone at the disintegrating wall, then smiled and star sixty-nined her. I felt very clever for about two seconds, but an automated voice soon told me it was sorry and my call could not be connected as dialed. Please check the number and dial again.

Then I got a fresh dial tone.

I threw the phone against the wall and it shattered pretty convincingly but I didn't feel any better. Eve was in some kind of trouble. Everyone was.

I touched the wall again, almost hoping I would fall through it. But the wall was solid. Then I noticed the damp, brown lump on the floor beside the couch. It looked like a hat, a crumpled sock. I bent to examine it, to touch it. The lump was a dead bird, its neck broken.

Jimmy Sky:

Christ on fire but he was fat. He was large. He caught a glimpse of his tubby profile just now and about lost his lunch. His belly boiled over the edge of his waistband and his thighs rubbed together as if they were in fact connected. It was no wonder he was soaking wet all day. He had no neck at all, really. There was a confounding clump of flesh there between his collar and chin that couldn't be called a neck, not by anybody's standards. And he had tits, okay. That was the big kick in the ass. That was the final straw.

Here was the thing about Jimmy. He only had access to this body on a very limited basis. Detective Moon was tooling around in it most of the time, and abusing it with pure suicidal flair. He was killing himself. Jimmy, though. He tried to eat right and lay off the booze. Jimmy sighed. All of this was going to change, and fucking soon. If he could only shake Moon out of this psychofunk he was wallowing in. Here was the thing. Moon wanted to kill Jimmy. He had asked his sketchy pal Phineas to find him, to find Jimmy. Hilarious, wasn't it. Except for the fact that Moon's intentions were unfriendly. He wanted to wipe him out. He wanted to strip Jimmy of his status as a character. It was annoying, to say the least. Jimmy had been Moon's very reliable undercover identity for two or three years now, an alias is what he had been. Nothing more. Moon had trotted him out now and again for a little police business and Jimmy would make the buy or solicit the blow job or kick the shit out of somebody while Moon took a breather. He had always known that Moon got a laugh out of Jimmy, for Jimmy was a lot cooler and sexier and had no worries about electric bills and taxes. Jimmy was a vacation from himself.

Then Moon got sucked into this game, this game of tongues. Which was interesting for a while. A nice, harmless fantasy ripe with vampires and magic spells, with medieval weirdness and good drugs and a fair amount of nudity. The drugs were a concern, though. Moon had got himself hooked on this sweet narcotic potion called the Pale. Or Jimmy did, as Jimmy Sky was his name within the game. Jimmy was a rare self-aware Fred who was angling to hook himself up as a Redeemer. But Jimmy had a problem, a nasty and fairly frightening problem. Moon and Jimmy were estranged. They barely knew each other anymore. His state of awareness was tenuous at best and he seemed to have no control over how and when he slipped in and out of the game. He would drift into Moon's world without warning and completely forget he had ever been Jimmy. Then he was helpless, he was trapped in daylight with no memory of the game and a powerful ache for the Pale that he didn't understand. And meanwhile, Jimmy was fucking tired of the game and he was mighty tired of being toyed with by Theseus the Glove.

Fuck the game, he said.

He wanted to end it, he wanted to blow it out of the water with a big, big splash and the first order of business had been to put a hit out on old Moon. That's right. He offed the fat bastard himself. He cut his throat and bled him dry. Okay, so he faked it. It looked good, though. It looked real. Beyond that, he had no idea what he was doing. He just wanted to stir things up and see what happened.

Dear Jude.

This shit is well out of hand and there's no reason to think it will change gears and become painless or dull anytime soon. I have to meet Griffin in less than an hour. Oh fucking joy.

Truly, I barely feel like myself. And it's not that I'm afraid of becoming Ray Fine, exactly. There is an ugly new sensation that I can only describe as degeneration. My physical presence is failing.

I am not real, okay.

The reflection that I seek in mirrors and blackened store windows, this is real enough. My reflected image is cruising up the street without a care in the world but I am nowhere to be found and how fucked up is that.

And I thought Eve was crazy. Her apartment was unstable, so what.
    Come on you neurotic piece of shit. Take out your knife and poke yourself in the thigh. Your shadowself will hardly bleed, will it. But the mirror version of Phineas will certainly lose its status in the ghostworld if it shows itself to have ordinary bodily fluids so go ahead boy, open up a fat vein.

This was no good, no fucking good.

I was talking to myself and of all my nervous habits, that was one I had never cared for. And I seemed pretty bent on cutting a big hole in my own leg. What a shivering mess I was. I turned around and around, looking for a safe place to roost. A place with normal, friendly humans. There was an open café across the street, yeah. I could have a five-dollar cappuccino and a piece of pie and read a few pages of *Ulysses* and with any luck there would be no mirrors in the place and just maybe that would do the trick.

Nervous bowels or bad coffee or too much sugar. Whatever the cause I was soon camped out in the public toilet with a horrible case of liquid shit. Which always makes me feel like I am probably dying. It just seems inherently bad to spray fluids from that particular hole. The bathroom was not filthy, at least. It was equipped with toilet paper. But the stall had been recently painted and the absence of graffiti was unnerving.

I pulled out *Ulysses* and flipped the pages around. For some reason, I couldn't read it in its proper order and I thought Joyce would forgive this. Why else would he write in such maddening circles.

Metempsychosis. The transmigration of souls.

I was with Molly on that one. Tell us in plain words, as she said. But I got the general idea and maybe this was my own problem. I was transmigrating.

Dear Jude.

I'm sure it's just residual sadness or some kind of projection but I can't read a word about Leopold Bloom without seeing Detective Moon. His round unhappy face. And I hope that doesn't cast me as Dedalus because he was one fucked-up person. He was tormented by memory, by false guilt. He was terrified of water and pregnancy and dogs. He was obsessed with the past, with the death of his mother. He had trouble with women. He had trouble with sex, like the rest of us. Stephen Dedalus was nearsighted and he was forever hallucinating.

He didn't much believe in reality.

Of course. It does sound very familiar.

But I think Dedalus was essentially good. He was frail and tortured and he had his doubts about the origin of sin but he was at least searching for the high ground. He wanted to be pure. He was a tragic hero, whatever that means. I would personally claw the eyes out of anyone who said that shit about me.

Chrome:

Love. He was in love with this one. He had spotted him at one of those automated cash machines where the humans line up like rabbits for a food pellet. Pushing buttons, their faces bright and fearful. They were always so relieved when the cash appeared. They smiled, as if they were chosen.

His target was of medium height, white or Hispanic. Dark eyes and very nice skin. Clean skin was a plus in all new relationships. He appeared to be healthy but not dangerous. And definitely a Fred. It was in the eyes, the emptiness of the Pale. Chrome had watched the man at the money machine, laboring to enter his code correctly. His card kept getting rejected. The Fred's little world was slipping and the machine hatefully spat out his card like a bad seed and he kept pushing it in until the machine finally ate it. The Fred remained placid all the while. He didn't wail at the sky or pull out his hair, he didn't strike the machine. He never blinked. Again, this was the Pale. And when the Fred had first flipped his wallet open to fetch out his card, Chrome saw the flash of a silver badge and felt his pulse jump. Another policeman.

Now. The hunt.

The Fred moved along at a turtle's pace, stopping every so often to obsessively examine his damned shoelaces. As far as Chrome could tell, the man's laces had not come undone yet. It was the very idea that seemed to plague the Fred. And each time the Fred stopped, Chrome was forced to stop as well.

His heart drumming crazily in the shadows. He was sure the Fred would hear it, if he only bothered to listen. But the Fred was busy untying his left shoe now, then tying it again. For the love of Mary. Did every serial killer have to put up with this sort of thing? He doubted that Hannibal Lecter would tolerate such foolishness. It was downright unseemly, is what it was. And he resolved to punish the Fred a little bit extra for the shoelaces.

They were moving east now. Away from downtown. Chrome nibbled at his own tongue and tried to think of ways to make this interesting. Eyes closed, perhaps. Hopping on one foot. Anything to give the Fred a fighting chance. And now the Fred did something that made Chrome smile, that brought the blood to his mouth. The Fred decided to take a shortcut through a graveyard. The ambiance would be divine.

Elvis was waiting.

Major Tom:

Black flies buzzing round and round behind his very eyes and something caught between his teeth, shred of apple skin or a piece of thread. A fingernail, maybe.

He sat at the best available table at the Paramount in his sharpest black suit, sort of a teddy-boy outfit with pants slim as knives and a jacket with no lapels, zip-up boots with squared-off toes perfect for kicking in the face of anyone who made the mistake of fucking with him. Dangling from his shoulder was Kink, his ethereal yet stupid-as-dirt girlfriend. Long dark red hair that looked wet, fine white throat and shoulders. She wore a thin plastic sheath of a bodysuit that appears to be transparent but was not, that stretched around her long muscled limbs like futuristic rubber. He was fascinated by this garment's construction, for there were no visible zippers or snaps and it looked like she had been dipped into the suit while it was still liquid and perhaps would have to be cut out of it later with a sharp knife. Tom stroked her tight inner thigh with one finger while smoking a thin cigar and chewing a piece of ice and keeping one eye well peeled for the elusive Poe.

Tongue like hot velvet dipping into his ear and he had to fight the urge to turn and bite it.

Careful, he said. Be careful, sweet Kink.

I'm thirsty, she purred.

Wait until my friend arrives.

I can't wait, Tom.

And don't call me that. It will only confuse him.

A cool, long-fingered hand crawled up his leg and stroked his gear through his pants with such delicious carelessness that he shivered and sighed. He wore no underpants with this suit, for the material was so fine and close-fitting that he had to be careful of unsightly panty lines and one consequence of this was that his rig was ultra-sensitive from all the incidental rubbing and touching and seemed to live in an ongoing state of half-erection. He pushed the hand away with some reluctance and pondered the chance of missing Poe if he took the dear girl off to the lavatory and screwed her to shreds in an unoccupied stall. He frowned, blowing a long stream of smoke into the glittering crowd. The mysterious Krazy Glue outfit might be a problem, however. For if he was forced to cut or rip it from her body, then she would have nothing at all to wear. He would have to wrap her up in newspapers and deposit her into a passing taxi. And this, he thought, might not be such a bad plan. He had a terrifying erection by this time and it would of course be a lot of fun to cut open her suit and besides, she would only be a nuisance later when he was trying to have an intelligent word or two with Poe. He smiled and smiled, for now the idea struck him that her outfit might well have come equipped with a small, discreet opening at the crotch for just such an occasion. An extra set of lips for the possibility of a good spontaneous public fucking, as it were. And a girl does have to pee, as well. Approximately twenty-nine times per hour, if she was anything like his girl. Right right right. Having settled this bothersome question, Tom was just gathering the strength to take Kink by the cold hand and breathe something vile and daring into her ear and drag her off to the Men's when he saw Poe ducking through the crowd in what at first glance appeared to be a psychotic clown's suit. Tom reminded himself to act more like Griffin and he smiled widely, for Griffin was proud of his fine white teeth and so he smiled with all his fury.

I was not the least bit thrilled by this scene. Too many disjointed arms and legs in sleek polyester, too much bad hair and too many self-conscious white people dancing badly by far. And I didn't much care for swing music. It was tolerable for about five minutes, amusing even. Then it got old in a hurry. I spotted Griffin now, sitting at a raised table with a not pretty but disturbingly sexy woman dressed like a very slutty version of Catwoman. I glanced down at Ray Fine's noxious clothing and shrugged. But I did take the hat off as I approached the table. I had a little pride left. Griffin didn't get up, but magnanimously pointed at an empty chair with the end of his cigar. I muttered a hello and sat down, lit a cigarette and looked around for a waiter. The catwoman regarded me with supreme disinterest.

Hello, I said.

Poe, said Griffin. I'm glad you could come.

Who's your friend?

This mad goddess? said Griffin. This is Kink, my beloved.

I watched his eyes for cruelty. He was such a good lawyer. He was relatively honest but his words were slick as jelly, veiled in hostility and despair.

Hello, said Kink. Her voice was hoarse.

I wanted to say hello, I wanted to be polite. Instead I just stared at her until she looked away.

What's the matter with you? said Griffin.

Never mind, I said. Then thought about it. What the fuck. I guess it doesn't matter. You were in the DA's office, Griffin. Did you know a Detective Moon, from the Ninth?

Griffin touched his forehead as if he had a sudden migraine. The girlfriend rolled her eyes.

You okay? I said.

If you don't mind, Poe. I would rather not discuss my daytime life, not now.

I didn't care for this answer. Moon got himself killed today, I said.

Please, said Griffin. I'm sorry, of course.

What about Jimmy Sky? Have you ever heard of him?

Griffin brightened. Jimmy Sky, he said. He said it twice, as if the name felt good to his tongue.

Do you know him? I said.

Afraid not, said Griffin. But it's a fine, sexy name.

Uh-huh. I need a drink, I said.

Don't bother looking for the waiter. There isn't one.

Then I'm going to the bar.

Griffin shook his head. That won't be necessary, he said.

He reached under the table to retrieve a bottle wrapped in plain brown paper and Kink promptly began to suck pornographically at her little finger. Her eyes flashing. Griffin removed the paper and I nodded, unsurprised. It was another bottle of the Pale. I had been thinking more along the lines of Jack Daniels, maybe vodka on the rocks with a pint of beer to chase it down, but this Pale stuff was not so bad. A little too sweet for my liking but weirdly potent and now I felt thirsty just looking at the bottle. Griffin reached into the side pockets of his jacket and produced two shot glasses.

I'll drink from the bottle, he said.

Griffin poured out two quivering shots and I swallowed mine before my heart took another beat. My head swam pleasantly. Kink took hers in dainty sips while Griffin had a long, greedy drink from the bottle. I poked my empty glass across the table. Another one, I said.

Griffin poured me another and I sucked it down. It was like drinking air.

Another one, I said.

Griffin smiled. Easy, cowboy. We have all night.

Another, I said.

You want to be gentle with this stuff at first.

I took a puff of my forgotten cigarette and smiled. It was maybe the best cigarette I had ever smoked and I knew I was in big fucking trouble. I looked around me. The crowed had faded away and I felt invisible.

The stuff you gave me earlier, I said. It was okay. But this is amazing.

I was having difficulty with my English.

That bottle was mostly water, said Griffin.

And I've had absinthe before, I said. It's not like this.

No, said Griffin.

Kink finished her drink and poured another one. I stared at her, my mouth open like a dummy. She was not so beautiful five minutes ago. Her skin had surely not been shimmering like this. This girl was made of silver and butterfly wings and she seemed to vibrate at some impossible high frequency. As if she might well disappear before my eyes. I was weak, I was a paper torso. I wiped at my mouth with some effort and found that I was drooling and I wanted this girl. I wanted to be inside her, to suck and bite and devour her. More than anything, I wanted to be eaten by her.

Relax, said Griffin. She's a Trembler.

What? I said. She's a what?

Phineas looked down from the ceiling and watched with mild horror as his disconnected body leaned across the table like a puppet with open mouth and splayed hands and he realized that he would do anything to kiss her, anything at all. He could possibly take a kiss by force but he didn't seem to have the strength. He was a worthless beggar and what under the sun did he have to trade her for a kiss? He had his shoes, his goofy hat. He had a few hundred dollars but he didn't want to insult her with an offering so profane.

Griffin poked the girl with a sharp finger. For fuck's sake, Kink. Will you cut it out? he said.

Just a small nibble, she said. Just a taste of his tongue.

Griffin's eyes were boiling now. No, he said.

But he's a Fred, she said. Like any other.

He's a friend, said Griffin softly. Leave him be or I will damage you.

The woman relaxed her gaze and I felt warm, then cold. I slowly regained a little muscular control but my tongue remained unfamiliar. As if it was not my own.

The fuck is going on, I said.

And slimy, my tongue was slimy oh boy.

Griffin nodded, smiling. You want to gather your wits, Poe.

Yeah, I know. Why did she call me Fred?

It's complicated.

My name is not Fred.

Griffin sighed. Have you ever heard of the game of tongues?

The what? I lit another cigarette, fingers shaking slightly.

Are you sure you're okay?

I touched my forehead. It felt like a blood vessel had swollen to almost but not quite bursting, like I should be unconscious now but was not. My vision was extraordinarily clear. I could see through my own skin. The club was dark but I squinted across the table like a traumatized rabbit with pink eyes.

Yeah, I said. Maybe I need a beer, or some regular water.

Griffin glanced at Kink, who pouted briefly then swiveled away.

When you were a kid, said Griffin. Did you ever play *Dungeons & Dragons*?

I shrugged. I was briefly a geek in high school, so what?

Griffin placed his hands flat on the table, palms down, his fingertips drumming the gouged oily surface and I stared at them for a while, unhappily waiting for the table to turn to butter. Meanwhile, Griffin's face and naked skull looked to have been cut from brittle green limestone.

You want to tell me what's in that Pale beverage, now?

Griffin shrugged. It's mostly herbs, vitamins: ginseng and gingko, various algaes and concentrated wheat grass. And the wormwood, of course. It's really pretty good for you.

It's a fucking smart drink? That's what you're saying.

I said mostly herbs. There's also a mild dose of Ecstasy and a touch of synthetic heroin.

That sounds…great, I said. It's just what I need, thanks.

Listen, said Griffin. Forget about the Pale, okay.

I hate Ecstasy, I said. I hate that shit. It makes people feeble and friendly.

Please shut up, said Griffin. The drugs are irrelevant.

I flapped my arms and felt confident that I was in fact made of sticks. I tried not to laugh. I was the stickman.

The Pale is only a means to an end, said Griffin.

Twitch and grin.

I jerked my head up and down like a stupid muppet.

Violent. I wanted to be violent and I was grateful for a concrete concept, for something I could properly wrap my teeth around. Fucking Griffin, though. He just sat there, staring at me. He wouldn't finish the train of thought, the bastard.

Then what is the end? I said, almost shouting.

Griffin smiled. He smiled. The game of tongues, of course.

Major Tom:

Oh, please won't someone give him a bullet. Did he truly not recall what a twisty nervous and altogether paranoid wreck Poe could be?

Fucking Poe. He was exactly like a chick, sometimes.

He wanted to show the old boy a good time and suddenly it was not unlike trying to squeeze a rape confession out of a deaf and dumb schoolteacher. Tom adjusted the knot in his tie and polished his scalp with the heel of his hand. Everything was fine, everything was fine. The first order of business was to get Poe the hell out of this dreadful place. Martha's Dead had begun to warm up, torturously tuning their inexpensive guitars and complaining about the monitors and hammering aimlessly at the drums. And Kink had apparently disappeared into the void, so fuck her. She could catch up with them at the Unbecoming Club. Right right right.

Let's go, he said.

Poe hesitated then bobbed to his feet like a rubber duck.

Tom sighed, watching him screw the moldy fedora down tight onto his head. They would have to do something about his clothes. The poor man was high, of course, but not unforgivingly so. In fact, Poe seemed very cooperative. He didn't ask where they were going and he expressed no concern over abandoning Kink. Tom imagined she was a bit too slithery for Poe's tastes. Poe generally went for women who looked like Catholic schoolgirls but carried a straight razor in their socks. He had always been attracted to false innocence, to girls who looked sweet and pious but might just cut his throat while he slept. He wanted a girl who looked like his sister, a sister who wanted nothing more than to be bound and gagged and fucked in the ass.

Anyway.

Poe stood there, waiting for guidance. Which could be attributed only to the excellence of the Pale. Truly, the game of tongues would not function without the stuff. There would be no new Freds and therefore no new victims. There would be fewer and fewer apprentices. There would be almost no economy, nothing to motivate the lower castes. It would be chaos.

Outside and the air was lovely.

Tom flagged down a cab and shoved Poe into the backseat. He tried to explain a few of these bald truths about the Pale to the pliable Poe, who stared back at him with one unblinking eye and nodded frequently. His other eye was clamped fiercely shut, for some reason, and Tom chose not to ask why. He instructed the cabbie to take them to a particularly isolated spot along Cherry Creek, hoping they would find a small pocket of the game so that he might show Poe the finer points of hunting tongue. Along the way he talked and talked and talked. He could only hope that Poe absorbed some of it.

Vibrating. I was vibrating and for some reason could only see out of one eye. I couldn't really talk, or I didn't want to. Griffin was droning on about something, which was nice. I crawled out of my body and settled into the narrow space below the rear windshield and remembered that when I was a child, my grandmother had owned a Siamese cat that always rode around with her in the car, and the cat had liked to nap in this spot. And I, the young Phineas, had often begged and pleaded for the opportunity to nap there as well. But my granny had always refused. It wasn't safe, she said. It was perfectly safe for the cat, who had superior reflexes and motor skills, but not for a five-year-old boy. And so I would gladly nap there now, or else listen to Griffin's voice if I couldn't sleep.

Where oh where shall I start, said Griffin. Of course you must first understand the caste system, as it's extremely rigid. Movement from one level to another is rare and difficult. But it's really all that the self-aware Freds and Tremblers may hope for, unless they are happy with their lot in life, eh? There is some sideways movement, naturally. Freds may become Tremblers and Tremblers may become Freds, although they surely wouldn't want to. The Freds are usually but not always men, and most of them are unaware that they have even entered the game. These are the most common victims of the hunt. The Mariners pull them down like sheep. The Mariners, mind you, hunt everyone. The Exquisitors too, may take an unaware Fred if they are desperate. They tend to prefer the mutual kill, though. The shared tongue. The Redeemers and Tremblers do not hunt, exactly. They practice various forms of seduction. They also prey on the Freds, and on each other. And the self-aware Freds often hunt each other in small packs. Have I left anyone out? The Breathers, of course. They do not hunt, and claim they don't need to. And the Gloves. They are masters of the game. Each chapter of the game is watched over by a Glove.

I don't know if they ever bother to hunt and no one, not even the boldest Mariner, would dare attempt to take the tongue of a Glove.

I was surprised, shocked to see my head turn to the side. I wanted to ask a question, it seemed.

Excuse me. What are you, then? My voice was dull and flat. I hated my voice.

Griffin shrugged. I'm a Mariner. It's the only thing to be.

And...what am I?

Hah, said Griffin. You are technically a Fred, but not for long. Already you are self-aware, and I want you to be my apprentice.

What if I don't want to play?

A brief sweet silence.

I watched the passing cars, lights trailing behind them like honey.

Griffin touched my face. It's too late for that, I'm afraid. Tomorrow you will awake with a mighty thirst for the Pale. And the only way to get it is to play.

The eyes were so heavy.

I pressed my cheek to the cool glass and wished for sleep.

And you will need a name, said Griffin. Everyone within the game has a name, except for the unaware Freds. They are simply Fred.

Okay, I said. I will be Ray Fine.

Ray Fine? said Griffin. It's not very sexy, but I suppose it will do. Who are you?

Oh, said Griffin. Have we not met? I am Major Tom.

Vibrating. I was vibrating and for some reason could only see out of one eye. I couldn't really talk, or I didn't want to. Griffin was droning on about something, which was nice.

Major Tom:

A wee bit sluggish from the Pale. He stood under a moonless sky and wished his neck did not ache from the various nasty toxins he had consumed this good night. And he wished he had worn underpants as he was nearly to the breaking point with all this rubbing and textile thrashing of his rig. He contemplated, then moodily discarded, the idea of sitting down right here and whipping the thing out for a fast hand job in the wet grass, if only to relieve a little pressure. But he wouldn't want to upset Poe, would he? Although that was not fucking likely. Poe stood alongside him and gazed into the gray and purple sky like he had never noticed it before and he would probably not blink if his pal Griffin commenced to hump a hole in the ground.

Never mind the pain. He would save this stunning erection and its brilliant load of gunk for dear Kink. How sweet it was to love someone, even such a manic ninny as the slippery Kink. Anyway. His bare skull was cold and for a moment he looked with some envy at Poe's crusty fedora. Then laughed softly. Poe turned to him, his face blank as a sleeping dog's and Tom smiled. Don't forget, this was his first apprentice.

Right right.

He pulled at Poe's hand until the poor fellow caught the hint and crouched down beside him. They looked down from a steep embankment of mud and recently transplanted grass at the paltry stretch of water known as Cherry Creek. The creek was dark and silent in its concrete bed and no one ran alongside it at this hour unless he or she was being chased by another.

Do you know where you are? he said.

Poe responded thickly. Denver. This is Denver.

Good. And your muscles, he said. How do they feel?

They feel numb. Not like my own.

Yes, he said. It's the Pale, it saps your strength. If you will be a Mariner you must find ways to overcome its effects, or resist it altogether.

How? said Poe.

Tom sighed. To resist is unpleasant, he said. Of course. But there are always pills and powders to be had that will restore the senses.

He pulled out a little gunmetal snuffbox and passed it to Poe, who took it from him with endearing caution. Poe's face was in shadows but Tom thought he might have seen a flicker of recognition in Poe's one good eye. The mad fucker had the left eye shut tight now, and Tom could have sworn that it was the right eye before. As for the flicker. The box was Griffin's, of course. And Poe had seen it earlier today. It was nothing to worry about. The identities bleed through easily at first. Eventually one learned to suppress them, or to live with them. He watched as Poe opened the box and tipped it with care, spilling a generous amount of cocaine into the palm of his hand. It was easily enough coke to stop his heart, and Tom was curious to see if the old boy was quite dizzy enough to suck it all down. But Poe hesitated, then separated the little pile with his fingernail and inhaled just half of it. Tom was pleased to see this. Poe's speech was rather impaired, but his movements were smooth and fluid and his judgment was sound. It was most common for a new apprentice to blink and stumble about like a defective robot for a few days, until his senses adjusted to the Pale. For physiological reasons that Major Tom did not quite understand, and couldn't be fucked to ponder, women recovered from the Pale much faster than men and were therefore less likely to be cast as Freds. He shrugged and smiled without showing his teeth when Poe offered him his open hand and what remained of the cocaine. Tom bent from the waist and sniffled and soon the little handful of coke was gone. He gently retrieved the box from Poe and

checked its contents and felt a rush of the warm and fuzzies upon seeing there was plenty more. He wet his fuckfinger and dipped it into
the box, smearing a bit of the sweet powder into his gums. After a
moment Poe did the same, then shrugged and said that he was ready.
Tom was proud of him, yes.

Let's go, then.

They dropped down to the edge of the creek, silent and shadowy
as wolves. Tom took the lead and they walked along the path, a body
length between them. Tom chewed softly on his own tongue. His skin
might as well have been on fire, what with the raw coke pushing and
shoving his blood through his heart as if death itself were on the
wing. He had a good feeling about this path, and soon proved himself a clever boy as the creek bent to enter a dark little grotto beneath
a viaduct.

Smoke.

Tom smelled smoke and raised his hand for Poe to stop. They
crept closer and saw the glow of a small fire. Four shadows around it.
Voices. The pulse of music. A droning and distorted bass line.
Deathmetal, his very favorite. He turned to Poe and smiled.

Like mice, he whispered. We will approach them like mice.

Three young Freds in various states of awareness. One little
Trembler, thin and pretty and not more than nineteen. She was perhaps overmatched by the Freds, who were filthy and starved to the
bone, dressed in black motorcycle leathers that no doubt stank of
blood and smoke and urine. They wore heavy boots that were surely
excellent for stomping and there were ugly chunks of metal driven
through their lips, their noses. Probably their tongues as well. On
another night Tom would have watched from the shadows to see
which of the Freds would be first to take the girl's tongue if she failed
to Tremble them. And then of course the Freds would turn on each

other and soon he would slither from the dark and say hello.

Tonight was different, however.

He wanted Poe to understand the fever, to taste one or more tongues and to know the fear that the Mariners strike in these others. He wanted Poe to recognize the opposite of love and so he whispered for Poe to follow him, to follow his own heart. Major Tom stepped out of the dark, holding his arms out like wings and for once he wished it were more practical to wear a cape. The drama would be delicious, it would be chocolate and strawberries and his throat was tight just thinking of it. But he would be forever tripping over the thing and therefore useless in a fight. Really, he didn't understand how Batman managed it.

Hello, he said.

Thick head and trying to think was not unlike trying to force a dull blade through overcooked meat while my arms and legs glittered bright with pins and needles from the big spoonful of coke I had just shoved up my snout. I didn't feel quite like myself, but I was trying. God help me. I watched as Griffin, who wanted to be called Major Tom for some reason, approached three punks and a hippie girl who sat looking stoned and fearful around a little campfire. Griffin had become a much more interesting freak than I had ever imagined.

"Major Tom" was the name of a David Bowie song, right? I tried to summon the lyrics but came up empty. Losing your mind, something about losing your mind in outer space. I shook my head and started to feel myself up for a cigarette but stopped in midgrope when Griffin reached into the little fire and pulled out a burning chunk of wood and without warning tossed it in my direction. Motherfucker. But my reflexes surprised me and I actually caught the thing, my right hand easily snatched the end that was not burning without any complicated guidance from my brain. And now I was twirling this chunk of fire around my head like a cheerleader from the bowels of the earth and of course the fire stretched against the dark sky like rippling orange ink and for a moment it was like I was creating fire, I was fire and this was pretty fucking cool. Then my hand was on fire and I wasn't sure if I could feel anything but I could hear the distinct crackle and pop of my own skin and I dropped the piece of wood telling myself not to scream, not to scream.

I peered fearfully at my hand, expecting it to be blackened and crispy or at least bubbled with gruesome blisters but hey, it looked okay. It was only hot, very hot. I looked back to Griffin and the four kids and they were all watching me and maybe the whole fire thing had only lasted two seconds or maybe they all knew I was new to this game or whatever it was so they were patiently waiting for me to stop freaking out and get my shit together and flow.

Then things started to move quickly, very quickly.

One of the punks had a huge silver nosering and oily black hair combed into a ducktail and he looked like Fonzie on acid. He looked pretty tough, or at least he fancied himself tough and he unwisely told Griffin to fuck off and zoom: Griffin was sitting on the sorry fucker's chest. And while I may have been high and my perception of speed and distance were not quite right, I was nonetheless amazed. This new Griffin was some kind of panther, he had reflexes like fucking Spider-Man and I moved closer now, fascinated. But one of the punks screeched at the sight of me and took off, disappearing into the dark and I felt a peculiar tug, like maybe I should chase the guy down and hurt him.

The girl and the other guy cowered together and maybe they were too scared or too stupid to run but maybe not. They clutched and grabbed at each other's clothing with a heavy sexual vibe and I was pretty confident they would have a go right then and there while Griffin and I tortured their pal but suddenly the male, who was probably twenty-two or -three and looked like a mean fucker with a scar on his cheek and long sideburns and a spiderweb tattoo across his throat and surely outweighed the female by fifty pounds, suddenly went all limp in her arms and opened his mouth. The girl leaned over him lazily and gave the guy a deep, penetrating and weirdly violent kiss. She looked like she was trying to suck his tongue right out of his mouth and now I suffered rapid flashes of Griffin's girlfriend leaning toward me in the club with hunger in her eyes.

Meanwhile.

Griffin had his guy by the throat and was flicking the big nosering back and forth with his index finger like he might just pull it out. Then he leaned over and hit the kid's cheek hard enough to draw blood.

Your blood is bitter, said Griffin. What have you been eating?

The guy made a weak choking noise but didn't, or couldn't, answer.

Hey, I said. But I said it too softly because I was curious. Honestly. I wanted to see what would happen.

Open it, said Griffin. Fucking open it.

I glanced over at the girl, who was now casually smoking a cigarette. Her new boyfriend wasn't moving, though. He looked dead, in fact. But there was no fucking way he was dead from a kiss. The man had to be unconscious or something and as I moved to help him an idiotic voice in my head that sounded a lot like my own voice said maybe what he needs is a little mouth-to-mouth. I kill myself, sometimes. I prodded the stiff with the toe of my boot and was not terribly surprised when he hopped to his feet and looked at us with something like shame and defiance and then turned and ran.

Ray, said Griffin.

Silence.

Then again, loudly. Hey, Ray.

And I turned, remembering dully that this was my name. I was fucking Ray and now I saw that Griffin had forced his guy's jaw open and was crouched over him like a mad dentist. The tip of the guy's tongue was exposed, a small pinkish triangle of meat and I thought of earthworms drowning in the rain.

Come here, said Griffin. His eyes shining.

What?

This Fred will be your first tongue.

I looked at the Fred, whose nosering was slick with snot and blood. It was strange, though. The guy didn't look so terrified. He looked meek and a little furious and yet he lay there with his mouth open, waiting for someone to bite his tongue and temporarily own him. I felt nothing I might call desire. And this is important, I think. I want to be clear about this. It wasn't a moral thing for me. It was an ordinary lack of desire.

I don't think so, I said.

What? said Griffin. His voice thick with disgust.

Let him go, Griffin.

Griffin shrugged. He bent and kissed the Fred, he bit and sucked at the guy's mouth and now I felt aroused. The Fred didn't go limp like the other one. His legs thrashed at the ground and his hips jerked against Griffin's ass. Then it was over. Griffin released him, he smiled and slapped the Fred's belly.

Disappear, he said. And to me he said, don't fucking call me Griffin.

The Fred grunted and clambered to his feet. He brushed himself off and began to fix his hair but Griffin was staring murderously at him and the Fred apparently decided to fuck with his hair later, for he hooted at us and ran away and now a thin, cool voice said, what about me?

I turned my head and the girl was standing very close to me.

Think fast Ray, said Griffin. Do you want her tongue?

What...?

Will you be a wolf, he said. Or a rabbit.

Kill the rabbit, said the girl.

Her breath smelled sweet, like green melon. Long yellow hair that hung in ringlets. A necklace of seashells and bright stones around her long throat. Fantastic eyes, blue with impossible splashes of black. Her lips were dark as berries.

Careful, said Griffin. Be careful, Ray.

I opened my mouth slightly. I did want to kiss this girl and why not, she was adorable and sexy and fresh as a damn flower. And she apparently wanted me to kiss her. I leaned forward dreamily, stupidly while the very paranoid little action figure version of myself was running around in my skull and banging the panic drum, howling don't do it don't do it you dumb motherfucker. The girl's mouth was not two inches from my own and I grabbed her by the face. And she looked pretty surprised.

But I trembled you, she said.

Uh, I said. Not well enough, I guess.

I had her face in my hands and it was ridiculously soft. She had perfect skin and edible lips and now I was not sure what I wanted to do.

You have really nice skin, I said.

Griffin spat. Jesus, Ray.

The girl was staring into my eyes like I was a mannequin. I assumed she was still trying to tremble me, whatever that meant. I let my hands slip to her throat and she rolled her eyes. Impatient, bored. Not afraid.

Are you afraid? I said.

No, she said.

Griffin began to whistle. Raindrops keep falling on my head.

I could hurt you, I said.

The girl shrugged, as if that was very doubtful. A tangible chunk of silence. Then I told her to open her mouth and for a long perilous moment thought that surely she would resist, that she would tell me to fuck off and the spell would break. The moment would shatter like ice. But then she parted her lips.

Tom and Ray, with Phineas:

Oh, brother did he need some love and understanding. This situation was not completely fucked but it was pretty well fucked. Major Tom was worried, very worried and for the first time in recent memory he was suffering an unwanted and completely unforeseen outburst of moisture beneath his armpits.

They had retired to a gas station restroom to clean up and discuss the matter behind a locked door. Tom stood before one of three mirrors, straightening his clothes with brittle fingers and washing the Fred's blood and snot from his hands and face. Ray Fine sat on a toilet with his legs crossed, smoking a cigarette. Tom was sweating because he had perhaps mistakenly lured an outsider into the game who, God knows why, did not want to be a Mariner's apprentice and worse, was too mentally competent to be cast among the hapless Freds. Otherwise, Tom would happily say fuck you, Fred. Have a nice life in the sewers and be careful with your tongue.

You have a problem, said Tom.

Oh? said Ray, as he blew a wobbling smoke ring.

I can only protect you if you're my apprentice.

Ray Fine laughed out loud, the insolent toad.

I'm not joking around, Ray.

What the fuck. Are you gonna protect me from girls who want to

French kiss me?

Oh, that's rich. That's a killer.

It's a gift, said Ray. I make people laugh.

Tom wet a paper towel and used it to cool off his skull, watching Ray very closely in the mirror and noticing that while the old boy was making a lot of smart-ass comments, he was looking pale as a ghost.

How was it, by the way?

How was what?

The Trembler, said Tom. Didn't you take her tongue?

Ray shifted his ass around on the toilet and stared back at him. He wasn't so funny now.

Did you bite her tongue?

Maybe, he said. What about it?

Blood. Did you draw blood?

There was a little blood, yeah. Ray flicked his cigarette at one of the sinks.

Tom gave a shadow of a smile. And how was it, Ray?

The sound of water dripping. Ray got up and wandered to the sinks, his blue eyes ghostly and vague. He was clearly drawn to the mirror and seemed to hate his own face at the same time. Tom watched him take one long, reluctant look in the glass and force his eyes away. Then back again.

Fuck me, said Ray Fine. That is an ugly hat.

He could still taste the girl's tongue, the Trembler's. Her blood had been warm and thick and good. And he had felt something he had never expected. He had felt safe.

And how was it, Ray?

The sound of water dripping. He felt dizzy and vague and he wished Griffin would stop calling him Ray. He got up and moved over to the sink, thinking he might wash his hands but there was his pale fucking face in the mirror, floating like a dead thing in still water. He looked like a paper target sometimes. All he needed were black circles around his torso and bloodless tears in the white. Who are you, who are you today. Who do you want to be. He looked away, then back. He was afraid his eyes would be trapped in the mirror.

Fuck me, he said. That is an ugly hat.

He looked away, at a crack in the wall. A long, narrow crack and he flashed to the idle childhood notion that a microscopic universe might well exist in that crack in the wall of a much larger restroom, that there were infinite cracks in the walls of infinite restrooms and here we go, he thought. Here we fucking go. Ray Fine slapped at the electric hand dryer and the white noise snapped him out of it and he found himself staring hard at Major Tom, who stared back without smiling, without breathing. A fat black cockroach scurried out of the dark and Ray heard the crunch of its hard little exoskeleton shattering under Tom's boot heel. The electric dryer died now and they dropped their eyes at once.

It was...very intense, said Ray. It was blinding.

Whoa, said Tom. I guess you're fucked. Have a nice life in the sewer.

Wait a minute.

You're in, man. You're in the game.

Ray stared at him. What is the fucking game?

The tongue is the game, said Tom. The game is tongues.

But isn't there some higher purpose to the game?

Ray was now standing a pubic hair too close to him and Tom felt himself getting edgy, very fucking edgy and he wondered what he wouldn't do for a shot of the Pale and some more attractive surroundings.

What sort of higher purpose, said Tom. He felt like his face was dripping.

Like a quest, said Ray. A noble quest.

Tom stared at him.

You know, said Ray. You could return the magic beans to the Fairy Queen. You could save Christmas. Something along those lines.

Why do you want to insult me, Ray?

Ray appeared to chew at the inside of his mouth and Tom shivered, watching him. He looked away and began to turn the hot water on and off, on and off. Then left it on and held his finger under the stream for as long as he could stand it.

I want you to stop calling me Ray, said Ray.

The tongue is the quest, Tom said softly. And I'm sorry. Your name is Ray.

And so that's it? said Ray. You...you're like a rapist, man.

Tom removed the damp towel from his head and regarded Ray with contempt. He had heard this morbid line of thought before, from soft and puny players of other castes. The Breathers, for instance. He told himself to be patient, to choose his words with great care.

The tongue is a powerful muscle, he said. A thing of beauty. And at the same time, it's weak. The tongue is soft and private and terribly vulnerable, like the genitals.

Unwanted intimacy, said Ray. There's nothing more terrifying, is there?

There's Elvis, said Griffin.

Oh, yeah. Elvis, said Ray. And what the hell does that mean, exactly.

Griffin laughed. To go see Elvis, he said. To die but not die.

Elvis is an imaginary death, said Ray. He nodded. I can live with that.

The taking of tongues is ultimately an act of compassion, said Tom.

Ray laughed. How's that?

Tom leaned close to him, hissing like a woman despite himself. If your tongue is between my teeth, then it's mine to sever. To eat. But I don't.

Why not? said Ray.

Because I'm enlightened.

Now you're a Buddhist, said Ray. This gets better and better.

And what did you do to that girl, the Trembler?

Ray frowned and sullenly twisted his head from side to side until the joints in his neck popped. He took off the hideous fedora and dropped it to the floor. He ran one hand through his matted blond hair, staring at himself in the mirror and finally Tom saw what he saw.

The face of another. One who was not Phineas, was not Ray.

Phineas began to cough, great hacking coughs that would rip him in two. He felt sick and he found himself wondering what Griffin's tongue would taste like. Fuck fuck fuck. He cast his eyes away, at the crack in the wall where another tiny shadow of himself was possibly having a better time. He took off the fedora suddenly and dropped it to the floor. He ran one cold skeletal hand through his hair and glared at himself in the mirror.

That chick wanted to kiss me, he said.

You are so hopelessly hetero, said Griffin.

Oh, really. Phineas smiled. That's odd. Because I'm thinking of your tongue right now. I'm wondering how sweet your breath might be, how your lips would be warm and cold at once.

Ah, yes. I think you will have a future as a Redeemer, said Griffin. The taking of tongues by way of sympathy and charm.

Whatever, man. What sort of thrill do you get from torturing some fucked-up kids?

Griffin rolled his eyes. The Freds are my daily bread. If I want a thrill, then I hunt another Mariner.

I could be a Trembler. I trembled that girl, said Phineas.

A fascinating idea, said Griffin. The male Tremblers do not lead such happy lives, I'm afraid. They are hunted ruthlessly by everyone, and soon they are left with no tongue at all.

Fuck it, then. You can just call me Fred. Or Freddie.

Griffin bent and picked up the fallen hat. He held it between two fingers as if it were a dead thing.

You dropped your hat, Ray.

Motherfucker, thought Phineas. Or did he say that aloud.

He was starting to hate the name Ray, he really was. But he reluctantly took the hat from Griffin.

Thanks, he said. It's not really my hat.

I promise you, said Griffin. You will regret this.

Whatever. Phineas put on the hat and shivered. He was Ray, though. He was Ray Fine. He lit a cigarette and blew smoke at the mirror and said, do you think you could take my tongue?

Now? said Griffin.

Phineas shrugged. Why not.

The sound of water dripping and they stared at each other for a long waxing moment and in a crack in the wall their microscopic shadows likewise stared at each other and Phineas was confident that his little shadowself would soon pin the shadow Griffin to the floor like a wriggling bug and maybe just rip out his tongue.

Mingus:

He was afraid of Chrome, very afraid. And he wasn't sure the women appreciated that. His poor brain hurt, all the time now. The game was too much for him. It had been days and days since he had slipped outside of it and it was like he could never sleep. He wasn't tired, exactly. But he might be losing his mind. He was beginning to understand that it was dangerous to stay in character all the time. He could not quite remember where he lived, for instance. And he had been fairly shocked to think of that genetics exam, to remember it at all.

It wasn't that he wanted to take the test. Doubtful that he would be able to comprehend the thing at all. The last time he had been to school he had found himself in a microbiology lab with a lot of frightening equipment that he no longer knew how to manipulate. The air had been thin and sterile, with a hateful undertow of chemicals.

Sometimes, though. It might be nice to visit his previous world.

His daylight self made him uncomfortable, however. His name was unimportant but he was a paranoid and sexually nervous computer yuppie who was failing out of med school with alarming speed and grace. He was just over five feet tall and he weighed 110 pounds when wet. He got by with shaving once a month and he had a sticky relationship with his mother. He was boring. He spent most of his time online, cruising the web and playing Doom. He was technically still married, but he and his wife were estranged and she had rarely bothered to sleep with him anyway. It was not a world that he wanted to rush back to, exactly. But sometimes he was curious to see if it had changed at all.

Dizzy's house made him feel safe, though. Familiar and strange, the memories were muted, like beasts held underwater. She kept a lot of candles burning and everything smelled of trees and he saw nothing but soft edges and shadowy landscapes. He sat in a leather chair, barefoot. He worried about Chrome, about what he would say or do if he knew Mingus had betrayed him. He sat with his arms crossed, staring straight ahead. In another hour or two, it would be midnight. It would be time to go out and play. He wondered if he could sit without moving until then, he wondered if he could stop his own breathing.

Goo had gone already.

She had been pacing around ever since he told her that Chrome was a madman. She had been smoking cigarette after cigarette and trying to hide the fact that she had slipped into her Eve persona and failing badly, he had thought. And maybe he should have followed her, he should have kept an eye on her. But she had given him a dirty look when he suggested it. It was funny, really. But little Eve was even more fearless than Goo. Anyhow. She was performing later and had likely gone ahead to prepare.

Change in temperature and the smell of Dizzy Bloom came around a corner. It was an unidentified spice, a color he had never seen. And before he could give it a thorough ponder, she was crouched before him with sweet glowing skin and brief sharp smile and long dark hair falling loose and he felt himself get a little warm. Females rarely came this close to him. He smiled, wondering what she wanted.

Are you okay, she said.

Not so bad. I'm worried, of course.

You're adorable, she said.

What?

Her hands floated to touch his thighs and his breath stopped. His breath shut down pretty efficiently. Dizzy Bloom ran her fingers up to his hips, tugging at his pockets. His brain was gone, long gone. And he let himself slide out of the chair to kneel before her as she stroked his face and whispered to him, kissed him.

Incredible.

Mingus wouldn't have believed another person's lips could be so soft. Dizzy offered him her tongue and he touched it lightly with his own. The room flickered around him as if the house was unstable. Dizzy Bloom shrugged out of her leather jerkin and now her little round breasts were in his cold hands and he felt something like nervous glee, pure shivering foolish glee. And when she slipped his trousers down and exposed his short thick penis to the naked air and lifted her skirt and moved to lower herself onto his lap and gently very gently helped him find his way inside her, well at this point he pretty much blacked out.

Concrete and barbed wire, concrete and barbed wire and I was trying to remember the words to this obscure country song that Jude used to sing when she was washing her hair or painting her nails, something about concrete and barbed wire and how the average state prison was an easily penetrated fortress compared to the human heart.

It was a country song, okay. I didn't say it was poetry.

Griffin or Major Tom was pretty bent on calling me Ray Fine and that was cool. I could walk and talk like Ray. I could be Ray Fine. I had created the poor stuttering bastard, hadn't I? I had purchased Ray's sad clothes and this moldy hat and even perfected the way he limped. Ray was my idea.

Good night, Phineas. I will most likely kill you in the morning.

Dear Jude.

It appeals to me, of course. The shadow world. The ability to slip in and out of the real. A fanciful subterrain where the lord of the rings and bladerunner become one and I can be a mad dwarf for a day, a thief or an assassin. I can be a mercenary with a soft spot for razor-girls and I daydream about this shit all the time, don't you?

When I was fifteen or so it was *Dungeons & Dragons*. A few of my friends had a game that ran for what seemed like forever and we gathered every weekend to play without stopping. We used Mountain Dew and nicotine for fuel because the Dungeon Master was kind of a fascist about drugs. We blacked out the windows but it didn't matter. At sunrise the game always lost its legs. My character was a thief, a halfblood elf named Grim. Don't remember his vital statistics exactly. Dexterity off the chart. Strength and charisma well above average and I wasn't bad looking. No magic skills, though. And I was no good at languages. What else. I was of questionable birth and not terribly stable. And my ethical designation was chaotic/good, which meant I would probably save a young maiden from a pack of orcs but maybe not. There were no promises and you wouldn't want to turn your back on me. I was a thief, after all.

I used to dream of Grim. In my sleep I was Grim. And even years later, long after the game was done, I dreamed of him.

It's easy. You stagger a hundred years forward, a thousand years back. You manufacture a world where the apocalypse has failed to manifest. Urban purgatory. The sun is a joke, a bad memory. The world is dark and wet and waiting to be fucked. The world is a great big pussy. Everything is sex and chaos. Rapidly shrinking human population due to HIV, ebola, mad cow disease. Whatever. The political elite live in orbiting space stations. Mutants born daily. DNA experiments gone wrong. Vampires and goblins. Elves. Werewolves. Androids and common humans. Cyber and weapon technology is at a standstill. Corporations are controlled by artificial intelligence. Evolutionary regression. Past and future merge, or blur. People ride camels and horses alongside landskimmers and hovercrafts. Traveling circus troupes wander nuclear wasteland. The road warrior model. Freak shows, blood sports, theaters of cruelty. Public executions and snuff films dominate the airwaves and pornography is common currency, etc.

Then again, I doubt you would need to daydream. This is pretty much the way you see things on a good day, isn't it?

Major Tom:

Convenience, he thought. Artificial light that made the skin look pasty and green and aisles swollen with bright, fascist packaging. Convenience. Oh, dear. That was rich. That was a regular killer. He stared down at himself from a big curved mirror overhead and tried unsuccessfully not to giggle. Shoplifters in the mirror may be closer than they appear and whoever had dreamed up the phrase "convenience store" was a born torturer.

Tom found himself staring at a long, tubular orange product mysteriously called "Pringles" and his mind began a bitter rhyming game: tingles jingles mingles shingles and what in hell was he looking for? The clerk was staring at him with bright green frog eyes and Ray was waiting outside. Ray, who refused to play the game.

Mouthwash.

Of course. He was on the wrong aisle, clearly. These products were all in the snack family. They were heavy with fat and starches and red dye #2, yellow dye #6. He needed the medicinal aisle, the cleaning creams and powders. He wanted some of that cool blue mouthwash. His tongue was a bit chalky, his tongue was sore and putrid from the mouth of that Fred by the creek and he suddenly wished he had taken a taste of that adorable Trembler. But Ray was a friend, he was a dear old friend and Tom had graciously let him have her without muscling in for even a nibble.

Eyes closed and hair wet from the rain. I am surrounded by dark water and the air is different, colder. The air has teeth and it must be winter. A noise like sweet kisses and the low croak of a frog, an old man coughing. I'm different, too. I'm smaller. Thick socks and rubber boots, long underwear. Heavy wool pants and a goosedown vest. Something in my hand, cool and slender. A composite bow. The shallow breathing of another and I'm not alone. Trevor is here, my cousin. A cruel and silent boy four years older than me who holds a shotgun in his steady hands and now I can smell oil and sulfur and bourbon. This is a duckblind and everyone laughed at me when I wanted to hunt ducks with a bow and arrow. And they were right to laugh. I never killed a single bird and check it out: that was a false memory, my first. I never had a cousin named Trevor and I never went duck-hunting as a boy. Pretty cool, huh. Psychological dislocation. Modality of the visible, the tactile. And like Stephen Dedalus I'm walking into eternity along Sandymount Strand.

Nacheinander and *Nebeneinander*. What is real and what is perceived as real.

Protean theory. The real is unstable. The real is self-consuming, like fire. And this seems to be a pretty big deal in *Ulysses*. The real. Stephen Dedalus is tormented by his own belief or disbelief in what he can see and hear and the way I understand it, *Nacheinander* refers to physical reality as it is perceived in linear time, to objects or events that occur once after another. While *Nebeneinander* is a spatial reality. Objects that exist on the same plane, or side by side.

Okay. What the fuck, right. But everything Dedalus sees is tangled up with memories real and false and reconstructed images. There's no separation. Meanwhile, his own thoughts are more coherent and more immediate than the noise around him and so it all blurs into this terrible internal monologue that shifts and changes and licks at the air like fire. Stephen Dedalus exists on four or five levels of reality at once.

Which seems to be what's happening to me.

The creepy little hunting scene might have happened to someone I know, or I might have pieced it together from a book or movie. It doesn't matter. I stepped in a puddle or heard a migrating duck cry in the distance. I smelled damp wool or brandy and the whole false memory was triggered. For five seconds it was real.

Dear Jude.

I'm freaking out, yeah. But it's a lot of fun.

Chrome:
Now this was quite the fucking pickle. He couldn't be certain but it seemed that he was bleeding very badly and his left arm may as well have been attached to someone else. His left arm was unresponsive. He could see it there, extending from his shoulder and resting in wet yellow grass tipped with frost, but he couldn't feel it at all. He couldn't

feel it.

Shot. The Fred had shot him.

Chrome sat with his back to a modest pink marble headstone that read: Lucinda Sweet, faithful wife and sister. His math was spotty but she seemed to have died just a few months ago, at twenty-nine. Chrome himself was twenty-nine. He was long in the tooth and slipping into winter.

S'il vous plaît, aidez-moi avec mes bagages.

Christian's favorite movie was *La Femme Nikita*, the original. The American version with Bridget Fonda was vile, it was beyond putrid. The producers of that shitty mess should be lined up and gutted like dogs. They weren't worth the bullets. He had heard from someone that Nikita was now a very hot blond starring in her own television series on cable and the show wasn't half bad, but Christian didn't own a television. He had sold it to his brother. His brother. He had not thought of his brother in months. What the hell was this. Chrome was slipping, he was actually slipping. His brother's name was Anthony. Two years younger and slightly better looking. Anthony had those killer green eyes and a perfect scar on his chin. It made him look tough and he liked to tell people it was from a fight but Christian knew it was a chicken pox scar and now Chrome bit his own tongue, hard. He was allowing the defunct Christian to poison his dying thoughts.

He would have to be careful, very careful.

Ironic, perhaps. But it was his own blood that was keeping him warm. It was like sitting in a hot bath. This was an illusion, though. He would catch a nasty chill if he didn't move along soon. But he was curious about the nature of the wound and he sent his good right hand on a casual scouting mission across bloodwet skin to get a clear notion of the damage. He had a cartoonish idea that the hole would be clean and round, the size of his fist. And as soon as the blood dried up his friends and lovers would be able to peek through it like a window. Those round windows they have on boats, he loved those windows and the bullet had struck him somewhere on the left side, obviously. The chest or shoulder. It had spun him around like a toy soldier hit by a stone. It had made him angry, very angry. And before the shock and pain had dropped him to his knees, he had managed to crush the Fred's skull with a handy chunk of concrete and then to eat out most of his tongue, like it was sushi. The tongue had been sweet as a nice cut of raw tuna and Chrome now sat with his boots resting on the Fred's soggy torso because he had always believed it was proper to elevate the legs when injured but he would definitely need to get inside, and soon.

Please, he said. Won't somebody help me with my luggage?

I smoked a cigarette and waited for Griffin, who had stepped into a convenience store to buy mouthwash, of all things. Time was unreliable, as ever. Griffin had been gone five minutes, or half the night. I stood on one foot, the left. Because Ray had a bad right knee, from an old basketball injury. The knee ached on these rainy nights. I smiled into the dark as Griffin walked toward me, sipping from a travel-sized bottle of Scope.

Docile.

I became docile. I allowed myself to be led on a crisscrossing and seemingly nonsensical path across town that threaded the inner eye and dipped in and out of memory and dream. That was it. If I had been dreaming and some person from a strange land had asked me to draw a map of Denver, it would have resembled the city that Griffin dragged me across. I couldn't have sketched it in two dimensions, however. It would require impossible three- or four-sided paper and the bright textured pop-ups of a children's book. There was a remote pain in my legs and Griffin seemed to be moving along at a fast trot, a jogging pace that I could never have maintained on an ordinary evening.

I followed Griffin along bright, crowded sidewalks without touching anyone, without making eye contact. Through damp, black tunnels and across scorched vacant lots and before long I was climbing. I was climbing a cold metal fire escape and never realized it until we had ascended a rooftop.

The Pale.

That shit was magical. Tar and gravel underfoot. Griffin's steady breathing in the dark. I looked around and around and the sky was curved around me, it was a hollow black dome bright with needles. My God it's full of stars. Laughing, someone was laughing. The soft and fearful laughter of a paranoid. I was laughing. Phineas was laughing. A voice hissed at me to shut the fuck up and now Griffin leapt to the next roof without a backward glance, rolled to his feet and grinned like a monkey and said, come on Ray, pull yourself together. It was five and a half feet across, maybe. The length of your average dead body. No problem. I sucked at my tongue and looked own. We were high enough that the ground below was invisible, the ground was purely speculative and I did a fast inventory of personal phobias. The fear of heights did not seem to be among them and while I couldn't speak for Ray Fine, I jumped easily across the narrow chasm.

Faith.

Eve and/or Goo:

How did she feel and oh God but that was a stupid question, so stupid and she hated herself for thinking this way. Unglued. She felt like she was in a dentist's chair waiting for him to cut into her gums and realizing that the painkiller had not taken hold and she wanted to tell someone but her mouth was full of cotton and mirrors and that sick little device they used to suck out your saliva. It was fear. The kind that bubbled up from deep in the tissues and paralyzed you. She wanted to run away but her arms and legs were so tight and she felt herself curling inward, tucking herself in crash position and she wasn't sure if this conflict of the senses was panic or rage or despair. Or nothing. She was bursting out of her skin, she was molting and she didn't want anyone to see or touch her.

One thing was clear. She was not Goo, not at the moment.

Eve was backstage at the Unbecoming Club and she was going on in like ten minutes and she wasn't ready. Or was she. Eve could do this, she could do this. And maybe this was her chance to get out. To get out of the game. An hour had passed since she learned that her boyfriend was a murderer and she was numb and stupid with goose bumps even though it wasn't cold at all. It was hot in here, the air was thick as soup but in her head she was walking along the top of a very high cliff, a place where she could stop and see for miles and miles on a clear day but the sun was much too bright and the wind was pulling at her, she was contemplating the plunge and it just didn't seem real. But this was enough, wasn't it. This was it. Christian had killed someone and that was reason enough to disappear. She wanted to go back to the world where your boyfriend was a bad driver or an asshole, a hypochondriac, a compulsive shoplifter. Or married. The daylight world was depressing but safe and predictable and she could at least relate. She could see for miles on a clear day. Her boyfriend was a killer, though. It was so melodramatic, so Hollywood. My boyfriend killed a guy, yeah. That's right. Fucking killed him. And I'm Courtney Love. Tap tap tapping. She sat on a circular green sofa that smelled of pee and her foot was nervously bouncing on the dirty stone floor and she remembered that she wasn't alone. Goo was here somewhere.

No, she said. Goo wasn't going to make it. But Adore was here.

Adore was ten feet away, talking in a hushed, conspiratorial tone with Theseus. One ghoul talking to another, oh God. Theseus was dressed in white, all white. Fine white linen suit, white shoes and hat. But his clothes were stylishly frayed and crusted with grime and mold. He looked more or less like Mr. Roark's corpse, freshly dug from the grave. Adore was dressed in pretty straightforward *Aeon Flux* gear: three banded leather straps across her chest that managed to cover some but not all of her muscular breasts. Obscenely tight, shiny green vinyl pants and black motorcycle boots. And Eve might have been seeing things but Adore appeared to be wearing a prosthetic penis tonight. She had a plastic banana or something shoved down her crotch. Adore had quite a package.

Eve hopped up now, jittery. She felt weirdly like a grasshopper.

The bathroom. She needed to pee, she needed to be alone and she skittered along the dark hall backstage, her legs were full of juice and she was trying not to hop. She was trying, God help her. She should never have shared the Pale with those guys. In the bathroom she got a look at her clothes and she looked fairly mild by Exquisitor standards. Dark suede jeans and a little black sweater that would probably better fit a twelve-year-old. It was thin and snug as a glove and her nipples looked like they were trying to escape but Adore would say she was much too conservative for this crowd of rubber and latex and aluminum clothing and she could always alter that before she took the stage, or not. Never mind that. Her hair was a fucking fright. Black tendrils, unwashed. Her hair stood on its ends as if she had just licked her finger and jabbed it into a socket. Eyes sunken, buried in hideous dark circles. White vampire skin and too-red lips. She pressed one finger to the big artery in her neck and measured her pulse. Fast and furious, her heart was violent. She was apparently terrified.

Eve peed.

Fuck it, oh fuck it.

A haze of blue smoke and endless, untethered shadows. The flicker of gas lamps. It was an old warehouse space with a gray stone floor and scattered sawdust and I briefly imagined I could smell the raw meat that had once been packed here. There was movement in the dark and I saw that maybe a hundred people were drifting, scurrying through the place. They slithered about like ghosts. Long fingernails and pale makeup. Bone and silver jewelry, tattooed flesh. Leather and silk and rubber, in relatively Goth colors. Black and black. In the far corners of the dark I caught the random mottled flash of naked skin jerking and grinding but there was altogether more fear than sex in the air and most of these freaks were just kids. They sat huddled in small groups, sharing unmarked bottles of the Pale.

I give you the Unbecoming Club, said Griffin. I give you beauty and chaos.

Paranoid murmurs. No one trusted the others.

It's a happy place, I said.

Hush, said Griffin.

A bar had been hammered together in one corner out of misshapen scraps of metal and wood. There was a large unfinished stage in the center of the space which was empty but for a curious pair of steel hoops under a single muted spotlight. There was an upright piano against one wall and there was a truly odd assortment of furniture: church pews and cast-iron tables and chairs that might have been salvaged from the dump. There were several torn and weathered sofas, water-damaged leather armchairs that might have once looked nice in a bank lobby. Rocking chairs and one bright blue La-Z-Boy recliner. Even a few wheelchairs. There was a terrifying fan mounted in one wall, the eye of Cyclops with seven-foot blades.

Griffin's face was glowing.

He clearly loved it here and I could only wonder if he saw this crowd as one big family or a lot of potential victims. And what was the difference. I sat down in an empty wheelchair and began to spin myself in slow circles. Now a sinewy, silver creature detached herself from a semiconscious cluster of trolls and came over to give Griffin a long, lurid kiss on the mouth and when she came up for air she turned to look at me and I recognized her. The creepy girlfriend, Kink. Who had wanted to eat my tongue. I was doubtful that she could hypnotize me a second time but one never knew. I would be careful with her.

Hello, she said.

I ignored her. I decided that if Griffin ever went to the bathroom I just might try to Tremble her myself, for kicks. Her tongue was probably nine inches long. I lit a cigarette and looked around and everyone seemed to be waiting for something to happen. And while some of the patrons had the pallor and attitude of zombies, there were plenty of others who looked like Griffin. Hungry and watchful.

So. What are we doing here? I said.

Hmmm. Do you want a drink? said Griffin.

That depends. Do they have anything but that Pale shit?

Griffin shook his head. Please, Ray. Will you keep your voice down?

I think there is some kind of sweet wine at the bar, said Kink.

Yes, said Griffin. There is usually a barrel of port.

Fantastic, I said. I'll see you later.

Griffin blinked at me and didn't smile. He obviously didn't think it was a good idea for me to wander off alone and unsupervised. What the fuck. That was as good a reason as any.

Wait a minute, Ray.

I rolled through blue smoke and although it did cross my mind that handicapped folks would probably be pretty unamused to see a guy with two good legs zipping around in a wheelchair like it was some sort of toy, I have to say it was a gas. And lately I hadn't been having much fun and I would have to take it wherever I found it. I rolled over to the bar and was about to ask somebody what kind of currency was accepted here, brass buttons or seashells or actual dollars, when I found myself staring into a familiar face. Long and gloomy and washed of color. The same self-administered haircut, the mental patient special. Crumb, of all people. And why not. Crumb would naturally gravitate to any underworld scene that featured drugs and regular nudity.

You son of a bitch, I said.

My God, said Crumb. As soon as you think the day is wasted you get a nice surprise.

Never fails, does it.

You're alive, said Crumb.

Pretty much.

Did you take a bullet in the spine?

What?

The wheelchair, said Crumb. Are you a paraplegic?

No, man. I'm just fucking around.

What are you doing here?

I'm looking for a drink that isn't laced with methadone.

Fancy that, said Crumb. You don't care for the Pale.

Not really.

I would have thought it was exactly your speed.

Yeah, well. Once upon a time.

I stood up and was so stupidly glad to see Crumb that I threw my arms around the old fucker and he still smelled like he never bathed. I lit a cigarette and wiped at my eyes. Fucking hell. I was lonely, wasn't I? Two days in the city and I had briefly touched three friends, with mixed results. Eve had promptly disappeared. Moon was dead. And Griffin was out of his fucking mind.

It's good to see you, I said.

Now I turned to the bartender and asked for a jar of the port, a request that was met with mild disgust and a trace of fear. For God's sake.

People are suspicious of nonconverts, said Crumb.

I shrugged and paid two dollars for a tall glass. It was strong and sickly sweet.

What about you, I said. Do you drink that shit?

The Pale? said Crumb. I take a drop, now and then. Purely medicinal.

Uh-huh. And are you involved in the game?

Crumb licked his gray lips. I am Gulliver, he said. The Redeemer.

Perfect, I said. I'm Ray Fine.

And have you chosen a caste?

I'm a Fred, I suppose. I'm self-aware.

Crumb grinned. He scratched at his dark, unshaven jaw. The harsh whisper of sandpaper against stone and I was surprised to find my senses were still unusually heightened.

Eve:

Out of the bathroom and right away she saw Dizzy Bloom and Mingus standing in an uneasy circle with Adore and Theseus and without even thinking about what they must be discussing she hopped over to them and was glad when Dizzy smiled and pulled her close. Eve needed that, didn't she. She needed someone to protect her, someone to tell her she was okay, to love her. Because everything was coming apart and Theseus was already spitting electricity.

What will we do, said Mingus.

Nothing, said Theseus. You will do nothing.

But Chrome is dangerous, isn't he. This is real, it's too real.

Adore scowled. What do you propose, little one?

I don't know. The police?

Theseus laughed richly. The police, he said. What an idea.

He should be severed, said Adore.

Yes, said Theseus. Amputated from the game like an infected limb.

You're going to kill him, said Dizzy.

Don't worry, pet. Chrome won't be harmed. The dear boy. I will take care of it and none of you will be the wiser. Chrome will simply disappear for a time.

Eve didn't want to say anything but she couldn't stop herself. Her voice was escaping whether she liked it or not, her voice was a desperate little air bubble.

Excuse me, she said.

They all looked at her and she tried to focus, to remember what she wanted to say but she couldn't help noticing something different about Mingus. He was not so pale and amorphous. He didn't look like you could just put your hand right through him. There was a touch of new metal in his eyes. Oh, well. This was obviously sex. He had finally fucked or been fucked by Dizzy and Eve wanted to give him a squeeze and say she was happy for him. It was about time.

Adore was staring at her. What do you have to say, dear?

His name was Christian, said Eve. He has parents somewhere, and a brother. He has a master's degree in French lit and he works in a video store. Or he used to.

Brief, unpleasant silence.

He loves movies, she said.

Theseus and Adore looked at each other, smoke trailing from their noses. Eve had hoped that Adore would be on her side but that was just silly.

I don't believe my fucking ears, Theseus said.

Maybe she's right, said Dizzy.

But she took a half-step back and Mingus grabbed for her hand as Adore extended one bony fingernail and traced a slow, hypnotic figure eight in the air before tucking a loose strand of hair behind Dizzy's ear. Mingus looked like he might faint but Dizzy never flinched.

Adore licked her lips and said, I detest Breathers.

Eve felt calm. Her blood was still furious beneath her skin but she was calm.

Open hunting, said Theseus. He smiled. I will spread the word among the Mariners that the three of you are to be hunted like dogs if I hear another word about the police. And it will get very bloody if I hear any silly rumors about a fictional person named Christian with a master's degree.

Adore turned to Eve. Are you performing tonight?

Eve stepped close to her and said softly, yes. I think so.

Adore smiled, showing two jagged rows of bright yellow teeth and Eve wondered how much the sick bitch had paid to have her incisors sharpened. Or had she done it herself, with a file.

I'm glad, said Adore. And what piece would you like to do?

The Scavenger's Daughter, said Eve.

How yummy. Who will be the victim?

They stared at each other for a perilously elastic moment and Eve wanted nothing more than to drop her eyes and look away but somehow she borrowed the guts from Goo to lazily grab Adore by the crotch and give her little make-believe cock a fierce, familiar squeeze. Theseus coughed, apparently embarrassed.

I will, said Eve. I will be the victim.

Hail of Frogs:

The blades of the giant fan had begun to move. The blue haze fell away and Phineas gratefully reclined on a lemon-yellow couch in the darkest corner of the space. He sat close to Crumb, his head lowered like a thief. Crumb was talking philosophy, however.

It's all about obliteration of self, said Crumb. The utter loss of self. I have failed at the game personally. It amuses me to be Gulliver for a day or two but I'm still Crumb.

And what about these others. Do they know their own names?

I'm never sure, said Crumb. Everyone lies to me, which is peculiar. I'm a Redeemer, a confessor. And still they lie. But a lot of them have day jobs so they must be able to come in and out.

Brief silence. Phineas thought about the fact that he would really have to find a job soon, or starve. It was a surreal notion.

Who did you come here with? said Crumb.

Friend of mine, a lawyer. He called himself Major Tom.

He's a Mariner?

Yeah, said Phineas. I took a girl's tongue with him this evening.

Disturbing?

A little.

The intimacy is fantastic, said Crumb. Obviously. But the transaction is strangely antisexual in the end.

It's fucking creepy. And I don't quite understand it.

What? said Crumb.

The tongue. The temptation.

Crumb smiled. It's not so complicated, he said.

You obviously have a theory.

Have you ever had a good look at hieroglyphs, said Crumb.

The sideways people? said Phineas.

The sideways people, said Crumb. They have very large mouths.

Okay.

Think about it, said Crumb. In religious art and literature, the mouth and tongue are always big symbols. They carry serious voodoo. The tongue is the spoken word, the tongue is Creation. Then you have the chaos of Babylon, the scattering of tongues.

Crumb paused, grinning. Phineas lit a cigarette because he knew Crumb didn't want his opinion, not yet. Crumb was only warming up.

But that's not really what this is about, said Crumb. The mouth is often fearsome, a source of destruction. The mouth devours, after all. And the most hideous beasts in medieval literature always breathe fire, right. The tongue of fire.

Phineas regarded the stoned kids around him.

The powers of fire and speech, said Crumb. The two skills that set us apart from the lower animals. Creativity and destruction are thereby intertwined in man.

No shit.

Have you read the *Upanishads*?

What do you think? said Phineas.

I suppose not, he said. But if you had, you might know that the mouth is said to represent an integral consciousness in the context of sleep. The mouth is the door between real and unreal worlds, between reason and madness. And if one is unlucky and sleeps too long without waking, then the soul must escape through the mouth.

But look at these people, said Phineas. They don't have a clue about that shit.

That's irrelevant, said Crumb.

And he was right. A child may not be able to explain how or why he is affected by the symbolism of a dream, but he knows he is affected. He can feel it in his skin. He is instinctively afraid of spiders, rats. He is charmed by beauty. He is moved to do things he doesn't understand. Phineas sipped his port and watched Crumb, who was now smoking a leisurely cigarette.

Do you know a guy named Jimmy Sky? said Phineas.

Crumb shrugged. He's a player, I believe. A Fred of some kind but I don't know him.

He's an undercover cop, said Phineas.

That's beautiful, said Crumb. Does he know what he's gotten himself into?

No, said Phineas. I don't think so.

And you want to save him?

Phineas laughed. I'm not sure, really. I think I'm looking to kill him.

Theseus stood by the bar, immaculate and white.

His lips were wet as he surveyed the crowd, his jaw clicking. A young Mariner named Peter Quince appeared at his elbow, whispering that there was a telephone call for him. Theseus frowned. He did not like to use the telephone at the Unbecoming Club. It intruded upon his dreams. But Peter Quince was a fine fellow, very discreet. He never touched the Pale and Theseus often used him for difficult errands. The call must be important.

Theseus turned and walked into the dark and through a doorway and into a sparse, box-shaped room with office furniture. He sat down at the desk, picked up the telephone and looked at it with distaste. Hello, he said. Hello.

Silence on the line. Theseus lit a cigarette and put one white shoe on the desk with dull thud of rubber against wood.

I can hear you breathing, he said. You fool. You sound like a dying bloody horse. Come on, then. Who am I speaking to?

He blew smoke and waited.

Theseus flared his nostrils and was about to hang up when a man cleared his voice on the line and said, this is Jimmy Sky.

Jimmy, he said. It's good to hear your voice.

Did you hear about Moon? said Jimmy.

Yes, yes. Such a shame. How kind of you to hold onto his cell phone, though. In case he needs it on a rainy day.

Fuck you, said Jimmy.

No, don't hang up. Long pause. I'm sorry, said Theseus.

Oh, yeah. I bet you are, said Jimmy. Please make a donation to the Negro College Fund in lieu of flowers.

Ha. That's very funny. What do you want, Jimmy?

Pause.

I want self-awareness.

Theseus smiled. Is that all?

The dead cops, said Jimmy. Are they Freds?

Of course.

Who's killing them?

You are, Jimmy. You are.

Motherfucker.

I'm joking of course. But then you did kill Moon.

Who is it?

A talented young Mariner, said Theseus. He's known as Chrome but his given name is Christian Wells.

Where can I find him? said Jimmy.

He's a houseguest of Dizzy Bloom.

The address, you fucker.

Look in the telephone book. It's her real name.

If I kill him, will Moon be self-aware?

It's possible, said Theseus. But not likely.

I hate you, said Jimmy.

Oh, by the way. It might interest you to know that Captain Honey suspects someone else entirely. I think you know him.

Who?

Theseus shrugged. An unstable person by the name of Ray Fine.

One face bleeding into the next and Tom had what he might best describe as an ice-cream headache. The slow rush of dirty skin. Twisting hair and scar tissue and pockmarks. Terrible eyes sleepless and drugged, bright and searching. A handful of men and women before him on a ratty Oriental rug in various postures of despair, some of them nodding in junk stupors while others twitched and vibrated and muttered about the intricacies of the rug's design. One girl of about seventeen lay with her cheek pressed hard to the floor as if she were listening to the earth. A single strand of oily brown hair fell over her visible eye and every five seconds or so she laboriously moved her bruised right hand to brush it away and not more than two feet from her, Kink was violently kissing a barefoot peasant girl with blond hair who could have been the first girl's twin. And at the center of the rug, where the design came to an angry climax of flowers and geometry, Major Tom soon found exactly what he was looking for. A beautiful man with black dreadlocks and dark chocolate eyes. The unspoiled face of a new Fred. Tom sighed. He contemplated the tongue.

Dizzy was loath to admit it, but she was happy. Mingus sat beside her on a slick black sofa, holding her hand. Their faces were pushed together, not kissing but close enough to share the same air.

Tell me about your parents, said Mingus.

I don't remember them.

What do you remember?

I grew up with my grandmother, Millicent Bloom Devine.

Tell me about her, said Mingus.

Why, though?

Because I have no memories of my own. None that I can trust. I see a man in the suburbs cutting grass. A thin man in bad clothes. A father. I see a sister, a little girl in a red bathing suit. But they aren't mine.

What else?

I remember walking through a silent green jungle armed with two 9-millimeter pistols and a box of flares. Terrible and beautiful at once. The foliage is so thick it's as if the sky is green. A tiger jumps at me and I shoot it five, six times. The chatter of unseen monkeys. I climb over a stone wall and jump across a pit filled with cobras. Then avoid the quicksand and enter a catacomb of ruins. And I'm a woman. I have tremendous breasts and a British accent.

That's not real, then.

I think it's a computer game called *Tomb Raider*.

Okay, said Dizzy. It's okay.

Tell me about your grandmother, said Mingus.

Dizzy smiled. I called her Grandma Milly. She was the firstborn daughter of Molly and Leopold Bloom.

And who were they?

They lived in Dublin, long ago. Leopold was a pervert, a Christ figure. And he was a kind of grifter, a complicated man. But very well-educated. Molly was crazy, I think. And she was a little slutty, or so they say. A prolific adulteress. I prefer to think that she was looking for true love.

What happened to her?

Chrome entered, bloody.

One arm cradled and useless. The other held out sideways for balance. His face white as death. Whispers from the slippery crowd. Oohs and aahhs. One kid with the furry hands and feet of a hobbit floated by on a skateboard and insolently patted Chrome on the back and murmured very real, brother. Very real. Chrome took one step. Then another. He was going to fall over any minute and there was nothing he could do about it. Mingus appeared, seemingly from nowhere.

Run away, said Mingus. You aren't safe here.

Mingus, Mingus. I'm hurt.

I can see that. What happened?

Shot, apparently.

Chrome fell forward and Mingus caught him.

You haven't heard me.

What? What…so tired.

Theseus knows. He knows about the kill.

You, said Chrome. You betrayed me?

Helpless. Mingus shook his head.

Not possible.

Yes. I told Goo, and Dizzy.

Why?

You have to get out of here.

But I should be safe here, I live here.

No. They want to remove you, to cut you off.

Help me. Je suis malade, s'il vous plait.

Mingus smiled as if he might weep. Chrome was leaking blood like a hatful of water and he wanted to tell the Breather not to worry but his strength was gone.

Je suis malade.

Dizzy came out of the throng and took Chrome's good arm. She threw it over her small shoulders like a wrap. Mingus held the bloody arm and together they led him away, his feet dragging between them.

Chrome relaxed. He would not die alone, at least.

Eyes dry and staring. Too much sugar in his system. Phineas watched as a very young girl sat down at the piano and began to hit random, discordant keys. Electric lights came up and a low hum and cry ran like a current through the crowd. Crumb nudged him and pointed to the main stage. The small spotlight was abruptly killed and now the only lights came up from the floor.

White fingers.

Eve walked onto the stage and Phineas opened his mouth, then closed it.

I should have warned you, said Crumb.

Another woman took the stage. Motorcycle boots, hot green pants and leather straps across her torso. Eyes hidden behind black mask. In one careless hand she held a long slender metal rod that most resembled a car's radio antenna.

Who is that? said Phineas.

Lady Adore, said Crumb. The Exquisitor.

Eve wore only white underpants and a black sweater with the sleeves hacked off. Her pale arms extending yellow and thin from ragged, gaping holes and now she pulled the sweater over her head in an abrupt, nonsexual motion. She walked to center stage and crouched to pick up the joined metal hoops, which she examined briefly before handing over to Adore without comment.

The hoops were approximately fourteen inches in diameter and held together by a steel clasp. Phineas didn't feel well, looking at them. Lady Adore separated them and dropped one to the floor, where it spun briefly like a coin.

Eve fell to her knees, as if to pray. Expressionless, staring. She sat with back straight and buttocks resting on heels. Thighs pressed together. Arms loose, palms upright. Lady Adore circled her with the single detached hoop in one fist. Now she whipped at the air with the antenna and Phineas looked away, to the crowd.

They were hushed, gathered close.

Phineas stood up, stricken. One hand touching his mouth.

What is this? he said. What is this?

Performance torture, said Crumb.

Phineas watched as Lady Adore crouched beside Eve and pulled the first hoop over her bended knees, then worked it slowly and with much effort up over Eve's thighs so that the metal rim circled her hips at one edge and the tops of her feet at the other.

Eve's face was sickening. Colorless, beaded with sweat.

Adore now placed one hand on Eve's head and forced her to bow until her nose was nearly touching the floor. Eve's arms remained at her sides as the second hoop was pushed down over her head, then forced over her shoulders and down to the small of her back. Now the two hoops were touching and Adore clasped them together.

Eve was fetal. Dark red streaks, a web of blood extending beneath her skin.

The hoops formed a terrible figure eight around her body.

Adore took a step back and turned a slow circle, slicing at the air with the antenna and grinding her hips suggestively. Then turned and uncocked her long left leg, touched the toe of her boot to Eve's trembling shoulder and gave just a tiny push. Eve flopped onto her side, she was a fish and she was bleeding from the mouth and nose. Adore raised the antenna above her head and when the crowd groaned, she hesitated, smiled. Adore dropped to one knee and kissed Eve on the mouth, then rolled away and bouncing to her feet lashed her twice across the back with the antenna.

Phineas pushed through the crowd. Sick and feverish.

He threw his elbows against unseen flesh and vaulted onto the stage. It was four or five feet off the ground and he shrugged, as if surprised at his own agility.

Adore turned to face him, visibly disgusted.

You, she said. You are the victim.

He was speechless, dreaming. And she whipped him across the face with the antenna, opening a long cut that extended from the corner of his mouth to just below the ear.

Fuck, he said.

Adore swung at him again and he tried stupidly to catch or block the flashing antenna with his left hand. Now his fingers were bleeding and he took two quick steps forward, striking Adore in the nose with the heel of his right hand and she went down, the nose likely broken. Phineas kicked her in the stomach, not terribly hard but hard enough to be sure that she stayed down, then turned to Eve and hesitated to touch her, for she was so white and her face was stretched like a drum and running with sweat.

Eve, he said. Oh, fuck.

Theseus leaned on one elbow, sipping a pale yellow drink from a martini glass. He was relatively serene, gazing at the stage with gross indifference until Ray Fine chose to interrupt the program. Theseus shrugged and looked away, scanning the crowd. He left his unfinished drink at the bar and sauntered into a throng of bodies. Angry. He was fucking angry and soon came to the rug of triangles and flowers and crouched to mutter furiously in Major Tom's ear.

Do you know that man? he said.

Major Tom turned, wary. Then smiled the smile of a lotus eater.

Phineas slipped one hand between Eve's thighs and belly, fumbled for one agonizing moment then managed to release the clasp and slip the first hoop from around her legs.

The metal surprised him, slipping so easily over her wet flesh.

He straightened her legs carefully, gently. He removed the second hoop and rolled her onto her back, checked her pulse. Eve was breathing but she was shaking, she was in shock. Phineas rubbed her arms and legs for a long moment, hoping to restore circulation. All the while he was talking to himself, to her. It didn't matter what he said to her. Anything, anything. He wrapped her in Ray Fine's wool jacket and carried her to the edge of the stage and stood there for a moment, the floor lights throwing shadows across his bloody face and he realized that he couldn't jump down while holding her, that he might drop her and so he laid her down and now the crowd began to grumble. Phineas jumped to the floor and faced them.

Who has a car, he said. Who has a fucking car.

There was no response and he picked up a wrought iron chair and hurled it into the dark with the crash and clatter of iron against wood and a fleshy thud as it struck a body. A car, he said. Come on.

Who has a car?

Crumb came from the shadows, his hands held out wide as if to show that he was unarmed.

Take it easy, he said. I have a car.

Dear Jude.

You can say what you like about me. I have a tender fascination for the obvious and I'm slow to process violent stimuli but I tend to think that men are much softer than women, more sentimental. They cry at the movies and pretend not to. The male of the species is weak. He doesn't tolerate pain well, he is quick to break down under interrogation.

And while two mostly naked women spanking each other under bright lights sounds like a good idea the reality is something else.

Perhaps if they had been strangers. Then I could have shut down, I could have relaxed properly. I could have tolerated open flesh wounds and crushed feet and eyes burned with bleach. I could have imagined fucking them, hurting them. I could have been shamed and abused to the point of massive and paralyzing despair.

And I suppose this is what the torturer meant, when she said I was the victim. Because while Eve was visibly suffering it was I who cried out first.

Funny because I remember something you said to me once. That I had an unfortunate tendency to fall in love with the victims. And you were right.

But who am I in love with now? Eve, do you think?

By the way. I am not a particularly stupid man, right? But when it comes to literary theory and existential philosophy, well. I am stupid. I'm thick. Crumb had to give me the lowdown on a lot of that protean theory in *Ulysses*. The business of realism is a favorite topic of his but you have to be careful with Crumb. If he's had too much to drink he can easily chew your ear off about the Greeks. And according to Crumb, Aristotle had it all figured out two thousand years ago. The universe, the big nasty. Human existence. God and consciousness and death. The serious shit. Aristotle was on top of it all and his Poetics and Ethics were like very detailed instruction manuals that the average human is too fucking stupid or lazy to sit down and read.

Yeah. When Crumb gets going in that vein, he doesn't smoke cigarettes. He's so worked up he eats them.

You never met Crumb, did you. He patched me together after you relieved me of my kidney. Wait, that's not true. They took care of that at the hospital. He made sure I wasn't dying, though. And he gave me the first shot of morphine, which I suppose made things that much easier for you. He's a friend and I don't have many.

A friend is like anything else. A dog, a plant. You ignore them and they tend to die on you.

Chrome:
Not quite conscious.

The taste of aluminum and a slow downward spiral. He was close to Elvis, too close. Floating like a scrap of wood in high water. The floating was a trick, an illusion. Loss of blood and so on. He was in fact being carried and dragged along by Mingus and a female Breather whose name he could not remember at the moment. His toes dragged and he wished he could lift them, raise them up. For the dragging sensation caused his teeth to ache. Where. Where were they going. He might have asked this. But there was no answer. The pace began to slow and he wondered distantly if he was heavy. No, surely he was not. Chrome was slender, so slender. He was a reed and he took pride in his narrow waist.

Headlights. The grumble of a motor.

Slam of a car door. Mingus speaking softly to someone, someone else.

Horizontal now and soft tissue under his head. The female's thighs. His head must have been cushioned in her lap but he could smell nothing but his own blood. Hum of rubber on wet pavement. This was the backseat of a car, a hired taxi. Fingers in his hair. The female. Hospital. They were taking him to a hospital and he believed this was not a good idea. Dangerous. He was shot, gun shot. And the hospital was the very very last place he should go, even if dying. The police would find him.

Mingus, he said. Mingus.

The little dwarf's worried face soon loomed into view and Chrome realized he had been unaware that his eyes were even open. He had mistaken the black vinyl seat before him for the inside of his head.

Hush, said Mingus. You have lost a lot of blood.

Don't, he said. Don't take me to the hospital.

You need a doctor.

The police will kill me.

Christian, said Mingus. I'm not sure if I can deal with this.

He groaned. Then stop the car and let me out.

No, said the female. We can take him to my house.

Who is that?

It's Dizzy.

Yes. Take me to Dizzy's house.

You're dying.

Then I can fucking well die there.

Dark skies and bitter relief to be outside again. The air was wet and if I opened my mouth I could soothe the tongue. Eve had stopped shaking pretty much but had not said a word and I wondered if this was pain or shame or what. She couldn't be that injured, could she. Those joined hoops had been like something out of the Inquisition, though. And the thing about torture was that the victim always confessed or died.

Always.

They didn't put you on the rack for a day and a half and then decide you were innocent. Eve wasn't guilty of anything but she might well have suffered internal damage. Those hoops were evil. The way her nose was bleeding had scared the shit out of me and I was sure she might have had a blood vessel or two burst in her brain. On the other hand, I have a fucked-up imagination and an irrational but profound fear of embolisms and brain tumors and maybe I was projecting.

And I was still flying high with adrenaline.

My mouth was bleeding pretty freely where the dominator had cut me with her metal whip and it struck me that I would probably need stitches. I would have a handsome faceful of thread and it was too bad I couldn't pass that little problem off on Ray Fine.

Truly. What else was an alterego good for.

Eve relaxed her arms now and moved her head, brushing my cheek with her lips.

Put me down, Phineas.

Are you sure?

I'm not hurt, she said.

I put her down and she stood there, barefoot on the wet sidewalk. She fastened the buttons of Ray Fine's wool jacket up to the throat and suddenly she looked about fourteen. Thin white legs and bruised, angry face. The sleeves were too long for her and she used them to wipe the blood from her nose. I lit a cigarette and gave it to her.

Thanks, she said. And I'm sorry about your jacket.

Don't be, I said.

She crouched down on the curb and smoked hungrily.

Hey, she said. How are you? We haven't really gotten a chance to talk.

Yeah. I'm fine.

How was Mexico?

Eve, I said.

Did you get to see a bullfight? she said. I've always wanted to see one.

You're in shock, I said.

But I think I would cry when the bull was killed.

Eve, I said.

It's cruel, don't you think?

Do you want me to call you Goo? I said.

She choked back a laugh or sob and I thought, here it comes. The embolism.

No, she said. Please don't.

I sat beside her and she passed me the cigarette.

I'm out of it now, she said. I'm out of the game.

Oh, I said. How do you know?

Because that was me up there. That was Eve.

Yes, I said.

What are we waiting for? she said.

Crumb, I said. Crumb went to get his car.

Who? she said.

And before I could remind her that she had known Crumb for years, that she used to work for him for God's sake, I saw the headlights of Crumb's car, a rusted yellow Rambler with what sounded like a rotten muffler. The car choked out an angry cloud of black exhaust and I found it disturbing to think that this ugly piece of metal had probably rolled off the line a few years before Eve was born.

Crumb didn't get out of the car. He just sat there, revving the engine.

I smiled and my mouth felt white with pain.

The Rambler would probably die if Crumb took his foot off the gas. Oh, this would be a fantastic ride. Crumb was notorious for getting lost and I was still confused by the madman's map of Denver that Griffin had spawned in my head. The car had a wide bench seat in front so the three of us could ride cozily. Eve slid into the middle, tugging at the jacket to cover the white triangle of her underpants. Now she turned to Crumb and looked at him for a moment.

But you're Gulliver, she said.

Crumb sighed. Yes.

I didn't like this at all. Eve seemed to know who she was, and who I was. But she was still so entangled in the game that she didn't know Crumb from Gulliver.

Do you know where you are? I said.

Denver, she said with a trace of disgust.

Meanwhile, Crumb put the car into gear and we lurched forward. He found the Rolling Stones on the radio: "19th Nervous

Breakdown." It was appropriate, I suppose. Though it generally alarms me when life has a soundtrack. I tried to relax and let the street outside become a blur. After a few minutes I turned to Eve and whispered, do you know Jimmy Sky?

No, she said. I don't mingle with the Freds.

Then how do you know he's a Fred?

Where am I going? said Crumb.

Don't know, I said. Eve's place, I suppose.

No, she said.

You need some clothes.

My place is slipping, she said. It's not safe.

Ah, said Crumb. The slip. Very nasty.

Shut up, I said.

He's right, said Eve.

Two minutes ago you said you were out of the game.

Eve stared at me. That doesn't mean it isn't real.

Oh, fuck. Will you please listen to yourself?

By the way, said Crumb. Your face is a mess, boy.

I touched my mouth. I know. It feels like hamburger.

Then let's go down to the shop. I can sew that up and we'll all have a cup of tea and a nice talk.

Jimmy Sky:

He was back, baby. He was back.

Jimmy Sky walked around and around the house, stomping on rosebushes and cursing the thorns. He was looking for easy access. It was such a cute little house, very Victorian and all that and he would hate to break a window. But that was not to say that he wouldn't.

Now.

Jimmy was well aware that Theseus was giving him some sort of happy fuck-around. On one level, anyway. But there wasn't much he could do about it just yet. He wanted to find this Mariner, what was his name again. Aluminum foil or magnesium boy or ironhead. He chuckled. Chrome, it was Chrome. And according to Theseus, the kid was taking tongues from cops who were dizzy and fucked from the Pale and leaving them dead and somehow, his fictional friend Ray Fine was the prime suspect. And that made Jimmy fucking grumpy.

Theseus. He would deal with that fancy boy later.

Okay. His feet were muddy and he was pretty well sick of walking around this house so he ambled up the back steps and used his formidable girth to huff and puff and kick down the door. It wasn't so easy. It took three tries and on the second he found himself flat on his ass.

But the door was only wood, and wood splinters in the end. It gives.

Jimmy Sky crashed through and found himself in a kitchen. Flicked on a light and commenced to explore. A lot of knives in here. He opened the fridge and found a leftover carton of moo goo gai pan, barely touched. Excellent. He grabbed a fork and walked into the living room, shoveling the stuff into his wide gob.

Nice fucking place.

The Breather who was said to live here was obviously thick with silver.

Jimmy stomped upstairs and took a cursory look in each of the bedrooms, his eyes peeled for human shadows. Everything was fine and white and fairy-tale clean and he was sorely tempted to take a long yellow piss on one of the sheepskin rugs but then couldn't be bothered. He couldn't be fucked.

However. He did need to pee and of course whenever he found himself alone in a stranger's house, one of Jimmy's favorite tasks was to find the nearest bathroom and root through the medicine cabinet for prescription drugs. But then he supposed everyone was this way. He shrugged and soon located the bathroom. Thankfully emptied his bladder and polished off the moo goo gai pan as he did so. Jimmy sighed to see it go and tossed the empty carton into a wastebasket, then hurriedly washed his hands. He opened the medicine cabinet and whistled at its contents. He had found the mother lode, hadn't he? And the little Breather who lived here was mad as could be.

Decisions.

Well, now. There were plenty of vitamins and expensive herbal smart-pills and a wild rainbow of antidepressants that didn't much interest him. But there were also quite a few muscle relaxers and painkillers and amphetamines that were exactly to his taste, and he thought a couple of Demerol tabs would go down nicely with a diet pill or two. He rolled four or five pills around in his mouth as he walked back down the hall because he always preferred to taste whatever he was consuming and so he favored the dry swallow. But now his mouth seemed to be full of chalk and his tongue was a bitter ashen lump so he rapidly steered himself back to the kitchen and took a pitcher of what he incorrectly assumed to be lemonade from the fridge and had a big unfortunate gulp of the stuff.

Grapefruit juice.

Which might as well be poison, in his book. And not only did it burn his sore gums and torture his glottis, but the juice did not integrate well with the moo goo gai pan and before he could say howdy doody Jimmy Sky was vomiting all over his shirt. And what a fucking mess. His shirt was foul beyond belief and he was standing in partially chewed noodles and bits of gray matter that upon closer inspection were not necessarily meat nor vegetable and to top it off, the pills he had just taken were gleaming like tiny extra buttons down his chest.

Now then.

He could have gone back to the bathroom and gotten a few more tabs of the Demerol but these little guys on his shirtfront were hardly dissolved and what was the difference anyway. Waste not, yeah. Jimmy Sky plucked the little buttons between thumb and ring finger and swallowed rather more carefully this time, washing his mouth out with water from the kitchen sink.

And he paused, thoughtful.

Jimmy Sky was a practical man. But this sort of behavior, the consumption of partially digested pills, that was pure Moon. Ah, well.

Bang.

Metal against metal.

Bang, bang and his ears perked up like an old dog's. That sounded a lot like the front gate.

The back room of the Witch's Teat.

The whorehouse décor and somber lighting. The whistling kettle. The peculiar smells. I found it familiar and terribly sad at once. Crumb peddled inexpensive sex toys, used records and relatively legitimate drug paraphernalia out the front door, and in the back room wielded his untrained medical skills on the mad souls who wanted or needed to avoid regular hospitals. Crumb was no butcher, and he would rarely reach for a scalpel when drunk. But his education was spotty. His run at college had been disastrous, from what I could gather, and irrelevant besides. Crumb had been a theology major. He had picked up a little medicine while working in a tattoo parlor, and later was apprenticed to a back-alley abortionist for a year or two. And beyond that, Crumb was self-taught. He subscribed to the *New England Journal of Medicine* and he kept an expensive video library of the medical dramas on TV. He swore by *St. Elsewhere* and complained that *Quincy*, while entertaining, was medically unsound. *Quincy* was a menace, he said. Crumb read every textbook he could get hold of and had faithfully practiced his surgical skills on rubber dummies, dead dogs and a few comatose friends. His specialty was extractions: bullets and other foreign objects, bad teeth, unwanted fetuses. Crumb could remove things from the body. And he was pretty good with a needle and thread. I had come to him quite a few times over the years, with minor lacerations and other flesh wounds that I might not have wanted to report to the department.

Crumb had acquired a dentist's chair in the year or so since I last needed his services. It faced the television and gleamed darkly in a corner by the sink. There was a Batman cartoon on the box, the sound muted. I stared at the screen for a moment, my brain clicking. It was so obvious, and kind of sad. But all superheroes had pretty much the same problem. Batman was flash and sexy compared to Bruce Wayne and even Robin the Boy Wonder was a lot cooler than Dick Grayson. As for Superman, well. It was a fucking miracle that Clark Kent had never committed suicide. I glanced at Eve, who was pacing around the little room as if she couldn't stay and she couldn't go. Obsessively twirling one finger in her hair, around and around.

Crumb steered me toward the dentist's chair and tottered off to scrub his hands.

No thanks, I said.

What's the matter? said Crumb.

Nothing. I've got torture on my mind, though.

So?

A dentist's chair?

It's perfect. I can clean your teeth while I'm at it.

Fuck that. My teeth are fine.

I'm joking, of course. But I do have a tank of nitrous, if that helps.

I had to admit that nitrous would help.

And five minutes later I was strapped into the chair with a mask over my nose and I could feel the needle tugging at my skin as if it wasn't skin at all, but a plastic sheath that I wore around my head. I could feel Crumb's fingers resting heavily on my face and I could see Crumb's eyes, round and never blinking bug's eyes. Crumb had bumped up the volume on the TV before he started, saying it helped him to relax and that if I didn't want my ear sewn onto my forehead not to complain and so now I listened as Batman exchanged dark nihilistic metaphors with the Joker and I smiled warmly with drool running down my chin.

Eve leaned over me, slow and sudden at once. It was stupid, she said. What you did was stupid.

I gurgled at her. Tried to smile but I felt vague about who she was. The dreambrain identified her as a conglomerate. My mother was in there, the sister I never had. My dead wife and a long line of forgotten lovers and characters from books and movies that I might have fantasized about.

I'm a creature of comfort, said the Joker.

I'm glad, though. I'm glad you were there, she said.

And I was pretty sure the needle would pull my face off. My poor skin could only stretch so far and no farther before it slipped from my knob like a wet bathing suit. It's terrible, isn't it. The way your skin clings to you.

Mingus:

He could hardly credit it but Mingus was losing his sense of smell. Overload or temporary freakout or some kind of total shutdown. Because he should have been able to taste Christian's blood by now. The stuff was all over him.

He glanced over at Dizzy Bloom and was struck with worry and nausea, a queer star-shaped feeling blossoming in his throat for her. What visions must she be suffering, he wondered. Dizzy Bloom was strong, though. She had borne her half of Christian's weight without a whimper. Maybe she was holding her breath. Dizzy Bloom was an alien, a beautiful creature, and he supposed the star-shaped sensation creeping up from his belly was love or something like it. This was unforeseen and perhaps a little frightening but he was too worried about his lost sense of smell to give it a lot of thought. He could see nothing behind his own eyes and he had no memories true or false. He had nothing.

Mingus took a deep breath as they lowered Christian onto Dizzy's porch swing but there was still nothing. He watched as Dizzy dug through what seemed like a thousand pockets for her house key. He closed his eyes. He breathed.

Wait.

Rotten chocolate, thick and pungent and it wasn't chocolate at all, it was the smell of fresh earth, of death. And as fast as it came it was gone and Christian was falling off the porch swing. Mingus crouched beside him, hugging his friend's cool damp body and waiting for Dizzy to unlock the front door.

Isthmus cerebri, said Mingus. Vena ascendens.

The door swung open and Dizzy turned to help him with Christian.

Tunica elastica. Quadratus menti. Corpus callosum. Sympathetic plexus and vitreus humor.

What? said Dizzy.

Mingus blinked. He was only remotely aware that he had been muttering these phrases aloud.

Medical terminology, said Christian. His voice like the faraway croak of a frog. Our friend Mingus, he said. He often quotes from *Gray's Anatomy* when nervous.

Mingus blushed, hoping that Dizzy would smile at him in the dark.

Christian, he said. Be quiet.

Why, said Christian. Why do you call me that?

Because you're failing.

Dizzy sniffed the air and stopped short and the three of them nearly tumbled into her living room.

There's someone here, she said.

Mingus felt the prickle of goose bumps along his arms. Fearful.

Theseus? he said.

No, she said. It's the smell of sick.

The overhead light was flicked on and a stout, balding man in vomit-streaked clothes stood before them, a gun in his right hand. He touched his own forehead with the barrel as if scratching an itch.

Fuck me, he said. You call yourself a Breather. A little kid could walk in here and smell puke.

You, said Dizzy. I know you.

Christian was slumping to the floor and Mingus moaned, holding him close. And as he always had, he felt safer with Christian beside him. Even like this.

No, said the man. You don't know me.

You're a policeman, she said.

Not tonight, sister. The man waved his gun and nearly fell over. I'm no cop.

Who are you? said Mingus. He had found his voice, it seemed.

I'm Elvis, said the man. I'm king of the fucking Freds. I'm Jimmy Sky.

Dizzy's face was white, her lips flatline. Our friend is hurt, she said. What do you want?

The man guffawed. I want him, of course.

What do you want with him? said Mingus.

That depends. His name is Chrome, yes? The Mariner.

Mingus hesitated. Yes, he said.

And the man who called himself king of the Freds stepped forward, he swaggered close with his gun held crooked. He swung his arm around, breathing crazily. He faltered, mumbled an obscenity or two and glanced upward as if looking for the sun. Then poked the end of the gunbarrel at Christian's mouth.

Chrome, he said. You have made the game real.

Mingus watched the man's chubby index finger tighten around the trigger, he watched the tiny creases in the skin of Jimmy Sky's finger turn white and he could already feel the hot spray of Christian's blood but there was a pause, a heaviness in the air. And Jimmy leaned close enough.

Don't you find it curious? he said. That I don't want your tongue.

Christian straightened, his cheeks deathly. Mingus knew that he wanted to be proud but he couldn't stand alone. There was no strength left in him. Dizzy said softly, wait. And the man never heard her, he never did. But he was staring at Christian with the sudden horror of recognition in his eyes.

I know you, he said. You work at the Video Hound. I rented *Star Trek* from you, just a few weeks ago. *The Undiscovered Country*. Last month. Last fucking month. Jimmy lowered the gun. Oh, he said. This is…unexpected. This is fucking strange. And look at you, he said. Look at you. Someone has already killed you.

Please, said Dizzy. Let's talk about this. I can make some coffee.

Coffee, said the man. Fuck that shit. Your friend doesn't need coffee.

Mingus made a rare, free-falling decision. He decided to say fuck it and he stuck out his left hand and took the gun away from Jimmy Sky. It was easy, really. The fat policeman yawned at him, unconcerned. Mingus turned the gun over and over in his hands, wondering how one might unload it and at that precise moment, Christian's knees buckled and he fell forward, pulling Dizzy down with him.

Oh, this is pretty. This is gorgeous, said Jimmy Sky.

The room collapsed into the glass eye of a fish.

The room curved inward and Mingus twisted the gun this way and that, careful to keep it pointed at the floor. He could not fathom how the bullets went into it and he cursed himself for never learning such things as a boy.

In warped space he could see Dizzy shoving at Christian, rolling him over onto his back and bending to breathe into his mouth and behind her the fat policeman was lazily removing his jacket and tie, his shirt. Dropping them to the floor like soiled rags then fumbling to release his belt buckle. This seemed terribly inappropriate and Mingus lifted the gun. The man's pants sagged but did not fall down and Jimmy Sky shrugged. He lifted one heavy foot and began to hop around in a circle, trying in vain to yank off his shoe.

The gun was unsteady and Mingus felt sure that it would go off any moment.

Dizzy breathed into Christian's slack lips. One of Jimmy Sky's shoes hit the floor, followed by a dirty white tube sock. Mingus fumbled with the gun and now Jimmy Sky sat down, cursing because his other shoe would not come off. There was a knot in the laces. Mingus lowered the gun. Dizzy was beautiful, he thought. Dizzy was silent and mournful and her eyes never left Christian's face as she offered him her breath. The gun was heavy, warm and heavy and suddenly Mingus darted back outside into the dark and grunted as he threw the thing onto the roof. And he stood there a long moment, waiting to see if it would fall back to his feet.

Silence.

The gun didn't fall and soon Jimmy Sky came outside, barefoot and eerily peaceful. His great white belly jiggling.

Horrorshow.

Mingus stared at him, unafraid now.

Nice fucking night, said Jimmy.

Yes, said Mingus. They stared at each other for another moment and Jimmy burped wetly, then gave a great sigh. He tottered down the steps and Mingus slowly turned and went back inside, his head full of noise. Dizzy looked up at him and he knew everything was bad. It was real.

We have to do something, she said.

There was bad air in his mouth and he didn't know what to say.

What? he said.

I don't know, okay. But there's a bullet in him and he's almost dead. If we get the bullet out, maybe he won't die.

His tongue felt thick. That seems naïve, he said.

Dizzy glared at him. Isn't he your friend?

Oh, God. Mingus touched his eyes and they were dry. Of course, he said. Yes, he said. And I keep expecting him to sit up. To laugh at me and say: quelle heure est-il?

Huh?

What time is it. Christian wishes that he were French, you know.

Why won't you call him Chrome?

Because Chrome wouldn't be dying.

Dizzy shook her head. Please, she said.

I didn't think you liked him.

Dizzy shrugged. I don't like him. But it's part of the game,

Mingus.

No, he said. No, it's not.

She stood up. Help me move him into the kitchen.

Mingus helped her. He could hardly say no, could he. And it was gruesome, the way Christian's body slid across the floor. They dragged him into the kitchen and the blood became a muddy streak across black-and-white tile.

Bright overhead light.

Mingus sat beside the body, his fingers pressed to Christian's throat and there was perhaps a faint pulse but he knew that if he touched the floor or the leg of a chair he would likely feel the same faint, faraway beating. Dizzy was opening one drawer after another and he realized she was looking for tools.

Do you have a knife in your pocket? she said.

No, he said.

Take this, she said. And she handed him a blunt little knife, the sort of knife one might use to cut cheese at a party. A soft cheese like Brie.

I want you to cut open his shirt, she said.

Mingus nodded. He stared at Christian's torso, at the fine silver mesh shirt. The gentle curve of pectoral muscles unmoving. He shifted his eyes to the brightly defined collarbone below Christian's throat.

Blood, the blood there was nearly dry.

Mingus slipped the point of the blade in at the neck of the shirt and sawed through the thin material and he was disgusted to hear himself grunting. The shirt fell away and Christian's chest was black with blood. Mingus reflexively pinched his nose but he needn't have bothered. There was no smell, not for him. Dizzy sat down across from him and he took one look at her and almost laughed because she knew it was inappropriate but he wanted to kiss her. There was a nice glow of sweat and urgency about her face and her lips seemed darker, almost brown and her hair fell in heavy black braids that touched the floor. The little muscles jumped in her arms. He saw that she held another knife with a black handle and serrated blade, an ice pick and a small sharpened spoon that he thought must have been intended for pitting olives. She laid these on a white linen napkin and together they gazed at the wound.

Which was not so bad, really. Torn flesh.

It was more of a rupture than a hole but they needed something to clean it with, alcohol or something. He mentioned this and she said, I looked. I don't have anything.

The Pale, he said.

There's none to spare.

He sighed and realized that he was only calm because his tiny reptile brain believed none of this was happening. This was a very intense video game, a first-person shooter from hell.

What about cough syrup, he said. Some of them have alcohol.

Yes, she said. Yes. I have NyQuil.

What color? he said. And it didn't matter, it didn't matter. Christian was dead.

Green, she said. I hope.

Yes.

Dizzy said she would be right back.

Okay, said Mingus.

He stared at the knife, at the funny little spoon. He wondered what in God's name would she do with the ice pick. And in a moment Dizzy came back, another linen napkin in hand. She stained it green and began to wipe the blood from Christian's chest and soon his chest was green, as if his blood were green.

This isn't necessary, said Mingus.

What? she said.

He touched her wrist, he grabbed it. There's no one around, he said. We could drop out of the game for five minutes.

You can't be serious.

Mingus sighed. He wanted her to call him by his proper name. He wanted her to kiss him again, he wanted to talk about tomorrow and beyond. They had a lot to talk about. But Dizzy was unwavering when it came to the game.

Look at him, said Mingus. He's dead.

Are you sure?

No.

Aren't you a medical student? she said. In the daylight, I mean.

You know I am, he said. And I'm on academic probation.

Dizzy shrugged. I don't care. We have to try, at least.

That six-fingered claw in his belly was love, he was sure of it. But when she offered him the serrated knife, he shook his head. He couldn't do it and he didn't want her to do it but she bent over Christian and felt for the bullet with her finger. She couldn't seem to find it and he heard her suck in a deep unsteady breath as she lowered the sunshiny little blade to cut at the flesh around the hole in Christian's dead chest. And Mingus was calm, he was far away. Dizzy made an opening the length of her finger above Christian's left nipple and stopped. She looked like she might faint and now Mingus took the little sharpened spoon away from her.

Fuck, he said. Oh, fuck.

He wished he could dig around in the area of Christian's heart and find the bullet, if only to give it to Dizzy so she could breathe again. But he couldn't.

Dead, he said. He's dead, Dizzy.

Yes.

Dizzy leaned forward and felt around in Christian's pockets until she found a packet of cigarettes, then sat back against a cupboard and lit one.

The gray sunken cunt of the world, she said.

Mingus took the cigarette from her.

What? he said. What did you say?

My great-grandfather, she said. Leopold Bloom. He called death the gray sunken cunt of the world and I never understood what he meant until now.

Mingus blew smoke at the ceiling and thought what a beautiful freak she was.

Dizzy, he said. Leopold Bloom is a fictional character. He was never real.

Oh, she said. I don't know about that.

Long silence. Mingus wondered about tomorrow.

J'ai faim.

Dizzy Bloom smiled. What?

I'm hungry.

The face was numb and I couldn't smile.

But I liked to think that smiling was unnecessary and now I looked down with mild effort to see that I was still strapped into a dentist's chair, hands flecked with the blood of Phineas and folded piously in my lap. I released the seat belt and maneuvered my legs into standing position and this was not so bad.

Breathed. The air was still and I supposed it must be approaching dawn. I spied a clock that claimed it was slightly past three. Technically it was Saturday. No sign of life but for a vaguely humanoid lump on the couch and I doubted they would have just left me in the chair because I might have had a seizure and thrashed myself to death but

Crumb had always been one to fade before first light and Eve, well. She was not quite herself.

Jesus.

Eve was freaking me out. She looked about thirteen sometimes but she was fierce, she was stoic. I would have been crippled and sobbing after two minutes in those rings.

Found her in brightly lit bathroom. Narrow.

A mirror directly to my left, I could feel it there. Eve sat on the toilet with the lid down. I was sick of fucking mirrors and I stared straight at Eve. She was so tiny. Her feet barely touched the floor. Her legs were crossed, one foot bouncing. She was reading a glossy magazine.

Crumb? I said.

Asleep, she said.

That lump on the couch, you mean.

Yeah.

What are you reading?

People, she said. It's very strange.

I nodded. Yes.

These celebrities, she said. They all look terrified.

I could feel the mirror beside me, a pale reflecting skin. I told myself not to look at it.

They are terrified, I said. They have lost themselves.

Eve touched finger to tongue, flipped another page.

Those cannibals are right, she said.

Breathe. One two three four five.

What cannibals?

The ones that claim the camera steals your soul.

Without a conscious thought I pulled an aluminum towel rack off the wall with a brief sparkling shower of white dust and turned and smashed the mirror beside me in one long circular motion.

Do you feel better? she said.

No.

But the spiderweb of glass that obliterated what would have been my face was a fair beginning.

Let's get out of here, she said.

How?

She rattled Crumb's car keys.

You want to steal his car, I said.

Eve shook her head. He gave them to me. I think he wants us to leave.

Saturday

Eve not Goo:

She hated herself and she could not sit still.

Eve squirmed like a worm on a hook and tried to whistle. She tried to whistle something pleasant like merrily, merrily your life is but a dream or maybe the theme to a Burger King commercial, something safe and normal. Have it your way. You can have it your way. But she was a poor whistler, she always had been. Eve was much better at spitting. And so she shifted around behind the wheel of Gulliver's yellow Rambler like she had sand in her pants, or spiders.

It's Crumb, she told herself. Crumb, not Gulliver.

Why was that so hard. She had known Crumb for like three years. And she (or Goo) had only encountered Gulliver a few brief times. The whole thing made her dizzy and she was glad to be out of it. But she was squirming because Phineas was sitting beside her, because he was looking at her. He hadn't said more than two words since they left and his mouth was probably sore with those stitches.

God.

When did he come back, anyway. Three or four days ago. Or was it a week?

Eve tried to remember how she had felt when she saw him on her doorstep. When she laid eyes on him. Warm. As if she had just swallowed a mouthful of brandy. She had felt like she was fifteen and she had a stupid, hopeless crush on her best friend's brother who had just come home from college and whose legs had rubbed briefly, innocently against hers beneath the dinner table.

Warm.

But the brandy fingers had been fleeting. They had flown away like five small birds and she wondered why she hadn't simply asked him to get her out of the game, to rescue her or something. But fuck that. She wasn't anyone's little sister. Of course. He had rescued her, in the end. He had pulled her from the Scavenger's Daughter even though she never asked him to.

If she had a therapist and she wanted to analyze it, she might say that she had been daring Goo to stop her, to save her. Or maybe she had been curious to see how long she could stand it. How long before she passed out. Or failing that, she might have hoped that Chrome would lift a finger, but he hadn't ever been there. Anyway, she didn't want to analyze it.

Where are we going? said Phineas.

To Dizzy's place, she said.

What is that, another club?

Laughing. Dizzy is a friend.

Phineas lit a cigarette, which he smoked out of the corner of his injured mouth.

You know what? he said. I think I've had enough of your sick friends. Let's go to your place.

Eve sighed. I told you. It isn't safe there.

Brief silence, tender.

Eve, he said. There's nothing wrong with your apartment.

And besides, she said. Dizzy isn't sick at all. She's nice.

Whatever you say. He blew a line of crooked smoke from the side of his mouth.

It's my life, she said.

I'm sure it is.

But she thought about it, she tried to see it from his angle. And somehow her life was not hers. It was a loose thread, a plot twist. It was a situation and situations get fucked up. Three months ago she was reasonably normal and enrolled in college and now she was bloody and bruised and anorexic and squirming behind the wheel of a borrowed Rambler.

Okay. It was fucked up, she could see that.

But she liked to think that once in a while the sun was meant to shine only for her. Eve squinted as she drove and it occurred to her that she wasn't wearing any pants. She carried no identification, no proof of her existence at all. She wouldn't want to get pulled over but she smiled and thought, if she was pulled over she could pretend she was a prostitute, she could let Phineas do the talking and she would love to hear what he had to say. It was still dark but the sun was shining somewhere, it was shining for her benefit and here was Dizzy's house. She slowed and let the Rambler drift to a stop.

This is it, she said.

Phineas frowned. Who is this Dizzy person?

I told you. A friend.

Right, he said. And is she in the game?

She's a Breather, said Eve.

Oh, good. I like Breathers.

They got out of the car and walked up to the house. Eve didn't flinch when he took her hand. The front door stood open, a crack of light. Phineas dropped her hand and eased through like he was made of smoke and shadows and she remembered that he used to be a cop.

Irrational, but she felt safe with him.

Discarded clothes on the floor. As if someone had undressed while drunk. White pants, green military belt. Blue shirt and blazer and wide yellow tie. Phineas picked up the tie, twirled it between his fingers and she wondered what he was thinking.

There was blood on the floor, a long brownish streak.

Phineas followed it into the kitchen and she followed him and they found Dizzy Bloom and Mingus sitting on the floor with Chrome's body stiff as a canoe between them. Blood and streaked with something sticky and green. Dizzy and Mingus were eating chocolate pudding cups and drinking ginger ale mixed with the Pale. They whispered to each other like kids drunk on sex and Phineas ignored them, bending to examine Chrome. Eve stopped in the doorway, a wide blank space forming in her head.

Goo, said Mingus. He tried to stand up but failed.

Eve looked at the blood, at the wound on Chrome's chest. Christian, she thought. Oh, my.

What happened? said Phineas.

He was shot, said Dizzy.

Yes, said Phineas. Who shot him?

A Fred, said Mingus. It seems.

It was a policeman, said Dizzy. I think.

Phineas blinked. Did you say a cop shot him?

He was hunting, said Eve. He was hunting and he went too far. Again.

Again? said Phineas.

Chrome killed a Fred yesterday, she said. Or was it the day before? Eve touched her fingers to her mouth, to her tongue. She didn't feel much of anything at all and Dizzy Bloom was looking at her, worried.

Goo, she said.

You have chocolate on your nose, said Eve.

Dizzy shivered like a scrap of fine cloth in the open air and after a bottomless silence she wiped her nose.

Phineas looked ill. The yellow tie clutched in his left hand. The stitches like black flies crawling out of his mouth. He leaned against the fridge and Eve watched as he fumbled through his pockets. He pulled out a cigarette and looked around.

You must be Dizzy, he said.

Dizzy shrugged and held out her hand, palm down. Eve felt the air turn stiff and she saw everything at once. The ice pick, the sharp little spoon. The linen napkins. The pudding packs. The blood, the green streaks of what she now saw was cough syrup.

Christian was dead.

His smooth pretty chest marred by a black and muddy patch of flesh over the left breast. Eve saw herself as Goo. She was in bed in another, much darker room, another pocket of time and she was kissing, sucking at his nipples. She was counting his ribs and marveling at his stomach muscles and still she didn't feel anything. Now she looked at Mingus, who was pale and blushing and confused. She wished he would get up and explain this scene to her. She wanted to know what her character should be thinking.

Hello. Do you mind if I smoke? said Phineas.

Please, said Dizzy.

Eve stood in the doorway. She looked at Phineas, but he was looking at Dizzy and so she tugged at him with her eyes, she tried to pull his skin apart with her thoughts and now he looked back at her, he held out one hand.

Are you okay? he said.

Yes, she said and suddenly she didn't want him to comfort her. She couldn't stand it.

Phineas turned back to the others. How do you know it was a cop who shot him?

Oh, well.

We don't, said Dizzy.

The two of them started talking at once and Eve smiled. Or you could call it a smile. Her lips slipped apart and she felt air on her teeth. They already sounded like lovers, she thought. Interrupting each other. Their words tangling together. Eve sighed. She looked at Chrome and didn't recognize him.

Hungry.

She stepped over his body and touched Phineas on the shoulder with one finger. He moved aside and she poked through Dizzy's fridge until she found a jar of dill pickles. Now she sat down and began to munch on a huge sour pickle, the jar between her legs in case she needed another one.

What should we do? she said.

Dizzy and Mingus looked at her. They shrugged as if joined at the hip and she remembered how irritating two people can be when they adore each other. Phineas coughed. He ground out his cigarette and fingered the yellow tie, he picked at a stain on the thin material. They all looked at him, waiting. Because he would know what to do. He was the adult.

Obviously, he said. We need to get rid of the body. Unless you want to tell this fantastic story to the cops.

No, said Dizzy. I don't.

Okay, he said. I can help you. But I want to know whose tie this is.

Dizzy sighed. Wow. I almost forgot about him.

Who?

He said his name was Jimmy Sky.

Phineas laughed out loud and now he sounded a little fragile, Eve thought. He sounded like there was a big handful of mad laughter in his stomach and he could only let it out a little bit at a time because if he laughed it all out at once he would go fucking crazy. Eve licked her fingers and took another pickle from the jar. She watched as Phineas tied the yellow tie in a crooked knot around his neck. He was smiling a thin, bitter smile and it occurred to her that he might not want to be the adult.

No, he said. This isn't high school and I'm not your big brother. I can make this body disappear but you can't just go to bed and forget about it.

Who is Jimmy Sky? said Eve.

He's no one, said Phineas. He used to be a friend of mine.

Well, she said. What did he want?

I think he came here to kill Christian, said Mingus.

And? said Phineas.

Mingus shrugged. Christian was already dying.

Jesus Christ. Phineas looked around the room as if he might be dreaming.

Dizzy touched his leg. What? she said.

I'm sick, he said. I feel sick.

It's okay, she said. Everything is okay.

Have you ever had someone die in your kitchen? he said.

Dizzy hugged her knees. No, she said. Never.

You're a Breather, right? he said.

Dizzy nodded. Yes.

And that means what? he said. That you're clairvoyant? That you can smell my clothes or fondle my keys and see my past, my future?

Sometimes, she said. Only sometimes.

Mingus got up suddenly, nervously. He climbed onto the kitchen counter and sat there like a very tired boy and began to take off his shoes. Eve was empty, she felt empty. The pickles were making her ill and her boyfriend, who was not really her boyfriend, was dead. His body was two feet away. It was too much, really. She tried to put on a new face. A cheerful face. That's what her mother would suggest and now she put a fist to her lips, trying not to laugh. Phineas pulled a fat paperback book out of his jacket pocket and Eve saw that it was a copy of *Ulysses*. He placed it on Christian's chest and Eve flinched.

His body isn't a coffee table, she said.

No, said Phineas.

He picked up the book and offered it to Dizzy, who received it gingerly, fearfully. As if it were made of lead.

That was Jimmy's book, said Phineas.

Dizzy opened the book and read aloud: tired I feel now. Will I get up? O wait. Drained all the manhood out of me, little wretch. She kissed me. My youth. Never again. Only once it comes.

Phineas stared at her. Fantastic. But where is Jimmy Sky?

Dizzy closed the book and stroked the smooth, worn cover with the tip of her ring finger, then lifted the book to her mouth and kissed the spine, licked it. But she did not smell it.

I don't know where he is, she said. I can't see him clearly. But he's cold, he's shivering.

Phineas rolled his eyes. Do you think so? His clothes are all over your fucking living room.

Eve laughed, she giggled. Oh, she tried not to but it came spilling out of her.

I'm sorry, said Dizzy. That's all I see.

I love this game, said Phineas. I love it.

Please stop, said Mingus. I want to stop.

Eve looked up and she felt bad for him. Mingus looked exhausted, he looked thin. Dark circles under his eyes. His hands trembling. Christian's dried blood on his clothes. Eve wanted to close her eyes, to sleep. She heard Dizzy exhale heavily, as if she had been holding her breath. Eve wondered what Goo would do if this was but another scene from the game. And she had no idea, no idea. All she could do was put the pickles away and wait.

Dizzy hesitated, then returned the book to Phineas.

His face was pale, apologetic. Eve hated it when he said he was sorry and she hoped he wouldn't do so.

I'm sorry, he said.

Dizzy stood up and she looked unsteady on her legs. She backed away from Phineas, from Christian's body. She was really beautiful, Eve thought. She was dirty and speckled with blood and her braids were falling apart but she was beautiful. Her arms were thin and muscular and she had nice hands and Eve realized that she was attracted to her, to Dizzy.

Her mouth felt dry.

Dizzy held out her hand and Eve wanted to take it but she didn't move. The hand was not reaching for her. Mingus hopped down from the counter. He kissed Dizzy's neck and Eve shrugged. They did seem happy together, safe together.

Flesh was flesh and bodies needed other bodies.

Eve looked at Christian and she could admit to herself that a thin faraway part of her was glad that he was gone. Chrome was dead and Goo would have no one to come back to. She looked at Phineas and wondered what she would do with him. What did she feel. She stared at his sick blue eyes. At his thin, hard mouth. His unshaven jaw and bright crooked teeth. And she thought of the way he had taken her hand in his as they had approached this house.

Flutter. She felt the flutter.

It's late, said Dizzy. It's very late and I'm going to bed.

Okay, said Mingus.

Dizzy tried to smile but it was like the muscles in her face were rotten. Eve smiled back.

It's not okay, said Dizzy.

No, she said. It isn't.

You can sleep here, said Dizzy. If you want. There are several spare beds.

Do you have any paint thinner, said Phineas. Or bleach?

His voice was dry, unflinching. Eve felt something twitch in her spine. Her breath slipped away from her. Paint thinner, she thought. This seemed like such a gruesome question but Dizzy was fairly untouchable, she was cool and weightless as a sparrow. She glanced down at the body and nodded.

Look under the sink, she said.

The two Breathers retreated from the room and Eve was left alone with Phineas and the body. Phineas went to the sink and began to dig through the cabinet. Eve stared down at Christian and told herself to touch him, to say good-bye. To feel something. His eyes were closed, thank god. He had such long, black eyelashes and she wondered how many times she had watched him sleep and felt invisible beside him, completely invisible. How many times she had curled up beside him like a little frog changing colors and wished one of them was dead.

Funny, though.

Because she never thought it would feel quite like this. Empty and cold and sick from lack of sleep, with the taste of pickles in her mouth. Christian's eyes were weirdly asymmetrical and she realized now that the left one was still swollen from the scratch that reached down the side of his jaw, where she had cut him with the sharpened doll. She touched the swollen eye, lightly. It felt rubbery and strange, it felt like a misplaced testicle and she was a little hysterical, perhaps. Can you see me, she said. Can you see me now.

Hand on her shoulder.

I need your help, said Phineas.

Her muscles were light and feathery. Yes, she said. I can help you.

Eve stood up and he handed her a metal jug of turpentine. Which made strange little echoes, like splashes at the bottom of a well. She watched as Phineas lifted Christian onto his shoulders, grunting with the effort.

He gave her dead lover the hug of a fireman.

Heavy footsteps. Out the back door, across Dizzy Bloom's dark, wet grass.

Brick patio, then more grass. Eve looked up at the sky and wished they could sit down to identify their favorite stars. The jug of paint thinner against her knees. Jack and Jill went up the hill. She opened the back gate and held it open for him. To fetch a pail of water. Parked cars and stretch of gravel. It was too bright and she realized how bad it would be if they were seen. Eve took the lead. Jack fell down and broke his crown. She didn't ask Phineas where he wanted to go.

Instinct.

She turned between a little red house and a vacant lot, she followed her feet along a dusty little path that might have struck her as charming under other conditions. Jill came tumbling after. The path curved through a gang of bushes and dumped them in a parking lot behind a fast-food place. Happy meals, she loved happy meals. Child-sized portions and always a prize. Every meal should include a prize. Two big blue Dumpsters like sleeping whales and she veered toward them without a thought. Is this far enough, she wondered. Is this far enough from the house and she could hear Phineas breathing hard and fast through his teeth. Between the Dumpsters and her eyes squeezed themselves shut as he shrugged Christian's body down like a sack of gravel.

Now, he said. Breathing.

He took the turpentine from her and she had to ask.

What is it for? she said.

Fingerprints, he said. Hair and fibers. Don't you watch television?

Not lately, she said.

Phineas sighed, hesitated. Then slowly and without ceremony, he dumped turpentine over the whole of her ex-boyfriend's body.

Goo's ex-boyfriend.

Her nostrils burned and Eve sat down abruptly on a wooden box that stank of tomatoes. She looked around and around. The air was bright and gray, the air was the color of metal under the pale winter sun. Phineas carefully wiped down the sides and handle of the empty jug, then tossed it into one of the Dumpsters.

That's it, she said. Do you want to say anything?

Eve looked at the body. Christian was deflated, he was much smaller than before. He was wet.

I can't, she said.

Phineas reached into his pocket and pulled out a handful of tobacco shreds and lint and coins and scraps of paper. He picked through and selected two dimes, which he placed on Christian's eyelids.

The dead suffer no laughter, he said.

What does that mean, exactly?

Phineas shrugged. Tell him a joke, if you can think of one.

Okay, she said. How many serial killers does it take to change a lightbulb?

Unwavering silence and shards of color now in the sky.

How many? he said finally.

One, she said. But it takes him a long time.

Phineas looked at Christian, then at her. Why?

Because he first has to dismember the old one, she said. Then masturbate on its remains.

Phineas nodded and she laughed to herself, brief and manic. He held out his hand and she took it and they walked back across the parking lot and along the twisting path, through the gate across Dizzy's dark garden. Phineas steered her around to the front of the house so they might avoid the kitchen and she was glad, she was warm. As they climbed the front steps she caught a flash of pink movement above. Thought she saw a fat pale gargoyle on the roof and was amazed that she had not noticed it before. Now she blinked, looked again.

But the gargoyle was gone.

Through the front door and Phineas still held her hand. He didn't say anything and he didn't once try to let go of her hand. He glanced around at the crumpled clothes on the floor and took a long shuddering breath. Eve lowered her eyes, she frowned at her own wet feet. There were bits of yellow grass between her toes and she wasn't going to let go of him. Of Phineas. She took him up the stairs and down the hall to the guest bedroom with the cloudlike white comforter.

Dead gray morning light.

But it was dark enough that his mouth and eyes were vague and shadowy as unfinished sketches and Eve wasn't quite breathing. The pillows were cool and grotesquely soft and she slapped at them, half expecting them to disappear. Phineas took off his hooded jacket and sat down on the bed, slowly took off his boots. He unbuckled his belt and he seemed terribly calm. He opened his mouth but Eve didn't want to talk and she pushed him down onto his back. And she pulled his socks off, his pants. Her fingers never quite touched his skin but she was sure that she could hear his heartbeat. Or her own. Eve dropped the wool jacket to the floor and now wore only underpants. White underpants and she wondered how white her skin must be. How thin she was. Her breasts felt heavy and cold and too large which was funny and unfamiliar but she folded her arms across them and when she moved she felt the deep bruise from the Scavenger's Daughter that circled her back and thighs and belly, an endless figure eight in her flesh. It would be purple tomorrow. Phineas still wore his shirt, a white polyester shirt with a red stain on the chest and a woman in a bikini down one sleeve. The faint smell of mothballs and he was naked from the waist down, he was apparently speechless but unashamed and she could see he had an erection. And she lowered her arms, she unbuttoned his shirt and lay on top of his chest with her legs drawn up like a grasshopper and at first thought that she only wanted his skin against hers but soon she was kissing him, she was kissing him. His tongue was slow and shy and she was absurdly wet but it was a long time before his cock was inside her, before he entered her. And when he did, he just held her. His face was pressed to her throat and she wondered if he could even breathe, his arms were heavy around her and he didn't rock or pound or thrust at her. They barely moved at all and after what seemed like an hour she began to rise and fall against him and over his shoulder she again saw the face of a fat pink gargoyle peeking at her through blackened window but that was impossible and she closed her eyes as Phineas said her name once or twice in a sweet faraway disbelieving voice and now he seemed to get bigger inside her and she began to shake and come apart and vaguely hating herself she kissed his ear and said please, don't come inside me.

Dear Jude.

The truth is that I don't know what I'm doing.

It might look like I'm trying to save somebody from something but I'm not. How can you save anybody when everything is reflex, everything is a muscular spasm. I saw a movie once where two guys are standing at the end of a tunnel, two guys named Frank and Joe. Frank is very cool, he's James Bond with long hair. He gets all the women and he can disarm a bomb while hanging upside down. He quotes poetry ever so casual. Frank is a gourmet cook, in fact. And Joe is a fuck-up. Every friendship has one. Joe is Barney Fife on speed. He shuts his hand in the car door and ejaculates prematurely and prefers cheap American beer. Meanwhile. There's a bad guy with a gun at the other end of the tunnel and I don't remember why he wants to kill Frank and Joe but that's not the point. At the precise moment that the bad guy pulls the trigger, Joe flinches. He lunges sideways, he throws himself between Frank and the gun and takes one in the shoulder. Frank is amazed. The audience is amazed. Because Joe was trying to save his life or something. But upon closer examination, the bullet was a ricochet and if Joe had never moved, the bullet would have missed them both. Joe couldn't deny it and he didn't want to. He wasn't thinking about Frank, he wasn't thinking anything at all. He just jumped. And that's what I'm talking about.

Now I stole my first sour breath. Eve beside me, soft naked thin with a surreal childish glow to her cheeks but then she was just twenty, still a girl. I had a feeling she would laugh at me if I let myself feel bad about fucking her. She would laugh and laugh. My eyes were not yet open. Yesterday I had felt like her brother, her big clumsy brother. But what had I really wanted.

I had wanted to adore her, to protect her.

Which was funny, wasn't it. I was so poisoned by Hollywood. I would open my eyes, soon.

Saturday.

Thank God. Friday had been too fucking long by far. When I opened my eyes there would be daylight, deadlight. Eve smelled good, she smelled like fire and spilled ink and bright cold glass and she was all angles beside me, she was bent knees and sweet sharp elbows and collarbones I could drink from and I need to get hold of myself.

Eyes still closed and I let my fingers flutter up one of her thighs.

I would open my eyes and the morning light would be thick and colorless, there would be no discernible shadows and I would blink and rub my sore blue mouth and look around for reckoning and resolution but resolution was a daydream, a phantom construct. My fingers now fell upon her hipbone and drifted down the hollow slope between her belly and pubic hair and for the first time I wondered what time it was and part of me wanted to slip out of bed and disappear but I remembered what she had said in the dark, her breath cold and urgent as she said please, don't come inside me and I had tried not to, I had come everywhere else, on belly sheets and hair and part of me wanted to wake her now and make slow hungover love to her by daylight and without hesitation, I wanted to eat her alive but my teeth were sore from grinding and this was it. I was taking control.

There would be no one else's point of view, no one else's voice. I was going to end this and I couldn't deal with the drift anymore. I could no longer filter the thoughts of other characters. The sinister bend, the false angles of a body held underwater. The secrets. I never said I wanted to be a filter and I was pretty sure I was not good at it. I dragged my hand away from Eve's sleeping body and sat up, I opened my eyes. It was late morning and everything was faintly, unpleasantly yellow.

Okay.

I felt sick. This was a lot like a hangover but not. There was something wrong with my bones and my stomach felt inside out. I had what felt like a mouthful of rust, of bloodorange metal flakes. There was a small bathroom five, maybe ten feet away and I pushed myself away from the bed with relative arrogance then crawled the last few feet to the toilet, where I vomited quietly, painlessly. The contents of my belly were clear, gelatinous, nonthreatening. It was a pure morning. I sat cross-legged on a fuzzy white bathmat and regarded my bruised genitals from what felt like a terrifying distance.

Nausea.

I had a fantastic erection but now I doubted that Eve wanted to be molested this morning by me or anyone else and anyway my skin felt weirdly rigid, my body was fragile and unfamiliar and it would probably take forever to successfully masturbate and what I really wanted was to gather my clothes and go downstairs, I wanted to smell the air and figure out where the fuck I was.

Griffin was right. I had an uncanny craving for a shot of the Pale.

Muscles. It was a good thing they operated on their own, most of the time. I reclaimed my clothes and managed to dress myself without too much horror or difficulty. I kissed Eve on the lips and wondered briefly if either of us had tried to take the other's tongue last night and was happy to realize this was irrelevant.

Downstairs.

I was amazed to find cigarettes in one pocket, unsmashed. The night came back to me in funky disconnected flashes and it seemed I had been pretty high and still there was no lost time that I was aware of. False memory was possible but I didn't detect the lingering scent of overripe oranges, I didn't feel the reverse tug in my arms and legs that signified the artificial.

This was Dizzy Bloom's house, I knew that.

Dizzy was twenty-two or maybe twenty-nine, she was dark and small and pretty and possibly fictional but I believed she was real and I found her in the kitchen. It was bright and hot and Dizzy was on her hands and knees, she was scrubbing the floor in a wrinkled white dress, her nipples protruding through the material like little brown beans and I felt a sudden headache that seemed to originate in my mouth at the sight of her but then she seemed to be one of those women who was really not trying to fuck with your mind by not wearing a bra but simply wanted to be comfortable. I hung in the doorway for a moment, watching her. My jaw hurt and I suspected this was more a consequence of worry and stress than of drugs and the fragmentation of my senses.

Hello, I said.

Dizzy Bloom looked up and suddenly I knew why she had reached for my copy of *Ulysses* with such sadness last night. Today she was sober and damp with sweat and red-faced. She was irritated and a little fearful of the unknown but I clearly saw Molly Bloom in her. Dizzy was skinny but she had a dislocated heaviness about her, there was a fat unshaven woman in her who wanted to lounge too long in bed eating sweets, who had not yet found the love she wanted.

Hello, she said. Did you sleep well?

Too well.

I was fucking thirsty, I was made of sand. It was on the tip of my tongue to ask if there was any of the Pale but I squashed this question like an ugly green bug. Then shrugged.

Is there any of the Pale?

Dizzy gave me a certain look. The look of one addict who knows another and I tried to smile. I tried to show her all my teeth because while I instinctively wanted her to like me and trust me, I didn't much give a fuck. This wasn't a narcotics anonymous meeting.

Yes, she said. In the freezer.

I walked to the fridge and slung open the freezer door. One unmarked bottle of honey-white liquid, thick but not frozen. I looked at it but did not drink.

Okay, I said. Do you want to talk about what happened last night?

Not yet, she said.

I chomped at my tongue. I wanted to smoke five cigarettes at once.

Are you hungry? she said.

I stared at her, at her dark lips and mild, forgiving eyes. She still held a yellow sponge in one hand. The floor was glowing wet, rubbed to a spotless black and white. Her hands, though. Her hands were stained red from squeezing blood out of the sponge. My stomach twitched and I looked around at her kitchen. Two windows. A fish-bowl with no fish and a lot of cookbooks. There were no modern appliances but there was a fond array of expensive knives and fine pots and pans that gleamed like silver. Dizzy Bloom was apparently childless and unmarried, a Breather who had somehow shorn herself of any real identity. I gazed at her now, my brain sore and dull. She probably had a trust fund and a degree from a posh university and was no doubt much smarter than me.

Who are you? I said.

Dizzy Bloom, she said. We met last night.

I know. But who are you?

What an archaic question.

No, I said. I'm not hungry.

Well, she said. There's a naked man on the roof.

A what?

The man who left his clothes in my living room, she said. Jimmy Sky.

Oh, I said. Oh, fuck.

I glanced down at myself, at my rumpled Ray Fine clothes. I hoped Jimmy would recognize me. I hoped someone would. Dizzy Bloom dipped her yellow sponge into a bucket of soapy water, she crushed it in her fist and resumed scrubbing the floor. I watched her and tried to think.

Well.

I had found Jimmy Sky without really trying and maybe the two of us should have a nice talk. I listened for Dizzy to murmur or sigh as I took the half-empty bottle of the Pale from the freezer. But she was silent, preoccupied with vanishing bloodstains. The cold bottle bit at my hands and I left the kitchen, intending to go outside. But instead veered down the hall, instinctively seeking a bathroom. I had been too busy throwing up earlier to give my psyche a proper shakedown. Now I locked the door behind me and peed, then turned to the mirror and stared. I didn't look much like myself and there was nothing I could do about Ray Fine's goofy clothes so I opened the medicine cabinet and saw that Dizzy had quite a few problems. She had a borderline personality, she had sleeplessness, she had seizures and a fuck of a lot of stress. She had bad dreams and psychotic episodes and while this was all very interesting I couldn't give it a lot of thought and for once I didn't want to drug myself. I wanted something more immediate and a pair of scissors jumped out at me. I breathed and thought about it and yes, I needed a haircut. I took one small sip of the Pale and stared cutting. The hair fell like dead leaves, random. I grabbed chunks of hair and cut them away without thinking of symmetry or logic, I slashed at my hair until the shape of my head pleased me and now I felt like myself.

I took the Pale and went outside. It was a nice day, sort of. It had the atmospheric freak show of seasons changing too close to the mountains. Green leaves winking back at me. Premature rosebuds and the possibility of a late snow made the sky appear farther away, a thin hostile blue. I walked backward over wet slick grass and scanned the roof and there, hunched next to a little brick chimney, was Detective

Moon or Jimmy Sky, pink and shivering. Facing the sun with eyes closed.

I lifted the bottle of the Pale to my lips and drank but didn't swallow. I rinsed my mouth and spat into the grass, trying to decide how best to climb onto the roof. The one tree that stood alongside the house had long frail branches that extended to touch the rain gutters but that tree looked pretty dead. That tree was dead, boy. There were holes drilled into the bark where someone had poisoned it, probably because its roots were fucking with the foundation of the house. Those upper branches would hardly support a child. I was inclined to holler at Moon and ask how exactly he had gotten up there or even chuck a rock at him and bring him tumbling down but I doubted that I would be able to put him back together again if he shattered into a thousand bits of Moon. Again, I rinsed my mouth with the Pale, allowing myself to swallow a few drops. I stared up at Moon, who had begun to rock back and forth like an autistic kid.

Poor fucker needed help.

I walked around to the side of the house, looking for a ladder or some of that handy white scaffolding that young lovers always use to sneak in and out of bedrooms in the movies. I moved to the back of the house and saw an upstairs window that seemed to open onto a sloping lip of the roof and now I remembered Eve saying something as she was falling asleep about a strange gargoyle at our window.

Quickly back inside.

I stopped in the front room to grab Moon's crumpled pants and jacket. Took the cell phone from one pocket and patted down the others. Found a butterfly knife but nothing else: no wallet, no keys, no gun. I hoped Moon was not armed and told myself that naked guys are almost never armed because they have no pockets. But then again, I hadn't seen Moon's gun lying around anywhere, had I?

Nothing I could do about it anyway. I slung Moon's pants over one shoulder like a scarf.

Eve was no longer in bed and I wondered if she was okay. If she had doubts about me. If she was standing now under the hot blast of a shower, scrubbing the stink of Phineas from her skin. I couldn't worry about it. The window wouldn't open so I calmly put my heel through it and tapped the remaining bits of glass from the frame, then stuck my head out and looked around.

The roof was steep with slick, balding shingles and I bent to unlace my boots. I slipped out of my socks and briefly considered stripping off all my clothes as Moon might feel more comfortable if we were both naked, but decided against it. I tucked the bottle of the Pale into my pants before climbing onto the roof. My bare toes gripped the rough surface and I leaned sideways, scrambled to the peak and over. I angled up to Moon slow and very joe casual, as if I had just happened along this way and maybe we could wait for the bus together. I pulled the bottle from my crotch and sat down beside the naked man without a word. We shared a moment of silence. Dizzy Bloom had a pretty nice view and I felt like I could see three sides of Denver.

I removed the pants from around my neck, dropped them in Moon's lap.

Moon glanced sideways. Get away from me, Poe.

Put them on, I said. You will feel better with pants on.

Bright cold air. The tops of trees against blue. The side of Moon's unsmiling face.

What did you do with that kid's body? he said.

Nothing. I just relocated it.

Why?

Why not?

He was killing cops, said Moon.

I shrugged the artificial cool. Part of the game, wasn't it.

He worked in a video store, said Moon. I knew him. I knew him. I probably had fifty conversations with him. The kid knew a lot about movies.

Moon made no movement to put his pants on but he did straighten his legs briefly as he scratched an itch and I saw the barrel of his big .45 clutched between his thighs.

Hey, I said. You want to give me the gun?

The coo of stupid pigeons.

No, said Moon.

Who am I speaking to, by the way?

Moon hesitated, smiled. It was a wide, shit-eating smile that I didn't recognize or like.

Jimmy? I said.

Moon shrugged. Yeah. We're both here, I guess.

I found you.

I didn't want to be found.

It wasn't hard, I said. Half the city can see your white ass.

What were you going to do when you found Jimmy Sky?

I don't know. I thought you wanted me to kill him.

Yeah.

Long cold breath and my lungs hurt. My ass was going to sleep and I really didn't want to wrestle Moon for the gun, not on this roof. I took a small sip of the Pale and offered it to Moon, who took it and held it up against the sky. He gazed at the liquid behind glass for a few heartbeats and I relaxed, reached for a cigarette, thinking: if Jimmy was high, he might be easier to deal with. But Moon upended the bottle and poured it out and I saw that his doglike brown eyes had become black in the last of the winter sun. The Pale was so thick it seemed to bead up and dart down the roof like a pack of silverfish.

Fuck, I said.

You're better off, said Moon.

For a moment, I saw myself scrambling down to the roof's edge. I saw myself trying to scoop up the disappearing Pale with my bare hands and I blinked as Moon smiled and swung the bottle at me in a slow flashing arc and I just managed to jerk my head down like a turtle and the bottle glanced off the top of my head and shattered against the chimney with a sudden white sparkle of raining glass and my eyes flickered shut again, involuntarily. I opened them and now had a good close look at Moon's big gun.

What are you doing, Moon? What are you doing? I said.

There was glass in my hair, down my shirt.

Moon sighed. I've been watching the birds. It's what rooftops are for, right. And these birds, they're just shitty brown city birds, sparrows or starlings or who the fuck knows and I keep hearing these doves but I can't see them. Anyway, I love the way these brown birds seem to vibrate, like their hearts are beating so hard and fast they might explode. And they don't even know it. They don't realize, they have no concept of self-destruction.

I nodded because I wanted to be friendly. I didn't much want to hear a schizophrenic birdman rant on the subject of what separates us from the beasts but Moon had the terrible glow in his eyes that said there was no stopping him.

The coolest thing, said Moon. The coolest thing is flight of course. To fly, right. Everyone wants to fly and I'm not going to jump if that's what you're thinking. I don't want two shattered legs, okay. I want to sleep. If anything, I want to sleep alone. But it's the way they float, they ride the currents. The thermals. They catch an updraft of warm air and just coast up to the sky and it's so effortless it's like they coexist with the fucking air. Can you imagine?

Meaning what? I said. That you want to coexist with yourself?

Moon swore softly and adjusted his crotch and I wished he would put his pants on. It would make this whole scene a little easier to take, I was sure.

I tried that, said Moon. I tried and tried.

Listen, I said. Let's go. Let's get off this roof, okay. Have some breakfast. Let's get out the yellow pages and find someone you can talk to, a private shrink or someone. Someone you can trust.

Is there some reason I shouldn't trust you?

No. I didn't say that.

Whatever. Do you like birds?

Whatever, I said. You know, I met someone yesterday who just about bit my head off for saying that word to him. Your partner, Lot McDaniel.

Moon clenched his fists. My partner.

Yeah. A dapper English guy.

You don't have a clue, do you.

What?

That fucker is running the game. He's the man behind the curtain.

Really. I swiped at my forehead, amazed that I was sweating in the cold.

Yeah, really. His name is Theseus the Glove.

I did think he was a trifle strange.

I've been meaning to kill him, said Moon. Or at least scare him. But he's evasive. He's smarter than me, he's smarter than Jimmy and what can I do. I'm just a Fred.

Let's go talk to him, I said. Fix his wagon.

Fuck you. You just want me down off this roof.

I shrugged.

And why? Why do you want me down and don't say it's because you care about me.

I worked my jaw, took a long look at the trees and sky. Okay, I said.

Thank you, said Moon. Because we both know it's bullshit. No one saves anyone else because they care so much. It's all about avoiding a mess.

Yes, I said. Your dead fat naked body would be a big mess in Dizzy's yard and I already dumped one body behind the Burger King so I can't go back there.

Dizzy, said Moon dreamily. He sighed. She's a peach, isn't she? She inspired me to buy a book, if you can believe that. A fat book with no guns or horses and so far I have only read a few pages. It's not something you can skate through while sitting on the toilet. I mean, it's not exactly a western even though Buck Mulligan sounds like the name of a deputy marshall.

Ulysses, I said.

You know it?

Vaguely.

Her great-grandmother is the main character, or something.

Not exactly, I said. But she does have a sexy monologue in the end.

Moon nodded. I met Dizzy Bloom yesterday and she looked right through me. She's a real honey.

A honey, I said. And she's in the kitchen right now, she's cleaning up blood.

I saw her last night, said Moon. She didn't recognize me and besides, she seemed pretty sweet on that little elfboy, that Breather.

Let's go inside, I said. Inside, okay.

Hey, fuck you. I saw you last night, said Moon. You were slipping it to that other little chick, that torturer. Did you tell her your real name?

I nodded. That was Eve, I said. She knows me.

Remember when you were a kid, said Moon. You always wished you were someone else: Tom Sawyer or Billy the Kid or Pistol Pete Maravich or even some cooler smarter faster kid you knew in school.

Yeah. I wanted to be Han Solo.

It's fun to be someone else, said Moon. Until you can't stop being them.

I held my breath and released it slowly through my teeth and I don't know. I think what I felt was sympathy. It was all I had.

I know, I said. Everything gets fucked up in the end.

Fucked up. Moon laughed.

Uh-huh. Why don't you give me the gun?

Moon shook his head. Get off this roof, Poe. Unless you want to get shot.

Nobody broke your heart, I said.

He smiled. I know. I broke it myself so why don't you fuck off. Disappear.

What are you going to do?

I don't know. I'm gonna have a little heart to heart with myself, I guess.

Moon or Jimmy laughed and rolled his eyes, rubbing his belly with the free hand. I felt like my eyeballs were sweating. I was staring at Moon's unsteady trigger finger. His whole hand seemed to be vibrating and the gun was going to go off, soon. I backed away as carefully as I had come.

Okay, I said. Do you mind if I call for an ambulance?

Moon shrugged. Go ahead.

I continued to edge backward, dropping to my belly now.

Do me a favor, I said.

What's that, said Moon.

Put your pants on, please.

Moon grinned and fired a single shot into the air. I bit the side of my cheek and tasted blood. If one of the neighbors hadn't called the cops already, they would surely do so now. I slithered wormlike down the other side of the roof and back through the window. Breathing, I counted to ten. I sat on the edge of Dizzy Bloom's big cozy guest bed and put my boots back on. I sniffed the air. It did smell like Eve had taken a shower. Her clothes were gone and the bed was made. I couldn't remember if it had still been disheveled before I went out to talk to the mad birdman and I just wished she was near me. Really the worst thing about being alone was that there was never anyone to turn to and say: hey that was fucking weird, wasn't it? I took out Moon's cell phone and turned it on.

Wonders never ceased for the battery still held a charge.

I found the cream-colored and very nicely engraved business card that McDaniel had given me the day before. The snotty bastard answered on the tenth ring, his voice dry and very British.

Cough. McDaniel.

Hello, sir. Detective McDaniel?

Yes.

This is Ray Fine. We met yesterday.

Forced warmth. I remember.

You said for me to call you tomorrow and here it is, tomorrow.

Pause. Crackle and hum.

Indeed, it does look like tomorrow. What can I do for you Mr. Fine?

I have some information for you about Moon, or about who might have killed him. I guess there's a nut running around out there killing cops.

Oh, well. Yawn. Anything you can tell me would help.

The killer's name is Theseus, I said. I don't know if that's his first name or last name or what but I figure he's a Greek guy. Doesn't that sound Greek to you?

I suppose so, said McDaniel.

Is there a Greek Mafia in this town, that you know of?

No, he said.

His voice was getting pretty frosty and I smiled.

Whatever, I said. He's definitely your guy.

Hmmm. Where did you come by this information?

Very reliable source. A fellow named Jimmy Sky.

McDaniel snorted. Jimmy Sky, did you say?

That's right.

And where is this person? I might like to ask him a few questions.

He's outside. Having a smoke.

Do you think you could entice him to come downtown?

Maybe. Will you buy us breakfast?

But of course.

You might regret that, I said. I can eat a stack of pancakes the size of your head.

I'm sure you can.

Do you have an expense account?

No, I don't.

Are you dirty? I said. Because dirty cops on TV always get free breakfast.

Mr. Fine, please. Let me give you an address. Do you have something to write on?

I have the back of my hand, I said.

And I managed not to flinch when McDaniel gave me the address. I didn't have to write it down. I knew it already. Griffin's office.

Have you got that, then?

Perfectly, I said.

Very good. I shall see you in oh, a half-hour or so.

Cheerio.

McDaniel grunted and hung up. I exhaled. There was something wrong with me and I couldn't seem to stop smiling. Maybe the universe was okay. I hesitated, then reluctantly dialed 911. Again, I identified myself as Ray Fine. I told the female operator that I had a friend on the roof suffering a psychotic episode. Dangerous to himself and others. The operator said not to worry, they had already received three reports of a naked sniper and the cops were on their way. I choked back an obscenity and told her calmly that he was no sniper. I told her the cops would only spook him and asked her to send an ambulance, a fire truck.

I knew they would send a carload of cops, no matter what I said.

But I told the operator five times that the subject was a cop, that he was armed and he would very likely resist. I suggested that they bring a net, maybe a tranquilizer gun. The operator told me not to worry and I said I would give it a try. I hung up and glanced at the clock by the bed. The average response time was nine minutes but it was early. It was Saturday morning. I would give them six and I hoped to god I was gone before they showed.

Moon, I said. I'm sorry about this.

Downstairs and I barely recognized anyone. It was like the mothership had touched down in my absence and reclaimed the pods. Dizzy

Bloom had tangled her hair into a complicated bun. Her face was different, too. Dark lipstick and round little steel-framed glasses. They were much nicer than Ray's glasses. She wore jeans and a black cardigan sweater and she was reading a newspaper, a cup of tea or coffee in her left hand. The swirl of steam around her face. There was a plate of bagels on the table and now she put down her coffee and reached for the cream cheese. A young man with a very serious posture sat across from her, smoking an unfiltered cigarette and staring intently at the screen of a laptop computer. Thin blond hair pulled into a severe ponytail and no jewelry. Expensive white dress shirt with cuffs buttoned, dark green twill pants and black shoes. If I was not mistaken, this was Mingus. His eyes were bright and not the least bit psychotic as he smiled and held out his hand.

Hello, said Mingus. I don't think we've met. I'm Matthew Roar.

Okay, I said. I'm Phineas.

We shook hands and I looked as far as I could into the man's face, his mouth and eyes. There was no hint that this was part of the game.

And you know my wife, I believe. Dizzy Bloom, he said.

You two are married, I said.

Dizzy smiled, a cruel flash. I kept my maiden name, she said.

Uh-huh.

I looked sideways and saw Eve. And I knew her, I recognized her. I had seen her in multiple incarnations and this was but another one. She wore black boots and white stockings and a silky black skirt with a thin blue sweater that she must have borrowed from Dizzy because the skirt was sexy but much too collegiate and the sweater was a little too small. There was a white line of flesh at her hips between sweater and skirt and the sleeves were too short. Her hair was tucked behind her ears and she held a coffee mug in both hands. She was blowing on it with pale puckered lips, staring at me.

You look nice, I said.

She flinched. Thanks.

I went to the stove and poured myself a cup of coffee that was hot and black as death and smelled of cinnamon and chicory. I sipped it carefully as Dizzy picked up a pencil and began to examine the crossword. Matthew was bent over his laptop, which now made a happy chirping sound to indicate that he had mail. I nodded. Dizzy and Matthew were not fucking kidding about this game of tongues. Their characters were so divorced from their real identities that they were probably going slowly but surely clinical. But I had a feeling they knew it was over. They must. Their friend had died in their kitchen last night and they were calmly eating bagels and cream cheese and they were probably sorry they had no smoked salmon to offer us but their worlds were going to crash soon. The cops were coming and I was tempted not to warn them. Eve came over to stand next to me.

Do you have a cigarette, she said.

I gave her one. I want you to come downtown with me, I said.

Okay. Why?

I have an errand to run. And I don't think you want to be here.

She lit her cigarette at the stove, careful not to set her hair on fire.

Why? she said.

Because the cops are coming.

Dizzy Bloom looked up. Do you know a six-letter word for "dark"?

Opaque, I said.

Thank you.

Did you hear me?

What? she said.

The cops are on the way. Two minutes, maybe three and they're in your living room.

What do they want?

I shrugged. Madman on your roof.

Dizzy smiled and nodded. Of course.

I felt hot, irritable. I poured the rest of my coffee down the sink and yes, I wished there was more of the Pale. The others were so fucking unflustered, like robots. Something was very wrong with them. They were all supposed to be junkies, right. Confused. Out of touch with reality. I looked at them and thought maybe they weren't real, maybe they were only pretending to be normal people for my benefit. I wiped at my face and told myself I had one minute left.

Eve and I are going, I said.

Will you be back for lunch?

No. I don't think so.

Matthew looked up and there was a trace of something like sadness around his mouth. I hesitated. The sun was coming through the windows and I could hear sirens in the distance and I realized I was going to miss the little Breather. I bit at my tongue and wondered when Chrome would walk in wearing a T-shirt and sweatpants, hungover and slack-jawed with ordinary life and carrying a basketball under one arm.

Do you want to shoot some hoops, he would say.

Dear Jude.

I have no soul inside, only gray matter.

I think *Ulysses* is finally getting to me. I jumped ahead to the end, to Molly Bloom's melancholy monologue and after two pages of somber cocksucking and the philosophy behind the mixing of urine and menstrual blood, I was freaking out. The physical details are heavy of course but pretty casual by modern standards. The consumptive nature of her voice, though. It's like cancer. Her voice is relentless and unwavering as a slow-burning fire. I can't read that shit anymore. Okay. I understand that Joyce was trying to re-create the random sound and fury of a human mind at work but I'm not sure why he would want to.

Painful and blinding. Trapped in the wheels of another's thoughts.

And moreover I'm not sure why Dizzy would choose such a tragic character to be her number one ancestor. Molly Bloom suffers a lot of weird and profound indignities as the object of her husband's whim. Leopold asks her to walk barefoot in horseshit as a kind of demented foreplay and when she is fat with milk he begs her to let him squeeze a few drops into his tea. And he torments her in the end with the seemingly innocent request for breakfast in bed which now strikes me as a truly frightening though nonaggresive act of marital sadism and I wonder if Dizzy truly hates Matthew Roar for being weak and vir-tuous and kind to her and maybe she wishes for a physically grotesque man like Leopold Bloom. If she wishes for someone like Moon, like Jimmy Sky.

A horse named Throwaway, I said. Throwaway.

Are you okay, said Eve.

No.

The belly wail of sirens were close and getting closer and they might as well have been inside my head. I grabbed Eve by her small hand and squeezed it, the bones moving beneath her skin fragile and rub-bery like the ribs of a bird and I only hoped she wanted to come with me. That she wouldn't resist or pull away because I needed her and was not sure how or why, but I did. It wasn't that I was particularly afraid but I had no plan, no idea what I would say to McDaniel. Maybe she could help me there. She apparently had some higher knowledge of torture and not to change the subject but part of me was happy, I was happy that Goo had not slept with Ray Fine, for instance. Although that might have been the least frightening and strange of all the possible combinations.

Outside and I pulled her across the backyard. Jimmy might have become sweaty and agitated by the sound of the sirens and I imagined he was up there flapping his naked arms like an angry crow and I didn't want him taking any potshots at us. One of the more annoying voices in my skull proclaimed that we should stick around and see him through this but I disagreed. Because you can only save yourself, right.

Yourself.

Running. Wet grass.

I told myself not to crush Eve's fingers because she wasn't resisting, she was light as a shadowpuppet and she followed me without a word through the back gate and across a curve of gravel and suddenly I knew that I wanted to have another look at Chrome's body because after that little scene in Dizzy's kitchen it seemed more and more likely that his death was just a crooked line in the script, a typographical error.

He's dead, said Eve. Her voice was sharp.

What?

Christian, she said. You're wondering if he's really dead.

Come on, I said.

I pulled her across the vacant lot, ignoring the little path. I was pretty sure by now that he would be reclining beside one of those blue Dumpsters, that he would be a blood-stained but unusually handsome homeless man. He would be scratching his jaw and dazedly contemplating his ruined clothes and wondering what exactly he had been up to last night. I pulled her across the parking lot, slower now.

The only footsteps were our own.

The parking lot stretched before us like the sky and suddenly we were upon him. His body was where we had left it, stiff and gathering flies.

Eve sucked in her breath.

I didn't need that, she said.

Oh, fuck.

Yeah.

It was a stupid idea, of course. I had carried him here just a few hours earlier and he had been cold and dead in my arms, he could have been a posterboy for death but dream and game and daylight had seemed so readily interchangeable that anything should have been possible. Eve backed away, one hand over her nose.

He stinks, she said.

That's the garbage, I said.

But that was a fucking lie and why did I want to lie to her.

Yeah, I said. He stinks.

Eve wrinkled her nose and I saw how pretty and young she was without Goo's face tangled up around her own. It would be inappropriate to kiss her now, standing over her dead boyfriend's body like this. The air ripe with his gasses. But I wanted to kiss her.

Let's move him into the Dumpster, she said.

Why? I said.

The cops will want to ask me a lot of questions. Won't they?

Probably. You're the girlfriend.

If we move him, maybe they won't find him today.

I stood there nodding like a dummy and it wasn't that I disagreed with her. Eve was right, of course. I had no idea why I had left him exposed like this. He should be moved and there wasn't a lot of time to stand around talking about it but I wasn't sure I wanted to touch him again.

He had such a pretty face, pale and puffy even as it was in death.

I made sure the Dumpster was not padlocked and threw open its jaws with a screech of metal that would send the rats running for shelter. I hoped that a pimply kid in Burger King brown wasn't on his way out with an armload of rotten buns and meat even though I could probably use his help.

The dead are heavy, after all.

I lit a cigarette and took two quick puffs, then gave it to Eve. I stepped over the body and without pausing to let myself freak out or feel sorry for him, bent down and sunk my hands into the soft fleshy pockets of his armpits. I dragged him up to a rubbery standing position and danced him over to the blue Dumpster and his knees dipped and buckled comically as I slipped one hand between his legs and got a firm grip on his crotch. I lifted and tried to throw him over the side of the Dumpster but I was too short or he was too heavy or something because he tumbled down on top of me and favored me with a damp, gruesome embrace.

Eve didn't laugh and for that I thought she was pretty cool.

Help me, I said.

And she didn't balk or hesitate at all. Eve locked her teeth together and held her breath as she lifted one end of the body. She was grim and almost smiling as she held him by the feet and I wondered how many times she had watched him tie the laces of those boots. Together we managed to sling him up and over and into the Dumpster and two minutes later while she crouched in the shadows wondering if she was going to vomit, I climbed in and covered her boyfriend's body with trash.

But first I patted him down for cigarettes, money, weapons.

Eve finished retching, or gave up trying. Now she walked quickly away from me, across the parking lot. I climbed out of the Dumpster feeling about as clever as a drunk raccoon. The stink of French fries in my clothes and hair. I followed her, glad to see she was not walking back to Dizzy's house.

Jimmy was on the roof, naked and angry.

I hoped the paramedics would be able to talk him down. I hoped we wouldn't hear screams or gunfire. I hoped we wouldn't hear the deadening silence that meant he had fallen. I followed Eve to a little plastic igloo that housed a pale green bench with the names of a hundred assholes gouged in the wood. I sat two or three feet away from her. I hoped there was a bus coming.

Do you want to talk about it? I said.

About what, she said. About Christian being dead, or last night?

I shoved my hands in my pockets to stop myself from scratching at my skin.

Either, I said.

No. I don't know.

Across the street a young man with a bullet-shaped head leaned out of a window and yelled at a barking dog. I looked up and down the street for something to focus on, something to talk about that wasn't dripping with realism.

Eve was an arm's length away, her hands restless on her knees. Her face pale and sober. She tugged at the hem of her borrowed skirt, as if it wasn't quite comfortable. I wanted to comfort her but I was too clumsy. And I felt like I was fading, I was blurry and unreliable. I was suffering a transporter malfunction, a pixel error. Every inch of my skin was shimmering. I wanted to take off my shirt and ask her to scratch a maddening itch down the middle of my back but I told myself the itch was not real.

The itch was not real.

I'm sure he deserved it, she said. And I didn't love him, if that's what you think.

Empty hands.

No, I said. I don't think that. But what's the difference?

I liked having sex with him, she said. Or my character did. But I think that when someone you love dies, you should feel something unbearable. You should feel crushed and lost and you shouldn't be able to breathe.

The bullet-shaped head came through the window and yelled at the barking dog to shut the fuck up.

And how do you feel, I said.

I need a bath, she said. And I think I have food poisoning.

That's bad enough.

I can breathe, she said. How do you feel?

Unpleasantly awake. Frustrated, empty. I want to get high.

You were a cop, she said.

Not a very good one, I said. And it was a long time ago. It was an alternate universe.

That Fred, she said. He said Christian was killing cops.

I stared at her. And?

Isn't that supposed to make you insane?

I shrugged. This isn't television, right. No one likes their coworkers to get killed and obviously it's scary when someone shoots a cop because it means they are much crazier than the average crazy person but I never swallowed that Hollywood notion that a cop's life is worth more to me than a bike messenger's or a drug dealer's or a homosexual dogwalker's. A lot of cops are bitter assholes and they can't wait to fuck you, to rob you blind and shit on you. And so are a lot of bike messengers. I don't know any dog walkers but they can't all be nice people. Meanwhile a lot of drug dealers are just guys who like cartoons and fast food and they have kids and dogs and student loans and they're basically harmless so the answer must be no, I don't particularly give a fuck.

No, I said. I don't give a fuck.

And what about last night? she said.

A bird flashed across the horizon of my brain, a speckled brown blur of words too raw and strange to be spoken aloud.

It was fantastic, I said. It scared the shit out of me.

I don't think it was real, she said.

Eve was chewing at her lip and the muscles in her throat were killing me. Her nipples were visibly hard and her thighs were long and slim and perfect in those white stockings. I felt like Humbert. I rubbed at my eyes, disgusted. I leaned close enough to kiss her but she turned and my lips brushed her cheek like a brother's. I am a suicidal romantic, or I was at that moment. I wanted to tell her it's never real.

Doubt, I said. It's everywhere, it's all around us. You can't see it or smell it but it's there.

Yeah, she said sourly. Like oxygen.

Do you want to try again? I said.

Eve's mouth was crooked and sweet, her eyes cloudy. She didn't have to say anything. I knew the answer was yes, she wanted to. But we wouldn't.

Here comes a bus, she said.

Yeah. Where's it going, though?

Dead cops meant nothing to me. I didn't know them and so they were just names, faces. They were characters in a movie that I wasn't watching. I was eleven years old when *Star Wars* came out and I have rarely been more shocked and heartbroken than when Obi-Wan Kenobi was killed but I had the distinct feeling that she wanted to get off the subject so I stood up as the big silver bus approached, rattling and heaving. The brakes moaned with the familiar whispering metallic sigh that echoed too long and always made me think there were people being tortured in the bowels of the thing. It was going downtown, at least. I wondered if I would see that blind guy again, the one that was tormented by his tongue. I fucking hoped not, because he did seem like the sort who rode the bus for days and days without stopping, from one end of the line to another. Eve took my hand and climbed aboard first, then turned to look at me with eyes wrinkled and amused.

No money, she said.

Oh. I forgot about money.

I dug around in Ray Fine's pockets and came up with a sticky wad of bills. The driver extracted two singles and gravely told me to take a seat. The bus was mostly empty and we found seats near the middle, near the center of gravity. I wanted to tell Eve that I have black-and-white nightmares about buses and I think they have something to do with the movie *Metropolis*. I have this recurring vision that I will wake up one day to find myself standing in a long line of black-faced men and women in dark, conservative clothes waiting to board an unmarked bus that will take us to hell and when I first pass the driver he seems normal enough but when he turns around his face is a skull with patches of raw skin and empty holes where the eyes should be and when the doors hiss shut I know they will never open again, not until we arrive in the first ring of hell.

I sat beside Eve, our legs touching. I liked the way she pressed her knees together, the way she picked restlessly at the thin stockings she wore under her borrowed skirt. I didn't know what to do with my hands, either. I wanted a cigarette, of course. Eve took my right hand and held it in her lap, she trapped it there like a nervous kitten and I laughed.

You're manic, she said.

The shakes, I said. But no worries.

Yeah.

Eve shrugged and turned to look out the window. I nodded, admiring the harsh line of her jaw. The uneven color of her cheeks. I met her a little over a year ago, when she was nineteen, when she was so unpleasantly sexy it left me stupid and weak.

If you saw her in a grocery store, stalking through the dairy section in jeans and army boots and a T-shirt that said she was tough and fragile and fully capable of fucking you to tears, you would sigh and clutch your belly as if kicked and duck down the frozen foods aisle. Because you would want to follow her, you would want to see what she was buying and you would want to get another good look at her in the odd shadowless supermarket light but you really couldn't stand it and instead you would buy ice cream that you didn't need. Eve was a year older now and she didn't quite paralyze me. Don't get me wrong. My jaw ached a little yet, looking at her. But I was a year older, too. I was relatively unchanged. I was a year closer to dying of lung cancer. The bus wheezed to a stop but no one got off. There was a tickle along the back of my neck and I looked up. The driver was peering at someone on the sidewalk.

Well, he said. You getting on or not?

There was no answer and the driver moved to shut the doors.

Hold it, chief.

I recognized that voice and could only stare as Jimmy Sky's round head heaved into view. Moon but not Moon. He stood alongside the driver, swaying slightly as he dug through his pockets and managed to come up with a dollar bill, which he pressed flat against his chest before surrendering. Jimmy was shirtless, barefoot. His belly jutting over the waistband of the white pants.

I glanced at Eve, who didn't blink.

Money, she said. It's something you forget about, in the game.

Yeah, I said. I imagine a lot of things are like that.

Jimmy ambled heavily down the aisle, staggering as the bus lurched forward. He caught hold of a safety bar overhead and hung there a moment, panting. I tried to catch his eye but he stared through me.

Your head is screwed on wrong, said Eve. Everything looks strange. The stuff that seems so important to your other self, your daylight self, is just funny. You wonder how you ever believed in anything. But then your character starts to run wild and you get almost homesick for reality.

Jimmy Sky regained his balance and continued down the aisle. His eyes were calm but his breathing was so loud it seemed deafening to me. Wind through dead trees. Moon might have been a giant talking frog and he would have looked just as strange to me. Now he passed without a flicker.

You feel like you're disappearing, said Eve. Your daylight self is like a little kid who fell down a well. You can hear her voice down there in the dark but it seems faraway and weak and you don't know how to get her out. You want to throw her a rope but you can't be bothered or something.

I glanced over my shoulder to see that Jimmy had found a seat in the very last row. He was wedged between two sinewy black men who wore gang colors and had the feral eyes of dogs that kill their own.

They were somehow unoffended by Jimmy and I shook my head, thinking, but he must smell like death. How can they tolerate him?

Eve poked me. Are you listening, she said.

My thoughts flailed. I am...yes. What is she like? I said.

Who?

Goo, I said.

She's a lot like me, said Eve. Only better. Goo has no morals, no inhibitions. She can step outside herself and use her body like it's a piece of machinery.

How is that better?

Eve shrugged and said, Goo is an Exquisitor.

Which means what, I said. Exactly.

It means that she can extract emotions from people that they don't realize they possess.

Isn't that what happened last night?

Eve frowned. Goo isn't nearly as selfish or paranoid as I am. And she's still here. She's not going to just go to sleep and disappear.

Really, I said. That's...comforting.

Eve breathed into my right ear and I flinched as if bitten.

What about you, she said. Did you have a character in the game?

Oh, yeah. I was a Fred named Ray. For about eight hours, anyway.

What was he like?

Ray? I said. He was a great fucking fool, a fearless idiot. He was a lot like me.

Eve giggled. And what happened to him?

Nothing happened to him. I made fun of his hair and stole his clothes and treated him like dirt and he just fucked off after a while.

I like his clothes, she said.

Aren't these nice?

You should be doing magic tricks for spare change.

I don't know any tricks.

Everybody's dying, she said. Just pick a disease.

I wasn't sure what she meant by that, but I liked the idea. I resisted the urge to glance back at Jimmy. I couldn't protect him and I doubted that he wanted me to. I doubted that he knew my name. I let my eyes flutter shut and soon I disappeared and daydreamed. I tried and failed to synchronize my breathing with the seasick rumble and drone of the bus.

Eve squeezed my thigh. Be careful, she said. You don't want to fall asleep.

Why not?

You might wake up and not know who you are.

Imagine that.

It isn't funny, she said.

Okay. Tell me about Mingus and Dizzy, I said.

What about them?

Are they really married, for instance?

They're separated, said Eve. But that's her real name.

Oh, well. That explains everything.

Today was a big day for them, she said. Those two never step out of character. And why would they want to. Look at them. Mingus and Dizzy are much more fun to be with than Matthew and Dizzy.

This was making my head hurt.

You truly become someone else, she said. You lose your previous self. You amputate it. I know a few gamers who have faked their own deaths and never gone back.

Moon. The poor bastard. I glanced over my shoulder and saw that Jimmy was staring straight ahead, grinning. The two black men had abandoned their seats and now stood in the aisle, their faces watchful and distressed. Jimmy had spooked them, apparently. I turned to Eve.

And then what happens? I said.

Eve shrugged. You live in the game. You gather tongues and drink the Pale. You act out complicated plots scripted by your Glove. You accumulate points.

But what do the points mean? I said. What do you get in the end?

Nothing, really. I suppose you can improve your power and status but the class system within the game is so rigid that mostly you try to stay alive. If your tongue is taken sixteen times, then your character dies. You become a wetbrain, a shadowfred.

A shadowfred?

Eve nodded. A dead character. You're too weak and disoriented to reenter the game and too fucked-up to go back to reality. It's really very sad. The Mariners hunt the wetbrains for sport, even though their tongues are worthless.

Whose tongue is the most valuable?

A Glove's, obviously. But no one would try to take one.

Why not?

Punishment, she said. The punishment would be severe.

The bus shivered but did not stop. I wanted a cigarette. If the bus didn't stop soon I might put my hand through the window.

Of course, I said. How is the game different from life, then?

Eve laughed, uneasily. I held onto her hand.

The city was two-dimensional behind shatterproof glass. It flattened out like stock footage that's been used one too many times. I wanted off the fucking bus. The *Metropolis* dream was twisting around in my little brain and I was having difficulty breathing but eventually we came to a stop downtown that was within walking distance of Griffin's office. It did occur to me that I didn't have to go there at all.

Eve and I could go have breakfast and talk about tomorrow and maybe go over to her apartment and check the walls for unwanted portals. But I had a feeling that it wouldn't matter which direction we took when we stepped from the bus. We could walk north or south and we would still arrive at Griffin's building.

The bus stopped and the doors whooshed open.

This is it, I said. This is our stop.

Eve stood up to go but I just sat there.

Are you sure? she said.

Yeah, I said finally.

I followed her down the aisle and hesitated at the steps. Jimmy would get off with us, surely. But when I looked back, he was reading a newspaper.

Oblivion, I thought. The destruction of self. I imagine it feels good.

Eve and I didn't hold hands on the sidewalk. There was no one about and the air fairly buzzed with silence. It was early, I guess. Or maybe it was just one of those lost Saturdays, one of those blank days where the color of light never changes from morning until dusk. The sky was on hold. Time and weather were nonexistent and it was like half the city was unconscious.

Griffin's building soon loomed against the empty sky and as we approached the dark reflecting glass doors, I wondered what we would do if they were locked. But the doors weren't locked and I stupidly told myself not to be surprised that the lawyers and other pinstripe types who had offices here would be working on the sixth day. How else would they get ahead. I held the door open for Eve and let her go in first, which meant she was between me and McDaniel when he stepped out from behind a big artificial plant with a gun in hand.

Theseus, she said. Her voice brittle.

If it isn't little Goo, he said. I love your disguise.

Her shoulders went stiff. What's that supposed to mean?

Nothing, pet. Nothing at all. I'm sure you have made quite the victim of this one.

Oh, shut the fuck up.

Ouch, he said.

And by the way, she said. My name is Eve and Goo is as good as dead.

McDaniel was glowing, he was so smug. And he looked very elegant in what appeared to be a deerskin suit. I don't know. It could have been human skin. He wore a tiny ruby stud in his left ear and his teeth were obnoxiously crooked and white when he smiled. I looked around for the security guard who had eyeballed me so nastily the other day but the lobby was white and silent as the moon.

McDaniel coughed. I relieved him of duty, he said. Official police business.

Thank God.

He shrugged and pulled a square key on a brass ring from his breast pocket. One eye on us and the gun held high, he inserted the key into a lock on the wall and turned. I could only assume the doors we had just come through were now electronically locked and the alarm system activated.

Where is Mr. Sky? he said.

Indisposed.

His teeth flashed. A poor choice, he said.

I shrugged. Eve was furious and I was very sorry that I hadn't told her who we were coming to see.

McDaniel waved the gun impatiently. Come along, then.

Eve shrugged and threw me a shivering glance that said she wasn't afraid, exactly. But she wasn't too thrilled about this. And without waiting for me to blink she turned on her heel and walked to the elevators. McDaniel frisked me quickly and seemed unsurprised to find that I wasn't carrying a gun. He took away my knife though, and Moon's copy of *Ulysses,* which he tossed sideways with a snarl of disgust. The book hit the marble floor with a tremendous echoing crash and slid to rest against an emergency exit door. He left me with the blue notebook, a pack of cigarettes, what little cash I had and Ray Fine's yellow-tinted glasses. There was no reason for him to prod me along with the gun at my ribs, and so we walked to the elevators side by side, like friends. McDaniel was a few inches taller than me and he smelled sweet as a clump of freshly killed flowers.

Eve had already pressed the Up button and she fidgeted against the wall, looking much like a restless and sullen teenager. The slash of her dark eyes and hair hanging forward. All she needed was a mouthful of gum to pull into a pink tangle between her fingers and lips and whatever McDaniel was thinking, I wanted nothing more than to let her go home. Eve was tired, she had done nothing to deserve this. The elevator would be there any minute and if I was going to do something it would have to be quick and very fucking fancy. McDaniel stood two or three feet to my left, his body at a slight angle so that he could watch both of us. The gun dangled in his right hand, against his thigh. I looked at his eyes and he was completely focused on Eve; on her slim white thighs and the line of exposed flesh at her narrow waist; on her firm little tits. The motherfucker. He was no weakling but he was tall and thin and likely had a poor sense of balance and I thought I could probably kick his legs out from under him and drop him like a scarecrow made of rubber bands and sticks, but if he didn't drop the gun he would easily shoot me in the face as I tried to jump on him and gouge out his eyes. And he looked like he had a fair grip on the gun. I glanced at Eve and as strong as she was I thought she was too far away to help much. What I wanted to do was kick the gun out of his hand and hit him in the throat with some kind of karate chop, or bite it off. As long as he dropped the gun, and Eve came up with it, everything would be cool. I would have a mouthful of blood but Eve could go home and take a bath or check into a hotel, order room service and figure out how to pay for it later. And she could seek a little psychological help. The two of us could even check into rehab together. A day and a half on the Pale and my own morphine problem had developed new legs.

Anyway.

All of this nonsense flickered through my head in the space of two seconds and as I was sucking in a deep breath and getting myself ready to launch a sideways boot at his gun, McDaniel turned and raised his right hand and I was looking down the thing's dark steel nostril. McDaniel smiled and a soft bell chimed to indicate that the elevator had arrived.

I backed away from him, into the mirrored chamber. Eve beside me, silent. McDaniel stepped through the doors and told me to push the button for the sixteenth floor. I resisted a smart-ass temptation to push every button, as I was reluctant to annoy him in such close quarters.

The box began its ascent.

You aren't very clever, he said. Are you?

No, I said.

McDaniel produced a set of handcuffs and gave them to me.

Who are these for?

He grinned. They're for her, he said.

I didn't move. What's up?

McDaniel hit me in the ear with the barrel of his gun, not so hard. But hard enough that I found myself on one knee with butter-flies and ringing telephones in my head. Four or five crumpled help-less reflections of myself in the mirrors around me. The elevator abruptly stopped in midair and hung there like a bomb waiting to fall and I guessed that he had slapped the red emergency button, which might well account for some of the ringing noise. Eve's face hovered into view and the chickenshit voice that does a lot of the talking in my skull at times like these began to howl and cry the word *bait*.

This was a trap and Eve was the bait.

Oh, me.

Eve pulled me to my feet and held one finger before my eyes.

One, I said. I could still count, by God.

She smiled and moved the finger back and forth and I suppose my eyes were still tracking because she looked relieved. The handcuffs were heavy in my left hand and I was ready to drop them when McDaniel told me to look sharp and cuff her to the handrail. In the far corner, away from the fucking buttons.

Both hands, please.

I sighed and felt my skin turn gray with rage and I wondered if he would actually shoot us if I refused but Eve suddenly pecked at my cheek, a sweet dry kiss and two whispered words.

It's okay, she said.

And so I clamped one metal ring around her right wrist and pulled the second one up and under the rail and locked the other wrist so that her hands were behind her back.

Perfect, said McDaniel.

What are you going to do? said Eve.

I don't know, said McDaniel. I really don't know.

He stepped close to me and pressed his mouth to my cheek in almost exactly the same spot where she had just kissed me and I wondered if he could taste her on my skin.

Don't worry, he said. After I've finished with your friend, I will come back for you. And I might amuse myself with you further, or I might just take you home. I might take you to Lady Adore and let her punish you in a really interesting way.

I'm not going back, said Eve. I'm finished, Goo was finished.

McDaniel chortled. Quite right, he said.

Adore will let me run, she said.

He shook his head. You don't know her very well.

I was anxious. And growling, I realized. I sounded exactly like a paranoid dog and so I lit a cigarette, reasoning that it might calm my nerves and that it would certainly be to our advantage if a fire alarm went off. McDaniel was not stupid, however. He slapped the butt from my mouth and crushed it under his heel. He stroked my cheek with the barrel of his gun and I flinched. The pain was irrelevant and I wouldn't mind so much if he hit me again but I was afraid I would be unable to stand up if I suffered any more damage to my inner ear.

You like her, he said. Don't you?

I didn't move or speak. I had a bad feeling.

Why not give her a kiss, he said. On the mouth.

I hesitated, then stepped close and kissed Eve's lips.

Very nice, said McDaniel. But quite dull.

Fuck you, I whispered.

Yes, he said. Later, perhaps. But now I want you to slip your right hand up her skirt and give her box a squeeze. And don't let go.

I turned in circles and the mirrors were bright. There were bits and pieces of me in every corner.

Quickly now, he said.

Four or five versions of myself. I slipped my hand under Eve's skirt and cupped her pussy like a peach that I would hate to bruise and she was hot, in fact. She was wet. I stared into her face and told myself to think of garbage and black flies, dead fish and horseshit. I told myself not to get hard, not to get hard because an erection would only rob my brain of useful blood and make me dumber than ever. If that was possible. Eve's mouth twitched slightly and she moved her hips to push against my hand and I was hard as can be.

And now with the other hand, said McDaniel. Tickle her titties.

That's enough, I said. Motherfucker.

McDaniel sighed. Oh, all right. This is just for fun. But I do want you to kiss her again, and this time please force her mouth open and take her tongue.

He doesn't need to take it, said Eve.

Take it, said McDaniel.

My reflection was in fragments and part of me was enjoying this. If I had to come back from the dead to hurt McDaniel for this, I would try. But for now I bent and kissed her again, my mouth open. Eve allowed me to bite her tongue, and I offered my tongue to her. She bit it just enough to draw blood. I felt dizzy and realized my hand was still tucked against her crotch like a glove and the fingers were moving. I pulled away and McDaniel laughed, apparently satisfied. He hit the red button and we continued up to the sixteenth floor. I kissed Eve once more, for luck. I wanted to promise her I would come back for her but was afraid it would sound false and much too dramatic.

I hope you aren't claustrophobic, said McDaniel.

Not at all, she said.

McDaniel motioned for me to remove myself from the elevator. I backed away from Eve and stood between the doors to stop them from closing. McDaniel placed the gun against Eve's head to keep me from getting any funny ideas, then pinched her nose shut between his thumb and finger until she stuck out her tongue but he didn't try to bite it. He laughed, and told her not to worry. He promised that he would be back for her. Eve closed her eyes and I threw my thoughts at her like furious hail. Don't worry, don't worry, don't worry.

I almost laughed.

Because one of us would be back and I was the only one armed with a blue notebook. But I did remember her telling me once that she had nightmares about open spaces, that in fact she loved to feel trapped. McDaniel roughly touched her ribs and belly with long white fingers, he was tickling her with unpleasant intimacy and now she lunged and squirmed away from his touch like an angry daughter. And before he disembarked the elevator, the fucker happily pressed all twenty-nine buttons.

Now he shoved me down the long yellow hallway, through the little waiting room and past the desk where the freakish and overtly sexual receptionist was not sitting, past the dark landscape of a drowning human brain and through the hissing doors to Griffin's pale white lair. And Griffin, or more likely Major Tom, was napping restlessly on the black leather sofa where just the day before he and I had shared some very nice coke. I could use some of that shit now. My reflexes were fucking poor, my reflexes were impoverished and now McDaniel pushed me toward the sofa where Griffin lay sleeping.

Wake him, he said.

I kneeled beside the couch and looked into Griffin's face. At first I thought he must be dead but his lips were much too rubbery and slick with drool. He wasn't easy to wake up, though. I thumped his nose with the blackened nail of my middle finger. I spat into my hand and palmed his bare skull like a basketball. I tugged open one eyelid and blew hot air onto his naked eyeball and still he snored until McDaniel grew weary of this and kicked the glass coffee table over, shattering it. Griffin sat up with a foolish grin on his face while I rolled into a nearby corner to pick small bits of glass out of my skin.

Theseus, said Griffin. Welcome, welcome.

McDaniel rolled his eyes and gave a mock bow. He stalked the length of the office with the cool inner fury of a stage villain whose head is so ripe with mischief that he can't begin to begin.

What can I get you, said Griffin. A drink, a cigar?

I would like a moist towel, I said.

Griffin sneered. Hello, Ray. Ever the prole, aren't you?

The what? I said.

Proletariat, he said. The dull, wage-earning class. Haven't you read *1984*?

No. I did see the movie, though. David Bowie, wasn't it?

William Hurt, you troll. McDaniel fairly snarled.

Whatever, I said. And I said it slowly, letting the word roll lavishly over my lips.

Excuse me? he said. His eyes like pinpricks.

Fuck you, I said. Fuck you, okay.

Griffin coughed and threw a pillow at me. Wipe your face, Ray. You're a fright.

Thank you.

Griffin stood up, then. His arms out wide and his posture grossly servile. He moved close to McDaniel and began to grovel and kiss his hands and virtually lick at his genitals in such a way that might have been fashionable two hundred years ago, in a surreal French courtyard full of bursting flowers and castrated male servants. McDaniel primped and preened throughout and I had to wonder what I was doing with these two mad fuckers while Eve was handcuffed to herself in an elevator.

Let's get this over with, I said.

Griffin literally purred as he helped McDaniel out of his jacket. He hung it up, careful not to crease it, and turned to look at me with disdain.

Your tone of voice is offensive, he said.

Offensive, I said. Are you serious?

Terribly.

I am not offended, said McDaniel. Yet.

Well, then. Who wants a cocktail? said Griffin. I have a pint of the Pale here somewhere.

I wasn't sure if Griffin was high or just acting high. McDaniel exhaled through his nose and murmured that he was not thirsty. I did want a drink, however. I wanted two fingers of dead memories, served over ice with a wedge of lime and a splash of tonic, chased with a fat line of coke that would leave my jaw numb and heavy. I told myself to change the subject.

McDaniel cocked his gun now, and uncocked it.

I smiled as my education finally kicked in. *A Midsummer Night's Dream,* I said. Isn't that right? Theseus was the Duke of·Athens.

McDaniel squinted at me. Very good. You are not quite the oaf I imagined.

I shrugged.

But did you know that the character of Theseus is generally played by the same actor who portrays Oberon, King of the Fairies? Both men are grand manipulators.

I scratched a phantom itch along the side of my neck and thought it small consolation that McDaniel had taken his name from a comedy.

No. I didn't know that.

And what is your given name? he said to me.

Phineas Poe.

I thought so, he said. The wife-killer from Internal Affairs.

The blood does not actually boil. It's a useful, if somewhat exaggerated expression. My skin was not even hot but I was sick of cool good-byes and reluctant eyes and while I would let this comment pass for the moment I was pretty fucking sick of this nursery-rhyme explanation for my wife's death.

McDaniel held the gun on me and I bit at my tongue.

Griffin himself looked fairly sickened. He sucked air through his teeth and I wondered if he now was my friend or McDaniel's toady.

McDaniel grinned at me. What is your intention? he said.

Excuse me?

You called me this morning, he said. Do you remember?

I don't know, I said. I'm making this up as I go along.

As am I, he said. But why did you not bring Jimmy Sky?

Jimmy was naked and suicidal on somebody's roof this morning, I said. He's probably in the hospital by now. If he's lucky.

McDaniel sniffed the fingers of his left hand.

Did you hear me, I said.

What does your hand smell like, he said.

What? I said.

I wonder if it smells like Goo, he said. I imagine she has a stinky package.

I sighed. He was definitely going to have to shoot me before I would discuss the smell of Eve's panties. Griffin went over to his desk and began to fiddle with the controls of a police scanner. He reached for a set of headphones.

Moon was a friend of mine, I said.

McDaniel waved the gun. Detective Moon was officially dead

yesterday, he said.

Tired. I was tired of his face, of his snotty accent.

You fucker, I said.

I created Jimmy Sky, he said. And just when I have a good role for him, he's gone mad.

What role was that?

His eyes flickered yellow. Two cops have been found dead and mutilated in the past two days. Three, if you count Moon. I was planning to package Jimmy as the killer. Major Tom there was going to tidy up the legal side. But then you came along and confused things.

I confused things, I said. That's hilarious.

When did you arrive in town? he said.

I nodded. Two days ago.

Perhaps you would like to be the killer.

I would love to help you, I said. But your killer is already turning green in a Dumpster behind a Burger King on West 17th. He was just a guy named Christian.

McDaniel either didn't believe me or didn't care. He raised the gun.

Whoa, I said.

On your knees, he said.

Griffin turned off the scanner. A naked gunman was shot and killed by police an hour ago, he said. Identified on the scene as Detective Walter Moon.

That can't be, I said. That can't be right. Moon is riding the crosstown bus with no shirt. He's on the bus. In fact, I'm expecting him to walk in here any minute and start taking names.

McDaniel smiled a crooked smile and even Griffin looked as if he felt sorry for me, because I was so ignorant. And I chose that moment, for good or ill, to pick up a little straight-backed chair made of steel and chrome that looked very uncomfortable and throw it at McDaniel. He ducked under it easily and the chair bounced off the massive window behind him like it was made of rubber. The same window that I had seen fall from its frame and glide down to earth the other day like the hand of God. The chair landed almost at my feet and McDaniel grinned like a cat, his lips turning purple. He took a step forward and I knew he was going to shoot me.

Easy, said Griffin. Everybody take it easy. This carpet is Egyptian silk and cotton, okay. And it's white. It cost two thousand dollars per square foot.

McDaniel snarled out of the side of his mouth and the veins in his forehead bulged nicely. He had a very long nose, I noticed. He looked like a pale, sickly dog-man. Half man and half dog and not quite civilized. He turned now and stared intently at Griffin, as if he might just shoot him for practice. He stared and stared and the air between them became elastic. I touched my forehead and found my skin cold, rubbery. The skin of a frog. I had a hangover, I think. This was withdrawal or something. I wanted a shot of the Pale and I was operating on fumes.

Griffin sat down abruptly, on the floor. He was trembling.

Don't look at me, he said. Don't look at me like that.

McDaniel stared at him.

I was beginning to wonder if I might just slip away when Goo walked into the room. She wasn't Eve. I knew this without quite understanding it. Her face was different, colder. Her eyes were far away. She wore nothing but a black bra and underpants. There was a smear of blood across her stomach and she held the rest of her clothes away from her body as if they stank.

These aren't mine, she said.

No, I said. Dumbly. They're Dizzy's.

She didn't know me. She looked at me without comprehension. But she veered toward me and dropped the clothes at my feet and I saw that her hands were bloody. I reflexively kicked the clothes away from me, as if they were diseased.

McDaniel beamed at her like a proud papa and I knew he was thrilled by this little distraction, because he wouldn't have to think for a few minutes.

But then, neither would I.

Meanwhile. Griffin still sat on the floor, his face blank as a scarecrow's. He was having a private little meltdown, an identity crisis. He had chosen the worst possible moment to crack apart and to be honest, I was tempted to sit down beside him but now Goo was drifting around the room in a slow, disintegrating figure eight, her bloody wrists held out away from her body. She had wriggled out of the handcuffs, somehow. I wasn't terribly surprised, when I thought about what she had been doing for a living the past few months. But I knew how tightly I had cuffed her. She held her hands out like a child, like she was shocked by the blood. But that wasn't it. Her hands were fucked up, I saw. I stepped in front of her and took her by the wrists, gently.

Jesus, I said.

She had broken both her thumbs and ripped away a handful of skin to get free of the handcuffs. Her eyes were glassy. Eve was not okay. I had thought she would be okay in the elevator, but she wasn't. Goo had come along and ruined her pretty hands and now she needed medical attention. She needed a shot of Thorazine.

I looked at McDaniel. I'm taking her to a hospital, I said.

No, he said. You're not.

I want to go home, she said. Home.

McDaniel aimed the gun at her. Torture us, he said. Entertain us and I will take you home.

No, I said. Fuck that.

Goo hesitated and I saw nothing familiar in her eyes. She had become a stranger again and now she pulled away from me. She lifted her arms over her head with the horrible elegance of a prisoner who has been told to dance for her supper or be killed. I will never know what she was going to do but I like to think that she was going to hypnotize him and eat his tongue and pretty much rescue us all from this game but I never found out because McDaniel relaxed at that moment, watching her, and I chose to end things differently. I bent and picked up the chair again and this time swung it like a tennis racket and caught him in the face with one of the legs and although the gun went off harmlessly as he went down, he was down and that was all I wanted and his face was like a burst tomato.

Fucked, howled Griffin. The carpet is fucked.

The gun was on the floor and I scooped it up. It felt good in my hand. I kicked McDaniel in the ribs, hard. He seemed to be unconscious and I kicked him again.

How much did the carpet really cost? I said.

Two hundred a foot, said Griffin. But two thousand sounds better. Nervous laugh.

I was still on edge. Legs like water and I was hearing things. There is a noise that people make when they can't breathe, a noise that isn't a noise at all but is the opposite of noise because without oxygen there is no sound and now I heard, or imagined such a noise and turned around to see that Eve was on her back. The bullet from McDaniel's gun had gone through her throat.

This was the result of my choice. I picked up a chair and five seconds later Eve was dying at my feet. Planetary alignment was irrelevant. I knelt beside her and pressed my hands to her wound but it was hopeless. Eyes hot and staring. The dark, bloody mess of her throat. Her pulse was a flicker and I held my hands there until it stopped. Blood in her black hair and I rocked back and forth beside her. I was humming. Eve was dead. Her eyes were closed and I wonder if she would have recognized me if the bullet had strayed six inches to the left and buried itself in a wall. Black cotton bra and underpants. Fine white skin flecked with blood and broken thumbs. I rocked back and forth. She had fallen awkwardly and lay twisted, her left leg was crumpled under her body and I saw for the first time how many bruises she had. She was a rainbow and I fell away from her.

I sat against the wall for a while. Five minutes maybe. Griffin stood up and began to pace around.

This is serious, he said. This is serious shit, Ray.

I ignored him. I covered Eve's body with my coat and turned my attention to McDaniel. He was still out and I hoped he was dying. I sat on his chest. I felt his pulse and it was strong, it was thumping like a drum and he would be awake soon.

This is bad, said Griffin. I don't know if I can fix this.

Here's your big chance, I said.

Griffin rubbed his bald head, frantic. My chance for what, Ray?

Fuck, I said. Will you not call me that anymore?

Yeah, he said. I'm sorry. This is just a little intense. I slipped out of character, back there.

When?

When he said that shit about your wife.

I spat. That's fucking great. And who are you now?

Griffin stared at me. My name is Griffin.

Yeah, I said. Do you want his tongue?

The room seemed to swell and shrink around us of its own accord, like a great beast breathing. The two of us were in its belly. The air was thin and Eve was outside somewhere. She was gone.

Do you want this man's tongue? I said again.

My god, he said. No, I don't. I want to wake up with both legs tomorrow.

Right, then.

I stuck the gun down my pants because I would need both hands. I retrieved my knife from McDaniel's breast pocket. The blade was sleek, bright, warm. It was comforting. I reached for his mouth, pushed his lips apart and ran my fingers over the sharp ridge of his teeth. I massaged his jaw briefly and his mouth opened. Took a breath and poked two fingers into the dark hole, fishing for his tongue. This was foul beyond belief. I don't know how dentists do it. The mouths of strangers are forbidding, grotesque. I touched his tongue and knew I couldn't do it. I looked at Eve's body and told myself I had to do something to him, something bad. I remember her scrawled logic notes that had spawned my diary and bit at my tongue softly. It was warm and familiar. My own tongue was not grotesque. It was not the source of horror that the blind kid had described on the bus.

I needed to hurt McDaniel.

The gun in my pants was pretty ordinary, a Smith & Wesson .38 Special with black rubber grip. It held five shots but I wouldn't need them all. I had noticed earlier that McDaniel was wearing very expensive Italian boots that came up to barely kiss the ankles and fastened on the sides with a chrome buckle. The boots were composed of a soft, glossy black leather and the soles were heavy lug rubber. They would look fine with a tuxedo. They would not slow you down if you wanted to climb a tree. The footwear of dreams. My own boots, meanwhile, had been killing my feet lately and his looked to be about my size. I removed them, fumbled with the buckles like a novice shoe salesman and left McDaniel in his stocking feet. I tried the boots on and they were perfect. I wanted to walk around in them and admire them but was afraid he would wake up soon and I needed to finish this before I freaked out and ran away without doing anything.

McDaniel lay on his back in the center of Griffin's nice white carpet.

Half of his body was obscured by shadows. Of course it was. I took a few steps back and without hesitating or stopping to think, raised the pistol and aimed at McDaniel's left foot and Griffin may have shouted at me, I don't know. I never heard him. I pulled the trigger and McDaniel's foot pretty much exploded. The bones in the foot are complex and fine and his would never be put back together. He would probably be up and around on a prosthetic in a year or so, but he would certainly need a cane and I imagined that if the game survived he would get one that doubled as a sword.

My head was ringing, my head was full of crashing waves.

I stared down at McDaniel and he appeared to regain consciousness for a moment. His eyes found mine before rolling back into his head and I doubted that he would ever forget me. I took a shallow breath and laughed, a brief glittering laugh. That first shot had been easy.

I lifted the gun again and calmly destroyed his other foot.

Griffin was sitting on the floor against the wall, his hands covering his ears. I glanced at the big unforgiving window where I had seen the three of us before and perhaps it was because of the clouds or the angle but there was nothing, no one reflected in the glass now. There was only a curved gray sky, and for a brief horrible moment it seemed to have no top or bottom and it looked very much like the inside of my head. I was sick, I was filled with vertigo and loss. I thought of the wall behind Eve's couch, the dead bird on her floor. I wondered if I could walk through that wall of glass, if there was another reality there that might sustain me. I was slipping. I turned and vomited into Griffin's wastepaper basket, which was of course made of black wire and did not hold liquids very well. The white carpet was truly fucked, now. It was time to go. I crouched beside Griffin and touched his face. I needed him to act like a lawyer and I guess he was finally thinking the same thing.

He took the gun from me and said, go. Get out of here.

I cast one last look at Eve, at Goo. I wanted to touch her, to say something meaningful but that was Hollywood. Her face and chest were hidden in my dirty coat and her naked legs stuck out at odd angles. She had the discolored plastic limbs of a life-sized doll.

My feet were heavy and unfamiliar in my enemy's shoes. Dragged myself back through the waiting room and this time I didn't look at the brain landscape. I found my strength and ran back down the yellow hallway and pushed the Down button. I practiced breathing. Thirty seconds passed, ninety. The doors opened and I stepped inside. The handcuffs dangled from the brass rail, unopened.

Blood on the metal, smeared and nearly dry. Fragments of torn skin like pink threads.

The elevator took me down to the lobby and I barely glanced at the mirrors on the way down. I hurried to the emergency exit door and picked up my copy of *Ulysses*. The fire alarm tripped when I opened the door and no one was waiting for me.

I stood in an alley surrounded by white stone and it was like the sky had simply fallen. There were sirens in the distance and I walked away from the exit at what I hoped was a normal pace. I came out of the alley and was facing a street.

Pedestrians, traffic. I looked at my hands, at the tips of my fingers. They were untrembling but still numb from pulling the trigger.

The sidewalk was new, freshly hardened concrete. There were no cracks in it at all, no impurities or scars. It was a little eerie and after a while I crossed over to the other side. I walked and walked and when I grew weary, I drifted to a bus stop. The thought of another bus ride fairly horrified me, but on a cellular level it seemed that I couldn't resist. I got on the first bus that came along.

The liquid sigh of the doors shutting behind me. The driver, gruff and unsmiling.

I paid and made my way along to a seat that looked safe.

Red, torn vinyl.

I scanned the faces of the other passengers but none of them was Jimmy Sky and none of them was the blind kid with the maddening tongue and my loved ones were all cartoon characters in the end. I pulled out the blue notebook and found that I had lost my pen.

Open windows and blank faces. Strangers all.

Dear Jude.

There is nothing but the greedy suck and churn of the engine beneath my feet and I feel serene. There is no motion sickness. I borrow a black ballpoint from a little old woman who smiles and coughs and tells me to keep it. I close my eyes and wait for Stephen Dedalus to come sit down beside me. I have saved no one but myself and now I watch for the other universe to unravel in my skull, for the sky to become my own skin and fill with stars.